THE DUKE
Who Loved Me

ON HIS MAJESTY'S SECRET SERVICE

BOOK I

PATRICIA BARLETTA

patriciabarletta.com

Published Internationally by Patricia Barletta
Boston, MA
Copyright © 2018 Patricia Barletta

patriciabarletta.com

Exclusive cover © 2018 mightyunicorn.ca
Interior design by Tamara Cribley www.deliberatepage.com

PRINT ISBN 978-1-7324769-5-0
EBOOK ISBN 978-1-7324769-4-3

Editor: Joanna D'Angelo

ACKNOWLEDGMENTS

This book might never have seen the light of day when it was first published back when dinosaurs roamed (well, maybe not quite that long ago) if I had not happened upon my local chapter of Romance Writers of America (RWA). Through workshops and chapter meetings, I learned about the art and craft of writing a romance. I made friends who connected me with people in the publishing industry. My dream finally came true: My first novel was published. So, my thanks go to those friends I made all those years ago, who are still my friends today.

I also want to give a shout-out to my present-day editor and all-around cheerleader, Joanna D'Angelo; Steve at mightyunicorn.ca. who created my swoon-worthy cover; Tamara at deliberatepage.com. who makes the inside of my books beautiful; and Kathy K. who made sure my i's were dotted and my t's crossed. Thank you!

ALSO AVAILABLE

Moon Dark
BOOK 1 AURIANO CURSE SERIES

Moon Shadow
BOOK 2 AURIANO CURSE SERIES

Coming Soon

Moon Bright
BOOK 3 AURIANO CURSE SERIES

Sign up for Patricia's newsletter at patriciabarletta.com.

Follow Patricia Barletta on BookBub

PROLOGUE

Hyde Park, London, 1806

Two small groups of men, dressed for the chill dampness of pre-dawn in greatcoats and hats, huddled beneath a towering stand of oaks and spoke quietly among themselves. Around them, the morning mist swirled, and dripping moisture pattered against the leaves. The call of the mourning dove echoed through the glen. As the bell from the nearby cathedral rang, dawn began to lighten the grassy clearing nearby, and the two groups broke apart.

Three individuals were left alone in the center of the clearing. As the others watched, two of the men positioned themselves back to back. They had discarded their outer garments and wore only their waistcoats over white shirts. The dark hair of the one and the light hair of the other contrasted sharply, even in the dim light. They each held a brightly polished dueling pistol. The eldest of the trio moved back to where the others stood waiting. Speaking clearly, he explained the Gentlemen's Rules.

"You will each walk ten paces on the count, turn and fire," he said. "Each man will be allowed one shot. Any man who turns and fires before the end of the count will be warned by the other's second and, if it is judged appropriate, will be shot by him. Do you understand the rules, gentlemen?" At a curt nod from each of the duelists, he went on, "May your honor be satisfied when this is finished. God go with you both. Are you ready?" When both men had indicated they were, he began, "One…Two… Three…" Each paced off at the count. "Five… Six…" They marched on. "Seven… Eight… Nine…" The moment was near. "Ten." They turned and fired.

The explosions of the pistols were startling, breaking the peace of the glen. Birds swarmed from their nighttime roosts, calling an alarm. The pistol reports echoed through the trees and across the fields beyond.

The fair-haired man grabbed at his chest and swayed. Several of the onlookers rushed to his side and caught him as he fell. They lowered him carefully to the ground. A dark, red stain bloomed across the stark white of his shirt.

The dark-haired man lowered his pistol as his friends gathered about him. His expression, one of dismay and puzzlement. He turned to his second who was holding his coat for him.

"I aimed away from him," he said, shaking his head. "I couldn't possibly have hit him."

His friend glanced at the fallen man and then back. He said nothing, but merely helped the duelist with his greatcoat and handed him his hat. Together, they made their way to one of the waiting coaches. The wounded man was carried to his own coach and driven away.

Eventually, the others dispersed, and the glade was empty once more. There was no evidence that a duel had been fought. The acrid smell of gunpowder faded away. The birds settled back on their perches. The early morning fog dissipated as the sun streamed through the tree branches, casting golden rays into the peaceful glen.

And a dark figure, hiding in the leafy undergrowth, skulked away through the woods.

CHAPTER 1

London, 1810

Lady Jessica Carlton watched as the cards were dealt. Five others sat around the table in the middle of the room. It was quiet except for an occasional murmur and the hushed slap of cards. Candles glowed from the elegant chandelier, hanging over the green, baize-covered table. As silent as statues, the servants in their livery stood in their inconspicuous positions.

She watched as the players scanned their cards and tried to hide feelings of disappointment or elation. Her own cards could not possibly lose. She feigned a dainty yawn behind a gloved hand as she hid her smile. The men placed bets and play went on, as one by one, they dropped out. Only two people were left in the game. Lord Hoxly shook his head.

"Well, that's it for me," he announced as he threw in his hand. "I say, m'lady, you've the Devil's own luck this evening."

Jessica peered out from behind her black-silk half-mask, and smiled sweetly. "Nay, Lord Hoxly, the Devil has none, for Luck is a lady."

Appreciative chuckles ran around the table as Lord Hoxly smiled his defeat. "Then may I compliment Lady Luck on her choice of companions? It is not every evening I can lose to such a beautiful victor."

"Why, thank you m'lord," Jessica said with a slight nod. "Perhaps next time you will allow me to win even more."

Guffaws came from the other players as Lord Hoxly shook his head in acceptance of his vanquishment, both verbally and at cards. They all, at one time or another, had been her hapless victims.

After gathering her considerable winnings, Lady Jessica, or Lady Fortuna as she was known at the gaming hell, bestowed a dazzling smile upon the gentlemen at the table.

"If you gentlemen will excuse me," she said as she rose, "it has been an exhausting evening. It is time I took my leave. Good night."

The men rose with her and murmured their farewells. Jessica could feel their eyes on her as she left. She knew they watched with varying degrees of interest, from gentlemanly appreciation to outright leering. She could imagine their conversation as soon as the door closed behind her.

The speculation over her true identity.

The fact that she hid behind a mask, possibly covering some disfigurement.

Her nickname, *Ice Witch*, gained during one very long, very close game of faro played against one of the more notorious members of the gaming hell.

And perhaps, the conjecture once again that she was the Regent's latest paramour.

Jessica could not be bothered by such idle chatter. She wearily leaned back against the seat of the carriage which was taking her to her lodgings. She had done well playing cards this evening. Perhaps, she would have to play only once more before she had to return home to Braeleigh. A tired sigh escaped her at the thought. There was a time when Braeleigh meant everything to her. Now, she was not quite so sure it did. The painful memories did not help.

Her mother's death, her father's remarriage to Margaret, and then her father's sudden, tragic death a year ago had combined to turn a place of peace into one of grief. Yet, Jessica would have been content to stay and try to heal her wounds and those of her twelve-year-old brother, Jason, had it not been for Margaret's cruel demands. It was because of their stepmother that Jessica was living a dual life — one of the adventuress out to win every penny she could, and one of the genteel daughter of an earl who dutifully traveled home from the city every month to visit her brother and stepmother.

She gazed blindly at the passing houses and storefronts. Normally, the excitement of the life she was living would cause her blood to pulse through her veins. The gaiety, the laughter, the concentration of the game combined to help her repress the true purpose of her sojourn in London, at least for short periods of time. But tonight, for some reason, a depression lay heavy on her heart. It was as if something dire were about to happen, only she did not know what or when. But she could not give up the struggle of wits she sustained with Margaret. She would never let her stepmother be victorious in her little scheme.

Jessica saw they were nearing her lodgings. Her bed, hard and lumpy though it was, would be welcome tonight. Her evening at the gaming hell had drained her. Lord Hoxly had been a formidable opponent. The Marquis of Bellingham had persisted in his advances to the point of being crude. It was a different life she lived now. She was no longer cradled in the warmth of her father's love and the companionship of her younger brother. She missed her brother, Jason, terribly, and she worried about him being subjected to Margaret, a shrew, who cared only for herself.

The carriage stopped before the rooming house where she had been living for nearly a year. Not exactly a palace, she thought wryly as she noted the stained whitewash and paint peeling off the door. Next door was the Green Dragon Inn. The sign, hanging above the door from one hook and creaking back and forth in the night wind, pictured such a creature. The poor dragon's fiery breath had turned to a pale yellow and many of his scales had flaked off with the paint. Not a very formidable dragon, she noted. She turned her attention back to her own lodgings. There was scant light coming through the street-level windows. The landlady had probably retired for the night and would not be pleased to be roused again at such an ungodly hour. Jessica would have to endure her dour looks and scathing comments once more. Even though the woman was paid extra for her trouble, she felt obliged to scold. At least the place was clean. And inexpensive.

She stepped down from the carriage, paid the driver and knocked. After several moments, she heard the bolt thrown back and the door was opened a crack. An eye peered at her through the opening.

"It's Jessica Carlton, Mrs. Cooper," she said, knowing her landlady's suspicious nature.

There was a grunt and the door swung wide. As soon as Jessica stepped across the threshold, the door was slammed behind her and locked. Muttering, Mrs. Cooper shambled back to her room and shut herself in. Relieved that she had been spared a tongue-lashing, Jessica started for her room. The front parlor was deserted except for a mangy dog sleeping before the dying fire. He barely opened his eyes as she walked past. The candles in the sconces on the staircase had burned very low and gave testimony to the very late hour.

Jessica knew Donny would be waiting up for her. The woman had first been her nanny. Now she acted as her lady's maid. Donny's acceptance of the situation and her mothering during the time they had been in London had been the only thing that had kept Jessica sane and able to go through with her scheme.

Quietly, she opened the door to her room. It appeared deserted. There was a single candle burning on the table beside the bed. The fire crackled brightly in welcome. Jessica tossed her wrap on the bed and went to stand before the fire's warmth. The carriage ride from the fashionable section of London where the gaming hell was situated, to the less respectable area of the city where the Green Dragon made its home, had been chilly and damp. Jessica had not wished to spend the few extra coins for a warming brick for her feet or an extra carriage blanket.

"Aye, and 'tis a God-forsaken hour ye be comin' in," Donny said from a dark corner.

Jessica laughed lightly. "Oh, Donny, stop complaining." She threw a pouch onto the bed. It landed with the heavy clink of money. "See what these late hours have brought us."

Mistress Donlin harrumphed and rose from a chair in the shadows. She picked up the pouch and hefted it in her hand. "And a good thing 'tis, too, what with ye havin' to make payment soon."

Jessica shivered. "Better I should have to return to Margaret every month with a payment than marry that over-stuffed, middle-aged baronet with thinning hair and red veins across his nose. Every time he looked at me, he made my skin crawl."

Donny lifted a loose floorboard under the threadbare rug near the fireplace and emptied the pouch into a box nestled in the hiding place. Carefully, she replaced the board and smoothed the rug.

"Aye," she agreed. "Sir Percival Lowry was no great catch for any girl. But he would've saved Braeleigh for ye."

Jessica's chin went up. "If my father were still alive, he would never have considered the marriage. He wanted a love-match for me and would have lost Braeleigh sooner than have me unhappy."

Donny turned to help Jessica undress. "The Earl was soft where his daughter was concerned."

Jessica turned on Donny. "Just because you have been my nanny all my life, Mistress Donlin, does not give you the right to criticize my father." Even as she said the words, she knew the woman was right. Her father had indulged her, but he would never have given up his ancestral home, not even for her. That was the reason she was in London and living a precarious existence—to save Braeleigh.

Donny harrumphed. "Ye know as well as I that yer father was never in his right mind after his lady died. All that gamblin' and racin' and schemes to make money. 'Twas the racin' that killed him and the schemin' that put ye here in the city."

Jessica shrugged and turned her back so that Donny could unbutton her dress. "With Napoleon rampaging all over the Continent and England's very shores threatened, the idea to build a new shipyard was the thing to do for a man loyal to the Crown. It was not his fault that the other investors ran off with the money and left my father with none to meet the Admiralty's orders."

"*Hmph.* Left you and yer brother with none, not to mention Margaret. Or have ye forgotten what it is yer about here in London?" Donny slipped a warm nightrail over Jessica's head.

"I've not forgotten. I believe I will only need one, or perhaps two more evenings at the card table this month before I have enough for Margaret. The fifteenth of the month is almost a fortnight away. I may be able to begin on next month's stipend before we leave for Braeleigh. Perhaps there will be enough left over for some of that marvelous scented soap I saw at the perfumer's."

Donny muttered, "Seems to me y'ought to stay in and try goin' t'bed early. Ye be too thin. Next thing ye know, ye'll be gettin' sick, and then where'll ye be?"

"I'm fine, and I am not going to get sick. Margaret will get her stipend," Jessica answered as she sat before the small dressing table so Donny could brush out her hair. She knew her maid's grumbling covered up her concern.

"Ye ought to find yerself a husband to take care of ye. Ye shouldn't have to go to that gamin' place." Donny pulled the pins from Jessica's hair and began to brush the long, ebony tresses.

"I have no connection. Who would introduce me to a suitable husband? Besides, I'll not marry till I'm ready. I'll not marry someone I don't love." It was an old argument, and Jessica said the words by rote, but she meant them.

"If yer father had lived, he'd'a found ye a husband," Donny said. "And ye would've wed him whether ye loved him or not. It's a husband's place to take care of his wife an' her family. Ye wouldn't have t' be runnin' around like some strumpet all night."

Jessica climbed onto the bed and slid under the covers as she hid a smile. "Are you suggesting that I should have been a dutiful step-daughter and wed Sir Percival?" She knew Donny's feelings about Margaret and her scheme, but she loved to tease her.

Her nanny-turned-maid gave her a sharp glance. "Yer stepmother had only herself in mind when she came up with that one."

Jessica giggled. "Come, Donny, I thought you wanted me to wed."

"Aye. To some nice lord who'll take care o' ye for the rest of yer days." She tucked the blankets around Jessica.

Jessica sighed. "I don't think I'll ever find one of those. The men who frequent the gaming houses are not looking for wives, and the women there are not…acceptable."

"Seems t' me a young girl with a decent name and good looks ought t' be acceptable," Donny grumbled.

Jessica only smiled as she snuggled down into her pillow. "This girl with a decent name is tired, so if you are through your grumping, I'll go to sleep," she murmured.

Donny gave the blankets one last pat, then did as she was asked, shaking her head.

But Jessica's smile faded as Donny closed the door behind her.

CHAPTER 2

The next night, Jessica entered the establishment of *Madame* du Barré once again. After greeting Jacques, *Madame*'s very large majordomo, and handing him her cloak, she turned to look out over the elite of London society who had come to titillate their excitement and slake their thirst for more than the usual round of balls, dinner parties, and theater. The establishment of *Madame* du Barré was neither coffee house nor club. It was a gaming hell, one with a reputation for fairness at the tables and wickedness elsewhere within its walls. *Madame* du Barré's was not for the faint of heart or pious of nature. Although many of the forms of entertainment provided by *Madame* for her guests were illegal, nothing had been done to close her doors, for many of the guests were members of His Majesty's government, including the Prince of Wales on occasion.

Jessica smiled at Jacques, who murmured that *Madame* was most anxious to speak with her this evening. Not everyone was allowed past the front door by Jacques, but to be told that *Madame* wished to speak with her was indeed an honor. Of course, once inside, it was customary to pay one's respects to *Madame*, but it was not always the rule that a person would be warmly welcomed or even acknowledged.

A burst of laughter carried over the noise of the crowd. It came from the gold salon where *Madame* usually spent her evening. As she moved through the crowd towards the sound of the laughter, gentlemen clad in the latest of fashions bowed to her, and women in the most daring of gowns nodded their greetings. The ladies for the most part wore dominoes, half-masks, as Jessica did, to conceal their identity and preserve their reputations. Yet, it was not usually difficult to discern the better-known members of society.

Jessica had come to this establishment when she first arrived in London. Strangely, it had been from Margaret that Jessica had learned of *Madame*'s establishment. On one of the few times that Margaret had talked about her life before becoming Lady Carlton, she had mentioned going once to *Madame*'s. She had told Jessica how exciting it had been to wear a mask and mingle with such a rakish crowd. Jessica, in her innocence, had been fascinated with the story. When she had asked her father if he had ever been there, he had become furious with Margaret for telling his daughter about such things and had told Jessica that should she ever find herself in London, under no circumstances was she to go near the place. The matter had been forgotten until her father's death and Margaret's insistence on her marriage.

When Jessica had first conceived of her plan to outwit her stepmother, she had decided that a gaming hell was exactly the type of place which would best suit her needs. Remembering Margaret's story, Jessica had gone to visit *Madame* during the afternoon, when no one else had been there. Margaret's name had gained her entrance and a meeting with the woman.

Jessica remembered her first impressions of the house itself and the woman who inhabited it. She had been led upstairs and only caught glimpses of darkened rooms that contained gaming tables and other shadowy shapes of furniture. The room where she was finally escorted to, however, was bright with sunlight and decorated in expensive velvets and brocades and furniture imported from France. An attractive, middle-aged woman dressed in a lavender silk negligee reclined on a chaise. Her dark eyes had watched Jessica approach with warm curiosity. She had invited Jessica to sit, and then had ordered hot chocolate.

That seemed a lifetime ago. Jessica stood now at the door to the gold salon and watched that middle-aged woman flirt outrageously with the men around her. *Madame* had accepted the frightened, eighteen-year-old girl and her desperate scheme to make money. She had even given Jessica money to get started and helped with her wardrobe. All *Madame* had asked in exchange was for Jessica to deliver a letter to a certain *Monsieur* Montaigne who lived not far from Braeleigh, and to keep these letters a secret. *Madame* had been more than generous.

Jessica's career as a professional gambler had been launched. That had been nearly a year ago. Since then she had visited *Madame*'s establishment with great frequency and had become well-known. But to the patrons, her true identity remained a mystery. *Madame* imparted little information about her, and Jessica imparted even less. The only information they had concerning her was the strange name she gave herself — Lady Fortuna — and that she was a very shrewd card player who rarely lost. *Madame* had told her bets had been taken to see who would be able to defeat her at the card table. More discreet bets had been placed to see who would be able to break down her virtue.

Madame caught sight of Jessica in the doorway of the gold salon and waved her lace fan at her. The men surrounding her opened ranks as they turned to see the newcomer. The gap in the crowd allowed Jessica an unobstructed view to the woman who sat royally among her fawning subjects.

Jessica's glance fell on a stranger who stood beside *Madame*'s chair. One hand rested on its back. The stranger was tall with hair the color of spun gold, and his skin was unfashionably tanned. He stood easily, appearing confident of *Madame*'s attentions, while the others about him jostled nervously for a word or a glance from her. What struck Jessica the most were his eyes. Even from across the room, she could tell they were the color of bright emeralds and seemed almost as hard. Those eyes watched her approach *Madame* with a speculative look that Jessica found terribly unnerving. She wished he would turn away.

"*Ma petite*," *Madame* greeted her as she held out both hands. "*Très ravissente*," she said in approval of Jessica's appearance.

Jessica smiled in thanks as she kissed *Madame* on both cheeks. She knew the dress she wore was becoming. Donny had made it for her, because Jessica couldn't afford a modiste. It was a simple, black, watered silk gown cut quite low over her bosom with a high waistline defined by a gold ribbon tied beneath her breasts. The sleeves were long and tight and ended in a point that covered the back of her hand. Her hair was piled in curls on top of her head and entwined with another gold ribbon, matching the one on her dress. She wore no jewelry except for a simple gold locket that teased the cleavage between her breasts.

Madame turned to the stranger who stood beside her chair. "*Monsieur le Duc,* do you not think *la petite fille,* beautiful? Ah, but where are my manners? You have not met our enchanting gambler. May I present the Lady Fortuna? *Ma petite,* this is His Grace, Damien Trevor, Duke of Wyndham."

Jessica, despite her wish not to, was compelled to look up into those green eyes. They seemed to mock the world. An aura of self-possession emanated from him and a strange magnetism demanded one's attention. He was dressed simply, yet elegantly, in a coat of rich, brown velvet with tight, faun-colored breeches which just missed being indecent. His waistcoat of pale yellow satin embroidered in white silk covered his white silk shirt. A very large topaz winked out from the folds of his intricately tied stock. He was easily the handsomest man Jessica had ever met. She curtsied politely and extended her hand.

"A pleasure, my lady." He smiled as he bent over her fingers.

"Wyndham has just been telling me news from the Continent." *Madame* sighed. "It is so long since I have been home."

Distracted by *Madame*'s words, Jessica turned to smile sympathetically at her and allowed the Duke to keep possession of her fingers much too long. She felt his lips touch the back of her hand. It was a bold, improper action, one which should not have surprised her in *Madame*'s establishment. She jerked her hand away as the feel of his warm lips sent a strange, thrilling sensation up her arm. She sent him a cold glance of warning, but was unprepared for the intense, calculating look in his eyes. It was gone immediately, replaced by an amused, mocking smile, but Jessica had seen something beneath the gentlemanly exterior of the man. It frightened, yet fascinated her. She searched frantically for something to say to give herself time to regain her composure. She focused on *Madame*'s words.

"…because of that man, Napoleon," the lady was saying. "Bah! He is a wily one. He says '*Liberté*! *Fraternité*! *Egalité*!' and then he makes himself emperor."

"Do you not wish to see your homeland grow more powerful, *Madame*?" Jessica asked, merely for something to say.

Madame smiled at her. "Not at the expense of so many lives, *ma petite*. I do not live in France any more, eh? I am here, in England, with all my friends."

"And we are so very glad that you are here, *Madame*." The Duke bowed graciously. "Where else would we find so charming a lady as yourself?"

Madame flipped open her fan and held it coyly before her face. "Ah, *Monsieur le Duc*, you have a golden tongue. Did you learn that from *Monsieur* Napoleon himself, or did the angels bless you at birth?"

The Duke smiled at *Madame*, but his eyes looked at Jessica as he said, "It was not I who was blessed by the angels, *Madame*."

Madame pouted. "Naughty boy," she scolded as she snapped shut her fan and tapped him on the arm with it. "It is impossible to flirt with two ladies. You will make them both sad, and then you will be left with none."

"*Madame*, with you, I wear my heart on my sleeve," the Duke said gallantly. "But I find I cannot ignore the charms of this quite intriguing lady." He lifted Jessica's hand and this time, kissed the inside of her wrist.

Jessica was aghast at his brazen action. Although dealing with men who made advances was not new to her, for some reason the Duke caused her a great deal of apprehension. Summoning up her courage and relying on her past experiences, Jessica gently disengaged her hand.

"You are too kind, Your Grace," she said coolly. "But surely, you have met other women more intriguing than I in your travels. Did not *Madame* say that you have just returned from the Continent? I have heard that the women of Spain are hot-blooded beneath their demure facades, and the women of Italy will take two men to their beds."

"I'll wager that after those women of Italy have had Wyndham, two men wouldn't be enough," someone said from the back of the group.

The Duke bowed his acceptance of the compliment in good humor, and the others chuckled.

"And the women of France?" *Madame* asked with a smile. "What have you heard of them, *ma petite*?"

Jessica smiled at *Madame*. "That they are urbane and witty and set the fashion for the rest of the women of the world."

"Perhaps that is so," the Duke said, "but none has the beauty of the English rose."

Jessica felt the caress of his eyes as if he touched her. In spite of her wish to remain cool, she blushed. *Madame*'s appraising glance made her shift uncomfortably.

The woman chuckled, then changed the direction of the exchange. "There is a game just beginning in the green room, *ma petite*. Perhaps, Your Grace, you would be interested to join in also?"

"That sounds intriguing," Wyndham answered without taking his eyes from Jessica. He offered his arm to her. "Lady Fortuna, may I have the pleasure of escorting you?"

Jessica had no choice but to take his arm, yet she almost wished it had been Sir Percival, the man her stepmother would have her wed. At the thought, she looked up at the Duke to compare the two men, which was silly. There was no comparison. The Duke was handsome and charming, where Sir Percival was ugly and vulgar. Realizing the ludicrousness of her comparison, she smiled to herself.

The Duke caught her smile and raised an eyebrow. "Is there something that the lady finds amusing?"

Caught off-guard, Jessica blushed again and was surprised into telling the truth. "No, Your Grace. I was just thinking of someone I knew."

"I see. And this other man, do you find him attractive?" he asked, his tone cool.

"How do you know I was thinking of another man?" she challenged.

He merely raised a brow.

Jessica shook her head and laughed at the idea of Sir Percival being found attractive by anyone. "He is not attractive at all. It was a ridiculous thought." She quickly changed the subject. "I have never seen you here before, Your Grace. You do not come here often?"

"As you heard before, I have been on the Continent for quite some time. When I am in London, I am an occasional visitor to *Madame*'s, but, perhaps, I may begin to come more frequently." His gaze turned thoughtful.

"Do not come to *Madame*'s only on my account, Your Grace, unless you wish to lose at cards," she said bluntly. "I am not looking for any amorous entanglements."

"Really," the Duke murmured, not at all put off.

Jessica was relieved to find that they had at last arrived at the green room. She did not like the Duke's last comment and the hint of challenge it held. The man was too handsome and too charming for her tastes. She had never heard of him before, and that was something quite unusual. Gossip about this baronet or that earl, this vicomtesse or that duchess was always making the rounds at *Madame*'s. Yet, he and *Madame* had acted as if they were old friends — or lovers. She would have to question *Madame* about him as soon as she had the chance.

He escorted her into the room, one of the smaller gaming rooms in *Madame*'s establishment. It was only large enough to hold one table around which seven or eight people could sit. At one end of the room were several chairs and a settee where the players could relax during breaks in the game. The room was, indeed, green, from the patterned carpet on the floor, to the dark green brocade on the walls, to the various shades of green satin covering the furniture. There was a sparkling crystal chandelier which cast its light over the whole, and crystal wall sconces helped illuminate the room. Jessica had gambled in this room many times and won quite large sums. She considered it a good omen that *Madame* had suggested this place on the evening she had met such a man as the Duke of Wyndham.

The other gamblers, all men, were already seated about the table, but play had not yet begun when Jessica and the Duke arrived. There were only two empty chairs at the table. Jessica breathed a silent sigh of relief that they were not next to each other. She did not wish to have to sit next to the Duke all evening. She needed to concentrate on the game, not some skirt-chasing man intent on making a conquest.

The men greeted the two newcomers to their table as they seated themselves. Jessica was again relieved to discover that everyone knew His Grace — relieved and intrigued. Who was this man that he was so well known by everyone but her? But she put it out of her mind. The less she had to do with him, the better.

There was something about him that was different from the other men she had met at *Madame*'s. It was not that he was so handsome, with his darkly tanned aquiline features and dark golden hair, for she certainly had met other handsome men. It was not even his charm or his smile, though she found his smile devastatingly attractive. It was, rather, the aura about him of an untamed animal, taking what he wanted when he wanted it. Yet, he was not vulgar or uncouth, for in the few minutes she had been with him, his manners had been flawless, and he had shown her every respect, despite the boldness of his caress on her hand. But he gave the impression of being slightly uncivilized, that perhaps he should have been a pirate instead of a Duke. In short, he frightened her.

After a few pleasantries, the game commenced. Jessica played well at first, winning most of the hands, but after the first hour of play her luck seemed to leave her. She was having trouble concentrating, for every time she looked up, a pair of brilliant green eyes seemed to be mocking her. As the hours passed, the pile of money before Jessica grew smaller, while the pile of money in front of His Grace multiplied. In desperation, she tried to bluff with a very large bet on the next hand. The Duke was not fooled. He held better cards and won the round. Nervously, she placed her hand over the few coins still before her. There was barely enough to pay for a hired carriage to get her to her lodgings.

It was several hours after midnight when she decided it would be wise to leave the game before all her money was gone. She had lost a considerable sum, almost a third of what she owed to Margaret. It would take several more nights at *Madame*'s to make up the amount needed to pay her stepmother.

She tossed her cards into the middle of the table. "I believe you gentlemen have outwitted me this evening," she told them with a smile. "You have repaid me in kind for winning so much from you on previous evenings. I bid you good-night, sirs."

The gentlemen stood and consoled her.

"Bad luck, m'lady."

"Next time will be better."

"The cards were against you."

As she nodded and smiled bravely, she noticed that the Duke called one of the servants over and spoke to him in a low tone. The servant nodded and left the room quickly. Jessica thought nothing about it as she listened to the words of sympathy from the other players. Only the Duke said nothing as he sat back in his chair and watched her with a curious glint in his green eyes.

Finally, able to take her leave, Jessica walked with dignity out into the main gaming room. Blinking back the tears in her eyes, she kept her chin up as she maneuvered through the people milling about the tables of chance. Fortunately, no one stopped her to greet her or pass the time. She was relieved when she finally reached the entrance hall and was able to ask Jacques for her cloak and to fetch her carriage.

While she waited, she tried to push her depression to the back of her mind, but her thoughts invariably turned to Braeleigh and her brother. She promised herself she would make back the money she had lost. Margaret would not have any reason to use Jason for her gain.

With one last sigh, she pushed away her dark thoughts as Jacques returned through the doorway.

"Pardon, *Mademoiselle*, but your carriage is gone," he said.

Jessica frowned at him. "That's impossible. I paid the driver extra to wait for me. I will see for myself." Impatiently, she pushed past the majordomo and stepped out the door. She looked up and down, but only a few private coaches waited silently for their wealthy owners. Her carriage was gone. It was impossible to find a carriage for hire at this time of the night. What could she do? How was she to get home? It was very dangerous to walk, for gangs of thieves and cut-throats roamed the streets, seeking out vulnerable victims. It was out of the question to go back inside *Madame*'s and ask someone for a ride. Her pride had suffered enough for one night. She could not face anyone after losing so badly. She was sure the news of her loss had spread as soon as she had left. It was too difficult to act as if losing meant nothing to her.

As she wondered desperately what to do, a deep voice spoke next to her. "Is there some difficulty, my lady?"

Jessica jumped at the sound. She had heard no one approach. Turning, she discovered the Duke at her elbow. He smiled engagingly.

"I apologize if I startled you, but you seemed troubled by something," he said.

The Duke of Wyndham was the last person she wished to see at that moment. Jessica pasted a smile on her lips as she said flippantly, "It would seem my luck has fled me completely this evening. My carriage appears to have left, so I am without a ride home."

"Then it is fortunate indeed that I also decided to leave *Madame's* early. I will give you a ride." He spoke as if there were no other alternative. It was nearly an order.

"That won't be necessary, Your Grace," she said. "I am sure Jacques will be able to find me some means of transportation."

"Nonsense. Besides, Jacques is occupied with other matters at the moment." He turned and gestured through the door.

Inside, Jessica could see two gentlemen challenging each other to a duel, and the lady for whom they fought had fainted into Jacques' very capable arms. She glanced quickly up at the Duke's strong face and found him waiting politely for her answer. Immediately, she dropped her gaze in order to think more clearly. She could not make a decision while looking into those shards of emeralds. The Duke did have a point. Truly, what other choice did she have? Knowing that she was placing herself in jeopardy, she resolved she would be very alert for any improper behavior on the part of the Duke. That decided, she began to tell him she accepted his offer, but he was already summoning his coach from where it waited beside the road.

As she watched the dark, shiny vehicle pulled by four matching bays approach, she had a moment of panic. He could not learn of her poor lodgings. It would dispel the air of mystery she had so carefully built around herself. He would realize that she was no better than an adventuress, out to win riches and perhaps a husband or benefactor, even though in her case that was not the truth. What if he told others where she lived? Would the men still wish to have her gamble at their tables? Would the women still include her in their gossip? She sent a furtive glance in the Duke's direction. His hard profile was turned to her. He did not seem the type to spread tales.

The carriage stopped before her, and she found she had little choice left. The Duke had his hand beneath her elbow and was propelling her up the small step and into the dark interior of the coach. "May I give the driver an address?" he queried.

Jessica hesitated only a moment before answering clearly, "The Green Dragon."

She watched carefully for his reaction. He merely raised an eyebrow and then passed the information on to his driver. The Duke climbed in beside her, then there was a slight lurch as the carriage started up.

Feeling the need to say something to him, she said shyly, "I hope I am not taking you too much out of your way, Your Grace."

"It is never out of my way to help a beautiful woman," he answered with a grin, as he turned those damnable green eyes on her. "I understand you rarely lose at cards. Were you so troubled tonight because your husband will beat you for losing so badly?"

Jessica sent him a sharp look. "I have no husband."

"Really?" the Duke murmured. "How long have you been a patron of *Madame*'s establishment?"

"About a year." Her answer fell involuntarily from her lips.

"Your parents do not object to their daughter frequenting such a place?" he asked, his tone a mixture of concern and curiosity.

"I really do not believe that should concern you, Your Grace, but since you ask, both my parents are dead," she answered coldly. This man was infuriating. He had discovered more about her in a few short minutes than any of the other patrons of *Madame*'s had discovered in all the time she had been going there. And she had been silly enough to answer him.

"I am sorry," he said simply.

His apology surprised her into one of her own. "You are forgiven, sir, provided you forgive me for being so sharp with you. I have no right to offend someone who is kind enough to offer me a ride to my door." Her smile was genuine.

"You need do nothing more than smile, my lady, and all is forgiven." Ignoring her obvious reluctance to speak about herself, he asked, "You live with your guardian at the Green Dragon?"

Jessica's smile faded quickly as she stared at him. The man's tenacity was incredible. Her temper flared at his question, yet she had enough common sense to realize that she should not anger him. He was a Duke, powerful and influential, and he was a man, strong and muscular. She was alone with him in his carriage, a dangerous circumstance.

"Please," she said firmly, "I would rather not discuss it."

He raised an eyebrow at her tone. "Of course," he acceded coolly. He turned to watch the darkened streets pass.

Jessica observed the Duke stare out the window and was relieved at his silence. He appeared to be ignoring her, and she was just as happy to be left to her own thoughts. His presence made her uncomfortable, and that alone gave her pause. No man had ever had that effect on her. What was it about him that made her afraid of his glance and shy away from his touch?

Hoping that the journey to the Green Dragon would be over soon, she sat tensely against the soft leather cushion and clasped her hands together in her lap. The Duke rode easily with one booted foot up on the seat across from him. Damn him for being so relaxed. What did he care that she had lost a small fortune this night? He did not have a furious stepmother to face if he did not have enough money to bring home. Or the threat of marriage to someone who repulsed him. What did he know of bill-collectors and creditors? What did he know of grief at losing a loved one? Jessica turned and stared out her own window.

The coach slowed and stopped before the inn. Jessica did not let on that she actually lived in the rooming house next door. She had decided that if this man wished to come looking for her, he would not find her where he thought she would be.

In silence, the Duke helped her from the carriage. His hand remained on her elbow even after Jessica stood firmly on the ground. She could feel its warmth through her cloak and dress. Taking a step back so that he was obliged to drop his hand, she boldly looked up into his face. Once again, that strange mingling of fear and fascination slid through her. Quickly, she lowered her eyes.

"Thank you for your kindness, Your Grace," she murmured. "I should still have been left at *Madame*'s if you had not happened along." She smiled shyly up at him.

"It was my pleasure to help a fair maid in distress," he said with an answering smile. "It was certainly a much better ending to the evening than I had anticipated. Having been so long away from home, I have lost track of many of my friends."

"How lonely for you," she said, sympathetically. "Certainly, you will reacquaint yourself with them after a short time. After all, the season will be starting soon."

"Yes, that is true." He nodded. "Perhaps I will make your acquaintance again at one of the balls or masques."

Jessica laughed at the irony of his statement. If her family had not fallen on such hard times and had it not been for Margaret, it might have been very possible that she would have met this man during the upcoming season. "Hardly, Your Grace. My name does not appear on any invitation list."

"If I knew what your name is, I could change that," he offered.

Wary at his gentle probe, Jessica stiffened. "That, Your Grace, is none of your business. Do not presume that because I accepted a ride from you, I am of easy virtue. I thank you for your generosity, and I bid you good night." Nodding once, she turned on her heel and stalked away into the shadows. It did not even occur to her that she had completely passed by the door of the Green Dragon.

Jessica slowly climbed the stairs to her room. Things had gone very badly this evening. But she could not give up. She would have to go back to *Madame*'s the following evening. There was no other place for her to go. She would not be allowed entrance to any of the clubs or private homes where the stakes would be high enough for her to regain what she had lost, and the other gaming houses would not accept her. In dejection, she pushed open the door to her room.

When Jessica tossed the empty coin pouch on the bed, Donny remained silent. Gently, the little woman immediately set about helping her get ready for bed. After Jessica's warm nightrail had been slipped over her head, she straightened her shoulders, as realization flashed through her mind.

"Damn him!" she exploded, as her fist banged against the bedpost. "I will not allow him to mock me!" She turned to Donny and her blue eyes blazed. "I'm going back, Donny. I will show him that I am not to be trifled with. Do you know, I believe he dismissed my carriage this evening so that I would have to ride home with him? The audacity of the man!" Fuming, Jessica lapsed into silence.

While Donny brushed out her hair, Jessica went over every hand that had been played. Somehow, the Duke had outwitted her every time. By the time she had crawled into bed, she was plotting how to get her revenge. She lay in bed and her eyes burned holes in the ceiling.

CHAPTER 3

Damien stood before his cheval mirror and examined his reflection critically. He nearly did not recognize himself, having been on that mission in France for so long. Scruff usually covered his cheeks and chin, and his floppy brimmed hat and long black cloak usually concealed his identity. The man who stared back at him was not the English spy, *Le Chat*, but a gentleman of society, the Duke of Wyndham. He looked forward to embracing his true persona. His attention, however, was not completely on the perfect fit of his wine-colored, superfine jacket and buff-colored riding breeches, nor on the soft gleam of his boots and the intricate new fashion of tying his stock. Rather he was thinking of the intriguing woman he had met at *Madame* du Barré's gaming hell the previous night.

The Lady Fortuna. She was a puzzle, but the most fascinating puzzle he had ever met. He had listened to the gossip about her at *Madame*'s, but had not really believed any of it. Until he met her. She was obviously well-bred and cultured, but as for her being the daughter of an earl, he was doubtful. She had played cards too well. He had beaten her, but he had seen the skill with which she played. No titled gentleman would allow his daughter to gamble, and certainly not at *Madame* du Barré's. The chit had to be an adventuress, albeit a very desirable one. He could still envision her sitting next to him in the coach. She had been remote and alluring. After he had left her, he could still smell her fragrance lingering in the air. She would be a delightful diversion, just the thing to make him forget the hardships he had endured. The Duke smiled to himself in anticipation.

Wilson, his valet, brushed the shoulders of his jacket and stepped back.

"If I may presume to say so, Your Grace, you are looking like your old self again," the valet offered.

Damien's eyes were mischievous as he caught Wilson's in the mirror. "And what, pray, did I look like before, Wilson?" He was well aware he looked a wreck when he had appeared at the door of his London house a few days earlier.

Wilson coughed uneasily. Damien watched his man for a moment, then relented. "That bad, eh? Well, those days are gone, Wilson. Where's my hat?" He turned, and his valet handed him a tall beaver hat, soft leather gloves, and riding crop.

"Good man." Damien threw him a quick smile and then headed out.

As he reached the bottom of the winding staircase, Jacobs, his majordomo, was waiting for him.

"General Drayton is here, Your Grace," the man said. "He is waiting for you in your study."

Damien's eyebrows lifted slightly. "General Drayton, you say? How curious. Thank you, Jacobs." He handed the man his hat, gloves and riding crop, then headed for his study.

Upon entering the room, he was met by a gray-haired gentleman who wore his soldier's uniform with distinction. He bowed formally to Damien. "Good morning, Your Grace," he said.

Damien hid a smile of amusement at the man's formality. It was strange how roles could be reversed so quickly. "Good morning, General." He held out his hand to his former commander and smiled warmly.

The general shook Damien's hand. "It appears that retirement agrees with you."

"It is so much easier than living in a hovel." Damien motioned to a chair and the two men sat.

"My visit will be brief," the general said. He cleared his throat. "This is not a social call. We have a problem, and you are the only man who can help us."

The Duke raised a cynical eyebrow. "I seem to remember hearing those words when you first recruited me as a spy, George."

General Drayton smiled. "The problem is here in London," he said, becoming serious. "*Madame* du Barré to be exact."

"The Barré, you say!" Damien shook his head. "A loss to the men of London."

"I daresay," the general agreed dryly. "She is spying for Napoleon. We know it, but we can't prove it. She rarely, if ever, leaves London, so we know she has someone relaying information to the coast. We captured her last courier, but the devil tried to escape on the way back to London, and he was shot by one of his guards."

Disbelief crossed Damien's face. "God's blood, General, how do you expect to win this war with such numskulls?"

General Drayton's gaze sharpened. "That was my thought exactly."

Damien sighed. "So, you want me to find out who the Barré is using as a courier and capture him for you."

"If you could, it would help us greatly." The general leaned forward in his chair. "Damien, you know I would not ask this of you if there were any other way. You are known at *Madame*'s, and so will not arouse suspicion. My other men are not suited to this sort of thing as you are."

"Spare me the arguments, George," Damien said caustically. He puffed out a breath. His gaze lifted to the walnut-paneled walls, the shelves of books, the portraits, as he gave himself a moment. Coming to a decision, he said, "I will do this one more thing for you, General, but I cannot afford to spend any more of my time in the service of His Majesty. I have to see to my own affairs which I have neglected for too long. Besides, it has become too dangerous. I cannot jeopardize the lives of my men. Fouché, Napoleon's Minister of Police, has come too close to discovering my identity and that of my men."

General Drayton nodded. "I understand perfectly, Your Grace." He stood to leave. "Thank you, Damien. If there is ever anything I can do for you, please let me know."

After Drayton took his leave, Damien sank back down into his chair and stared thoughtfully after him. This assignment would not be all work. It might even be enjoyable. Although he regretted that London would lose a witty, entertaining lady in *Madame*'s arrest, he knew before that could take place, he would have to spend many nights at her establishment, a pleasant task. There was also a certain young lady with eyes like sapphires and hair like ebony whom he had met at *Madame*'s. He smiled. At least he could live in comfort and enjoy his pleasures while he accomplished his task. Whistling, he left the house for his ride.

During the week after her encounter with the Duke of Wyndham, Jessica frequented *Madame* du Barré's every evening. She had won back all she had lost, plus a sizable amount more. The stipend for her stepmother was secure. She was now playing to solidify her reputation as a shrewd gambler. She would be leaving for Braeleigh on the morrow, so this would be the last time she would be at *Madame*'s for several days.

The gown Jessica was wearing this evening was of blue silk, the same color as Jessica's eyes. The bodice was cut low and the skirt was composed of tiny, vertical pleats which rippled and clung to her body as she walked. It was a sensuous dress, made to cause heads to turn and keep men's minds from the cards in their hands.

Jessica arrived at *Madame*'s somewhat later than usual. After paying her respects to the woman and receiving her approval, she went to the private room where she would be playing cards. A game was already in progress when she arrived. One chair was empty, its back to the door. She recognized all of the players but one, who was in the chair to her right. Before she had time to speculate on the identity of the man, however, the round ended, and her presence was noted. The men stood as she approached the table.

"Good evening, gentlemen." She smiled as she glanced around at them. She turned to the man to her right to introduce herself. Her smile froze on her face as she recognized the green eyes watching her. She nodded a greeting. "Your Grace," she murmured.

"Ah, good show!" Lord Patterson exclaimed. "You two children have met."

"Yes," Wyndham said. "The lady and I spent a most interesting evening together."

Jessica did not miss the interested glances that were passed about the table at the Duke's remark. Not wishing to cause more gossip, she remained silent. To her dismay, Wyndham held her chair, not

Lord Hoxly who was to her left. Jessica fumed. Why did the Duke have to be here tonight of all nights? One more evening and she would have been gone for several days. He could have come to *Madame*'s then. Besides that, he was sitting next to her. Fate was not being fair.

As Jessica waited while the cards were being dealt, she noticed there was a considerable pile of money before His Grace. Did he never lose? Well, tonight, she was ready for him. Tonight, she would win.

Play continued for several hours. Except for an occasional witty or charming remark from the other players at the table, the time seemed to drag on forever for Jessica. The pile of money before her became smaller and smaller, while that before the Duke grew. Becoming desperate, Jessica decided to do something she had never done. She decided to cheat. Her father had taught her how to do this when he had taught her to play cards, only because he wanted her to know when other people were doing it. She had become so proficient at it that even her father had been unable to tell when she had dealt from the bottom of the deck. She doubted that the Duke, who was her only target, would be able to catch her.

It was Jessica's turn to deal. She held her breath as she dealt the cards around the table. The Duke said nothing. He merely picked up the cards before him. Bets were placed, and play went on. Jessica won the hand. The Duke lost.

The turn to deal traveled around the table twice more. Each time she dealt, she won, and the Duke lost. She was convinced he did not realize what she was doing. It was so easy. Perhaps she should have tried this before.

It was her turn to deal again. She picked up the cards, shuffled them. Just as she was about to deal them out, a darkly tanned hand snaked out and grabbed her by the wrist. With wide, frightened eyes, she looked up into twin shards of green ice.

"It would seem that the lady is dealing from the bottom of the deck," the Duke said. His voice was quiet, menacing.

Jessica blinked, but hid the fear that slithered through her. "What are you accusing me of, Your Grace?" she asked innocently.

"I think that is quite evident," he said. "I believe it is called cheating."

"How dare you, sir!" she demanded. The only thing to do was bluff. She jumped up, knocking over her chair. She hoped he would release her wrist, but his grip became even tighter as he remained seated—bad manners as well as an insult.

"But I do dare, my lady," he answered, his tone deadly quiet. "You see, I have been watching you. It is only to me that the cards come from the bottom of the deck. Would you care for a demonstration?"

One of the other men at the table cleared his throat and tentatively suggested, "I really don't think that is necessary, Your Grace."

The Duke acted as if he had not heard. Never taking his eyes from Jessica's face, he turned the deck of cards face-up and began to recite each card as he took it from the top of the pile. "Four of hearts. Seven of spades. Jack of spades. Trey of diamonds. Shall I go on?"

Jessica's eyes closed, and she felt the blood drain from her face. Suddenly, he was on his feet. He seemed to tower over her.

"If you were a man, I would demand satisfaction with weapons tomorrow at dawn," he told her roughly. "But since you are a woman, there will have to be another way." He paused for a moment, then his voice became silky. "I believe I have just the solution." One arm went about her waist and pulled her close against his unyielding body. He forced her head back with a thumb under her chin as if he meant to kiss her. "Perhaps *Madame* would not be pleased to discover that one of her patrons has been cheating in her house."

Jessica's eyes widened in fright. She tried to wriggle away from his hard body. "No, please!" she gasped.

His arm tightened around her, preventing her escape. "Then you will have to convince me otherwise," he said coldly.

Lord Hoxly leapt to his feet. "This has gone far enough, Your Grace," he said stiffly. "I demand that you leave the lady alone."

The Duke's chilling glance fell on the man. "You *demand*, sir?"

"Yes." Lord Hoxly stood tall. "If you require satisfaction from this young lady, I will gladly stand for her."

Jessica glanced from one man to the other in uncertainty. She was relieved that someone at the table saw fit to protect her from the rogue who held her, but she did not wish anyone harmed because of her. Before she could gather her wits enough to speak, she saw the Duke's eyes narrow dangerously.

"This does not concern you, Hoxly, nor any of the other gentlemen present. If you value your life, I would suggest you remain silent. You know I do not speak idly if I tell you that I will call out every man at this table if there is a hint of rumor concerning this night. The insult was to me and me alone, and the satisfaction I demand will come only from this lady. I presume I make myself clear, gentlemen?" His glance swept around the table.

The men either nodded or lowered their eyes. Even Lord Hoxly sank back into his chair.

The Duke turned back to Jessica. His thumb casually caressed her cheek as he murmured, "Remember, my sweet, persuade me." He released her without warning and strode from the room.

Deathly silence fell after his departure. Jessica's head swam, and she swayed. Lord Hoxly steadied her, as everyone began talking at once, and Hoxly helped her into a chair.

"Are you all right, my lady?" he asked solicitously.

Jessica managed a weak smile for him. "Yes, thank you. It was merely a slight dizzy spell. The man frightened me."

"He is, indeed, a very frightening man," Hoxly agreed. "Allow me to get you something to drink."

Jessica nodded her agreement.

As he was occupied, Jessica saw a servant slip into the room and gather up the Duke's winnings along with her own. Before she could stop him, he left. By the time Lord Hoxly had returned with a glass of brandy, her mind was racing. She had to recover what remained of her winnings. And she had to get out of there and speak to the Duke. She could not allow him to tell *Madame* about the cheating.

She took a small sip of the brandy, sighed deeply, and stood up. "If you will excuse me, gentlemen, I bid you good night. Thank you for your kindness, Lord Hoxly."

"Of course, my dear, not at all," Hoxly said with fatherly concern. "May I escort you to the door? Or perhaps to your home?"

"No, please don't trouble yourself," she told him, not wanting any witness to what she intended to do. "I feel much stronger now, and I am sure the Duke will not bother me again this evening. Good night, sir." The other gentlemen were deep in conversation, so she was able to slip out unnoticed.

She walked quickly to the door and collected her cloak, but before leaving, she asked Jacques if he was acquainted with the address of the Duke of Wyndham. When she explained her intention was to return something the Duke had left behind that evening, the major-domo gave her the address. Then she went out into the night. Her hackney-coach was there waiting. She gave the driver the address, and they sped off.

As the coach drove up to the house, Jessica saw it was in darkness. Perhaps he had not come straight home, after all. Well, she was prepared to wait for him all night if necessary. She dismissed the hackney and walked up to the front door. It was slightly ajar. She thought that a bit strange, but terribly convenient. At least she could wait for him inside without waking the household. It did not occur to her that there might be others, like parents or siblings, living in the house who might discover her.

Without another thought, she pushed open the door and walked in. She was in a large foyer, but it was dark, and she could not see any of its details, yet she could feel its size extend above her head and stretch out before her. Looking about, she spied an open door into one of the rooms. After a brief hesitation, she decided to wait in there. Discovery of her creeping about a strange man's house in the middle of the night would be the ruination of whatever shred of a decent reputation she had, but her desperation to set things right overrode everything else.

The room was dark as well, but a fire blazed on the hearth. She thought it odd that a fire would have been lit in a deserted house, but the warmth of the flames beckoned to her. She went to stand before it and held out her cold hands to soak up its heat.

"I'm glad you came, Jessica," a voice she recognized too well spoke from her right.

Gasping, she spun around. He was there, sitting in a chair, a brandy in his hand. He had been there all the time. Waiting for her. She felt like a small child who had been discovered with a hand in the jar of sweets.

To give herself time to regain her composure, she asked, "How did you know my name?"

The Duke shrugged. "A simple matter of asking *Madame*. She enjoys making love-matches."

Jessica opened her mouth to protest his term for their relationship, then decided she had better keep silent. This was not the time to argue about insignificant things. Turning back to the fire, she took a deep breath to steady her nerves.

"I…I had to talk to you," she said.

He said nothing.

Swallowing, she pressed on. "Please, you mustn't tell *Madame* that I cheated. I have never done it before, and I will never do it again. Please." She turned back to him and tried to read his expression, but his face was in the shadows.

Finally, he spoke. "How do I know that you will never cheat again? You appear to be quite expert at it, which leads me to believe it is something which you do quite often. Since I have been wronged, you seem to be asking rather much."

Jessica could see this was going to be quite a bit more difficult than she had originally thought. The Duke was not one to be easily swayed by a coquettish smile or a pouting lip. He was not a man who would forgive easily. She was not going to be able to charm her way out of this predicament. Nor could she tell him the truth and risk her stepmother finding out, giving Margaret the leverage to force her into marriage with Sir Percival.

"What else can I say, Your Grace, except that I am sorry?" she asked.

He merely raised an eyebrow.

"What do you want of me?" she whispered desperately. "I will do anything you ask."

Carefully, he placed his glass on the table beside him. In one graceful movement, he rose from his chair and came to stand before her. Jessica forced herself not to back away. A strange tension enveloped her with his nearness. She fought to keep her feet planted where they were. He gazed down at her a long moment before he spoke.

"Anything, Jessica?" he queried softly.

She looked up into those green eyes, darkened from the shadows. The firelight played across his face and made it appear demonic and handsome in turns. She knew what he wanted, what she would have to pay to keep his silence. A thousand thoughts raced through her mind. Was the price really too high to continue in her current existence? The memory of Sir Percival floated before her eyes. There was only one answer to his question.

"Yes," she said. "Anything."

He watched her plead with him. And submit. He was torn between his righteous anger and his foolish desire for her. He had never met such a beautiful creature. She was an enigma, one minute seductive and alluring, the next cold and aloof, the next naïve and innocent. He did not believe her ploy of innocence. She was an adventuress, playing the odds for her own gain. But this time, she had overreached. She had played him for the fool, and for that she would pay.

He untied her mask and slowly removed it. Her beauty was completely revealed. She had not been hiding ugliness, but rather a perfection that would cause the angels to be jealous. The blood raced in his veins. He needed to see more.

He unclasped her cloak and pushed it from her shoulders. A tremor ran through her when his hands brushed her skin. Faked or real? He stood gazing at her a moment, drinking in her loveliness. He did not care if her innocence was a sham. He wanted her, despite her deception. Pulling her to him, wrapping his arms about her, he brought his lips down on hers, searing them with his passion.

This was Jessica's first taste of a man's kiss. It was pleasant at first. She enjoyed the strong feel of his arms holding her, the hardness of his body against hers, the warmth that enveloped her. Then the kiss became more demanding. Jessica felt as if she were being smothered. He took her breath, and still he did not stop. She began to panic. She had never felt this way before. She pushed against his chest.

"No," she murmured. "Please, stop."

When he released her, a puzzled expression crossed his face, but he did not move away.

She gave a small, nervous laugh. "I…," she started, then realized she could not explain herself. She was too embarrassed to admit she had never been kissed by a man. Besides, she was supposed to be worldly. That was part of her persona at *Madame's*.

"I'll not force you, Jessica," he said, his words matter-of-fact. "It is your decision. You know the cost of my silence. If you wish to pay the price, you'll find me upstairs."

Jessica watched him move with controlled strength and feline grace to the door and out into the foyer. His footsteps echoed in the dark as he crossed to the stairway. She heard him begin to climb the stairs.

She turned back to the fire as she worried her lower lip between her teeth. His touch had been exciting, his kiss frightening. Jessica had known no man intimately, and the prospect of making love with this stranger, handsome and intriguing though he was, struck fear into her heart. Not only that, she would be ruined, losing the one thing which she could bring to her husband should she ever marry — the fact that she had saved herself only for him.

Jessica closed her eyes and sighed. It had not been easy living by her wits these last several months. She had been very cautious about becoming too friendly with anyone — male or female. Self-preservation prompted her to react with coolness toward everyone. Being a lone female in a place like *Madame's*, without the benefit of protector or benefactor, she had been fair game for any man who wished to try his luck at seducing her. Only *Madame's* very thin blanket of guardianship had saved her on several occasions. What would happen now if she succumbed to the Duke? Could she pay his price and still remain aloof?

She glanced sideways to the door. She could not allow him to inform *Madame* of her cheating. Even though *Madame* was the one person with whom she had a close relationship, she could not impinge on that friendship. *Madame* did not countenance any form of dishonesty in her establishment. Jessica would be barred from ever playing there again, and she did not have entrance to any other gaming house. She would be unable to pay Margaret. She would be forced to wed Sir Percival.

Jessica came to her decision. There was no recourse but to climb the stairs and go to the Duke. Taking a deep breath, she started on her journey.

As she came to the top of the stairs, she wondered if he often had women guests in his bed. Thinking back on the gossip she had heard about him since his arrival, she thought it very probable that he did. Although not the usual course for a gentleman to entertain his paramours under his own roof, the Duke did not seem to be the usual sort of gentleman. The absence of any servants in the house was quite noticeable. They were probably accustomed to his late-night assignations.

One door stood ajar at the end of the hall. Firelight flickered through the opening. She turned in that direction. When she arrived at the dark-paneled door, she hesitated, her heart pounding a nervous tattoo. She swallowed once, trying to beat down her fear. Placing her hand on the door, she slowly pushed it open.

The interior was dark and masculine, subtly lit by a group of candles in one corner on a table. A fire crackled warmly in the hearth. A large, four-poster bed with simple, but elegant, blue velvet hangings dominated the room.

The Duke was sitting on the bed, leaning back against the headboard. He'd removed his jacket and waistcoat and untied his stock. His shirt was open halfway down his chest. He'd drawn up one knee and rested a casual arm across it. The other long, muscular leg hung over the edge of the bed, his bare foot on the floor. Jessica had never encountered any pirates, but she thought they would resemble Damien Trevor, Duke of Wyndham, as he looked this moment.

She stopped just inside the door. A chill ran down her spine. It had been a mistake to come to the Duke's bedroom. It was still not too late to turn and run, but she felt rooted to the spot. Her eyes were riveted on the lean figure who relaxed on the bed.

"Come here, Jessica," he said softly from the dimness.

His voice was like a crack of thunder in the silence of the room. Jessica jumped. Slowly, as if drawn by an invisible string, she moved forward, closer and closer, until she reached the foot of the bed. Another few steps and she would be standing right next to him.

"Closer," he said.

Gulping, she stepped forward.

"That is far enough." Although his words were quiet, his eyes reflected the candlelight and made him appear like the Devil incarnate.

Jessica drew in a shaky breath. Her hands trembled. Her heart pounded. She did not know what this man meant to do. He was a Duke, arrogant and powerful, and in comparison, she was no one. If he hurt her — or worse — no one would question it. Margaret would not care, and Jason was too young to do anything about it.

"Undress," he commanded.

Jessica hesitated. She had never been unclothed before any man.

"Take off your clothes, Jessica." The Duke's tone was firm, allowing no disobedience.

She pulled the dress from her shoulders. It fell to the floor with a sigh. Her petticoat followed. Blushing hotly, she stood clad only in her stays, chemise, stockings and shoes. She fought the desire to cover herself.

The Duke indicated her shoes and stockings. "Remove those," he ordered.

She did as she was told.

"Take down your hair." Another order, spoken with authority.

Slowly, one by one, she pulled the pins from her hair and allowed it to cascade about her shoulders and down her back to her waist.

Finally, she was able to find her voice. "Please," she whispered, "do not hurt me."

At her words, the Duke stood swiftly. Jessica took a step backward. The Duke's teeth flashed white in a smile.

"Contrary to what you may have heard, I do not make a practice of harming women," he said as he advanced. "You need not be afraid."

His hand landed lightly on her arm. Then slid down to her hand. The caress made her shiver. He tugged her easily toward him. Cupping her face in his hands, he softly brushed her mouth with his lips. This kiss was near to Jessica's idea of love-making. She decided that it was rather pleasant. Perhaps this would not be so terrible, after all.

Damien was stirred by her more than by any other woman. She was an entrancing vision as she stood nearly naked before him. The swell of her breasts, her tiny waist, the curve of her hips created a perfect picture. Her thick lashes shaded her clear blue eyes, making them dark in her pale face. Her softly shaped lips had parted slightly. Whether she knew it or not, her whole being beckoned to be loved, softly, gently. So, his kiss had been tender.

He was vaguely aware of her apparent inexperienced response. Somewhere, in the back of his mind, he was surprised. At *Madame's*, she had been self-possessed and assured. He assumed she was experienced in intimate relations with men. But if not, she played the charade well, pretending to be an innocent. He did not dwell on the thought. He was too intent on the sensuous creature in his grasp.

His fingers tangled in the mysterious depths of her hair, holding her in just the right position as he deepened the kiss. He drank in the soft feel of her and the faint scent of jasmine surrounding her like an aura. He traced one hand down her back to her perfectly rounded bottom and pressed her close. His desire for her tipped on the verge of madness. He wanted to ravage her. But something warned him to go gently.

Her arms crept around his neck and she squirmed against him. It was not the move of an innocent. But he would play her game. She was too delicious to deny. When he raised his head, her eyes had darkened from her arousal.

His hand slipped from the tangle of her tresses, down the slim column of her neck, over her shoulder, to one rounded breast. He teased its rosy tip as he kept her gaze locked in his. Her breath came quickly through her parted lips. Her lids drooped languidly over her eyes.

He unlaced the strings of her stays and whipped them away. Then he pulled at the ribbons holding her chemise closed over her breasts and allowed them to come free. Glorious. His hand brushed across her softness as he pushed the thin material away. He leaned her back on his arm, and kissed his way down her throat, across her shoulder, to her breast. As his mouth closed on its tip and his tongue flicked at it playfully, her breath caught in her throat. Gratified at her response, he kissed his way back to her mouth. Her lips parted, allowing his tongue to ravage the sweetness within. She gave a little moan. Raising his head, with a little smile, he released her. She was his now. He stripped off his shirt and breeches.

Jessica felt bereft when he let her go. The feelings he had awakened in her were intoxicating. She wanted more, much more. As he discarded his clothes, she watched him in a trance. She swayed slightly as if she were drunk, because she was—drunk on the passion and desire he had aroused in her. Her body tingled all over. Her skin had come alive, responding to his every touch. She had never realized that the touch of a man could feel so magical.

His body was magnificent, even to her naïve eyes. Broad shoulders tapered down to narrow waist and hips. The muscles in his arms and legs were hard and sinuous, and rippled under his skin when he moved. In spite of her embarrassment, she could not look away. She wanted to watch his every move.

When he turned back to her, her eyes caught on the thatch of golden fur covering his chest. A thin, white line, from shoulder to breastbone, marred the symmetrical beauty of it. Without thinking, she reached out and traced the scar. The soft, dark gold hair on his chest tickled her and she drew her hand down to his flat stomach almost to his— She jerked away, appalled at her boldness.

He huffed a laugh. "Don't be shy, my sweet."

Her cheeks flamed. "I…" Words failed her. She could not tell him she had never even kissed a man, and certainly never touched one there.

With a smile, he took her hand and kissed her palm. The feel of his lips made her melt. Then scooping her up, he deposited her gently on the bed.

He straddled her on his knees, leaned over her and kissed her again. His mouth made her insides fluttery and tingly. She held on to his shoulders, warm and firm beneath her hands. His tongue traced a line down her throat, between her breasts and over her stomach.

His fingers intimately stroked her inner thigh. A sigh of pleasure escaped her when his tongue branded a tattoo in the same spot. But when he came too close to her secret place, she pressed her legs together. Fear made her stiffen.

Damien raised his head. That niggling voice came again questioning her innocence. He wanted to taste her desperately, but he would not force her. She would have to give herself freely. He stretched out beside her on the bed and nibbled at her ear. His hand claimed her breast and he rubbed his thumb across its rosy tip.

"Are you still willing to pay my price, Jessica?" he asked and swirled his tongue below her ear. He would give her every opportunity to back down, but he would persuade with every weapon he had.

Her lashes swept down. "Yes," she whispered on a sigh.

Jessica did not allow herself to think beyond the immediate present. The Duke, so far, had been gentle, and what he had done to her made her feel wonderful. She had come this far. There was no turning back now. Surprisingly, she found the sensations he aroused far from horrible. In fact, she rather wished they could go on forever.

His hands and mouth roamed over her body. They teased and caressed, creating sensations deep inside her she had never felt before. She opened herself to him like a budding flower. She found herself moaning with pleasure, squirming and wriggling so his fingers touched here, his mouth sucked there. And then he lay on top of her, covering her body, pressing her into the bed. She marveled at the way their bodies fit together so intimately. His skin against hers made her tingle and want. She held him close and ran her hands over his back. He buried his face in her hair.

"You are a witch, Jessica," he whispered.

Then he drove into her.

The sudden pain made her arch up and cry out. Confused, she froze, her eyes squeezed shut. She had been told she would feel pain her first time, but the Duke had aroused such exquisite sensations, she had forgotten. Now, the truth frightened her. Would she feel more pain if he continued? Would she feel pain every time? But perhaps, she would never lie with a man again after this night. Whatever the answers, she prayed this encounter would be over soon.

Damien, surprised at the barrier he'd broken through, waited for her pain to subside. Her nervousness and shyness and unpracticed naïveté had not been an act. A pang of guilt surged through him. He'd seduced a virgin. Why had she said nothing? But perhaps the game she played was bigger than he first thought. Was she trying to entrap him? Was she out for herself, or was she connected to Fouché through *Madame*? Whatever her reasons, she'd made a fool of him, had cheated at the card table. His injured pride reared up. He had not forced her. And he wanted her. Something primal made him glad he'd been her first. He would make her remember this night.

His thumb found the hardened peak of her breast and he stroked it gently. Slowly, she relaxed. When his mouth took his thumb's place and he sucked, she breathed out a moan. Hesitantly, she moved against him. He smiled. She might have been an innocent virgin when this night began, but she was becoming a vixen. Her wriggles and sighs fanned his need. Holding her hips, he thrust into her, savoring her hot sweetness.

Jessica gave herself up to the insistent, driving desire that engulfed her. Her mind reeled, and she lost all sense of reality. There was only the man above her in her world. She felt as if she were in a whirlpool, being drawn deeper and deeper into the vortex. Down, down, they fell, clinging to each other, until the bottom gave way and the sudden, great release came. Never in her life had Jessica experienced anything like it. She thought she was going to die. As if he were her only lifeline, she grabbed at the man who held her.

As the waves of sensation receded, her world came back into focus. What had she just done? Tears threatened, and she strangled the sobs that constricted her throat. The Duke rolled off her and held her close. Despite her best efforts, those tears spilled down her cheeks and wet his chest.

His hand rubbed soothingly up and down her back. "Why didn't you tell me you had never been with a man, Jessica?" he asked softly.

She sniffed and wiped at her eyes. "You would not have believed me if I had." She sat up quickly and pulled away from him. As if she did not care, she shrugged one shoulder. "What difference does it make now, anyway? The deed is done. You have your payment, Your Grace."

He sat up next to her and with a finger beneath her chin, made her look at him. "Was it so bad, my sweet? Did you not enjoy giving payment as much as I enjoyed taking it?"

She had enjoyed it. Too much. But his arrogance made her furious. "You are despicable!" she spat at him.

He laughed. "And you are beautiful." He pulled her down and rolled over her, balancing himself above her.

Jessica glared up at him. "Have you not had enough, Your Grace? You have deflowered a virgin and avenged your honor at the same time. Not every man can make that claim."

Damien winced. "You are very blunt."

"I am only speaking the truth," she said. "You forced me into your bed."

"I did not force you. I asked you. And I did this." He swirled his tongue in the hollow of her throat. "And this." His hand slowly caressed her breast. "And this." He sucked gently where his hand had been.

In spite of herself, Jessica moaned as once more he began to fan the fires of her passion. A part of her brain told her she was crazy to succumb to him again, while the rest of it decidedly ignored its warnings. What this man did to her was exciting beyond belief, and she wanted more of it.

He made love to her again. And she let him. He brought her alive in a way she had never felt before. When it was over, she sighed, exhausted, contented, and fell asleep in his arms.

Jessica dreamt of green fields and her mother and father playing with her. She was a young girl again, and there was Braeleigh, and everything was right. But, then she was alone, and it was dark. She was lost. Her stepmother's face floated before her. She was smiling cruelly. Her stepmother turned into Sir Percival. He was surrounded by faces she did not know. She was at *Madame*'s, and the faces were yelling at her. Get out! Cheater! Liar! Get out! A pair of mocking green eyes stared at her. She tried to run away, but she fell. Hands grabbed at her.

"Jessica. Jessica."

Those eyes. His eyes.

She realized she was awake, and he was looking at her. Then she remembered where she was.

"Are you all right?" the Duke asked. "You're shivering." He pulled her close and smoothed her hair until her tremors stopped.

His warmth and gentleness comforted. In his embrace, she felt safe from Margaret and her cruel demands. But his protection was an illusion. He was a threat to her and her precarious existence. Slowly, her shivers stopped.

"I'm all right now," she said, her voice muffled against his chest. She felt foolish for being so afraid of a dream. She pulled away from him, turned in the bed, and glanced out the window. The sky had begun to brighten. "I have to go."

"Go where?" he demanded. "Why do you have to go?"

She sat up, arching her brow. "I have to go where all creatures of the night go, Your Grace. Back to my lair. You did call me a witch, didn't you?" She gave him a wry smile. "Or was I mistaken? Perhaps it was the Devil whispering in my ear."

He ran his hand up her back under her hair and laughed. "It was not the Devil, my sweet, only a man bedeviled by your beauty."

"Truly, sir, you are the Devil, for no mere mortal man could seduce a witch such as I so easily." She slid out of the bed before she succumbed to his touch again and gathered her clothes.

Jessica glanced up to find his eyes on her. She wore not a stitch of clothing, and she quickly donned her chemise. Her dress was slipped from her grasp before she could put it on. The Duke stood with the ripple of blue silk dangling from his hand.

She held out her hand. "Please, Your Grace. My dress."

His eyes held determination. She was just as determined that he would not have his way with her again.

He held her dress away from her. "Not until you stop calling me 'Your Grace'. My name is Damien. Say it." His arrogant command allowed no disobedience.

Jessica's eyes widened. Even after a night of love-making, he still intimidated her. He was the powerful Duke of Wyndham.

"Say it, Jessica," he said in a softer tone.

She swallowed. "Damien," she whispered.

He smiled. "Was that so difficult?"

When he smiled at her like that, her resolve melted. Then she remembered how she had come to be where she was. She meant nothing to him beyond a single night's enjoyment.

With her emotions well under control, she allowed him to slip her dress over her head. He turned her around to fasten the back. Pushing her hair aside, he brushed his lips across her nape. At his caress, she moved away, but was stopped by his hand on her arm.

"Don't be so skittish." He laughed softly. "I promise to behave."

When he finished doing up her dress, she thanked him and walked to the mirror. Her hair was a riot of tangles.

"Will this help?" he asked as he held his brush out to her.

"Thank you," she murmured shyly and began brushing her hair. Using his brush seemed very intimate, even after their night of love-making, but she could not leave looking like a wild woman.

While she was occupied, Damien dressed quickly. When she had finished, he held the door for her. They descended the stairs in silence. He collected her cloak from the floor of the salon.

As he placed it about her shoulders, he asked, "Will you come again tonight?"

Jessica stepped away and whirled to face him. He had received double his due for the injury she had done to him. His pride should have been soothed many times over. She was not about to pay any more.

42

Her fists clenched at her sides. "Do you think because you have stolen my maidenhood that I will come meekly to you whenever you ask? I have paid your price for silence. I am not your whore."

Surprise flashed through his eyes. His tone was level as he said, "I am not asking you to be a whore. I am asking you to be my mistress, my lover."

Her chin went up proudly. "It is the same thing. I will be no man's mistress."

"An adventuress has few options." His words whipped at her. "What man will have you for wife when he finds out that you are no longer a virgin? Or did you plan to never marry and become an old maid, to sit at home and knit for no one but yourself?"

"Who would know that my maidenhood has been taken?" she demanded. "I would not be stupid enough to let on."

The Duke's answer was merely the lift of an eyebrow.

Jessica felt as if she had been struck. He would not, could not ruin what little reputation she had. He could not possibly be so cruel to gossip about what had occurred in his house this night. Fighting back the tears, she struggled to answer in a level tone.

"I cannot keep you from speaking about this night if you wish to do so. I will not beg you to keep silent. I have given you my most precious possession in payment for your silence on another matter. I cannot give you anything more."

"Give me yourself, Jessica," he said softly.

His words tugged at her. But she would never become any man's mistress. "I cannot. Why do you want me? There must be hundreds of women in London who would gladly tumble into bed with the powerful Duke of Wyndham. Please, let me be—"

"I do not want hundreds of women," he interrupted, "I want you."

"No."

"I will have you, whether you want it now or not," he went on as if she had not spoken. "Jessica, the Lady Fortuna, will be the sole property of Damien Trevor, Duke of Wyndham. I will make you want it."

His arrogance made her furious. First, he wanted her as his mistress, and now she was chattel, his property. The man was unbearable. What would he ask of her next? She decided not to wait to find out.

"You presume too much, Your Grace," she answered haughtily. "You know nothing of my life, nor why I came to you tonight. But I will be considered the property of no one—not even you. Now, if you will excuse me, I will be leaving. I am taking an early coach out of London, and I have much to do."

She turned and stalked to the door, into the foyer, and across the floor to the front entrance. At each step, she expected a hand on her arm, detaining her. She did not take a complete breath until she was outside.

Jessica walked down the steps and out to the street. There were no carriages in sight. She resigned herself to a long and possibly dangerous walk back to her rooms.

After several minutes, she heard the clatter of hooves on the cobblestones of the street behind her. They slowed as they came abreast. In the dim light of dawn, she saw a rider on a magnificent black stallion. Of course, he would come after her. She began to walk more quickly.

"It's a long walk back to the Green Dragon," Damien said. "May I offer the lady a ride?"

"The lady would prefer to walk, thank you," Jessica answered coldly. She pulled her cloak closer about her and lengthened her stride.

An arm went about her waist, and she was lifted off the ground. Jessica found herself seated on the horse in front of the Duke.

"As I said, it is a long walk, and I will have nothing of mine abused," he stated sternly.

"Nothing of yours?" Jessica repeated incredulously as she twisted about to face him. "I told you, I will not be owned like a piece of furniture. You have no right."

Her words were cut off by his mouth. Jessica fumed and tried to wriggle free, but his hold was too tight. Silently, she called him every foul name she could think of, and she even made up a few new ones. He had no right to do this to her.

He finally raised his head. Jessica's temper exploded. She whipped out to strike his arrogant face. Just as fast, the Duke caught her wrist, his gaze cool and amused. She was so furious she could have spit. Realizing that it would do no good to struggle or berate him, she jerked her arm out of his grasp and faced forward, trying to ignore the fact that she sat intimately between his thighs.

They rode in silence until they came to the Green Dragon. Before she could slip from the horse, he turned her face to him and lowered his lips to hers again, this time with more gentleness. Possessively, he cupped her breast. It took every ounce of Jessica's will not to melt against him. His touch was devastating. His kisses could make her forget who she was. Instead, she held herself stiffly away.

"You will be mine, my sweet. Sooner or later, you will be mine," he whispered against her mouth.

Jessica jerked away and glared. He gazed back at her, those green eyes dancing, then he guided her as she slipped from the horse. She straightened her cloak, and stalked away, past the door of the inn, with as much dignity as she could muster.

After only a few steps, something landed with a clink in front of her. A pouch lay just beyond the toe of her shoe, and the shine of coins peeked through its opening. She scooped it up and swung around to face the Duke as he sat smugly upon his horse.

Her cheeks flamed in indignation. "I will not accept payment for anything I did this past evening. You may keep your money." She lifted her arm to fling the pouch back at him, but his words stopped her.

He shrugged. "You may throw it back at me if you wish, but I would discover exactly what it is you throw away."

Jessica lowered her arm and narrowed her eyes.

"The pouch contains your winnings from this past evening at *Madame*'s. It seems I collected them by mistake," he said with a grin.

"By mistake!" She remembered the servant, obviously following orders, who had collected both her winnings and those of the Duke. Words failed her. She spun on her heel and stalked away. She never wanted to see the overbearing, cocksure devil again.

CHAPTER 4

The coach ride from London to Braeleigh was long, and Jessica would not reach home until the next day. She had plenty of time to consider the events of the past evening. She was very confused. Usually, she was aloof and cool, which discouraged men's advances and kept them at a distance. Those who would not behave felt a sharp rap from her fan and the biting edge of her tongue, her only defense in the unconstrained atmosphere of the gaming hell.

Last night, something had shifted. She had given in to the Duke too easily. She had lost more than just her maidenhood. The Duke had breached a secret part of her that no one else had ever touched before. And it frightened her.

For most of the trip, Jessica kept her thoughts to herself, and Donny dozed as best she could while being bumped around from the ruts in the road. They were the only two passengers in the coach. Not many people traveled out of London at this time of year. The spring social season was coming up soon and people were preparing for the fêtes and balls they would give. The weather was very unpredictable, making travel unpleasant and sometimes hazardous. Just that morning, the sky had been gray and angry and had promised rain before the day ended.

As they stopped to change the horses at a post station, the threatened rain began. Jessica decided that the weather matched her mood perfectly. After a quick refreshment, they embarked again. Dark had fallen by the time they stopped for the night, and they were chilled to the bone. Jessica was very quiet during their supper, and she could feel Donny's worried looks. When they reached their room, Donny confronted her.

"All right, out with it," she demanded. "What be yer problem? Are ye sick? Don't ye feel well?"

"I feel fine," Jessica protested.

"Ye don't look fine. Ye be glum all day, hardly said two words, ye did. Aye, and I be thinkin' it's got somethin' to do with that man ye met at that gamblin' place."

Jessica forced a laugh. "What man? I have met many men there."

"Don't ye be tryin' t'get out of it. Ye know very well what man I'm talkin' about. That one that made ye lose."

"Oh, him." Jessica pretended indifferent innocence. "Whatever makes you think that? I can't tell you the last time I saw him." And that, she thought grimly, was no lie. "Now, are you going to undo my dress, or will I have to do it myself?"

Donny harrumphed and looked like she was about to say something else, but instead, she said nothing. Jessica could tell that Donny did not really believe her. The matter was not discussed any further that night, and Jessica was relieved when they both went to bed without too much more conversation.

The next day dawned sunny and bright, a forerunner of the spring days soon to come. Jessica's mood lightened considerably. Having slept well, her state of mind was quite different from the day before. She was excited about seeing her brother, Jason, and Braeleigh again, despite the presence of Margaret. The Duke was far away in London, and had no control over her here. She had a feeling of freedom, a feeling she had not felt in a long time.

Jessica made Donny hurry through her breakfast so that they could wait outside for their coach. There was a cool wind, and the older woman grumbled about the cold making her bones ache.

"Oh, Donny," Jessica laughed. "It's too beautiful out here to complain."

Donny scowled. "Hmph. Get yerself in the coach before ye catch yer death."

Jessica laughed and climbed into the coach, for it was just about ready to leave. In a few hours she would be home. She smiled in anticipation as they started off.

The longer they rode, Jessica began to recognize familiar landmarks. She shook Donny's arm and pointed. "There's the Whittington farm. We get off at the next bend in the road."

She rapped on the roof of the coach, and it slowed and came to a halt. She and Donny descended, and their valises were tossed down. They would now have a long walk to get to Braeleigh, unless someone passed by and could give them a ride. Margaret did not see the need to send a carriage to pick up her stepdaughter and a servant.

Jessica and Donny had not been walking long when they heard a horse and wagon behind them. Looking back, Jessica recognized one of the farmers from the area. He pulled up beside them and stopped.

"Good day to ye, Yer Ladyship, Mistress Donlin," he greeted them with a bob of his head and lift to his hat. "Can I be givin' ye a ride to the manse?"

"That would be very kind of you, Mr. Stockham," Jessica answered.

"Well, then climb aboard. I be on my way there now with a load of eggs." He helped them clamber to the seat beside him, then clucked to his horse and they started off.

"Home again to visit Her Ladyship, I see," Mr. Stockham observed. "Yer a good child, Lady Jessica."

Jessica smiled at him but remained silent.

"Won't be too peaceful at the manse, I fear," he went on.

"Oh?" Jessica asked.

"Yep. Her Ladyship be fixin' the ol' place over. Workers there all the time."

"Really?" Jessica said as she exchanged a glance with Donny. "Well, I suppose it needed it."

"Ye know that better'n I, Yer Ladyship."

Mr. Stockham lapsed into silence then, and Jessica wondered what Margaret was up to. Several minutes later, the wagon turned into the drive of Braeleigh. It was not an overly large house in comparison to other country manors of the nobility, but it was old and had an honorable history. It had been built by the first Earl of Braeleigh. The land had been bestowed on him by Edward III for the earl's heroics in the battle of Agincourt during the Hundred Years' War. The original square stone structure had been added to with a wing on each side, yet it had lost none of its charm. It was built of stones of an unusual tan color, and sitting on a rise as it did, it was visible from a great distance. A parapet topped the roof of the oldest section, where the first earl's men could stand guard, and a moat surrounded the hill where it stood.

As they crossed the small drawbridge which was now permanently lowered, Jessica's eyes widened in shock. Workmen swarmed around the house and in and out through the great, wooden door. What was Margaret up to this time? And where did she get the money for all these workmen? Certainly, the stipend that Jessica brought her every month was not enough to pay all these people.

Jessica and Donny looked at each other in anger and shock, then back again at the house. Mr. Stockham pulled up in front of the door and jumped down from the wagon. After helping Donny down, he helped Jessica. Tipping his hat, he said, "Good day to ye, Lady Jessica. 'Tis good to have ye home again."

"Thank you, Mr. Stockham," she said and smiled through her embarrassment. The villagers were obviously gossiping about the strange goings on at Braeleigh and Lady Margaret's antics. She even suspected they were aware of why she went to London and came back every month. It pained her to see the dignity of the family title degraded so.

Holding back a sigh, Jessica went to find Margaret to ask her the meaning of all the activity that was taking place. She had to walk around several ladders and groups of paint cans, and climb over piles of rolled-up carpets. She finally found her stepmother in the study. As usual, Margaret's blonde hair was coifed to perfection, her long-sleeved, yellow and blue striped woolen dress the height of fashion. She was still beautiful despite the passing years, but to Jessica, it was a cold beauty. A mask that hid an ugly heart.

Various swatches of material were spread out before her, and she was studying them intently. Several moments passed before she looked up, condescending to acknowledge Jessica's presence. Her hazel gaze was cool.

Without a greeting, Margaret said, "Jessica, my dear, come, sit down and help me decide on a color for my dressing room."

Jessica did not move from her spot several paces inside the door of the room. Instead, she demanded, "Margaret, what is all this? What is going on here?"

"Why, I am redecorating, of course," Margaret answered, her voice full of amazement at Jessica's slowness of wit. "Anyone with half a brain can see that."

"Margaret, don't play games with me. You know what I am talking about. Where did you get the funds?" Jessica's voice remained hard.

"My, my, your months in London have certainly made you cynical." Margaret leaned back and coolly looked Jessica in the eye. "Don't you have a friendly hello for your stepmother?"

Jessica fought to keep her temper in check. "Believe me, Margaret, when I tell you that any greeting I give you will be far from friendly. How can we afford this redecorating?"

Margaret sighed as if her patience were taxed. "Ah, well, if you must know. It would seem that your father was not such a fool as I thought. He had invested in quite a large parcel of land in that wretched place, America. Land-wise, Jason is a very rich little boy. Since he is too young to control his estate, as his stepmother and guardian, I have taken that worry out of his hands."

"So, you are using my brother's inheritance for your own pleasure." Jessica tried to assimilate the fact that Jason, at least, was no longer poor.

"I am using it only as collateral, my dear," Margaret explained as if to a slow–witted child.

"When did you discover this land?" Jessica asked suspiciously.

"Why, just several weeks ago, after your last visit. You don't think I would have kept it a secret from my lovely stepdaughter, do you?" Her question was sly.

"To be truthful, Margaret, I do not know what to think." Jessica finally sat down. The shock of the news of the inheritance had turned her knees weak. A thought occurred to her. "Why didn't we find out about this land at the time of my father's death?"

Margaret raised her eyebrows and asked mildly, "Are you questioning my integrity, Jessica?"

Jessica looked back at her stepmother without saying a word.

With a shrug, Margaret mused, "I suppose the young are always suspicious." She smoothed her skirt. "The solicitor arrived shortly after your last visit and informed me that your dear father had large holdings in America. Imagine! And he never even told me."

Jessica thought he probably did not tell her many things. "Then you will no longer require the stipend that I bring you every month?" she asked casually.

"On the contrary, my dear. And let us not quibble over words." Margaret gave an airy wave of her hand. "Let us call it what it really is: ransom."

"Ransom?" Jessica repeated, feeling rather stupid for not understanding.

"Yes, my dear, ransom. Ransom for your…ah…freedom."

Jessica's brow wrinkled in confusion. "Margaret, what are you talking about?"

"Do not be stupid," Margaret answered in a hard voice. "Do you think I was going to marry you to Sir Percival just for the legal right to get you in his bed? You certainly cannot be as naïve as that. I want you out of this house, you simpering little fool, and I want Jason out of your influence. You can either get married, or you can pay me every month. Either way, it makes no difference to me. Just remember, I am still your legal guardian. If you find some young buck who is willing to marry you, just make sure he has plenty of money so that he can pay for that dubious honor."

Jessica was stunned by her stepmother's cruelty, yet her thoughts fastened only on the least of Margaret's dictates.

"But my father assured me I would have a dowry," she protested.

"Then you do have a problem, don't you, my dear?" Margaret's smile was cruel.

"What of Jason?" Jessica asked, trying very hard to remain calm. "Will you throw him out, also?"

"On the contrary," Margaret answered. "He is the Earl of Braeleigh. He needs guidance and help in running the estate. Who better to help him than his loving stepmother?"

The conversation was making Jessica feel ill, but before she left the room, she had to ask one last question. "Will I still be able to visit my brother?"

Margaret laughed as though she found her stepdaughter very amusing. "Of course. How else will I get your payments every month? Our agreement still stands as it did before. It is only the reasons which have changed. Now, be a good girl, and find the cloth merchant for me. I think I will do the walls of my dressing room in yellow silk… or perhaps the pink brocade."

Margaret leaned forward and studied the cloth swatches in front of her.

Jessica rose slowly from her chair and walked from the room. She ignored Margaret's demand to find the cloth merchant and climbed the stairs. Her mind was reeling. She could not believe she had just been thrown out of her own house. Somehow, she had thought that eventually she would have been able to quit her life in London and return to Braeleigh. Now, that did not seem possible while Margaret was still alive.

The hard words of the Duke came back to haunt her. No man would pay to marry a woman of questionable reputation, especially one who had been thrown out of her own home. Jessica sighed deeply. The prospect of becoming the Duke's mistress did not seem such a terrible fate. At least, she would be well cared for. Jessica shook her head to dispel her gloomy thoughts. She would not think of these things now. She would fetch Jason, and they would go riding together.

When she reached the door of the schoolroom, she found Jason in the middle of a fencing lesson. After several minutes, Jason finally scored. The fencing master called out the required, "*Touché*!" Jessica sensed Jason grinning behind his mask, and then he saw her.

"Jessica!" He dropped his sword, ripped off his mask, and ran to his sister's side. Jessica gave him a quick hug. He had grown in the month she had been away, the top of his dark head nearly reaching her own.

The fencing master cleared his throat. "I beg your pardon, m'lady, but the young lord has not finished his fencing lesson."

"Yes, I know." Jessica nodded with a smile. "Thank you. That will be all for today. You may inform the Earl's other tutors that he will not be at lessons for the rest of the day."

"Yahoo!" Jason yelled. "No more studying today! Thanks, Jess."

The fencing master bowed to Jessica and then saluted Jason with his sword. Her brother sloppily returned the salute.

Jason turned to Jessica, his blue eyes bright with expectation. "What'll we do, Jess?"

Jessica laughed. "First, you are to change your clothes, then we'll have something to eat, and then we'll go riding. How does that sound?"

"First rate!"

Jason put his sword away, discarded his fencing mask and padded vest, and raced out of the room. Jessica watched him go, and the smile faded from her lips. She would never let on to her brother how cruel Margaret was. But she could share her troubles with Donny while the woman helped her change.

After donning her riding clothes, Jessica met Jason in the kitchen. Before she had left Braeleigh, she would very often forego dining in the great, empty, formal dining room so that she and Jason could eat together in the kitchen. There, they would be able to laugh and tell each other stories without incurring Margaret's wrath. Jessica had continued the tradition on her visits home.

After a delightful lunch together with much laughter, the brother and sister headed out to the stables. Their horses were saddled and waiting for them. Jessica's horse, Aphrodite, had been given to her by her father when it was just a foal.

Jessica greeted her softly and rubbed her velvety nose. The animal whinnied and shook its head in greeting. She missed not being able to ride while in London, and always looked forward to it when she came home. She and Jason mounted, then trotted out of the stable yard.

When they were out in open country, Jason called to her, "I'll race you to Eagle Rock!" Without waiting for his sister's reply, he dug in his heels and galloped off. Jessica laughed and raced after him.

They both rode very well, but Jessica had the advantage of several years more experience than her younger brother, and she easily caught up with him. They raced side by side until they had almost reached their goal, then Jessica eased up and allowed Jason to win the race.

As they slowed their horses and brought them to a stop, Jason looked at his sister with disappointment. "Aw, Jess, you let me win," he complained.

Jessica looked aghast. "How can you think such a thing?"

Jason sent her a suspicious look.

They dismounted and allowed the horses to graze. Jessica took a deep breath of clear country air. Eagle Rock was an outcropping of several large rocks on a small rise at the edge of the land belonging to Braeleigh. It overlooked the countryside in one direction, and the sea in another. This had been Jessica's private spot to think. It was now their refuge away from their stepmother and her servants who always reported everything back to their mistress.

"This is so peaceful," Jessica said. "It's all yours now, Jason. How does it feel to be an earl?"

The boy shrugged. "All right, I guess. Margaret doesn't give me much time to enjoy it."

"Has she been very terrible?" Jessica noticed the shadowy smudges beneath his eyes.

"She has me taking fencing lessons, history, French, Latin, Italian, etiquette lessons and dancing lessons. I never get to ride." At this last he made a face. "I wish you could live here with me again, Jess. It's no fun anymore." He looked very sad and young.

Jessica put her arm around his shoulders and sighed. "I know, Jason. It's not really fun for me either. I miss you terribly. But Margaret doesn't like me for some reason, and until I can think of a way out of this mess, we'll have to go along with what she says."

Jason brightened suddenly. "I have scads of money now. Did you know that? I can help you."

Jessica laughed. "I know you have scads of money, my lord, Earl of Braeleigh."

"Well?" he asked. "Why can't I help you?"

Jessica shook her head. "It's not that simple. Margaret has control of your money. She wouldn't let you use it to help me."

"That's not fair. I hate her!" Jason exclaimed.

Jessica gave her brother another hug. "I know, but for now, we'll have to do as she says. Things won't always be like this. Come on," she said, poking him in the ribs. "Let's go to the village. Maybe the baker has made tarts."

They spent the rest of the afternoon in the village visiting and exploring the businesses and shops. Jason was delighted to watch the blacksmith work. He was fascinated by the rhythmic clanging of hammer against anvil, and the change that occurred in a piece of metal as the smithy worked on it. The baker had made tarts, and Jessica bought some, which Jason devoured.

The sun was beginning to set when they finally left. They galloped back to Braeleigh, so they would arrive before dark. Jessica guessed that Margaret would be fuming because she had spirited Jason away from his tutors.

When they finally walked into the house, Jessica knew she had not been wrong. They received the message from Foy, the butler, that Margaret was waiting for them in the salon. Glancing at each other with a knowing look, they entered the room.

"Did you wish to see us, Margaret?" Jessica asked.

Margaret was drumming her fingers on the arm of the chair where she was sitting. "Don't play the innocent with me, Jessica. Where have you been all afternoon?"

"Out riding," Jessica said. Jason edged closer to his sister.

"Obviously," Margaret stated dryly. "You were in the village, weren't you?" she accused. "I have given Jason specific orders that he is not to associate with that riffraff." Turning to him, she said, "You deliberately disobeyed me, Jason. You will go to your room and go without dinner tonight. Tomorrow you will spend at your lessons and will not be allowed to see your sister."

"But Margaret, she's leaving tomorrow!" Jason wailed.

"I cannot help that," Margaret said coldly. "You should have thought of that before you disobeyed me. Now, leave us. Jessica and I have some matters to discuss that do not involve bad boys."

Jason looked to his sister in confusion, tears bright in his eyes. Jessica squeezed his shoulder and nodded that he should do as he was told. She watched as he walked from the room in dejection. Her heart ached for him, but she knew that if she had come to his defense, his punishment would have been much worse.

When he had gone, she turned back to her stepmother. "That was cruel, Margaret," she said boldly. "He has done nothing wrong. I was the one who suggested we go to the village."

"It is not your concern any more how I discipline Jason. You are no longer a member of this household. Now, there is the matter of a payment due. I would like to receive it before dinner."

"You will have it," Jessica answered stiffly, as she held her emotions in tight check. "Is there anything else you wish to discuss with me?

"Yes. If you persist in disrupting this household when you come, then I will not allow you to visit with Jason when you are here."

"You cannot mean that," Jessica protested in spite of her resolve to remain calm.

"Oh, but I do mean it. And I think I will require that you bring me double what you are bringing now. After all, you have had nearly a year of experience, so it should be much easier for you." She flicked an imaginary piece of lint off the skirt of her dress.

"I cannot bring you that much money, Margaret. I need money to live."

"Then you will have to find another way to raise it." She yawned behind her hand. "I believe I will take a short rest before dinner." She rose abruptly and swept from the room.

Jessica stood for a moment, not quite believing the conversation she'd just had with her stepmother, then wandered from the salon. Encountering Foy, she informed him she would be dining in her room. As she slowly climbed the stairs, she could feel the tears welling up in her eyes. Damn! She was not going to let that woman make her cry.

She ran the rest of the way to her room and closed the door firmly behind her. The last rays of the sun were shining through the window and turned everything a fiery gold. Jessica smiled wryly to herself. Too bad one couldn't catch the sunbeams. Then Margaret could have all the riches she wanted.

Jessica undressed down to her chemise and crawled under the covers of the bed. She was so tired. Tired of the gambling, tired of the cruelty of Margaret, tired of the arrogance of the Duke. Why couldn't things have remained as they were? But she knew that could never have happened. Tomorrow, it was back to London. On her way, she had to deliver the letter to *Monsieur* Montaigne from *Madame* du Barré. With these thoughts running through her mind, she fell asleep.

When she awoke, it was dark. It took her several seconds to remember why she was lying in bed in her old room. Memory was not sweet when it returned. She still had to give Margaret her stipend. She rose, pulled on a dressing gown and tied it carelessly. Her hair had come undone during her nap, so she pulled out the pins and ran a brush through it. Then, picking up the pouch containing the money, she went in search of her stepmother.

Margaret was in her own room. She was primping before the mirror and did not even look up when Jessica walked in.

"I've brought your money, Margaret," Jessica said as she threw the pouch on the dressing table before her stepmother.

Margaret picked it up and weighed it in her hand. "Is it all here?" she asked sweetly.

"Margaret, I hope you burn in Hell," Jessica said hotly, then turned and fled.

She stalked down the hall, her thoughts on what she would like to see happen to Margaret. As she turned a corner, she bumped into a footman, one who had been newly hired by her stepmother. She gasped as he grabbed her arms and yanked her close.

"Well, now, ain't we a sight?" he leered as his gaze focused on her cleavage which was plainly visible beneath her gapping robe.

"Let go of me this instant!" Jessica tried to pull out of his hands. "I'll have you dismissed for this impertinence!"

"Now, don't go gettin' all upset there, m'lady. How's about a little kiss for ol' Dickie?"

Jessica was shocked into immobility, and her mouth dropped open. Recovering quickly, she struggled to get away. "How dare you! Let go of me!"

The man was short, but built like a bull, with hardly any neck and muscular shoulders. His fingers dug painfully into her arms, and her efforts to free herself proved fruitless. She found herself crushed against his barrel chest. Her head was pulled back by the hair, and he planted his wet, foul mouth on hers. For once, she was grateful for the experience she had gained at *Madame*'s. Using all her strength, she slammed her knee up into his groin. With a yowl of pain, he released her and clutched the injured area. As she turned to flee, she saw Margaret standing not far away with a smile on her face. Jessica ran down the hall to the safety of her room. Her step-mother's laughter chased after her.

Locking the door behind her, she wondered if her stepmother might have instigated the footman's advances. Matters were getting worse every time she came home. She had to think of some way to get out of this predicament, something that would also get Jason out of Margaret's clutches. Even if she married someone, that would not guarantee her brother's safety, for Margaret would still be his guardian.

Ideas and plans swirled inside Jessica's head all evening. Her dinner came, but it remained untouched. By the time the clock in the hall had struck eleven, she still had not arrived at any solution.

Remembering that Jason went to bed without any dinner, she decided to smuggle food to him. She hoped Margaret had already retired for the night. Carefully she unlocked her door and opened it. The house was quiet. Noiselessly as possible, she made her way downstairs to the kitchen. There, she found some apples, cheese, and bread, tied them in a napkin, and tiptoed back upstairs.

As she opened the door to Jason's room and crept in, a small voice came from the bed. "Who's there?"

"Shh. It's me," Jessica whispered. She crossed to the bed and sat on its edge. "I've brought you something to eat." She placed the napkin on Jason's lap and opened it to reveal her treasure.

"First rate! Thanks, Jess," he mumbled, popping a piece of cheese in his mouth.

She waited quietly while he ate his snack, then, when he was done, she took the napkin and stuffed it in her pocket. "So, I won't get you in trouble again," she explained with a smile. Becoming serious, she said, "I won't be able to see you tomorrow. I'm leaving early because I have to visit someone on the way back to London. Besides, if Margaret caught us together again, she would probably tan your hide."

"Can't you take me with you, Jess?" Jason asked wistfully.

For just a moment, Jessica was tempted to say yes, but then reality wiped away the temptation. She remembered the first time she had tried to leave with Jason, and Margaret had caught them.

Jason had not been able to sit down for a week, and Jessica had been locked in her room and unable to leave for London until Margaret decided she wanted the money more than the enjoyment of watching Jessica suffer.

Jessica shook her head. "I can't right now, Jason. But one day, I'm going to bring you with me, and then we won't have to worry about Margaret any more. Until then, I want you to do as she says. She has complete authority over you, so if you disobey her, she can punish you."

"She's so mean," Jason protested, his lips trembling.

"I know."

Jessica put her arms around him, and they sat holding on to each other, gaining strength from the other's nearness for several minutes. Her resolve hardened to free her brother from Margaret. After the episode in the hall with the footman, she was not sure that their stepmother was completely sane. But for now, Jason was better off at Braeleigh than in London.

Jason yawned.

"I think it's time that you went to sleep," Jessica said.

"Stay a few minutes longer, Jess," Jason pleaded.

Jessica shook her head. "I can't. It's late, and you should be asleep. What if Margaret found me in here with you?"

Reluctantly, Jason nodded his agreement and lay back on the pillows.

"Now, be brave, and I'll be back at Braeleigh before you know it." Jessica leaned down and kissed him on the cheek.

Before she could straighten, Jason put his arms around her and gave her a hug. "I'm going to miss you, Jess," he whispered.

"I'm going to miss you, too." Gently, she disengaged herself and stood up. "Watch from the window early tomorrow. I'll wave to you when I leave."

She turned and rushed out, not wanting him to see how upset she was. Jessica knew that would only make it harder for both of them. Returning to her room, she made sure her door was locked, then climbed into bed. Sleep did not come easily. Thoughts of Jason and Margaret and the Duke kept chasing themselves around in her head. After several hours of tossing and turning, she finally fell into a troubled sleep.

Morning came much too early for Jessica. The sun was streaming through the window when she opened her eyes, but she felt as if she had not slept at all. Knowing she could not remain in bed, she forced herself to rise. *Madame* du Barré's letter had to be delivered before she caught the coach back to London, and she wanted to be away from Braeleigh as soon as possible. She had the feeling that Jason had an easier time with Margaret when he was here by himself.

Dressing quickly, she went down to breakfast. The dining room was empty, for which she was very grateful. She was in no mood to spar with Margaret.

As she was finishing her meal, Foy entered to announce that her horse was saddled and in the front drive. She would ride to *Monsieur* Montaigne's on horseback to deliver the letter, then ride to the inn where Donny would be waiting for her with their luggage. From there, they would board the coach for the ride back to London. The innkeeper would make sure that Aphrodite would be returned to Braeleigh.

As she was rising from the table, Margaret sauntered in. "All ready to leave?" she asked. "What a pity you can't stay with us a while longer. Dickie was so disappointed he was unable to finish what he began last night."

Jessica did not bother to answer. She walked out of the room with Margaret's cackle ringing in her ears.

Quickly donning her hat and gloves, she left the house. She glanced up at the front of the house and saw Jason in a window. She smiled, threw him a kiss, then waved as she wheeled her horse and cantered down the drive.

Being out in the open helped to clear her mind. Her thoughts were still troubled, but she felt a weight had been lifted from her shoulders because she was away from Margaret. The problem of the Duke which now faced her seemed small in comparison to the villainy of her stepmother. She forced those thoughts out of her mind. She was free for several hours, and she was on her way to visit a very charming gentleman.

After an hour and a half of easy riding, Jessica came to the home of *Monsieur* Montaigne. It was a neat, compact house, barely bigger than a cottage. Standing on a grassy cliff, it overlooked a stony beach about twenty feet below. A steep path zigzagged down to the water. Except for his housekeeper, he lived alone.

As Jessica dismounted from Aphrodite, *Monsieur* Montaigne came to the door. "*Mademoiselle* Jessica!" he exclaimed. "I was hoping you would come today," he said in French. "You look more lovely each time I see you, like a flower ready to bloom."

Jessica laughed. "*Bonjour, monsieur*, and thank you. Your compliments always make my head spin."

She had answered him in French. Their conversations were always in that language, for *Monsieur* Montaigne said it made him feel as if he were back in his own country. He was a middle-aged man with twinkling brown eyes and hair beginning to gray at the temples. He wore it tied back in an old-fashioned queue. His clothes were modest, and instead of a cravat or stock, he wore a red kerchief about his neck.

After tying Aphrodite to a hitching post, she held out her hand. *Monsieur* Montaigne bent over it gallantly, then strolled with her to his house. Jessica noticed he leaned heavily on his cane, and realized his leg was giving him a great deal of pain. He'd told her he'd been badly injured fighting for King Louis during the Revolution. Because of his loyalty to his sovereign, he was forced to flee France or be executed with the other Royalists. Now, an ex-patriot and outcast in his own country, he lived in England.

Jessica stopped to admire the early flowers beginning to bloom beside his door. A movement in the trees beyond the house caught her attention, and she peered in that direction trying to see what it was.

"*Mademoiselle*, what is it?" *Monsieur* Montaigne asked.

Jessica squinted against the sun, then turned to her host with an apologetic smile. "I thought I saw something move in the woods, but there seems to be nothing. It was only my imagination."

"Ah, the mind does like to play tricks on us, yes? Come, I will make you some tea. My housekeeper has gone to the village." Taking Jessica's hand, he tucked it into the crook of his arm and escorted her into his house.

Jessica spent a very enjoyable hour with the gentleman. She always delighted in these visits, for her host was a charming and gallant man. It was easy to understand why *Madame* du Barré was so fond of him. The time of her departure came much too soon. When she left, she carried a missive back to *Madame*. She would deliver it the following evening.

CHAPTER 5

"Excuse me, Your Grace."

Damien glanced up from his breakfast to find Jacobs standing in the doorway of the dining room. The majordomo's face was carefully expressionless, a look he wore when he disapproved of something.

"Yes, Jacobs, what is it?"

"There is—ah—a person here to see you, Your Grace. He says it is most urgent that he speak with you."

"Who is it, Jacobs? You know I dislike having my breakfast interrupted."

"Yes, Your Grace." Jacobs's impassive veneer cracked slightly, and he grimaced. "He would not give me his name. He said it was a question of utmost secrecy. He is waiting in the front hall."

Damien raised an eyebrow. For Jacobs to leave a visitor standing in the front hall meant he regarded the individual as little better than riffraff from the streets. However, the man must have had some redeeming quality for Jacobs to allow him past the front door, rather than being sent to the back entrance.

The Duke tossed his napkin down beside his plate and stood. "All right, Jacobs. I will see him."

"Very good, Your Grace. I will be nearby should you wish my services."

Damien hid a grin. He would like to see very proper Jacobs in a tussle with some vagrant. Solemnly, he thanked his butler and went to see about this mysterious visitor.

As the Duke entered the front hall, he saw a man gazing up at a recently acquired painting by J.M.W. Turner. The man's clothes were mud-stained, and it appeared he had worn them for quite some time.

Mud streaked his face, making him almost unrecognizable. Several days' growth of beard shadowed his jaw. Damien had barely entered when the man swung about, snapped to attention, and saluted him.

"Edward!" Damien grinned as he walked toward the man and held out his hand. "You haven't saluted me in four years, Leftenant. There's no need to start now."

Edward grinned back as he took Damien's outstretched hand. "I like to practice occasionally."

"I didn't expect you until tomorrow. My apologies for Jacobs's inhospitality. He obviously didn't recognize you. Come into my study and I'll pour you a brandy. You look like you could use one."

When the two men had settled themselves and Damien had supplied his guest with a generous helping of his brandy, the Duke gazed at the man who was next in command in his group of spies. He watched with amusement as Leftenant Edward Johnson took a large gulp of the amber liquid and sighed in pleasure.

"That helps to warm my bones," Edward said. "It's damned uncomfortable living in the woods."

"I thought you enjoyed hunting," Damien teased.

Edward glared at him. "Not for five days running. I didn't expect to be playing the spy in my own country."

"Hmm. Yes, quite an odd situation. Well, what have you found out for us?"

The Leftenant began his report. "I watched *Monsieur* Montaigne's house, as you ordered, for five days — three of which were bloody rainy, by the way. Nothing unusual happened on the first four. No visitors. He and his housekeeper went about their normal routine. On the fifth day, his housekeeper left early in the morning. It appeared she was going to market. While she was gone, Montaigne had a visitor."

"Ah." Damien nodded in satisfaction.

"How the devil did you know the courier would show up?"

Damien smiled. "Information concerning England's negotiations with Turkey had been revealed to *Madame* du Barré. We knew she would rush to get this to Fouché."

Edward gave a low whistle.

"Yes, her boldness is incredible, isn't it?" Damien agreed. "Now, about this visitor. Can you describe him?"

It was Edward's turn to grin. "It was not a *him*. It was a *her*."

"The devil, you say!"

Edward chuckled. "Yes, a woman."

Damien's eyes narrowed as he remembered his last attempt to get information before he and his men had to flee from France, when they had been made fools by one of Fouché's male spies. "I don't suppose you could have been mistaken?"

Edward shook his head and snickered. "I was not the one who decided that '*Madame* Duquènes' would make a good hostage."

"I seem to recall your agreeing with me. Fouché's man made a damned convincing woman. You were convinced that Fouché's clerk was madly in love with her... him." Damien watched his second in command squirm, then said, "Well, what about this one? Could we be mistaken a second time?"

"No, not this time. This was very definitely a female."

"All right. Describe her." Damien sighed. He disliked having to arrest women. He felt they should not be involved in something as dangerous as spying.

"She was petite in stature, rather young, jet black hair. From where I was standing she was quite a stunner. I dare say you're in for a pleasing assignment."

Damien scowled. "All I want is a description, Leftenant, not a commentary."

"Sorry." Edward grinned, not in the least repentant.

"What else?"

"From her mannerisms and the way she carried herself, she appeared gentle-born," Johnson went on. "The horse she was riding was of excellent stock. Arabian, it seemed. And she spoke French."

"Could you hear what was said?"

"Only the usual pleasantries, then they went inside."

"Interesting," Damien mused. "Did you discover any clue to her identity?"

"I did visit the local inn. It seems she comes from the area, but does not live there any longer. She visits once a month, usually around the fifteenth, but I could not discover her name, nor where she resides now, nor the purpose of her monthly visit, unless it is merely to act as courier for *Madame* du Barré. The people in the area are suspicious of strangers asking questions. It seems this woman, whoever she is, is important to them. They appeared to be protecting her."

"Well done, Edward," Damien nodded with satisfaction. "Perhaps *Le Chat* will be riding again soon."

"Here? In England?" Edward's brow rose in surprise.

Damien had told him and the others who rode with them that he was ending his career as the notorious spy *Le Chat*.

"Yes, just one more time. It takes a cat to catch a rat." He stood to signal the end of the interview when he saw Edward stifle a yawn. "Go home and get some rest, Leftenant. I will contact you when I need you and the rest of the men."

Leftenant Johnson rose as well, after he tossed down the remainder of the Duke's excellent brandy in his glass.

Damien watched with amusement. "I will give you a cask of that when this job is over," he said.

Edward grinned. "It's been a long, wet, cold assignment. And I have always enjoyed your brandy." He added as an afterthought, "Your Grace."

Damien chuckled, and shook his friend's hand, then rang for Jacobs. When the butler appeared, the Duke told him, "See Leftenant Johnson to the door, Jacobs."

He watched his majordomo's eyebrows lift ever so fractionally as the man realized whom he'd left standing in the front hall. Jacobs bowed his acknowledgment of the Duke's request, then turned to Edward and apologized with great dignity. At Jacobs's admission of his mistake, Edward lifted a comical eyebrow at Damien, then followed the man out the door.

When the two had left, Damien sank back into his chair. So, it was a woman he was after. A woman of small stature with black hair. One who usually appeared at Montaigne's around the fifteenth of every month.

A tiny, nagging suspicion began to gnaw at the back of his mind. He frowned at his thoughts. It was too easy, too coincidental. There were many black-haired women who frequented *Madame*'s, several of whom were petite. But how many of them left London around the middle of every month? He remembered her words, that she was taking the early coach out of London. It had been two days before the fifteenth. He cursed under his breath.

The evening of Jessica's return to London found her at *Madame*'s. She had delivered the letter from *Monsieur* Montaigne, and now she wandered about the establishment. As she watched the play at the various tables and listened to the gossip, she discovered that quite a bit of the conversation concerned herself and the game she was involved in the night before she left for Braeleigh. Her sudden appearance again after being absent for three nights after the incident raised more speculation than she cared to think about, especially when her name was repeatedly linked with that of the Duke of Wyndham.

Jessica was reluctant to leave *Madame*'s, for that would be running away. She needed to pretend that the gossip did not affect her. Too tired from traveling to play, she lingered among the tables. She watched a game over the shoulder of one of the players. The man was going to lose heavily if he continued to pick at his buttons every time he had a bad hand. The others at the table could easily discern his nervousness.

Becoming bored with the game, she glanced around the room. Then she saw him. The Duke was here, but he was not alone. A lovely, blonde woman hung on his arm. He leaned close and smiled at something she said. A surge of anger made Jessica's insides contract. He certainly hadn't wasted any time finding someone else to warm his bed. She refused to examine why she was so angry, and instead, consoled herself with the knowledge that he would not be bothering her any more.

Turning away from the table, she made her way to one of the private gaming rooms that was empty at the moment. She had a splitting headache and needed to be away from the noise for a while.

She sat at a table covered in green felt and picked up a deck of cards. She would give the Duke time to become involved in a game and then she would leave. That way, she would be sure of not meeting him again. Absently, she began to shuffle the cards. Again, and again the cards slipped together. The monotony of the movement helped to ease the ache behind her eyes.

Suddenly, she felt another presence in the room. Looking up, she saw him standing on the other side of the table. He had an uncanny ability to sneak up on her.

"May I sit in on the play, or is this a private game?" the Duke asked with a smile.

Shrugging her indifference, Jessica motioned to a chair across from her. She would not let him see that he affected her in any way. Returning her gaze to the cards in her hands, she asked coolly, "What happened to your companion?"

His smile widened into a grin. "Is the lady jealous?"

"No," she stated flatly, "merely curious."

"I see," he said, still smiling, obviously enjoying himself. "Well, to satisfy your curiosity, my love, she is occupied with trying to lose a substantial amount of coins I just bestowed on her. And to further satisfy your curiosity, she is just a friend, someone with whom I occasionally dally, but who means little to me. I do not live the monkish life."

The bluntness of his last statement caused Jessica finally to look at him. "I did not inquire about your *petites amours*, Your Grace," she said evenly. "We have no commitment to each other."

The Duke sighed. "That is true. Sad, but true. Something I hope to remedy in the near future." He leaned back in his chair. "Was your business concluded successfully?" he asked.

"It was," she answered without thinking. Then realizing what she had admitted, she asked suspiciously, "How did you know I was away on business?"

"No one leaves London for only three days for pleasure," he told her. "Especially not at this time of year."

Jessica watched him, waited for him to go on with the conversation, to tell her that he had discovered her identity, or at least to give a reason why he came to speak with her, but he just sat and looked back at her. Finally, she could stand the silence and his gaze on her no longer.

"If there is nothing else you wish to say to me, Your Grace, I would appreciate your leaving me alone," she said tiredly.

"I have a great many things to say to you, my love," he replied softly, "but this is neither the time nor the place." He paused for a moment. Then, in an offhand manner, he said, "I am having a small dinner party tomorrow evening. I would like you to be my guest."

"No." Jessica did not even have to think about her answer.

"Fine," he went on as if he had not heard. "I will send my carriage for you."

Jessica stared at him in disbelief. "I beg your pardon, Your Grace. Perhaps you did not hear me. I said no. I will not be a guest at your dinner party."

The Duke's eyes narrowed dangerously. "You will be there tomorrow," he contradicted. "You will be ready, or my footmen will drag you from your lodgings in whatever you might be wearing at the time."

"You have no right..." she began. The forbidding expression on his face made her voice falter.

"I disagree. I would say I had every right to do as I wish with you. I am remaining silent in order that you may continue as a patroness of *Madame*'s house."

She gasped. "That is blackmail."

The Duke smiled and nodded. "Precisely." He stood. "Until tomorrow, m'lady," he said as he gallantly bowed to her. Then he turned and sauntered from the room.

Disconcerted, Jessica gazed after him. How was she to get out of this predicament? Evidently, the Duke's interest had not waned with her absence from *Madame*'s. She had thought that if she ignored him, he would leave her alone. Obviously, that was not going to work. Damn him.

She sighed and rested her head in her hands. The only thing she could do was to oblige him. She could do nothing else. She believed him when he said he would have his footmen drag her out of her lodgings, and the threat of his reporting her cheating still hung over her. She decided to leave *Madame*'s for the evening. She was too tired to care what he did. Perhaps tomorrow some solution would occur to her.

The following day, Jessica pondered how she was going to escape being the Duke's guest that evening. Then, while she was dressing for the dinner, she arrived at the obvious answer to her problem. She simply would not be at her lodgings. She would go to *Madame*'s. He would not cause a scene there and drag her out. *Madame* would not allow it. Jessica smiled triumphantly to herself. Quickly, she finished her toilette. She had to be gone before his carriage arrived.

When she was ready, Donny checked her appearance. Jessica wore a simple gown of deep red velvet with no lace or frills to hide the plunging décolletage. Tiny puff sleeves barely hugged her shoulders, leaving a generous expanse of bare skin. The gold locket which she always wore was her only adornment. Her hair was swept up into curls atop her head, and tiny tendrils escaped to frame her face and tickle her neck.

"Aye," Donny nodded approvingly. "If he catches sight of ye tonight, he'll be eatin' out of yer hand."

Jessica made a face. "I don't want him eating out of my hand, Donny. I don't even wish to see him. If he comes tonight, tell him… Tell him I am out with another gentleman." Jessica smiled wickedly. That would teach him she was not to be owned.

Donny's look was disapproving. "Ye be playin' with fire, lady fair. He be a duke, and ye don't anger them high-born gentlemen. Besides, ye might be better off if ye was pleasant to him. He might ask ye to marry him."

"Marry? Ha! The last thing on his mind is marriage. Besides, I wouldn't marry him if he were the last man on earth. He's arrogant and overbearing and despicable, and I hate him." Jessica clasped her cloak about her shoulders and raised her hood. "Don't wait up for me, Donny. I will probably be quite late."

"Hmph, I'll wait up fer ye if I've a mind," Donny grumbled as Jessica walked out the door.

CHAPTER 6

When Jessica arrived at *Madame*'s, very few people were about, for it was much too early for the members of society to be there. To pass the time while she waited for an interesting game to begin, she sat on a settee, sipped a cup of tea and watched the people arrive. As it grew later, games were begun in the main room. Jessica did not join any of these, for she would be playing for much higher stakes at a game later in the evening, but she enjoyed going from table to table to watch the play.

Nervously, she watched the clock as the time came and went when the Duke was supposed to collect her. Gradually, she began to relax. The Duke would not be coming after her. Soon, she would be involved in a card game, and she would be able to forget him altogether.

As she watched a particularly lighthearted match among several men and women, she felt a presence at her elbow. Laughing, she turned to make a witty comment to the newcomer. Instead of some innocuous stranger, she came face to face with the Duke. The fury on his face was frightening. His jaw was tightly clenched, and his eyes were like green ice. Jessica could only stare.

"Where is this other gentleman whom you are supposed to be with this evening?" His voice was quiet with repressed fury.

Jessica opened her mouth to reply, but no sound came out. Desperately, her mind groped for something to say, but all she could manage was a shake of her head. She had never believed anyone could look so angry and forbidding.

"No other gentleman?" he asked as he took hold of her elbow.

Jessica shook her head.

"Then you have two choices," he said. "You can come quietly with me, or I will carry you out."

She looked again into those green eyes and swallowed. She had no choice at all. The players at the table were drinking in every word, every glance, every nuance that passed between her and the Duke. To keep the gossip in check, she had to go with him. But even her acquiescence would be discussed behind fans and in quiet corners.

She nodded and allowed him to guide her to the door where he collected her cloak. He had not bothered to remove his own when he had come in, evidence of his intention to collect her quickly and be gone. Outside, he helped her into his waiting carriage, and they drove off.

The ride to his house was made in silence. The Duke stared out the window, and Jessica kept her eyes on her tightly clasped hands in her lap. Fearfully, she wondered what would happen to her once they reached their destination. What would the Duke do to her for defying him? He had told her he did not harm women, yet he was frightfully angry with her. She did not wish to contemplate her immediate future.

After what seemed like hours, but was only a matter of minutes, they arrived at the Duke's house. Again, no words were exchanged as he helped her from the carriage and guided her up the front stairs and in through the door. He took her cloak from her shoulders and handed it to the butler with the directive that they were not to be disturbed. With a firm hand beneath her elbow, he steered her into the salon where he closed the door behind them.

Finally dropping his hand from her arm, he walked several steps, turned and faced her. With an obvious effort to keep his temper in check, he said, "I will not be made a fool, Jessica."

Jessica's temper flared, overcoming her fear. What about her feelings? "Then do not order me about, treating me like one of your servants," she spat back at him. "I have told you before. I will not be owned."

The Duke raised an eyebrow, but said nothing.

"I told you last night that I would not come," Jessica stated vehemently.

"It would seem that you were wrong, for you are here now." His tone was sardonic.

"Do not mock me. If I had not come with you, there would have been a scene, and the resulting gossip would have ruined the respect *Madame*'s patrons have for me. As it is, it will be difficult to defuse the speculation concerning our relationship."

"Why defuse it at all?" he tossed out.

"Because we have no relationship," she snapped. As she spoke, she realized the house was very quiet, too quiet for there to be other dinner guests. "I thought you said you were having a dinner party. Where are your other guests?"

"There are no other guests," he said quietly.

Her mouth dropped open. "You lied to me."

He finally smiled, a wry twist of his lips. "On the contrary, my love. I said it was to be a small dinner party. I did not say how small."

She stared at him, not trusting herself to speak. How could he be so arrogant, so insufferable? Taking a deep breath and raising her chin, she said with as much dignity as she could muster, "If you would be so kind as to have your carriage brought around, I will be leaving. If you deny me the use of it, I will leave on my own." She turned to walk out.

"Jessica." The tone of his voice made her stop, but she did not turn around. He paused, as if what he had to say was very hard. "I apologize for my rude behavior. Have you dined yet this evening?"

She whirled to face him. Was he mocking her again? His expression was earnest.

"I asked you a question," he said softly when she did not answer.

She shook her head. "No." Eating had not entered her mind. She had been so anxious to evade him that she'd had no appetite.

The corners of his mouth twitched upward. "How fortunate. My chef has created a magnificent feast, but alas, my dinner guest was last seen heading out the door. Will you take her place, my lady? Please?"

She hesitated. He could be so damned charming. There he stood, no longer arrogant, but thoroughly engaging, entreating her like some wounded lover to stay and dine. Against her better judgment, she decided to remain.

"You are very persuasive, Your Grace," she said. "How can I refuse such a gallant request?"

He stepped forward and removed her mask. Taking her hand, he smiled. "You will not be sorry that you stayed, my love." He kissed the palm of her hand, then led her to a small table that had been set up before the fire.

She thought she would be unable to eat anything with him sitting so near, but he teased and gently cajoled. The food was delicious, and she discovered she was quite hungry. He enticed her to try the many dishes and different wines. Although she only sipped at the wine, by the end of the meal she was quite light-headed.

He held her chair for her as she rose from the table. She lost her balance and grabbed his arm. Instead, she found herself leaning against his chest. She giggled. When she looked up at him, she was surprised into silence by the intense, hungry look in his eyes. He stared down at her a moment and ran his fingers across her cheek. Then, as if coming out of a trance, he smiled.

"Come," he said. "Let's sit before the fire and watch the flames dance."

She allowed him to lead her to a settee. She sat at one end, and he sat very near. He draped his arm behind her. She could feel the soft velvet of his sleeve. It sent warm tendrils through her. Leaning back, she relaxed against him. She felt comfortable and content, and wanted the night to go on forever.

She realized what she was thinking. Would she really want to spend forever with him? She glanced up at him. His profile was turned to her as he watched the flames. It was a strong, aristocratic profile, and now that he was relaxed, it had softened and become gentle. He had shown her a side of himself tonight that was very endearing. Yes, she thought, she would very much like to spend forever with Damien… but not as his mistress. She sighed.

He looked down at her with gentle eyes. "What is it, my love?" He pulled her close.

The touch of his hand on her bare skin sent a delicious shiver through her and brought back memories of his touch on her body. She smiled up at him. "I was just daydreaming."

She reached up and touched his cheek. She could not allow herself to become deeply involved with him. Margaret still demanded money, and Jason needed her. But tonight… Her body and her heart played traitor to her mind. She was drawn to him like a moth to a flame. She was being stupid and irresponsible.

"Make love to me, Damien," she whispered, ignoring the tiny voice of caution that murmured in her head.

He gazed down into her eyes, two bottomless pools of limpid blue, now darkened by her desire for him. He was surprised by her advance and wondered briefly if this was some game she was playing. She was, after all, a courier for *Madame*. Besides the fact that he enjoyed her company, he had planned to get her to disclose information. That had been the purpose of the evening. At least, that is what he told himself.

He had expected some resistance on her part, so he had plied her with wine. But his plan was working far better than he thought it would. He felt her hand at the back of his neck, her fingers curling in his hair. As she pulled his head down to place her warm, inviting lips to his, he decided that any game he lost this pleasantly was worth the price.

He kissed her deeply, probing her sweet mouth. Her tongue met his. He was drawn to this beautiful enigma. She was shy and coy one moment, then passionate the next. He wanted, needed to unravel her.

He stood, pulling her up with him. He tasted and nipped along her jaw and down her neck as he enfolded her in his arms. She was silky, supple. He cupped her bottom and held her tight against him. Her gasp of surprise was swallowed by his kiss. His need throbbed. Sweeping her up, he carried her upstairs to his room.

He stood her beside the bed in a shaft of moonlight and drank in her beauty. Slowly, she raised her arms and began pulling the pins out of her hair. He watched it tumble down to her waist. Then she held her arms out to him. He embraced her and claimed that soft mouth once more. He drowned in her.

Jessica's senses reeled. A fire kindled inside her. That strange, wonderful pulsing made her throb. With her arms about him, she pressed close, feeling his hard, unyielding body down the length of her.

He stepped back, and she discovered he had unbuttoned her dress. Gently, he slid it from her shoulders, and it fell to the floor. She stepped out of her shoes and removed her stockings and petticoat. Nothing but her thin chemise covered her. With her eyes locked on his face, she untied the ribbons holding the garment closed and slipped it from her body. Naked, she stood before him and offered herself to him.

Not taking his eyes from her, he removed his clothes. When he had finished, she stood for a moment and admired his magnificent body. In one step, she pressed herself against him and slipped her arms around his neck.

"Make love to me, Damien," she repeated.

She gazed into his eyes. She knew precisely what she was doing. The consequences be hanged. His lips crushed down onto hers, and they tumbled onto the bed. Their passion carried them far into the night.

It was still dark when Jessica awoke. The curtains had never been drawn, so the moonlight shone through the window. Damien was sleeping soundly, one arm and leg thrown possessively across her. She shifted beneath him. He sighed and turned in his sleep. Feeling the need to be away from the magnetism of his body, she eased out of bed. His shirt lay in a white puddle on the floor, so she picked it up and slipped it on as she walked to the window.

An enclosed garden spread out below her. Little was growing there at this time of year, but in a week or so, green shoots would begin to appear. The thought of spring brought a pang shooting through her chest. Spring was for new things and new love, something which she could not have.

Her feelings for Damien overwhelmed her. She could not afford to spend any more time with him, for she had to take care of Jason.

Becoming the mistress of the Duke of Wyndham would solve her problem with Margaret, but it would not help her brother, still too young to help himself. Besides, Damien did not love her. To him, she was only a plaything. The heat of shame rose through her. To him, she was only the adventuress, the Lady Fortuna. Tears, which she had not allowed herself to shed since her father's death, began to fall in silent streams down her cheeks.

A pair of warm arms wrapped themselves around her from behind. "Why are you crying, my love?" he whispered as he held her close.

She had not heard him get out of bed. If she had, she would have composed herself. She could not tell him her problems. He would not be able to help her. His arms gave her a sense of security that she knew was false.

Swiping her cheeks, she turned to face him. "Please," she begged, "do not force me to come here again. You know nothing about my circumstances. I cannot be your mistress, Damien."

"Tell me about these circumstances," he demanded. "Let me help you."

She shook her head. "No one can help me." She laughed bitterly. "I can't even help myself." She pulled away from his embrace, and loneliness enveloped her. Aimlessly, she wandered to the center of the room, into the anonymous dark. "Things are never as they seem. Events never happen the way they are planned. I am not what you think I am."

Damien thought he understood what she was saying. Yet, there was another dimension to her words that baffled him. He supposed she was speaking of her involvement with *Madame*, but she sounded as if she were desperately in need of some sort of assistance. What that assistance was and the reason for it eluded him. For some inexplicable reason, he wanted to help her, an adventuress, albeit, a very desirable one, a woman who had made him look the fool and, except for tonight, had rebuffed him at every opportunity. He chided himself for being soft. Had he not wanted her in just this state so that she would reveal what she knew of *Madame* and her spy ring?

"Tell me who you are, Jessica," he demanded softly. He could just make out the white of his shirt covering her as she stood in the shadows.

"I am the Ice Witch," she whispered mysteriously, then gave an ironic laugh. "That is what the patrons of *Madame*'s call me, you know. The cold-blooded woman who uses sorcery to make the cards do as she wishes. They are wrong. I am not a woman at all. I am too young. Too young to decide my own fate, to make my own decisions."

She stepped into the moonlight and stood defiantly before Damien. Grabbing the front of the shirt she wore, she ripped it open down the front and exposed her body to his gaze. "Do I look like a young girl to you, Your Grace, or a woman, fully grown?"

Damien approached her. He would get no other information from her this night. She needed to be reassured. The information would come once he had gained her trust.

With a finger beneath her chin, he tilted her head back, so he could look into her troubled eyes. "You are a very beautiful woman, Jessica." His other hand cupped her breast, his thumb caressing the pink tip. "Let me prove to you that you are a woman."

She sighed. "Even as a woman, I cannot control my own fate." She placed her hand over his to make him stop his caress. "Please, promise that after tonight, you will no longer pursue me."

His mouth flattened, then he gave a short nod. "I make no promises that I will not keep, but you have my word that I will not force you to come to me if you do not wish it."

"Thank you," she whispered. She reached up and touched his lips with her fingers, tracing their outline. "Now, make me feel like a woman."

He gladly followed her command. He brushed his lips across her ear and tickled her neck with his tongue. Leaning her back across his arm, he kissed her shoulder, then trailed kisses to her breast cupped in his hand. He teased its rosy tip until she moaned — passionate music.

Jessica gave herself up to the delicious tension he created within her. Her instincts made her rock her hips enticingly against him. She heard him gasp, and her lips curled at his response.

He smiled. "No innocent would move like that, my lady."

She grinned, turned and sashayed to the bed, discarding his shirt along the way. Turning to face him, she stretched, catlike. Her whole body felt alive, sensuous, smoldering.

"I am no longer an innocent, Your Grace," she teased. "You have seen to that. I am a wanton woman with no good reputation left to my name. Come, let me show you how wicked I have become." She held out her arms to him.

In three long strides, he crossed the space between them. He gathered her to him tightly and captured her lips. She pulled him down onto the bed. Her hands roved over his strong back, and her legs entwined with his. She could feel his desire for her, hard against her hip. Her blood raced through her veins. She wanted him, needed him, more than she had ever wanted anything in her life. His hands were everywhere, touching, teasing, making her moan with pleasure.

He paused and framed her face in his hands. "You are mine, Jessica. You belong to me."

She gazed into his green eyes and knew he spoke the truth. Her only answer was to pull his head down and kiss him passionately. He thrust between her legs, becoming part of her until the world seemed to explode inside of her. Her scream of pleasure was cut off by his devouring mouth. Afterward, they lay together. His arms around her comforted. Her head rested against his shoulder, her leg intimately laid across his thighs.

"It will be dawn soon," she sighed with regret. "I must leave."

"You could stay." His fingers persuaded with a caress up the back of her neck.

"Please, let's not argue again. You made a promise to me."

"I did, but I don't have to force you to stay." His eyes glinted mischievously. "I can make you want to remain here if I wish."

Despite his teasing manner, she was alarmed. His words held a great deal of truth, for just a simple caress of his fingers caused her to forget everything. Would he keep her here, a prisoner, making love to her whenever she would leave?

He laughed, the noise rumbling in his chest. "Do not look so frightened, my love. I am no fiend who keeps ladies imprisoned to await my pleasure." He pushed her into a sitting position. "Go and dress before I change my mind."

Jessica scrambled from the bed and dressed quickly before he did as he threatened. She felt his gaze on her, a warm tickle on her skin. Then he rose and dressed. As he reached for his shirt, she grabbed it away. She looked down at it sheepishly. It had not been her intention to rip it when she had put it on.

"I will take this and sew it for you, Your Grace," she told him.

Damien took it out of her hands and held it up. He examined it critically, then handed it back to her with a grin. "I'm afraid it is beyond repair, my lady, but if you wish to keep it as a remembrance, I won't mind."

"Arrogant scoundrel," she said as she threw it back at him, then turned her back.

He laughed, grabbed her by the arm, and swung her about to face him. He pushed a wisp of hair away from her face and let his hand linger in her curls. "Do you know that you are beautiful when you are angry?"

She scowled. "How many times have you said that to other women you have held in your arms?"

"You wound me deeply, my lady," he said in mock seriousness. "I do not pay compliments unless they are true, and with you, my love, I have seen you angry more times than not."

She poked him in the chest. "Then do not goad me into anger, Your Grace, for I harbor a sweet side to my nature, as well as a thorny one."

"I know," he agreed softly, and lowered his mouth to capture her lips.

When he finally raised his head, she was breathless. "I think you have changed your mind, and mean to keep me here to satisfy your shameful whims," she accused with a grin.

"Perhaps." He smiled. "I do not think you would mind that overly much."

Jessica feigned shock. "What do you take me for, Your Grace? I am not some strumpet off the street who will covet the body of every man who passes by her. I am a simple maid who fell victim to an unscrupulous knave." With that, she gave the hair on his chest a playful tug.

Damien winced. "Unscrupulous knave, am I?" He tugged the hair on the back of her head. "I think, perhaps, the lady needs some manners taught to her. She should not repeat things which are not true, for it was the lady, I seem to recall, who did much of the seducing this evening." Relentlessly, his mouth lowered, and he kissed her thoroughly.

When he released her, she said, "If you do that again, the morning will find us again in your bed, and no closer to separating than we are now."

"Would that be so terrible?" he asked with a squeeze.

No, it would not, but fear that he would follow through, that she would be unable to deny him raced through her.

"You promised," she reminded him as she tried to wriggle away.

With a reluctant grin, he released her and finished dressing. When they were both clothed, Jessica waited while Damien roused the footmen to bring around his coach. She smiled. This departure from Damien's house would be made in more comfort than the last.

It was not long before the coach was ready, and they sat close to each other in the dark interior. Jessica could feel his hard thigh pressed tightly against her. His arm was warm and comforting about her shoulders. The ride was bittersweet. She had found something wonderful this night, only to realize that it could never be fulfilled. She relished these last few moments alone with Damien. For once, the silence between them was not strained, but was filled with an easy companionship and contentment.

The trip to her lodgings ended much too soon. After Damien helped her down from the carriage, he drew her to him and kissed her.

When he raised his head, he warned, "Do not think this is the last you will see of me, Jessica. I do not easily relinquish my hold on those who are mine."

Where once she would have rebelled at his words, now they only made her leaving that much more difficult. She put her hand to his cheek and smiled with regret. She could never be his.

"Goodbye, Damien," she whispered. Pulling out of his embrace, she turned and fled into the shadows.

CHAPTER 7

During the weeks that followed, Jessica won a great amount at *Madame*'s. It seemed that no one could beat her. The games in which she played had stakes that were incredibly high, even for *Madame*'s establishment, but Jessica was forced to risk losing everything in order to win the large stipend which Margaret wanted.

The gossip concerning her, and Damien had died away, to be replaced by speculation about the games with the tremendously high stakes. At the end of the evening, everyone would watch as her game finished to see if she had won again. There were some who even placed bets on whether she won or lost on a particular evening.

For Jessica, it was a very exhilarating time, but her nerves were stretched to the limit. She could not go on in this manner much longer and remain sane. Her one, steadying influence was Damien. She did not speak with him. The most she ever did was exchange a smile across the room. He was keeping his promise to her. But knowing he was near gave her a sense of security.

One evening about a week before she was due to leave for Braeleigh, she arrived at *Madame*'s a bit earlier than usual. After paying her respects to *Madame*, she wandered to the room where her game would be played. It was empty. Not even any of the servants were about. She strolled to the table set up with new decks of cards and surveyed her battlefield. Tonight, if she played well, she could make the balance of the stipend which Margaret had demanded. She took a deep breath to calm her nerves.

"She hath forsworn to love; and in that vow do I live dead, that live to tell it now."

Jessica swung about at the deep voice quoting Shakespeare's *Romeo and Juliet*. Damien stood in the doorway.

"Hello, my love." He smiled.

He looked magnificent. The green of his silk coat enhanced the color of his eyes, his black trousers fit his trim legs closely, his pale yellow waistcoat embroidered in white threads set off the intricate knot of his stock which held a glittering emerald in its folds. Jessica's heart hammered in her chest. She felt her throat close up as a delicious thrill ran through her.

Smiling happily, feeling foolish for allowing her feelings to be so transparent, she managed to whisper, "Hello."

"Is that all I get?" he asked as he strolled toward her.

Torn between a desire to fling herself into his arms and the restrictions she had placed on their relationship, she retreated a step. "You startled me," she said, disconcerted at his approach. She retreated another step. Unable to think of anything else to say, she asked, "You have been well?"

Damien raised an amused eyebrow. "Do I look like I have been ill?" He advanced another step.

She backed away and smiled at her foolishness. "No."

He grabbed her hand and drew her to him. "Why are you running away, my love? Do I suddenly repulse you?"

"You know that is not true." Feebly, she tried to wriggle out of his embrace, then gave up.

"Then what is it?"

"Please," she pleaded. "I have a game soon. Someone will see us."

"What if they do?" he murmured as he nibbled at her ear and rained light kisses on her neck.

Jessica felt her willpower weakening as the effect of his touch took hold of her. "Please, Damien," she tried once more. "Not here, not now. I cannot be connected in any way with a man. Any man. The gossip…"

"The gossip be damned," he growled as he captured her mouth with his.

Jessica resisted for as long as it took to draw a breath. She finally gave herself up to the inevitable and melted against him. It had been torture for her these past few weeks. Seeing Damien every night, knowing he was near, yet not being able to be with him had been painful. Hungrily, she drank him in, his touch, his taste, his scent. For just a few moments, she would allow herself this tiny glimpse of heaven.

Some sixth sense brought her back to reality. She heard a small movement in the room. She stiffened and pulled away from Damien. When she looked up, she saw Charles Durham, Marquis of Bellingham, standing just inside the door.

"A thousand pardons, my lady, Your Grace," he leered. His bow was sarcastically perfect. "I was under the impression that there was to be a card game in this room this evening. Perhaps I was mistaken."

The Marquis of Bellingham was the worst person who could have caught her with Damien. He was always trying to put his hands on her, but her obvious disdain of a relationship with any man had kept her reasonably safe. Now, he would look upon her as fair game.

Jessica turned away to hide the deep blush rising in her cheeks, but her voice was cool as she answered, "You were not mistaken, my lord, but the game is not scheduled to begin for another half of an hour. If you would be so kind to find the other players, perhaps we could begin earlier."

"Of course," he agreed smoothly. His eyes flicked to Damien. "My congratulations, Wyndham, on your victory. I should have realized it would be you who would breach the wall."

Insulted, Jessica's chin went up. "Cities have walls, sir," she said coldly, "not ladies."

The Marquis gave Jessica a long stare. Bowing once more, he said again, "Of course. Excuse me." Turning on his heel, he left.

Damien glared at the empty doorway. "Bellingham's manners need some improvement," he muttered, then turned to Jessica with a grin. "But you have put the dog to rout. Bravo."

Jessica's fear of Bellingham made her lash out. "You made a promise to me. I cannot abide that man, and now he thinks he is free to impose his attentions upon me. You have ruined everything."

Damien sobered. He wrapped his warm fingers around her arms. "If I have ruined anything, I apologize, but I did not break my promise to you, Jessica. I have not forced you to be with me. If you need help, you only have to ask for it." He brushed his lips lightly across her mouth. "For luck," he whispered, then he was gone.

Jessica put her fingers to her lips. Damien's touch still lingered. Her anger gone, she smiled to herself. It was going to be a very lucky evening. She could feel it.

Damien had used every ounce of willpower he possessed not to carry Jessica off to his home and make love to her for the rest of the night. He berated himself for allowing even the one, stolen kiss. But she was so vulnerable, so desirable, as she'd shied away from him. He'd wanted to envelope her in an invisible cocoon of safety. Instead, he had held himself tightly in check, remembering the true purpose of his watch over her.

She had been in his thoughts constantly since the last time they had been together, much to his dismay. Unbidden, her face would appear before his eyes when he least expected. To remedy the situation, he spent hours each day pouring over the accounts of his estate. In the evening, he accepted all the invitations to dinners and other social gatherings which had begun to pour in when news of his return to society had become known. Nothing had helped. Jessica still haunted him.

He made a point of stopping at *Madame*'s every evening to check on Jessica. He told himself it was because of the job he was doing as *Le Chat*, but he would not admit the truth to himself. He wanted to see her. He found himself comparing every woman with whom he came into contact with Jessica.

He did not know why she bewitched him. He could have almost any woman he wanted. Mothers were throwing their unmarried daughters at him whenever they had the chance. Married women gave him sultry looks of invitation. Neither interested him. He'd decided he was not about to be married to anyone, especially some scatterbrained twit, and the thought of fighting a duel with a jealous husband over some unsatisfied, hot-blooded woman with the morals of an alley cat bored him. Perhaps what intrigued him so about Jessica was that she always seemed remote, always kept a part of herself secret. The reason behind her gambling was part of her secret, but the reason for her helping a spy baffled and angered him.

On the one hand, he wanted to make love to her, day and night, and on the other, he wanted to strangle her. He'd decided she was probably in the spying business for the money, although it most likely did not pay as well as her gambling. Or, perhaps, she was in it merely for the excitement, seeing it as just another game.

He knew women who attempted dangerous liaisons with their lovers just for the excitement of possible discovery by their husbands. He did not think Jessica was that type of woman. Jessica had no jealous husband with which to contend. He surmised there was not even a jealous lover. He had been her first, and as far as he knew, her only one. She could not have time for another, for she spent all her nights gambling. She was an enigma that he could not decipher. Truly, she was the Ice Witch.

His moods swung from elated, to dark and brooding. He felt as if he were caught in the throes of some mysterious disease without a cure. His one consolation during these times was his knowledge that he would soon find out exactly what Jessica's secret was.

Several days after her meeting with Damien, Jessica was in the middle of a game when she received a message from *Madame*. The note asked to meet with her in one of the upstairs rooms. Jessica thought the request odd, for *Madame* never interrupted a card game for anyone or anything. She decided that *Madame* wished to see her about the letter she would be delivering to *Monsieur* Montaigne in a few days.

During a break in the game, Jessica excused herself. As she emerged from the room where she had been playing, she saw the Marquis of Bellingham staring at her. When their eyes met, he grinned lecherously. Ever since that night he had seen her with Damien, he had been a nuisance. He engaged her in conversation several times, always when Damien could see him, and usually, his hand just happened to land on her arm or take hold of her fingers. Jessica tried desperately to discourage him without making a scene, but he would not be put off.

One night, he had gone so far as to corner her in one of the quiet cubicles that *Madame* had about the main room for intimate conversations. As Jessica tried to get past him, he had ripped off her mask and tried to kiss her. She had slapped him soundly across the face for his efforts. Damien had appeared as she was replacing her mask, and just his threatening presence had made the Marquis scurry away into the crowd. Since then, she'd stayed as far away from Bellingham as possible, but his leering, knowing smile followed her whenever their paths crossed. When she saw his lecherous grin on this night, a chill ran down her spine. She needed to speak to *Madame* about him.

The room where *Madame* had asked for the meeting was on the third floor of her establishment, an unusual spot. These rooms were used for illicit liaisons, perhaps if a woman had lost a bet to a man, or vice versa, and they wished to settle the debt with something other than a monetary exchange, or maybe secret liaisons where one or both of the partners had a spouse to deceive. Jessica had never been above the second floor apartment in which *Madame* lived. She supposed the strange meeting place had to do with the secrecy involved as messenger for *Madame*.

When Jessica reached the room, she knocked, but there was no answer. Finding the door unlocked, she opened it. Curiously, she glanced around. It appeared as any other bedroom would. Candles were lit, but the room was empty. *Madame* was not there.

Jessica walked in to wait for her. A footstep behind her made her turn, but it was not *Madame* who stood there. Instead, the Marquis of Bellingham blocked the door.

"Lady Fortuna," the Marquis leered. "What an unexpected pleasure to find you here."

Jessica raised her chin, determined not to show her fear. "I am waiting for *Madame* du Barré. We have private matters to discuss."

"How mysterious," he said as he walked into the room. He closed and locked the door behind him.

"What are you doing?" Jessica demanded. Apprehension slithered through her.

"I do not think *Madame* will mind if I keep you company while you wait for her." He sauntered toward her.

"Why did you lock the door?" Jessica stepped back. Her heart raced. "*Madame* will be here any moment."

"I think not, my lady." His smile was evil. "You see, *Madame* does not know you are here. As a matter of fact, no one knows where you are."

She understood now why the game had been interrupted. "Then it was you who sent the note." Her temper rose.

"How very perceptive you are, Jessica." He snickered.

She blinked in surprise. "How do you know my name?"

His gaze turned crafty. "I have made it my business to know everything there is to know about you, everything, that is, that one can discover about the mysterious Ice Witch. But, to me, you are no mystery. I know whom you see when you leave London. You would have no letters to deliver for *Madame* if it were not for me."

As he spoke, he stalked closer. She retreated.

"What do you mean?" she asked, pretending ignorance. "What letters?" While she tried to protect the secret of *Madame*'s letters, her attention was on keeping her distance from the Marquis.

Bellingham ignored her question. "Don't run away, Jessica. We can have a wonderful time together."

"Don't touch me or I will scream," she warned. She glanced around for a weapon. She saw only a candlestick on a table in the corner. She had to keep him talking until she could reach it. "Everyone will hear, and you will be embarrassed and dishonored."

His smile turned smug. "Scream all you wish. No one will care, that is, if anyone hears you. These rooms are quite soundproof."

She saw her chance and darted toward the table and the candlestick. He lunged, grabbed her, and dragged her hard against him. He pinned her arms against her sides. She tried to push away, to escape, but she was helpless in his grip. His cruel lips descended on her mouth, crushing her lips against her teeth. She stood as stone in his arms, not even fighting to free herself.

She wanted him aware that she felt nothing for him. His mouth violated where Damien's seduced and loved. His fingers clawed at her skin, where Damien's touch had been tender. When he became conscious that she was motionless and unresponsive, he raised his head, but kept hold of her arms. Anger burned in his eyes.

"Am I not good enough for you?" he sneered. "Or do you only tumble into bed for a duke? What does he pay you? I will triple it."

"You are not man enough to polish his boots," she spat.

His nostrils dilated, and his eyes narrowed at her insult. "You little slut," he rasped.

His hand lashed out and struck her face. Pain erupted across her lips and cheek. Her head rocked back, but she remained tight in his hold. She could taste blood. Tears blurred her vision.

"I was willing to pay you handsomely," he sneered, "but now you will have to make do with the pleasure you'll get from our coupling."

Jessica's fear paralyzed her. Then an idea flashed in her mind. If she could reduce his urges to nothing, she might be safe.

"What coupling?" she taunted. "Am I supposed to drool over a eunuch?"

His face twisted in cruel anger. With a tremendous shove, he pushed her back onto the bed. She missed the mattress, banged her head on the bedpost, and fell heavily to the floor. Lights exploded in her brain. Stunned, she lay in a heap, knowing she should do something, but she could not get her brain or body to work.

The Marquis pulled her up and tossed her onto the bed. She tried to crawl away, but he pounced on her. He straddled her and yanked up her skirt. She heard the sound of rending cloth.

"I will show you what a true man feels like, you whore," he panted as he fumbled at his breeches. "We shall see if I am man enough for you." He laughed viciously.

Jessica shoved at him, trying to fend him off, but he was too heavy. Her head spun. She could not think clearly. Fear turned her cold.

"Stop," she protested. "No!" She tried to squirm away.

He caught her wrists and loomed over her, blocking the light. With a deft movement, he forced her legs apart. She felt him between her thighs, pushing at her, trying to gain entrance. Horror overwhelmed her. She screamed until her throat was raw.

The sound of splintering wood exploded into the room. The heavy body of the Marquis was swept off her. She heard a flurry of blows, the crack of knuckles against flesh, thumps, grunts and moans that indicated a fight. And then it was over. Damien had the

Marquis pinned against the wall with a hand around his throat. Her attacker's face was turning purple.

"If you even look at her again," Damien warned, his tone cold and dangerous, "I will cut off your balls."

Bellingham pulled at Damien's grip around his throat with one hand. The other hand slipped into his pocket and pulled out a deadly little pistol.

"Look out!" Jessica warned.

Damien grabbed Bellingham's wrist. The gun waved wildly back and forth as they struggled. Her attacker tried desperately to aim at Damien, while Damien fought to deflect it away. The barrel swept around and pointed at Jessica. She rolled off the bed, huddled as close to the floor as she could, and watched in horror as the Marquis forced the pistol between them. They grappled, barely moving, evenly matched in their intent, one man desperate, the other furious.

And then the pistol fired, the sound muffled by their two bodies.

The two men stood motionless. All Jessica could see was Bellingham's stunned expression and a muscle working fiercely in Damien's jaw. Dread and anxiety sat like two weights in her chest. Had the bullet pierced Damien? Was he bleeding from a death wound? She was paralyzed, terrified to discover what had happened.

Damien stepped back. Bellingham slumped to the floor. A large, red stain spread across the middle of the Marquis's yellow-striped, satin waistcoat. His eyes stared blankly at the ceiling. Jessica covered her mouth with both hands, as she sobbed with relief.

Damien dropped the pistol, and, as if the world had slowed, she watched him turn to her. She could not move. Now that she knew he was still alive, now that she knew Bellingham was dead, she became aware of all her hurts. She felt a trickle of blood from her split lip, and a bruise throbbed on her temple. Her gown was ripped in several places, exposing bruises and scrapes and bare skin in intimate places. She shivered as cold from inside out seeped through her, and she curled into a ball on the floor. Damien placed his coat about her shoulders and rearranged her skirt and bodice to cover her. He pulled her up to sit on the bed, then sat beside her and dabbed the blood at her mouth with his handkerchief.

Jessica allowed him to do as he wished. She had no energy left to dissuade him and she could not stop shivering. In an expressionless tone, she said, "You're not dead."

His mouth quirked. "No."

"How did you know where I was?" she asked.

"I was just arriving when I saw you go up the stairs," he said. "Then I saw Bellingham follow you. I became suspicious, so I followed." He pushed a stray hair out of her face.

Jessica nodded. She was relieved that Bellingham was dead. She was grateful to Damien for saving her. And very, very glad he was still alive. Yet her brain circled around one painful thought. If Damien had been discreet on the night he had kissed her when the Marquis had seen them together, or if he had left her alone as she had asked, would this have happened?

And now that she was involved in a murder, what would happen next? Would *Madame* banish her? How could she survive? She had no means to earn money, other than gambling. How would she be able to fulfill her obligation to Margaret and keep her brother safe?

"Jessica, are you all right? Is there something I can do?" he asked.

She gazed at him. She felt numb except for the dull ache of despair. "Please," she pleaded, the words wrenched from her body. "Leave me alone. You have ruined everything."

He stood swiftly, as if she had threatened him with a weapon. Before he could respond, *Madame* burst into the room, followed by two burly servants.

"*Qu'est-ce que c'est?*" she demanded. What is this? Then she saw Bellingham's body. "*Oh, mon Dieu!*" She glanced from Jessica to Damien. "You protected her," she said to him. "*Merci.* Now go. We will take care of this, and I will care for *ma petite.*"

Madame motioned to the two servants to remove the body, then she rushed to Jessica and enfolded her in her arms. As *Madame* crooned to her and examined her bruises, across the woman's shoulder, Jessica watched Damien stiffen, then without a word, he turned and left.

Damien shut the door quietly behind him. All he could see were Jessica's stark eyes in her very pale face. Her lack of tears or emotion in reaction to the horrible ordeal she had just been through disconcerted him. He'd wanted to hold and comfort her, but her stoniness prevented him. Her cold words had initially cut him deeply and yet desperation had been stamped clearly on her face. Her life was not as carefree as she wanted it to appear. Was she truly an adventuress or was there something more going on? Either way, it was his fault. Unwittingly, he had caused this attack, as she had accused. He had erred, allowing his lust to overcome his good sense. Guilt twisted through him. Even if she was an adventuress and *Madame*'s courier, she did not deserve what Bellingham had done. Satisfaction at the man's death mingled with the revulsion of taking a life. He needed a drink. And he needed to decide what to do about the entrancing woman he had just saved. A woman who was fast becoming too important to him.

By the time he reached the main floor, his concern for the woman who caused the blood to sing in his veins made his decision for him. He would warn Jessica, the Lady Fortuna and possible messenger for *Madame*, that she was navigating through very treacherous waters. At least then, he might still be able to protect her from what could happen.

For the next several days, Jessica remained in her rooms as she recuperated from the attack by the Marquis of Bellingham. She'd won the sum of the stipend she was to deliver to Margaret the night before Bellingham's attack, so she did not have to go back to *Madame*'s until after her return from Braeleigh. The Marquis was buried. The gossipmongers had enough tidbits to chew over for weeks. Jessica just wanted the nightmare to end.

The day before she was to leave for Braeleigh, a messenger arrived with a single rose and a note. He did not wait for a reply, but disappeared as soon as the items were in her hands. She thought Damien had sent them and debated whether to throw them out the window. Resentment against him smoldered and sparked. He had caused her enough problems with his arrogant pursuit. She was glad he had not been injured in his struggle with Bellingham, but as much as it pained her, she wanted nothing more to do with him.

The note remained on her dressing table with the rose for most of the morning. Finally, her curiosity overcame her anger, and she opened the parchment. It read:

A simple rose is not so simple. It hides its essence under many layers. One by one, the petals are peeled away until its heart is laid bare. Beware that all your secrets are not opened to the light. The countryside is no place for a delicate flower.

The note was signed only with the footprint of a cat.

Jessica realized it was a warning of some kind, but the reason behind it eluded her. No one except *Madame* knew of her secret, and she did not think *Madame* would betray her identity and the reason for her gambling to anyone. And no one except Damien knew where she lived in London. The signature of the cat's paw was another puzzle. If the note had been sent by him, why be so cryptic?

Jessica threw the note and flower back onto the dressing table with impatience. She had enough things to worry about without puzzling over some silly note. She had not bled at her usual time this month. Perhaps it was because of the stress she had been under to meet Margaret's demands. Perhaps because of the trauma of the attack by Bellingham. Or perhaps, a more likely reason, she was carrying Damien's child. She had been stupid and careless. Now she would pay the price.

If she was truly *enceinte,* she would have only another three or four months before she would have to stop her visits to *Madame's* because of her swollen belly. How would she manage after that? Could she swallow her pride and go to Damien to beg for her child? His child? Their child? The thought of begging repulsed her. She would not be a kept woman. She knew Margaret would disown her when she found out. What, then, would happen to Jason?

Jessica could not arrive at any acceptable solution. Putting the troubled thoughts out of her mind, she decided she would only concern herself with the present. The need for a solution was still several months away. For the moment, all she would think about was leaving for Braeleigh on the morrow. And delivering *Madame*'s letter to *Monsieur* Montaigne.

CHAPTER 8

Jessica's arrival at Braeleigh was uneventful. The workers had nearly finished their refurbishing, and the house was again quiet. Margaret was obnoxious, as usual. The only change in Jessica's normal routine was that she did not stay the night at Braeleigh. She remained only long enough to give the stipend to Margaret and visit with Jason a short while. Her relief at leaving Margaret behind was overshadowed by her regret at leaving Jason. She had to find a solution to their situation soon. A little voice in her head kept saying that Damien would help if she became his mistress. But her pride kept rejecting that advice. She was distracted when she left on horseback to deliver *Madame*'s letter to *Monsieur* Montaigne. As usual, Donny had traveled as far as the inn. She would wait for Jessica there, where they would spend the night and then travel back to London the following day.

The sun was beginning to set as Jessica rode into the yard of the house belonging to *Monsieur* Montaigne. She was too preoccupied, her thoughts still on Jason, to notice the unusual stillness, although she did think it strange that the gallant gentleman did not come to the door to meet her as was his custom. He knew when she was coming and always remained at home.

Her horse gave a nervous whinny as she tied it to the hitching post. Jessica calmed it, then walked to the door and knocked. When she received no answer, she tried the door. It was unlocked, so she walked in. There were no candles lit to dispel the oncoming gloom of dusk. The house was in shadow.

"*Monsieur* Montaigne!" Jessica called. "It is Jessica!"

There was no reply. Perplexed, she walked several steps farther and tried again.

"*Monsieur*! *Monsieur* Montaigne!" Again, there was no answer.

Jessica frowned and worried her bottom lip with her teeth. Now what was she to do? There was no one to whom she could deliver the letter. She could not wait for *Monsieur* Montaigne's return, for it would be dark soon, and she had to leave for the inn. As she turned to retrace her steps to the door, something moved in a corner. She peered into the shadows. A form detached itself from the gloom and stepped into the dim light from the doorway. She fell back and gasped, her imagination turning it into a ghoul. But no. It was a man, dressed completely in black, except for his shirt, which was a startling white. His jacket was of superfine, his waistcoat of satin, his breeches of soft, black buckskin, his shirt of silk. His boots gleamed in the dull light, and the wide brim of his peasant hat placed his face deep in shadow. He wore a black, silky half-mask across his eyes.

He made a sweeping bow, then spoke in French, "*Bonjour, mademoiselle*. Perhaps I can be of some assistance?"

Jessica took another step back. Now that she saw she did not face a monster, her heart rate slowed, but she remained wary.

"Who are you, *monsieur*?" she demanded, also in French. "Where is *Monsieur* Montaigne? Where is his housekeeper, *Madame* Souchet?"

The stranger shook his head. "I regret they are no longer here. They were forced to leave on very urgent business. Could I deliver some message, perhaps?"

Jessica stilled, suspicious. Could this man be after the letter she was carrying? Had he been sent by the enemies of *Monsieur* Montaigne and *Madame* du Barré? But why? Who was he?

"No, thank you. That will not be necessary," she answered smoothly. "I came merely to pay a visit to my friend, *Monsieur* Montaigne. Since he is not here, I will leave." She began to back toward the door.

"I do not think that would be wise, *mademoiselle*," he said softly in a voice edged with steel.

The dim light that was coming through the open door was cut off. She swung around. Another man, also dressed in black, blocked her escape. She turned back to the caped figure. Panic seized her. The memory of the night she was attacked by Bellingham made her shake.

To hide the trembling of her hands, she clutched them together. She prayed her knees would not buckle.

"What do you want of me, *monsieur*?" She was surprised her voice sounded steady and strong. "I have nothing of value."

"What one person thinks of as worthless, *mademoiselle*, is another person's treasure. You are carrying something of great value to many people."

Jessica caught the gleam of white teeth as he smiled. She raised her chin in brave defiance. She would not be fooled into handing over *Madame*'s private correspondence to anyone, especially this stranger who could be working for Napoleon's Minister of Police.

"I believe you are mistaken, *monsieur*." She spread her hands before her. "As you can see, I have nothing that could be of such great importance to so many."

The man signaled to his friend blocking the doorway, who backed out and shut the door, but his departure only heightened Jessica's apprehension. She was alone again with the man wearing the cape. He stepped toward her.

"Perhaps, if I described this important item, you would remember that you carry it," he suggested.

He leaned negligently on the back of a nearby chair. His air of nonchalance did not fool Jessica in the least. But perhaps it would give her a few extra seconds to get to one of the rooms at the rear of the house and then make her escape through a window. She inched back a few steps.

"Yes," she agreed. "If you could tell me what it is you want, then maybe I could help you."

"It is a letter," he said. "A letter from someone you know in London written to *Monsieur* Montaigne. Do you know of such a letter, *mademoiselle*?"

"A letter, *monsieur*?" Jessica frowned as if in thought. She was amazed at how easily she pretended with this dangerous stranger. She shook her head. "No, I know of no such letter." She edged away a bit more. "There must be someone else coming to visit *Monsieur* Montaigne. He must have the letter you want."

At her last word, Jessica turned and fled. She heard the stranger behind her. If she could only reach that doorway, she could close and lock the door on him. He was so close. Just a few more steps. He grabbed for her. She slipped away. Then into the room. He was too close for her to shut the door. To the window. His hand closed around her arm, jerked her back. Her impetus swung her about and slammed her against the wall. The wind was knocked from her. He held her, face to the wall, pinned by his body, one hand pressed against the wall on either side of her.

She tried to wriggle free, but he caught her wrists and pulled her arms above her head. His grip was firm, unyielding. He would not let go. Against her back, she could feel his heart beating. His warm breath fluttered tendrils of hair on her neck.

"I am sorry if I have hurt you, *mademoiselle*, but it was not wise to try to run away." His words were soft. "You would not have gone far had you escaped. My men surround the house, and they do not take kindly to people who cause them trouble. Nor do I. Not even someone as beautiful as yourself." He paused. "Now, *mademoiselle*, you have a choice. Either you give me the letter that we both know you carry, or I will take it by force. I assure you, the first alternative will be more pleasant for you, and the second, well, that will be more pleasant for me, *non*?"

His last words sent a shiver down her spine. She had no doubt that his threat was sincere. The thought of having his hands tearing at her clothes turned her stomach nauseous. All she could think of was Bellingham above her, pushing her thighs apart, attempting to breach and defile her.

"I will give you the letter, *monsieur*," she said, barely above a whisper.

"A very wise decision, *mademoiselle*. I warn you not to try anything foolish that will anger me. You would not like me when I am angry." He released her wrists and stepped back.

She swung around to face him. "I do not like you now, *monsieur*."

He let out a mock sigh. "That is most unfortunate." Then he grinned. "Because I like *you*."

Jessica scowled at him.

Becoming grave, he said, "The letter, please, *mademoiselle*."

She glanced left and right, considering escape. He took a step closer, threatening with his proximity. She would never get away from him. She was caught. She could only give him what he wanted.

She hoped *Madame* would understand why she turned over her correspondence to this outlaw. She turned her back on him and lifted her skirt. Tucked into a frilly garter was the sealed letter. She pulled it out and allowed her skirt to drop into place. As she handed him the letter, she tried to see his face beneath the hat. Something familiar about him niggled at her.

He smiled as he took the letter. "Many thanks, *mademoiselle*. You have saved us both a great deal of aggravation."

He took her by the elbow and steered her back to the front parlor. Gallantly, he motioned her to sit.

"Please, remain here, *mademoiselle*," he said. "I will not be so gentle if you decide to try to escape again."

As he walked away from her, he pulled a pistol out of his belt and placed it on a table. Jessica did not doubt that he would use the weapon if she tried to move. Fearfully, she swallowed. Would he release her now that he had what he wanted? Or would he keep her and…? She could not finish the thought.

Outside, twilight was turning to night. She watched as he lit a candle. He became engrossed reading the letter. He was turned away from her, but the light glinted on his hair that curled below his hat. Golden hair. Jessica's eyes widened as she studied him. That profile. It could not be, could it?

He finished the letter and turned to face her. The candle threw its light under the brim of his hat. Jessica gasped.

"You!" she blurted. She clutched the arms of the chair. She needed to hold onto something solid.

Damien flinched as if he'd been struck. The look on her face tore at him. He had wanted to get through this evening without revealing his identity. He removed his mask.

"Yes," he said, switching from French to English.

"Were you the one who sent the warning?" she asked.

"Yes."

"But why? What do you want with *Madame*'s letter? Why are you dressed like that? Why did you do this to me?" Her questions tumbled one after the other.

"Do you know what is in *Madame*'s letter?" he demanded, trying to ignore her bewilderment and tamping down his desire to soothe her.

"Of course not. I do not read other people's private correspondence," she said, affronted.

"Perhaps you should." His tone was grim. He walked to the door and told his men he had the situation under control. Then he returned and stood over her. He forced the next words out of a tight throat. "I am placing you under arrest for treason, Jessica."

Her mouth dropped open. Then, nearly hysterical, she began to laugh. "Treason!" she gasped. "Damien, how long did it take you to figure out this little charade to get me to come to you?"

Damien blanched. Not only did she not believe him, but she had impugned his honor.

"Jessica."

His voice cut through her laughter like a blade.

Her amusement died abruptly.

"I have not broken my promise to you, and I am not lying," he said coldly.

Jessica stared up at him blankly.

Damien watched her carefully. Her eyes had gone dead. She was in shock, retreating into herself, protecting herself from any more hurt. He hated himself for what the situation required of him, but he was her jailer now. He had to make her see that.

He grabbed her arms and pulled her out of the chair. He knew the signs of shock and hysteria very well. He could not allow her to fall apart. He wanted to save her.

With a little shake, he commanded, "Listen to me, Jessica. The letters which you have been delivering for *Madame* contain information which she should not have. You have been helping to deliver secrets to Napoleon. I am working undercover to stop anyone who is delivering that information. Do you understand me?"

She stared at him. Slowly, her eyes focused.

"Treason?" she asked in a small voice.

"Yes."

She blinked. "I am under arrest?"

"Yes."

The finality of his single word landed on Jessica's ears like a stone. He released her. Her knees buckled, and she sank back into the chair. How could this be happening? The mess of her life had gone from awful to disastrous. Her mind skittered away from the overwhelming repercussions of her arrest and settled on curiosity instead. She frowned.

"How can you arrest me?" she asked. "What authority do you have?"

"The authority of His Majesty the King. I am a colonel in His Majesty's army." His words held the ring of truth.

She frowned. "Then you are not truly a duke?"

"I am that, too," he said with a little sigh, as if burdened by both responsibilities.

Jessica was confused. "But why are you both?" she asked. Few men, she knew, bought a commission in the army if they were to inherit a title. Buying a commission was left to second and third sons of the titled.

Damien smiled grimly. "It's a long story."

He turned away and collected his pistol, mask, hat, and the all-important letter. He paused beside the table holding the lit candle. "Come along, Jessica. It is time to leave."

She gathered her strength. Then slowly, as if she were an old woman, she rose and walked to his side. He blew out the candle and guided her to the door. Outside, she saw several other men dressed like Damien. Aphrodite was still tethered where she had left her.

"Who owns the horse?" Damien asked.

"She is mine," she said without thinking. "A gift from my father."

"Where do you stable her?" he pressed.

Jessica did not answer. She had already said too much.

One of the men approached with something dangling from his hand. She heard the clang of metal against metal.

"Excuse me, sir," he said. "Will you want these?" He held up manacles.

Jessica stared at the wide iron bands held together by a heavy chain. She could already feel them around her wrists — the hard cold of the iron, the weight of the chain. Bleak desperation overwhelmed her. Blackness swept over her. She swayed against her horse.

Damien's hands closed around her arms and steadied her. A concerned frown furrowed his brow. Then it was gone, wiped from his face as if it had not been.

"I will not put the irons on you," he said quietly, but firmly, "if you give me your word that you will not try to escape."

She had no need to give her word. "I have nowhere to escape to."

He nodded and waved his man away. As they rode out of the yard, the men surrounded Jessica. It was done subtly, with no command spoken. Damien rode before her, at the head of the group. Jessica kept her eyes on his broad back, her mind a complete blank. She could not let herself wonder what would happen to her or to Jason. She just had to do as she was told for now. Later, she would begin to think, to question.

The ride to the inn was made in silence. Occasionally, Damien would drop back to ride beside her, but he made no effort at conversation and neither did she. Jessica had nothing to say to him. She could not explain anything for she was still dazed. Damien likely held her in contempt, and she would not plead with him for mercy. Keeping her dignity, she rode with her back straight and her chin up.

By the time they reached the inn, she was exhausted and chilled to the bone. A light mist had begun soon after they had started out and made the trip seem much longer and more miserable. Jessica's riding clothes had not been made for long rides in the damp of night. She was shivering uncontrollably, and her teeth chattered.

"Why didn't you say that you were cold?" His voice held a hint of exasperation.

"You didn't ask me," she snapped. She did have some pride left.

Damien pulled her against him, enfolding her in his arms, his cloak shielding her. The warmth of his body was reassuring. The gesture evoked memories of the last time she had been with him. She longed to put her arms around him, but knew she could not. He was her jailer now. She was his prisoner.

As soon as they entered the inn, Donny accosted Damien. "Here now! Ye take yer hands off her!" She tugged at Damien's arm. "Ye'll not be puttin' yer filthy hands all over my lady." When her tugging did no good, she tried to wrest Jessica away.

Damien turned cold, green eyes on her. Jessica did not want his anger to spend itself on Donny, so she intervened.

"Donny," she said softly. "It's all right. I will explain later."

"Hmph," Donny grumbled. "It doesn't look all right." But she retreated back a step.

Damien removed his cloak and draped it over Jessica's shoulders. Then he took aside the innkeeper. While they spoke, Jessica kept her chin up proudly and stared at one of the far beams of the ceiling. Donny warily watched the men who stood stiffly about. The silence was awkward. Jessica breathed a sigh of relief when Damien returned.

"A meal will be sent to your room," he said. "I took the liberty of ordering a bath. It will cure your chill. I will come to see you later."

"Thank you," she said, then started up the stairs with Donny.

One of Damien's men followed.

Donny blocked his way. "Where d'ye think ye be goin'?"

Jessica put her hand on the woman's arm. "Please, Donny. It's all right. He will not bother us." She met the man's eyes and gave him a small smile. Then she continued up the stairs.

Donny followed, grumbling the whole way. She nearly growled when he stationed himself outside the room. As soon as Donny shut the door, she demanded an explanation. Jessica told her what had happened at the house of *Monsieur* Montaigne, and who had brought her to the inn. She only omitted that Damien had been her lover.

When she'd finished, the little woman asked, "What about his babe that ye be carryin'?"

Jessica gasped and stared at her in astonishment.

"Don't ye look so surprised," Donny said. "I've taken care of ye all yer life. Don't ye think I know what ye be about?"

Fiercely, Jessica said, "Donny, don't you breathe a word of this, especially to him, or I will tan your hide."

Donny sniffed. "I can keep me mouth shut. But if ye weren't so proud, ye'd tell him. He might be able t'make things easier for ye."

"No, I'll not take his pity. Or anyone else's." Jessica turned her back. She was relieved Donny remained quiet.

Jessica was huddled in a chair by the fire when Damien came to her room. She wore her dressing gown and had left her hair loose. She knew she should have been properly dressed, but she had no strength. He stood, cool and remote, just inside the door. She wanted him to gather her in his arms and tell her everything would be well. Instead, he looked every inch the soldier, despite his clothes. Why couldn't their relationship have been different? Why couldn't she hate him?

"I came to inform you we will be leaving at dawn tomorrow," he said. "There will be a man posted outside your door tonight. Do not cause him any trouble."

She smiled wryly. "I will still be here in the morning, Your Grace. I think you overrate the ability of your prisoner."

"The success of what I do depends on not overrating anyone or anything," he said seriously.

Jessica nearly laughed at the ludicrous idea of being considered dangerous. Instead, with a wry twinkle, she said, "I suppose I should be flattered that you think me that important."

Something flashed through his eyes. He looked about to say something, then stopped, cleared his throat. "I am only telling you, so you may be warned." With a formal bow, he said, "Good night, Jessica."

As he turned toward the door, she stood. "Damien."

He stopped with his hand on the latch.

"What is going to happen to me?" Her words came out small and frightened.

He did not answer immediately. A muscle twitched in his jaw. She thought she saw compassion—or was it contempt? —cross his face, but it was gone too quickly for her to be sure.

"I believe traitors are hanged," he said. Then he was gone.

She gasped, and her hand flew to her mouth, as she sank back into the chair.

His words were like hammer blows. How long before the sentence would be carried out? A month? Two? Certainly not long enough to allow her child to be born. There would be a trial. Perhaps she could throw herself on the mercy of the court. Perhaps they would postpone carrying out the sentence long enough to allow her to bear her child. Would Damien accept the babe as his? Would he care for it? Love it?

Tears slipped down her cheeks. The Ice Witch's icy façade was cracked. There was nothing she could do. Her own foolishness and naïveté had gotten her into this mess. But what else could she have done? Margaret had tied her hands — holding the threat of an unwanted marriage over her head while keeping Jason hostage. She'd had no other recourse but to raise the funds through gaming and no other choice but to do as *Madame* had requested in order to gain access to her gambling den.

Wiping her tears, she heaved a watery sigh. She supposed she was better off leaving this life. She could never belong to Damien anyway, not the way he wanted, not with Margaret's evil hanging over her head. And what of Jason? Her heart broke for her brother, who, with her death, would be left at the mercy of Margaret's wrath and no one to watch over him. Dare she ask Damien to help Jason after she was gone? Weren't the condemned allowed one last request? She would tell Damien about Jason and the child. But not now. She couldn't risk putting her brother at greater risk than he already was. She had to protect Jason and her babe for as long as she could. She would tell Damien when she could hide it no longer. With those decisions made, she went to bed, to wait for the next step down in her degradation.

The next morning, Jessica was escorted outside by another of Damien's men. A coach waited with the Wyndham heraldic device emblazoned on its door. Damien, dressed in an officer's uniform, was speaking with several of his men, who were also dressed as soldiers in His Majesty's army. She felt a catch in her throat at the way he had been transformed. He was just as handsome, just as magnetic, but with a military bearing, a commander at ease with his men.

He approached and without any greeting, he said, "You will be more comfortable riding in the coach. We will be traveling all day with only a few stops to rest the horses. Since you will not tell me where you stable your horse, we will have to take her with us. Is there anyone in the area whom you wish to inform of your arrest?"

Jessica looked into his face. There was no softening of his features. He was merely being courteous. He had become the soldier, her jailer, completely.

Dropping her gaze, she said, "There is no one."

Damien nodded, then offered his hand to help her into the coach. He had not missed the faint, dark shadows under her eyes that spoke of her sleepless night. Evidently, his parting remark the evening before had done what he'd intended. She was scared now, as she should be for what she had done. He wanted her to dwell on the consequences of her actions. Treason was a very serious business. He would alleviate her fears later, and persuade her to incriminate *Madame*. Even if she did not, the letter was enough evidence to arrest *Madame* du Barré, the hub of the spy ring.

As he walked to his horse, he tried to decide whether Jessica was guilty or innocent. He wanted to believe that she was telling the truth when she said she knew nothing of the contents of the letter. If only she was not so secretive about who she was and where she came from. What was she hiding? Whom was she protecting?

The ride back to the city was agony for Jessica. She conjured up grim and ghastly scenes, most of which had to do with Newgate Prison, and most of which ended in her horrible death. Rejecting even the small, yet very important fact that the contents of the letters she had delivered were unknown to her, she believed that just because she had delivered them made her guilty of treason. She had been so gullible.

By the time they reached the city, Jessica no longer cared what happened to her. She'd tried and convicted herself and found herself guilty. She'd brought shame and scandal to the family name. Jason was better off without her.

CHAPTER 9

Night had fallen when Damien's coach entered the city and finally stopped. Jessica had paid no attention to the passing scenery. She was too caught up in her shame and misery to care. When she glanced out the coach window, she expected to find herself in the dark, dreary, prison courtyard. Instead, the coach had stopped before the steps of Damien's house. It was lit as if their arrival had been anticipated.

Fury washed over her. What was he scheming now? She exchanged a confused, angry glance with Donny before she descended from the coach with the help of one of Damien's men. In silence, she allowed him to escort her up the stairs and through the door. Damien was waiting for her at the bottom of the grand staircase. As she stalked up to him, he bowed gallantly.

"Welcome to my home, my lady."

Ignoring his polite greeting and the guard beside her, she demanded, "What kind of cruel joke is this, Damien? Why am I here?"

Damien's face turned stony. "You are here, Jessica, because I requested it," he answered coldly. "You will be detained here, under house arrest, until your innocence or guilt has been determined. At that time, you will either be released or sent to trial. Being the mistress of a duke has its advantages."

Jessica felt as if he'd slapped her. How could he say something so cruel before all his men? With her cheeks flaming and her eyes brimming with tears, she opened her mouth to berate him, but his icy, green gaze froze the words in her throat. He turned to a maid who hovered nearby.

"Show Lady Jessica to her room, please, Lucy," he said calmly as if nothing had happened.

Lucy hurried forward and motioned to the stairs. Jessica was quite happy to comply. All she wanted was to be away from Damien's presence. She had been mortified and hurt by his admission of their intimacy before all his men. How could he be so callous? Did he despise her so much?

When Jessica was halfway up the stairs, he called to her. She stopped and turned slowly, not knowing what to expect, hoping for an apology.

"Dinner will be at nine o'clock," he said. "Please be prompt. My men and I do not like to be kept waiting."

She felt the blood drain from her cheeks. She could not endure sitting through a meal with him. Not tonight. Not with all his men in attendance. Not with all of them knowing of her intimacy with Damien. A black pall suddenly dropped over her eyes and her knees buckled beneath her. She crumpled to a heap on the stairs.

When her eyelids finally opened, she discovered Damien kneeling beside her, cradling her head against his shoulder. Blankly, she stared at everyone standing around her. Realizing she still leaned against Damien, she struggled to sit up, but he would not allow it.

"Lie still, Jessica," he ordered. Was that concern she heard disguised in his curtness?

"I'm sorry," she apologized. "I don't know why I fainted."

He raised an eyebrow and one side of his mouth twitched upward. "Obviously, the thought of dining with five men," he said dryly. Lucy appeared beside him and passed him a glass of brandy. He took it and held it to Jessica's lips. "Drink this. It will put some color back in your cheeks."

Jessica took a sip, swallowed and gasped. It burned all the way down her throat and hit her stomach with a jolt. She coughed and pushed the glass away.

With watery eyes, she looked up at him and said, "I'm better, now. Thank you."

Again, she tried to get up. Instead of helping her to her feet, Damien scooped her up in his arms and carried her the rest of the way upstairs.

"Please, Damien, I can walk," she protested, although she appreciated his warmth and strength.

"Perhaps," he said, "but I did not bring you here to kill yourself by falling down the stairs and breaking your neck. If I am to hand you over to a judge, I would prefer that you be in one piece. Besides, I like you better alive than dead."

He turned his head to look at her, and Jessica found her face only inches from his. If she moved just the tiniest bit, she could kiss him, and she very much wanted to do that. He stopped just outside the door to a room. He stood still, gazing at her. Jessica was caught in his intense gaze. Her lips parted, and she saw his head bend ever so slightly toward her.

Behind them, Donny cleared her throat. Damien blinked. The spell was broken. His spine stiffened, and he entered the room with her. As soon as he placed her on the bed, she began to sit up.

"Stay there," he ordered. "I will have your dinner brought up to you." He turned to Donny. "Put your mistress to bed. She seems to be too stubborn to do so on her own." With that, he left.

Jessica and Donny looked at each other a moment, each thinking their own thoughts. Donny was the first to break the silence.

"Aye, he's a hard one, but he seems fair enough. Ye be lucky he's a duke, and he cares for ye. Ye could be in prison, now."

Sadly, Jessica shook her head. "He does not care for me, Donny. I am only something to amuse him."

"Hmph. Amuse, is it? Ye can't see what's before yer own eyes," Donny grumbled. "Well, come on with ye. Into bed. He'd not like it if ye disobeyed."

Donny helped Jessica get undressed and into bed, then she began to unpack the few belongings Jessica had taken with her to Braeleigh. When she opened the armoire, she harrumphed, pulled out a blue silk dress and held it up.

"Look at this," Donny said.

"Why, that's just like mine," Jessica exclaimed.

"It *is* yer dress," the little woman replied. "They're all here, all yer clothes."

"But why?" Jessica wondered. "How did he know?"

"He knew. That's all ye need t'know. Ye don't cross a man like that. Ye tell him everything tomorrow."

Jessica's chin went up defiantly. "I'll do no such thing. He will not find out about Jason or the babe from me. He does not have to know yet. And you keep quiet, Mistress Donlin."

Donny's mouth tightened into a straight line. "Aye, I'll keep quiet," she reluctantly agreed. "But ye'll be gettin' yerself into deep trouble with him."

Jessica made no reply. She slumped down into the bed and pulled the covers up to her chin.

Lucy came soon after with a light meal of broth, fresh bread with butter, and tea. She told Donny there was a meal for her in the kitchen, and that if Donny wished to retire after that, she would take care of the Lady Jessica.

After Donny left, Jessica pondered her situation. The room she had been given was large and expensively furnished. It was evidently one of the better guest rooms in the house. Damien had been quite solicitous of her comfort. But his manner baffled her. He had turned so cold, almost cruel. Except for that one moment when they would have kissed. Her fingertips touched her lips, a faint smile crossing her face at the memory of his kisses. Her smile faded. She was a fool. He might still harbor a physical attraction to her, but any tenderness he'd had for her had certainly evaporated now that he thought her guilty of treason.

Sighing, she pushed the tray away and leaned back on the pillows. The food and hot tea had relaxed her. Later, she would decide what to do.

Damien had dined with his men, but his gaze strayed often to the empty chair to his right that would have been occupied by Jessica. His glances had not gone unnoticed, particularly by his leftenant, Edward Johnson. Edward had escorted Jessica into the house, and had witnessed Damien's ungentlemanly comments about his relationship with her. Edward glowered at him now.

With a twinge of guilt, Damien muttered impatiently, "Mind your own business, Leftenant."

At the end of the meal, he had given his men their orders for the following days while Jessica remained his prisoner. It was an easy assignment to keep a young woman under house arrest, but he had cautioned them against losing their diligence. The men had accepted his warning, but he felt their disapproval in their silence. He dismissed them in exasperation, not quite sure whether he was angry at the men for having been captivated by this slip of a woman, or at Jessica for arousing their pity, or at himself for being bewitched.

He sat alone now, in the dark before the fire. Having gone through a good portion of the brandy in the decanter at his elbow, his thoughts chased themselves in circles. He kept coming back to one simple question whose answer was not so simple: Why? He could not find any of the answers that the question prompted. Glancing at the almost empty decanter, he smiled wryly at himself. The brandy certainly had not made him think any clearer, and he was going to have a roaring headache in the morning. With extreme care, he set the glass on the table, pulled himself out of the chair, and started for bed.

In the upstairs hall, his feet stopped before the door of Jessica's room. Hesitating only a moment, he turned the knob and walked in. He stepped silently to the side of the bed and held the candle high, allowing its light to fall on her face.

She was so beautiful, this young woman, too young to have become involved in something as treacherous as espionage. He reached out and smoothed a lock of hair away from her face. His fingers trailed down her cheek. She sighed softly in her sleep, threw her arm wide, and turned onto her back. Her breasts softly thrust against her thin nightrail.

His breath caught in his throat, and he swallowed with an effort. What he wanted to do was climb under the covers and make love to her, to feel her beneath him, her body enticing, responding. Biting down on a groan, he lowered the candle and looked away. He could not, not yet. Their positions in this nasty game would not allow it. Quickly, he walked to the door and let himself out as quietly as he had come.

The following morning when Jessica awoke, she thought for a moment she was at Braeleigh, in her own bed. When she looked about, she realized she was in a room in Damien's house.

It was a pretty room, decorated in pale greens and yellows, reminding her of spring. She decided it was definitely better than prison, and was grateful to Damien for using his influence so that she would be allowed to stay at his home. Stretching with feline grace, she luxuriated in the satiny sheets. She felt rested and ready for anything, possibly even a meeting with Damien. As she was lying there, a knock came at the door, and the maid, Lucy, entered with a cup and saucer on a small tray.

"Good morning, m'lady." She smiled pertly. "I brought you some hot chocolate."

Jessica smiled back at the girl. "Thank you, Lucy."

Lucy opened the drapes, then stopped at the foot of the bed. "His Grace would like to see you in the dining room for breakfast when you are dressed."

The door opened, and Donny bustled in. "All right, out of bed with ye," she commanded. "Are ye going t'spend the rest of yer life under the covers?"

Lucy's mouth dropped open at a servant giving orders to a highborn lady. Jessica gave the girl a grin and a helpless shrug.

Donny turned on Lucy. "They be wantin' ye, girl, in the salon to help with the polishin'." She waited until Lucy had hurried out the door, then she turned back to Jessica. "Ye be feelin' all right?"

"I feel fine, Donny," Jessica assured her.

"Good." Donny nodded. "Yer Duke's walkin' around lookin' like a thundercloud. Ye'll be needin' every ounce of yer strength today."

Jessica sighed and climbed out of bed. She was not ready to meet with Damien. The day was going to be very long.

When Jessica walked into the dining room, Damien was sitting by himself at the long table. He was staring out the window and tapping a spoon absently upon the folded napkin beside his plate. Jessica stopped hesitantly just inside the doorway. Finally, he glanced up and saw her.

"Come in, Jessica. I will not grow fangs and attack you," he growled.

Jessica frowned at his bad manners. "That is quite possible," she sniffed.

His mouth flattened, and he scowled. Slowly he stood as if moving caused him pain, and motioned to a chair at his right. "By all means, my lady, please come in and be seated," he said sarcastically.

Regally, trying not to show that she was in the least intimidated by him, Jessica sailed into the room and waited as he held the chair for her. Her nerves only allowed her to perch uncomfortably on its edge. When Damien had resumed his seat, he rang for the servants to bring in breakfast.

After their plates had been filled, he asked in a more civil tone, "Are you feeling better this morning?"

"Much better, thank you," she answered quietly. Jessica noticed his bloodshot eyes, and could not help adding, "A good night's sleep will cure almost anything."

With a raised eyebrow, he said, "I thought I should inform you of what will be expected of you while you are here. You will be allowed the freedom of the house and grounds as if you were a guest. However, if you stray beyond the boundaries, my men have orders to treat you as an escaped prisoner. In other words, they will shoot first, then ask questions. I would appreciate if you did not put them in that position. They truly do not enjoy shooting women. Do I make myself clear?"

"Perfectly, Your Grace," Jessica baited him with the formal address for his bad manners. "Or should I address you as Colonel?"

His eyes narrowed, but he ignored her barb. Instead, he said, "You will be questioned later in the morning concerning your activities. Your cooperation, or lack of it, will have a large part to play when your fate is decided."

Jessica blinked. "What will happen if I do not know anything?"

"That is a problem," he said, then dropped his gaze. "Eat your breakfast." He gave a vague wave at her plate, then turned his attention to his own meal.

They ate in silence. Uncomfortable and tense, Jessica barely touched her food. She was relieved when they had finished, and Damien's good humor seemed to return. He held her chair when she rose from the table and walked with her out of the dining room. She would wait in her room to be summoned for questioning. As she started up the stairs, he caught her hand. She turned on the bottom step.

"It will go easier for you if you tell the truth, Jessica. I will help you all I can," he said.

He was a step below her, and so his face was level with hers. His expression was intent, serious. Was there a hint of sympathy there, too? She longed to reach out and touch his cheek. Instead, she bit down on her bottom lip to keep her emotions under control.

"Thank you," she murmured, then turned and fled up the stairs.

About an hour later, the summons came. She was to meet with Damien in the salon. Her nerves were as frayed as the handkerchief she had picked at while she waited. Soon, she would discover her fate.

No one was in the room when she arrived. Jacobs told her that His Grace would be with her presently, then left her alone. She sat on the edge of a chair, her hands clasped in her lap, her eyes downcast. Several minutes went by before Damien entered the room with another man, a soldier, quite a bit older than Damien.

"Jessica," Damien said, "this is General Drayton. He would like to ask you some questions."

The General bowed over Jessica's hand. He reminded her of someone's grandfather.

"I cannot recall ever being presented to so lovely a prisoner." His smile was kind.

"Thank you, General." Jessica smiled back at him. Perhaps this would not be such a terrible experience, after all.

The General sat down across from her. "I am sure you realize that you are in very serious trouble. The more you can help us, the easier it will be for you in the end. We are very willing to be lenient with someone who cooperates. Do you understand, my dear?"

Jessica nodded, nerves gripping her insides.

"Good," the General smiled. "Now, suppose you begin by telling us how you came to be delivering messages for *Madame* du Barré."

Jessica swallowed and began her story. She told how she had gone to *Madame* to gain entrance to her house, how *Madame* had offered her a loan to start gambling. Then she explained the way she was to repay the loan: by delivering the letter once a month to *Monsieur* Montaigne.

"Did you not think this an odd way to repay a loan?" the General asked.

"Ye-es," Jessica faltered. "But *Madame* was so nice. I had planned to repay her anyway when I could afford it. Delivering the letters was such a small favor to ask. I had no idea what the letters said."

The General became thoughtful. "Why was it such a small favor to deliver a letter every month to *Monsieur* Montaigne? He lives near the town of Osmington in Dorsetshire. That is a fair distance to travel just to deliver a letter."

Jessica nearly blurted out the truth, but she stopped herself in time. Lowering her eyes, she said, "I cannot tell you."

"Then tell me, my dear, why a well-bred young woman like yourself would want to have anything to do with a place like that of *Madame* du Barré?"

She watched her knuckles turn white as she clenched her hands in her lap. "I needed a great deal of money," she said barely above a whisper.

"Why?"

"I cannot tell you." She raised anguished eyes to the General.

"Whom are you protecting, Jessica?" The General suddenly did not look like someone's grandfather. He had changed to a steely commander who was not used to being thwarted.

Jessica pressed her lips together and remained silent.

"All right," he conceded. "We will let that go for the moment. Can you tell us if you ever saw anything unusual at *Madame*'s? Was there ever anyone there who did not seem to belong? Or was there anyone to whom *Madame* was particularly friendly?"

Jessica tried to remember if she had ever seen anything or anyone like what the General had described, but nothing came to mind. She shook her head.

"I'm sorry," she told him. "I cannot remember anything like that. I spent very little time there when I was not involved in a game. I…" Her voice trailed off, and she stared off into space as a thought came to her.

The General leaned forward. "Yes?"

Her eyes came back to focus on the gentleman across from her. "Charles Durham. The Marquis of Bellingham."

"Yes? What about him?"

Jessica felt Damien tense behind her. "He said something… odd… the night…" She halted, not able to speak of the horrible night the man had attacked her. She had tried not to think of that night, had tried to put it out of her mind. Now, however, the words of the Marquis came to her clearly.

She took a breath and forged on. "Several nights ago, the Marquis told me that if it were not for him, I would have no letters to deliver for *Madame* du Barré."

General Drayton exchanged a glance with Damien, who was no longer lounging on a window seat, but was now sitting forward, intent on every word.

"I'm glad I killed him," Damien muttered.

The General made a placating gesture with his hand, then turned back to Jessica. He asked, "Did he ever say anything else about these letters that you delivered?"

Jessica shook her head. "No. Just that once."

The General nodded. "I believe you have just given us the name of the traitor in our midst. You see, the Marquis worked closely with His Majesty's Foreign Minister. He was privy to many state secrets."

Jessica's eyes widened in shock, but she said nothing.

General Drayton went on, "What you have told us, my dear, is a great help, but I am afraid the story of your own involvement in this matter is not very plausible. How can we be sure that you are not lying to us about being ignorant of the contents of those letters? We must have some proof of your innocence. His Grace informs me that you refer to yourself as 'Lady Jessica'. Are you truly the daughter of some lord?"

"Yes."

"Then who is your father?"

"My father is dead, sir," she answered quietly.

"Then you have my deepest sympathies. However, that does not help. Your family. Who are they? Where are you from?"

Jessica did not answer. She was not going to dishonor her family name by revealing whose daughter she was. She was also not going to give Margaret the satisfaction of knowing what had happened to her.

At her silence, the General asked, "Could it be, perhaps—and please excuse my being indelicate—that you are the illegitimate daughter of some lord?"

Jessica felt the heat rise in her cheeks. "No!"

The General sighed. "All right, if you cannot reveal your family, then tell us why you have a need for such a large amount of money. I understand that you have won a fortune at cards, yet you live very simply. Where does the money go, my dear?"

Again, Jessica remained silent. How could she explain that her *dear* stepmother was holding her only brother hostage on his own estate? Who would believe her?

She heard Damien move impatiently. Not even his aggravation would make her reveal her secrets. Let them put her in prison if they wished. She would keep Jason safe and free from scandal.

General Drayton cleared his throat. "I see. You will not tell us. Very well, my dear. I feel I must warn you that your fate still hangs in the balance. If you change your mind and wish to tell us your story, just inform His Grace. Now, if you will excuse us, we have some things to discuss."

So, she was dismissed. She had told them everything that she had dared. There was nothing more she could do. Damien escorted her to the entrance of the salon and held the door for her. It closed behind her like the door to a prison cell.

She supposed they would decide to bring her to trial, for she could not expect the General to believe her story. It sounded like a fabrication, even to her. Would Damien believe her?

About an hour later, she watched from her bedroom window as the General left. Not long after, a knock sounded on her door. She thought it was only one of the maids, so she called to enter. But Damien walked in. He looked angry.

"How can someone," he said without any greeting, "who is so shrewd at cards, be so foolish with her own life? You have not helped your cause any by remaining silent about who you are, Jessica."

"I know," she said simply, and turned back to stare out the window.

He crossed the room in several long strides, and taking her arm, swung her about to face him.

"Why?" he demanded.

Jessica answered his question with one of her own. "Would you dishonor your family, Damien? Would you not prefer to die in obscurity than drag your family name through the mire?"

He dropped his hand from her arm and blinked. "Jessica, if your story is true, then you have nothing to fear," he said. "There would be no scandal, for there would be no trial. General Drayton only needs some proof that you are telling the truth."

"Oh, there would be a scandal. How else would *Madame* be convicted if not with my testimony? How was it that someone like me came to know a woman like *Madame*? What was I doing in her establishment?"

Damien raised an eyebrow. "Well?"

Instead of answering him, she asked, "Do you believe that I am telling the truth, Damien?"

He stared at her for a moment, then his gaze slid to the window. "I don't know."

Jessica nodded, understanding his indecision. Why should he believe her? He had met her in circumstances that would cause anyone to have grave doubts about her integrity. She had even cheated him in a card game.

"Thank you for being truthful." Ruefully, she smiled. "I would probably have trouble believing my story, too, if I were not the one telling it."

Damien looked at her, his eyes reflecting the pain of his uncertainty. Then the instant was gone, and his expression was once more impersonal, that of her jailer.

"I will leave you to think over your silence," he said. His tone was cool, detached. "Perhaps you will change your mind. If so, just inform one of the servants. They will know where to find me." Bowing formally, he left.

CHAPTER 10

Jessica remained in her room for the rest of the day, even requesting to have her meals there. Damien did not come again, and she did not try to find him. There was nothing left to say.

After she'd finished her dinner, she wandered to the window. She seemed to spend a great deal of time staring out at the drive, seeing nothing, thinking less. Her mind was brought back into focus by the arrival of Damien's landau. She saw him emerge from the house and enter the carriage. He was dressed for the evening. He looked magnificent. His evening cape swirled about his legs and reminded her of how he had been dressed the day of her arrest.

She realized she was truly a prisoner and could not come and go as she wished. She might never again see her brother, walk through the halls of her childhood home, ride across the verdant fields and enjoy fresh tarts in the village. With a sigh, she turned away from the window. She wondered where Damien was going to spend his evening, then put the thought from her mind.

She decided to go to bed. She would not think about anything. She would sleep.

But sleep did not come. For hours, she lay listening to the house become quiet as the servants retired. She knew Damien had not come home, for she had not heard the carriage on the drive. Tossing and turning, unable to sleep, she decided to go in search of something to read. She had not seen a library in the house, but perhaps she would find books in Damien's study. Slipping into her dressing gown, and taking a lit candle, she started her exploration.

On the main floor, Jessica opened several doors before she found the right one. As she walked into his sanctuary, she felt her pulse quicken. This was where Damien ran his estate, conducted his business. Another side of him revealed itself in this room.

Holding up her candle, she looked around. There were no lamps lit, but the fire burned brightly. Evidently, this was where he secluded himself when he returned home. It was a typically masculine room with walls paneled in rich, dark mahogany and the floor covered in a deep, red Persian rug. The various chairs, large and comfortable looking, were upholstered in red or black leather. Along one wall, from floor to ceiling, were bookshelves filled with volumes. In a corner of the room was a massive desk of dark, polished wood. A portrait above the fireplace caught Jessica's eye, and she went to examine it more closely.

The man portrayed in the painting bore a marked resemblance to Damien. Except for the color of the eyes and the wig the man wore, it could have been Damien. Even the expression was similar. She had seen Damien's eyes glint in just that way. The nameplate attached to the frame told her that this was the fifth Duke of Wyndham, Damien's father. She wondered if this man had been as adventurous as his son.

Jessica turned her attention to the books. For a small collection, it was very diverse. It contained many works of the older writers, as well as those of the modern period. She took down a volume by Sir Walter Scott. It had been signed by the poet with a personal inscription to Damien. She replaced the book on the shelf. One of Shakespeare's comedies was what she needed to lighten her spirits. Curling up in one of the chairs by the fire, she began to read.

Several hours later, a noise startled her awake. She was about to uncurl from the chair and scurry back to her room when the door opened, and Damien walked in. His gait was careful, as if he expected to step on something at any moment. Jessica realized he'd been drinking heavily.

As he stopped before the fire, she stood, the book falling unheeded from her lap. She wanted to leave as quickly as possible. He swung about in a crouch, ready to pounce, surprised at finding someone else in the room. A small, sharp, deadly-looking knife appeared as if by magic in his hand. Jessica remained pinned where she stood.

When he saw her, he straightened, and a slow grin spread across his face. He pushed the weapon back into his sleeve where Jessica assumed he must have had a sheath. His gaze fell on the book lying at her feet.

"What is this?" he drawled. "A raid on my library? Or were you waiting up for me?"

Jessica could smell brandy. She wanted to get out of his way. His mood was dangerous.

"I could not sleep, so I came to find something to read," she explained as she began to edge away. "I only meant to stay for a little while." Out of his reach, she turned to leave.

"Wait," he ordered.

She stopped.

"Turn around."

Slowly, she did as she was told. She did not believe he would harm her, but decided she should not take any chances.

"Why do you still wear the nightclothes of a young maid?" he demanded. "Is it to disguise yourself, Witch?"

Jessica's mouth dropped open at his unexpected question. She remained frozen as he approached. He untied her dressing gown and unbuttoned several buttons down the front of her nightrail.

"There," he breathed. "That is better."

Jessica immediately began to re-button her gown. Her heart could not endure another night of making love with Damien.

"I think I had better leave," she said firmly.

"Why? To recite your incantations and weave your spells, Witch?"

"Damien, you're drunk."

He grinned. "I know. You should feel great remorse, Witch. It is because of your sorcery that I am in such a sorry state."

"I'm going to retire," she said, ignoring his comment.

"Ah, now that, Witch, is a very good idea." He put his arm around her shoulders. "I believe I will come with you."

She slid out of his grasp. "Damien, please."

"*Please*? Do you not wish me to see your cauldrons boiling with your magic brews? Are you afraid to let me see your lair, Witch?"

"This is your house. You may go where you wish." She stood coolly before him and hoped her manner would dissuade him from any thoughts of making love.

"You are right," he agreed. "It is my house, and I wish to walk with my arm about you up the stairs to your room. You have fallen into your own trap, Witch." He smiled triumphantly and chucked her under the chin.

Jessica ground her teeth together in exasperation as he put his arm around her shoulders once more. His grip was tighter this time, and she knew he would not let her go again. She glanced up at him from beneath her lashes.

"Beware, lest I turn you into a toad," she warned. She could not help the flutter in the pit of her stomach at the feel of his hard body pressed against her.

He chuckled. "So, the sorceress shows her true colors. Perhaps it is you who should beware. Being a toad, I could give you warts." He laughed at his own cleverness.

Jessica rolled her eyes. They climbed the stairs together, and she brushed his lips away from her neck several times before they reached her room. He walked in after her and closed the door.

"This is a very pleasant room," Damien observed. He took off his coat. "I believe I will spend the night here." He removed his stock and unbuttoned his shirt.

"Oh, Damien," Jessica said in dismay. "Please, don't."

She began to re-button his shirt. Her fingers shook. She very much wanted him to spend the night with her, but he could not.

He caught her hands to stop their clumsy fumbling. "Look at me and tell me no," he ordered quietly.

She looked up into his eyes. "Please," was as far as she got. His mouth stopped any other words she might have said.

Jessica melted against him. She hungered for him, wanted him so badly. Her mind told her that she was being stupid, that she would despise herself in the morning for being so weak, but she did not care. Urgently, she helped Damien out of his clothes and removed her own. Naked, kissing, touching, exploring each other, they staggered to the bed. When Jessica shivered in the cool air, Damien pulled the blankets over them. As they snuggled under the covers, he gave a huge yawn.

"I fear my endurance is at an end, Witch," he said. "What spell did you put on me to make me so weak?"

Jessica giggled. "How much brandy did you consume this evening?"

"Oh, gallons." He nuzzled her neck and held her close. "Stay with me, my love," he whispered.

As Jessica held him close, a soft snore reached her ears. Smiling, she fell asleep, cuddled against his warm, hard body.

The next morning, Jessica awoke with a wonderful feeling of contentment. The other side of the bed was empty, but the pillows gave testimony that Damien had slept there. She ran her hand over the sheet beside her, remembering the night before. Sleeping the night in Damien's arms had been wonderful. If only her life could be like that forever. Knowing that it could never be, her sense of peace faded.

Damien had already breakfasted and was about his business by the time Jessica arrived in the dining room. But the room was not empty. The man who had escorted her into the house when she had first arrived was seated at the table. He rose when she entered the room.

"Please." She smiled. "Sit down and finish your meal." She slid into a chair across the table from him. "I hope you don't mind sharing the table with your prisoner."

"Not at all, Lady Jessica," he replied. "It is a pleasure to share the table with one so lovely as yourself."

"You are very kind, sir." She glanced at him from under her lashes. "I feel I am at a great disadvantage, for you know my name, yet I do not know yours."

"Forgive me, my lady. I am Edward Johnson, Viscount of Winslow, third son of the Earl of Mark, Leftenant in His Majesty's Army."

Jessica smiled at his thorough introduction. "Then I am very happy to make your acquaintance, Leftenant. You must find the duty of guarding one woman rather tedious."

"As I said, my lady, the duty is a pleasure."

He smiled back at her, his hazel eyes crinkling at the corners. Jessica decided she liked this man.

"But would you not prefer to be attached to some unit that is fighting Napoleon in Austria? Or perhaps Italy?"

"We have been fighting Napoleon, my lady, but not in the manner you suggest," he replied, then grinned. "This duty is much more pleasant than some others I have been assigned."

"Oh? Have you been under the command of His Grace for very long?" she asked.

"As long as I've been in the army," he replied. "About four years."

"Then you must know him very well."

The soldier shook his head. "Not as well as you might think, but better than most, I suppose."

"Do you know why he joined the army? It is so unusual to find a duke with a commission." Jessica knew she was prying, but thought he might be a good source of information about Damien. She was not about to let her chance of finding out more about the Duke escape her.

Leftenant Johnson gazed at her for a moment, obviously trying to make up his mind how much to tell her. Finally, he said, "He was not supposed to inherit the title. He had an older brother."

Jessica blinked. "Had?"

"Yes, he was killed in a duel about four years ago, just after I entered the army."

"How tragic!" she exclaimed. She shook her head. "Dueling is such a waste. Why can't men find some other way to settle their differences?"

"Perhaps because men often duel over women," the Leftenant said. "Someone has to be the victor and take possession." His smile was mischievous.

Jessica smiled back at him. "Women aren't possessions, sir. I think you have been with His Grace too long, Leftenant. You sound suspiciously like him."

"I consider that a compliment, my lady."

Jessica regarded him seriously. "You respect him a great deal, don't you?"

"It is deeper than respect," the Leftenant told her. "He has saved my life several times, as I have saved his. That creates a strong bond between men." He drained the last of his coffee and stood. "If you will excuse me, my lady, I must attend to some things."

Jessica nodded and watched him leave the room. She remained at the table and played thoughtfully with the food on her plate. So,

Damien had an older brother who had been killed in a duel. She remembered her father had been in a duel once, when she had been much younger. She was not supposed to have known, but she had heard her father and Margaret arguing about it. Jessica had never heard him so angry. Evidently, it had been because of Margaret that he had been forced onto the field of honor. At the time, she thought dueling to be very romantic, her tender age preventing her from seeing the truth of it. Now, she knew it for what it was: a stupid and dangerous tradition. Her heart ached for Damien. What a devastating way to inherit a title.

Her appetite had left, so she decided to retrieve her book from Damien's study. The door to the room was closed. She knocked, and Damien's deep voice bade her enter.

Opening the door quietly, she stepped inside. "I'm sorry to disturb you," she said.

He leaned back in his chair and smiled. "I wish all my interruptions were as pleasant." He held up her book. "I was wondering when you would come to get this."

Jessica took hold of the book, but he would not let it out of his grasp. Instead, he guided her around the desk, so she stood before him. Embarrassed at revealing her desire for him the previous night, she kept her gaze lowered.

"I only came to retrieve the book, Damien. I did not know you were here," she said.

"I will not keep you from your reading. Witch." He whispered his last word.

Was he mocking her? She met his eyes. His gaze glowed with desire. Her cheeks flamed, and she turned away.

"Do not look at me so," she said. "Someone may come in."

"I will look at you any way I wish, but if I embarrass you, we can retire to an upstairs room," he suggested.

"No!" She took a breath to steady herself. "Please, just let me have the book."

"You did not wish to read last night," he reminded her.

He gave her hand a tug, pulling her off-balance into his lap. She tried to wriggle free, but he would not let her up.

"Damien, please, let me up."

"No one comes in here unless they are bid." His voice soothed as his hand slid up her side and cupped a breast. "There is no need to worry about discovery." His free hand went to the back of her neck and slowly brought her lips down to meet his.

Wonderful sensations coursed through her body at his caress, but she knew that unless she did something immediately, she would end up making love to him right there. Gently, she pushed herself upright.

Running a finger down his cheek and over his lips, she sighed with a pout. "Oh, Damien, you do not play fair." When she saw that his attention was on her touch, she jumped up quickly and moved out of his reach. "Neither do I." She laughed, blowing him a kiss as she hurried out of the room, taking her book with her.

As she closed the door behind her, she heard Damien call, "Witch!"

CHAPTER 11

Later that morning, as Jessica sat reading by the window of her room, a coach arrived. When she saw the Wyndham crest emblazoned on the door of the coach, she wondered who could be inside. She watched a woman descend from the vehicle. Her hair was streaked with grey, yet she had the bearing and figure of a younger woman. Who was she?

Jessica couldn't recall hearing any gossip about any female relatives, nor was a wife ever mentioned. The women at *Madame*'s spoke of Damien as if he were an eligible bachelor. But only immediate family rode in the ducal coach. Perhaps his marriage was only one of convenience, an arranged marriage between families. Perhaps Damien and his wife had an agreement, each going their separate ways and taking lovers, certainly not unheard of in the London ton. She hugged herself as reality settled like a chilly cloud about her. It didn't matter in any case. Jessica's relationship with him would now change. He was her jailor, nothing more. She could no longer hold onto the dream that someday he would marry her. She laughed bitterly to herself. *Marriage*. As though that had been an option after her arrest — or even before it.

Jessica watched to see if there were any children who followed, but there were none. Perhaps the woman had left them at Wyndham, or perhaps there were no children. If his wife were barren, then at least Jessica could give him the gift of a child. She would at least be comforted by the thought that her child would be cared for after… She swallowed…after she was gone. She hoped that his wife would accept the child of another woman. She shook her head, realizing the depths she had sunk to — unmarried and carrying the child of a married Duke. What kind of woman had she become? How had she gotten herself into this situation? Silly, naïve fool!

She straightened her spine and turned away from the window. Now more than ever, she had to be strong and resist his charm, his seductive touch. No more secret trysts.

Uncomfortable in her situation, Jessica remained in her room, but by the middle of the afternoon the sunshine and spring weather began to beckon to her. If she were careful, she could get to the enclosed garden in the back of the house without being noticed. She took her book and slipped out. The garden was lovely, even now before the flowers were in bloom. She always enjoyed the spring and summer months. Everything was so alive.

She had been reading for a while when the woman she had been trying to avoid walked into the garden. The woman had not seen her, for Jessica was sitting partially hidden by a bush. The woman was much older than she had guessed at first, but she was quite lovely, a woman of ageless beauty.

She looked up suddenly, surprising Jessica into a blush for staring.

"You must be the house guest whom Damien mentioned," the woman said with a smile as she advanced and held out her hand. "I am Lydia, Duchess of Wyndham."

Jessica took her hand and curtsied. "It is a pleasure, Your Grace." She wondered fleetingly if Damien had informed this woman what type of house guest she was.

"We missed you at lunch," the Duchess went on kindly. "Were you not feeling well?"

"I did not wish to intrude. I understand that you have not seen Da—His Grace for some time."

"How thoughtful! Yes, I have not seen him for a very long time." Her tone was wistful, and Jessica wondered at that. "But, we will have plenty of time to catch up on each other's news. Promise me that you will not stay away at dinner."

As Jessica agreed, she noticed the fine lines around the woman's eyes and mouth, indicating the maturity of middle age. The Duchess also had the same uncommonly green eyes as Damien. Something about the woman's smile reminded her very much of Damien. The physical resemblance was remarkable. A little spark of joy erupted near Jessica's heart. The lady had to be his mother. Not his wife.

"Damien will be pleased," the Duchess was saying. "He was disappointed that you did not come to table. I will see you at dinner then." She began to turn away to leave, but turned back with a laugh. "I am very sorry. My manners are not usually this bad. I did not give you a chance to tell me your name."

Jessica smiled as she tried to control the giddy rush at discovering this woman was Damien's mother, not his wife. Her response to the question was automatic. "Jessica Carlton, Your Grace—" She caught herself too late. She didn't know what had prompted her to give her full name. It slipped out so easily because the older woman had been so kind.

The Duchess stared for a moment, then asked slowly, "Daughter of James, Earl of Braeleigh?"

Jessica hesitated, then nodded abruptly. "Yes," she answered, puzzled and surprised that this woman would know her father.

At Jessica's response, the blood drained from the Duchess's face. Her eyes glazed, and she swayed as if she might faint any moment. Jessica rushed to assist her to a stone bench.

"Your Grace. Are you all right?" Jessica asked in concern.

The Duchess did not answer. She only gaped at Jessica.

When she got no response, Jessica patted her hand, "Please stay here. I will get help."

Jessica ran to the kitchen door and collected the cook and several maids. After sending for Jacobs, the cook followed Jessica out to the garden. The Duchess was sitting where Jessica had left her, her face white and drawn. As the cook and maids fussed about their mistress, Jessica quietly slipped away and returned to her room. She felt terrible, that somehow, she had caused the attack.

About an hour later, Donny entered Jessica's room, carrying a stack of clean linens.

"Have you heard how the Duchess is feeling?" Jessica asked.

"Aye," Donny answered grimly as she put the linens in the armoire. "She be fine. Just a touch of the vapors."

"Then why are you looking so glum?"

Donny turned to face her. "Ye be in fer it, that's why. When His Grace found out who ye be, his eyes went all hard. Gives a person the creeps, it does. He's in with her now. Seems they be talkin' about ye. The Duke is lookin' t' tear ye apart. But it seems the Duchess be on your side. I told ye, didn't I, t'tell him everythin'."

At that moment, a hard knock sounded at the door. Before either Donny or Jessica could make a move to open it, Damien walked in. His eyes were as Donny had described them, glittering and cold. He turned to Donny.

"Leave us, please," he said in a voice to match his eyes. "I have some things I would like to discuss with your mistress."

Donny remained where she was. Jessica knew the woman would defy the Duke and stay if she gave the slightest hint she was needed. Jessica only shook her head. With a glare at the Duke, Donny left.

Damien closed the door firmly, then crossing his arms across his chest, he leaned against it. No one was going to get in to defend Jessica. Nor was she going to escape.

He was dressed for riding. His breeches fit him like a second skin. The dark green of his jacket contrasted sharply with his piercing eyes. He carried a short quirt. Swallowing, Jessica decided to take the offensive.

"How is the Duchess?" she asked.

"She is fine, now, though a bit shaken, no thanks to you," he said coolly.

"I am sorry. I don't know what I did to upset her."

"Don't you, Lady Jessica Carlton?" Her name became a sneer on his lips.

Jessica's head went up proudly. "Who I am does not concern you."

"I disagree." Damien pushed away from the door and advanced toward her. "It concerns me a great deal. Not only am I harboring a traitor under my roof, but now I discover she is the daughter of a murderer and the stepdaughter of a whore." He stopped barely a foot away from her.

Anger at his accusations turned her hot. Jessica's hand lashed out and connected soundly with his cheek. The blow hardly affected him. A savage smile curled his lips.

"How dare you!" she gasped. "What are you saying?"

"You know what I am saying, my sweet," he answered with mock gentleness. "Margaret has schooled you well in the wiles of allurement. How she must have gleefully clapped her hands to discover the second brother had fallen so easily into her clutches."

Jessica backed away in horror at his words. "I don't know what you are talking about."

"No? Playing the innocent to the very end, Jessica? I must admit, you do it very well. You are quite convincing. That little story you told General Drayton was so touching. You even had me convinced you were protecting your family name." He barked a short laugh. "What a fool I was."

Jessica took another step back. Damien stopped her with a soft touch of his quirt on her shoulder. "Do not back away, my sweet," he told her menacingly. "It is too late to run."

Jessica was dumbfounded and confused at what he was saying. What was going on?

"Damien," she tried to reason, "I have never lied to you."

"Perhaps not," he allowed. "But that is a very small point in your favor. Your omissions are just as damning. Those monthly visits to *Monsieur* Montaigne were conveniently scheduled to coincide with a visit to Margaret, were they not?"

"Yes," Jessica answered miserably.

"Ah, now we get the whole truth. She must have gone into fits of laughter when she heard her protegée had made me the fool."

"She has no idea that I know you," she protested. "I have never spoken your name to her."

He whipped his quirt down on the arm of the chair next to him. Jessica flinched. His blow left a sizable mark on the wood.

"Do not play games with me, Jessica," he warned. "You told me you have never lied to me. Do not start now."

Jessica's chin went up defensively. "I have not lied to you. I do not know what this is about, but what I have said is the truth."

Damien's eyes narrowed, and a muscle twitched in his jaw. "Very well, if that is how you wish it." He spun on his heel and walked to the door. He turned with his hand on the knob. "While my mother is here in residence, you will remain cloistered in your room. There will be a guard posted at your door at all times. Your presence here has greatly upset her." He yanked open the door and left.

Jessica sank into the chair where Damien had vented his anger. Absently, she ran her finger across the welt as she tried to make sense of what just happened. Damien obviously knew Margaret, and from the way he spoke, he despised her. Because Jessica was her step-daughter, he held her in contempt as well.

His reasons were beyond her understanding. His condemnation shocked her, turned her cold. Her insides felt like lead.

Donny came back into the room and puttered about, remaining silent. Jessica realized she might know something, for she had been with the family since Jessica had been a babe.

"Damien said my father was a murderer," Jessica said. Her voice sounded flat to her own ears. "What did he mean? And he said something about Margaret getting her clutches on the second brother."

Donny stopped her fidgeting and came to sit in the chair across from Jessica. "Aye," she began. "There was a scandal. Be about four years now, maybe a little more. And Margaret in the middle of it. Seems yer papa found out she be seein' another man. This time weren't the first, but he found 'em together in his own bed. Margaret was the clever one, though. Made yer papa believe she'd been forced. Said th' other man had some hold over her family. Nothin' else yer papa could do but challenge th' other man to a duel. He be a young 'un, too. Well, yer papa shot 'im. Didn't die right away though. Lingered for a few days. Yer papa weren't never the same after that. The man he killed was th' Duke o' Wyndham."

Jessica eyes widened. She felt nauseous. Faint. She could not breathe. Damien's older brother had been the man Margaret had dallied with, and her father had killed him in a duel. No wonder the Duchess had become ill when she heard her name. Jessica felt the same.

She got up and wandered to the window. The futility of her situation overwhelmed her. She leaned her forehead against the glass.

"He thinks I am involved in some sort of plot with Margaret to destroy him," she said.

As she stood there, she watched Damien ride out proudly on his horse. The soldier standing guard at the gate saluted him as he rode past. An ache so deep she nearly sobbed grabbed her heart.

"I have to be alone for a while, Donny," she said in a strangled tone. "I have to think."

Without a word, Donny got up and left.

Jessica spent the afternoon in despair. She realized nothing she said or did would convince Damien of her innocence. He was so caught up in his grief and his contempt of her family because of what Margaret had done that he would never see that she had been an unwitting pawn.

A knock came at her door close to teatime. Damien had not returned from his ride, so Jessica knew it was not him. With a sigh, she went to open it. Lucy, the maid, stood there. The soldier standing guard outside her door watched them curiously.

"May I come in, my lady?" Lucy asked. "I think I left my duster in your room when I was cleaning."

With a nod, Jessica allowed her in. She could not remember seeing any duster, and she could not imagine any maid in this house being so careless. Lucy closed the door carefully behind her once she was in the room. Instead of looking about for her duster, she held out a note for Jessica.

"A messenger brought this for you, my lady," Lucy told her. "He said it was from His Grace and not to let anyone know about it."

Jessica took the note. She thought the messenger's request rather curious. Why would Damien send her a note and be so secretive about it? He could have easily sent the message through one of his soldiers. She opened the note and read:

Jessica,

Damien has been badly injured. He is here with me. Come quickly.

A. du Barré

Her heart slammed against her chest. Her knees went weak. Damien was hurt! She had to go to him. When Lucy turned to leave, she stopped her.

"Please wait," she said. "I need your help."

The girl stood by patiently as Jessica's mind raced. Something about the note raised her suspicions. Why would Damien have gone to *Madame*'s? He certainly would not have gone alone to arrest the woman, not when he had all of his men with him when he arrested her at *Monsieur* Montaigne's cottage. But how did *Madame* know where to send the note? Had she already learned that her secret correspondence had been confiscated? Did she know Jessica had been arrested? Perhaps Damien had told *Madame*. But why? Jessica could not think of any plausible explanation why Damien would be at *Madame*'s, whether he was injured or not. Perhaps the note was a trap, and *Madame* was so furious at Jessica for getting caught that she wanted to punish her. But what if Damien really was injured?

Anxious thoughts and questions swirled in her brain. Even if it were a trap, she had to risk it. She had no choice. Damien needed her. She just had to figure out how to escape from the house.

Jessica glanced at Lucy and wondered how much she could trust her. The girl was her only option. "I have to leave," she said. "It is a personal matter."

"But, m'lady, the guards," Lucy protested.

Jessica waved away her argument. "I know. I am under arrest. I'm not supposed to go anywhere, but I have to attend to this. It is a question of life or death. His Grace is not here for me to ask permission, and the guards won't allow me to leave if I tell them. You have to help me escape. Do you think you can help?"

Lucy looked doubtful.

"Please," Jessica entreated.

"Well…" Lucy's gaze skittered about the room.

"I give you my word that I will return as soon as I can."

Lucy nodded. "All right."

"Good. Is there another door to the house that is not so well used as the front or kitchen doors?" Jessica asked.

Lucy thought for a moment. "There are French doors in the salon, and they lead to a veranda, at the side of the house, close to the street.

"Of course." Jessica remembered them now. "That's perfect. Now, all I have to do is get there."

Lucy grinned. "I can take care of the handsome soldier standing outside your door."

Jessica nearly hugged the girl in her relief. Instead, she smiled and said, "You are very brave for helping me, Lucy. I am sure when His Grace finds out about this, he will reward you handsomely."

Lucy blushed bright red. As she turned to leave, she said, "I hope everything will turn out all right."

"I'm sure it will," Jessica assured her, hoping she was telling the truth.

Lucy opened the door, saying as she did, "I'm sorry to have disturbed you, m'lady. I can't understand what happened to that duster." As she began to close the door, Jessica heard her say, "Sergeant, since you're so strong, do you think you could do me a tiny favor and help me move a chair?"

"Well, miss," the sergeant answered, "I'm not supposed to leave my post, you know."

"Please, sir? I have to clean under it, and I just can't move it myself. If I don't do it, Jacobs will have my head. It will only take a minute, Sergeant. Please?"

Jessica heard a mumbled reply and then footsteps retreating down the hall. She hurried to change into her riding clothes, leaving her dress on the floor where it fell. Bless that girl, she thought. She left *Madame*'s note on the bedside table. She wanted no suspicion that she had tried to escape.

She waited until she was sure that Lucy and the sergeant were gone, then she left her room and hurried down the hall. She stopped to listen at the top of the stairs. Hearing no one near, she glided down the steps and across the foyer. Outside the door to the salon, she stopped again and hoped no one would be inside at this time of day.

She opened the door and peeked inside. The room was empty. Slipping inside, she closed the door quietly behind her. Across the room were the French doors, just as she remembered. She ran to them and tried the latch. It turned smoothly. She stepped onto the veranda.

The veranda was on the side of the house and overlooked a small orchard. Through the trees, she could see the street and the iron fence which surrounded Damien's property. The fence appeared to be about four feet in height. She would have to jump it, for she could not risk going past the guard at the gate. She hoped the shock of seeing a woman on horseback jumping the fence would cause his aim to be off the mark.

She looked down over the veranda railing. The distance to the ground was not too far. She climbed over and let herself drop. Time was working against her. She only had a few more minutes before her escape was discovered. Discarding caution, she ran to the stables. She could not waste precious minutes in stealth.

Aphrodite's stall was at the back of the building. Fortunately, no stable hands were about. So far, her luck had held. Quickly, she saddled her horse, led her to a low stool and mounted. Jessica leaned over and patted the horse's silky neck.

"All right, girl, it's now or never," she whispered, encouraging both her horse and herself.

She dug in her heels and they took off at a gallop. As they reached the fence, she glanced over at the guard at the gate. His mouth hung open in amazement.

"Halt!" he called.

Jessica and Aphrodite sailed over the fence with ease.

"Halt!" he called again. "Halt or I'll shoot!"

She cringed against Aphrodite's neck as she waited for the shot. It never came. The soldier's threat had been false. Running feet followed, but she was on horseback and faster. She breathed a sigh of relief and did not slow down as her horse galloped around the corner. The soldiers would mount up and be after her soon. If she could just reach *Madame*'s, she would be safe. Damien's men would not come after her there for fear of ruining all their hard work in incriminating the woman. Besides, that was where Damien was. She would still be his prisoner.

As she galloped through the streets, passing coaches, making people jump out of her way, her mouth tightened. She had a few questions for *Madame* herself. The French woman had been heartless to involve her in treason. Jessica had done nothing to *Madame* to make the woman wish to entangle her in crimes. Other than being a foolish innocent. She pushed her angry thoughts away for the moment. Her first priority was Damien and helping him.

She reached *Madame*'s in only a few minutes. Slipping from her horse, she flew up the steps and pounded impatiently on the door. A lifetime passed before Jacques came to the door and showed her into the salon where *Madame* was pouring tea.

Jessica did not bother to greet her. "Damien," she blurted breathlessly at the entrance to the salon. "Where is he?"

"Ah, *ma petite*," *Madame* smiled. "Come, sit down. Calm yourself."

Jessica strode into the room, but she did not sit. "Where is Damien? I have to see him. How badly hurt is he?"

"He is upstairs. He is being tended by the doctor," *Madame* said calmly. She poured a second cup of tea. "Please, Jessica, sit down. Join me for a cup of tea. You may visit with him later. There will be plenty of time when the doctor has finished."

Jessica reluctantly perched on the edge of a chair across from *Madame* and accepted the cup. She took a small sip. "How did it happen?"

"A fall from his horse." *Madame* shook her head. "Damien must have hit his head. He was…How do you say…?" She searched for the word.

"Unconscious?" Jessica offered.

"*Oui, c'est ça*. Unconscious."

"Where did it happen? Why was he here?" The questions tumbled out of Jessica as she tried to read *Madame*'s placid expression.

"Here?" *Madame* shook her head. "No, no, no. He was not here. It was an accident down the street. A delivery cart and a coach — Boom!" She clapped her hands together to demonstrate. "His horse must have been spooked and threw him. When I heard all the noise, I ran out. There he was, lying in the street. Of course, I had him brought here. How could I not care for my dear friend?"

Jessica pondered *Madame*'s words as she continued to sip her tea. She had known *Madame* far longer than she had known Damien. And the French woman had always been good to her, protected her, kept her safe from lecherous men so that she could earn the money she needed.

But questions and suspicions kept her on edge. Something did not feel right about the situation. And then she thought of something else.

"Where is Damien's horse?" she asked. "I didn't see it out front."

Madame shook her head sadly. "The poor animal broke its leg and had to be shot."

Jessica remembered the times Damien had put her before him on that horse and taken her back to her rooms. What a tragedy that such a magnificent animal had to be destroyed. Unsettled and distraught, Jessica lifted her cup to her lips once more and sipped the tea to fortify herself. She noticed it had an odd taste, but attributed that to *Madame*'s French chef. No one made tea like the English. She glanced anxiously toward the entrance of the salon. How long was that doctor going to be?

A sudden thought occurred to Jessica. If Damien had been unconscious when he was brought here, how could he have told *Madame* that she had been under arrest at his house? Something was not right. The woman was watching her closely, almost as if she were waiting for something to happen.

Casually, Jessica placed her cup on the table before her and stood. Trying desperately to act nonchalant, she walked around to the back of her chair. For some reason, she felt the need to put something solid between herself and *Madame*. Her knees felt strangely weak, but she thought it was only because she was nervous.

There was something very wrong. Had she been lured into a trap? Was Damien even here? As she stood with one hand on the back of the chair, a wave of dizziness swept over her. Her hand flew to her head. What was happening to her? *Madame* was looking very smug about something.

"Are you not feeling well, *ma petite*?" *Madame* asked. Her expression showed triumph, not concern.

And then the realization came to her: *The tea*.

"What did you do to me?" she demanded weakly.

Madame smiled. "It was only something to make you sleep for a little while. You will feel better when you wake."

"Damien is not here, is he? You tricked me to get me here," Jessica accused.

Madame smiled. "*Non*, he is not here."

Jessica swayed and caught herself by grabbing the chair. She felt dizzy and confused.

"Do not fight it, *ma petite*," *Madame* soothed. "It will do you no good."

Jessica heard her voice as if from far away. She felt herself falling, then blackness.

CHAPTER 12

Twilight was falling by the time Damien returned home. He was not in the best of humor, having spent the afternoon trying to convince General Drayton to leave the arrest of *Madame* du Barré to him and his men. The General thought that since Damien had captured *Madame*'s courier, he no longer needed to involve himself in the case. Damien, on the other hand, was not content to allow the matter to be taken out of his hands so easily. He knew *Madame*'s wily tricks and trusted no one but himself to bring her to justice. The argument had ended in a stalemate.

Besides being overruled by his commander, the woman he had under house arrest had deceived him, betrayed him. She was the daughter of the man who had killed his brother. She was the woman who fired his blood, made his heart race. She was the woman who haunted his dreams.

She could be a traitor.

And then he had received that urgent summons from Edward to return home with no explanation. His mood had never been so black. When he found no guard at either the gate or the front door, his temper boiled over. Something had happened in his absence, something he did not want to hear. Leftenant Johnson met him in the foyer as he walked in the door.

"Edward, what the devil is going on?" he demanded harshly. "Where are the guards? Why is there no one on duty?"

Edward Johnson cleared his throat nervously and walked to the door of the salon. "I think you had better come in here, sir," he told Damien with unaccustomed formality. He opened the door as proper protocol for a lower-ranked officer for his commander.

Damien glared at him. As he entered the room, all his men jumped to attention. His eyes narrowed dangerously. He had taught his men never to come to attention when he walked into their midst. It had been too dangerous for any remnant of army etiquette to appear while they had been in France.

Damien sat on the arm of a chair and looked at Johnson. "All right, Leftenant," he said quietly, holding his temper in tight check. "Perhaps you had better tell me what this is all about."

Johnson picked up a note from a nearby table and handed it to Damien. "I think you'd better read this, sir."

As Damien took the note from Johnson, he realized his men were still standing at attention. "Dammit, sit down!" he barked. They immediately complied.

He had a cold feeling in the pit of his stomach. The feeling became worse when he read the note Jessica had left behind. How did *Madame* know that he had Jessica under arrest in his home? Someone had to have given her that information. But who?

What Jessica had not known was that he had placed guards on her not only to keep her from trying to escape from him, but also to keep her safe from *Madame*. He had expected the woman to try to get to Jessica, and through her, to him. He had been proven correct. But he had not expected it to happen in his house. And that did not absolve his men for allowing it to happen. He ran his gaze around the room, meeting the eyes of each of his men.

"Do you mean to tell me, gentlemen, that one rather tiny woman outwitted four of the best men in His Majesty's Army?" he asked scathingly. There was no answer, only an uncomfortable shuffling of feet. "How did she get away?" he demanded.

Johnson answered. "She slipped past Walker with the help of a maid—Lucy. The same girl who gave her the note. We questioned her, but all she did was cry and say how sorry she was, and that the Lady Jessica said it was a matter of life or death." He took a breath. "We tried to follow the lady—"

"But you lost her," Damien finished.

"Yes, sir," Johnson answered. He shifted uncomfortably.

Damien did not berate his leftenant for the failure. The man already felt guilty enough. Nor did he waste time castigating Walker for failing his guard duty at the bedroom door. Instead, his mind focused on Jessica. She had been clever to deceive his men. He rose and walked to the French doors, most likely the ones through which Jessica had made her escape. Staring blindly out into the darkness, he crushed the note in his hand. How could she fall for such a ruse? Didn't she realize what a crafty, dangerous woman *Madame* du Barré was? Fear for Jessica's safety threatened to overwhelm him before he squelched it. Now was not the time to allow his feelings to interfere with what he had to do. He stood lost in thought.

A knock at the door of the salon drew him from his musing. He was about to tell whoever it was that he was not to be disturbed when his mother pushed open the door.

"I'm sorry to disturb you, Your Grace," she said.

She only used the formal manner of addressing him when she had something serious to say.

"I believe you might wish to speak with this young woman." The duchess stepped aside to reveal the maid, Lucy.

Damien's brow crinkled in bewilderment. "Shouldn't Jacobs be dealing with her?"

His mother shook her head. "This is not for our butler."

"Go on, girl. Tell 'im," Mistress Donlin said from behind Lucy and gave the girl a push into the room.

Lucy shook, and tears streamed down her cheeks. "I-I'm s-s-so s-sorry, Your Grace." She gulped and twisted her apron in her hands. "She-she promised me a-a new frock."

Mistress Donlin tsked.

"Who offered you a new frock?" Damien asked, a cold feeling of dread taking hold of him.

"Th-the F-french lady in the park." Lucy sniffed.

"*Madame* du Barré." Damien spoke the name as if it were a curse. He felt his men's attention focus on the maid. Anger surged through him that his men had failed to get the truth from the maid. His house had been invaded by a spy. "Tell me everything."

"She s-said all I had to do was deliver a note to the Lady Jessica. She said you wouldn't mind. I'm so sorry!" Lucy bawled into her apron.

Mistress Donlin grabbed Lucy by the arm and shook her. "Quiet, you silly baggage."

Damien watched Lucy and a suspicion formed. "Did the French lady ever ask you to do anything else?"

Lucy's eyes widened guilessly and her tears stopped. "Oh, no, Your Grace."

He did not believe her. His gaze met his mother's. "How did you discover this?"

"Mistress Donlin overheard the girl telling one of the other maids about the frock and other fine things she would soon acquire," the duchess said.

Damien gave a nod to Jessica's nanny. "Thank you, Mistress Donlin." He turned his attention back to the maid. "I should arrest you, Lucy."

"Oh, no, Your Grace!" Lucy began to bawl again. "I promise I won't ever speak to that French lady again."

Grimly, silently, Damien agreed. If everything fell into place, that "French lady" would be in an English prison very soon. But first he had to save Jessica. He had no time to deal with the foolishly greedy and hysterical housemaid.

Turning to his mother, he said, "I think Jacobs should handle this."

His mother sent him a little smile. "I thought the same."

Jacobs would dismiss the girl and make her feel fortunate that she had not been sent to prison and grateful to get references.

With a regal nod to his men, the duchess said, "Gentlemen." Then she turned and sailed out of the room with Mistress Donlin following, holding a firm grip on Lucy.

"Blimey," Walker said when the door had shut behind the ladies. "A traitor in your own house, beggin' your pardon, sir."

Damien raised an eyebrow at Walker, for he had been the one guarding Jessica's door and had been fooled by Lucy. The young soldier ducked his head and a flush colored his neck.

Damien said nothing further, for his mind was already on the confrontation with *Madame*. Determination to save Jessica wiped out every other thought and emotion.

"It seems, gentlemen," he said, "that *Madame* du Barré has played her trump card. By using one of the maids in my household to take the Lady Jessica, she has nothing else to do but run for the coast. She'll want to lure us to France. I believe she has played right into our hands."

"How has she done that, sir?" Wells, the youngest of his men asked.

"She will have to come out into the open to make her escape, Wells," Damien answered. "We will capture her, retrieve the Lady Jessica, and then lay *Le Chat* to rest."

There was a general murmuring as the men approved of Damien's plan.

"Aren't we going to break into the gaming house, sir?" Higgins asked.

Damien shook his head. "I would like to, but it would be foolhardy to try. The house is built like a fortress. The walls are twice as thick as an ordinary house, and the doors are strong enough to secure a vault. We would never be able to get in, find the Lady Jessica, and escape with our lives — or hers." Dropping the note on a nearby table, he went on, "I suggest that we discuss this over dinner. We can do nothing but wait until *Madame* sends word to us regarding her demands. When that happens, we may not get another meal for a long time."

Resigned, his men dispersed to change for dinner.

As he watched them file out, Damien vowed, one way or another, he would get Jessica back.

As soon as his men reconvened about the dining table, Damien explained his plan.

"*Madame* will send word to us that she has the Lady Jessica, for I am sure she expects us to follow. As soon as she does that, she will begin her escape to France, but not too quickly. She does not want to lose us. She would prefer to have us catch up with her on French soil. It would be a victory for her if she could capture us as spies, instead of the other way around.

"I assume she has more than one escape route to France. We know of at least two. One of them was from the beach at Montaigne's house. She won't use that one. Now that we know of it, it's too risky. She must have another somewhere around Dover, that she uses when she is pressed for time." He glanced around the table at his men. "Any other ideas where she might cross?"

"Someplace in Cornwall, sir," Higgins offered. "Smugglers land in those coves as if they were free ports."

Damien nodded. "You are probably right, Higgins, but Cornwall is too far away for *Madame*'s purposes. Remember she has a hostage with her. She would have us on her trail for too long. She couldn't risk us overtaking her."

"If I were her," Johnson said thoughtfully, "I'd head for Dover. It's the quickest way out of England and closest to France. More people would be travelling on the road, more witnesses so she could leave a visible trail for us to follow."

"That seems to be the logical way for her to run," Damien agreed. "Something tells me, however, that she will not do the logical thing. I don't think we should trust to luck on this. Higgins, I want you to watch *Madame*'s house. When they leave, follow them to the edge of the city and observe which road they take. Then wait for us there. Wells, go with him. When *Madame* leaves her house, come back and let us know. We must be quick to follow. I will wait here with Johnson and Walker for *Madame*'s message that she has the Lady Jessica. Any questions?"

"Suppose she has already left for France?" Wells asked morosely. "Suppose she doesn't want us to follow?"

Damien had already thought of this, but had tried not to dwell on it. If it were true and *Madame* reached France secretly, then any chance of ever finding Jessica was lost. Despite his anger and mistrust, he could not bear thinking about never seeing her again.

He answered, "We have to assume that *Madame* has not done that. I truly don't believe she has. *Madame* wants me to follow her. She has a score to settle with me for fouling up her plans. We have to work on the assumption that she will be trying to lure us to France so that we may be captured as spies. For that reason, we will have to be very alert if we wish to come out of this alive." He glanced around the table. "Any other comments?" There were none. "All right, gentlemen, you know what you have to do."

The men dispersed to their various duties: Higgins and Wells to change from their uniforms to their less conspicuous peasant garb and then to leave to watch *Madame*'s; Johnson and Walker to change and ready the horses and other gear they would need. Damien remained at the table for some time, hoping that he was correct in his assumptions, hoping that Jessica had not been harmed, that he would find her safe and be able to free her from *Madame*'s clutches. Finally, he rose from the table and went to transform himself into *Le Chat*. He hoped he had guessed correctly.

Jessica returned to consciousness very slowly. She became aware of lying on a bed long before she was able to open her eyes. Her eyelids felt heavy, as if they were glued shut, and her head felt as if it were stuffed with cotton. Several moments passed as her mind cleared of its fog and she remembered where she was.

When she tried to move, a sharp pain made her realize her arms had been pulled above her head and her wrists had been tied to the bedpost. Moving her legs experimentally, she discovered that her ankles were bound as well, but had not been tied to the bed.

She raised her head as best she could and glanced around the dark room. She couldn't see much of anything as the only light was coming from a crack beneath the door. She heard the faint sounds of many people speaking, as if they were far away.

Once more *Madame* du Barré had tricked her. Damien must surely believe she was deceitful and a traitor. And once more, she had been naïve, escaping from his house like the spy he thought she was. But she had left the note for his men find. Surely that would explain her actions. She hoped.

She had to escape from *Madame* and turn herself in to Damien. She was sure *Madame* wanted her as a captive because of the spy business the French woman was involved in. But would Damien believe that she was not a willing participant?

She tugged at the ropes binding her wrists, but they were too tight. When she sat up to try to loosen the knots with her teeth, nausea gripped her insides. She fought down the waves of sickness, then tried again. But the knot about her wrists was just out of reach. With a groan of frustration, she slumped down.

Jessica lay on the bed for what seemed like hours. Occasionally, she pulled at the ropes and tried to reach the knots, but her efforts were futile. She heard people walk past the door, couples conversing, and the giggles of women. But when she called out for help, no one answered. Exhausted, she fell into a fitful sleep.

She did not know how long she slept, or what it was that woke her, but she was suddenly alert. She lay listening. It was very quiet. The silence had awakened her. She heard footsteps approach and stop before her door. A key turned in the lock, and the door swung open. *Madame* walked in.

"So, *ma petite*, you are awake finally, eh?" she said. "*Bon*, just in time. We have to go on a little journey."

"Where are you taking me?" Jessica demanded. "What do you want with me?"

"Ah, always the questions. First, eat a little something, and then I will tell you." *Madame* turned to Jacques who had come into the room with her. "Untie her and bring up the tray I prepared."

Jacques took out a knife and sliced the ropes binding Jessica's hands and feet, then he left. Jessica sat up and gasped as she rubbed her hands and feet, her circulation painfully returning. *Madame* sat on the edge of the bed. She took one of Jessica's hands and began to massage it.

"That oaf," she complained. "He does not realize that a woman does not have to be tied up like some angry bull. It is painful?"

Jessica nodded. "*Madame*, why are you doing this? I have done nothing to harm you."

"Nothing, *ma petite*? Do you mean that you have said nothing about the letters you have delivered for me?" she said with a raised brow.

Jessica lowered her gaze before the woman's accusation.

Madame shrugged. "Ah, well, I expected that. You are the innocent. It is too bad you became involved with *Le Chat*."

"*Le Chat*? Who is…?" Jessica started to ask, then as she met *Madame*'s eyes, she realized who it was. Damien, of course. That warning she had received, signed with the paw print of a cat, must have been sent by him. He had been trying to protect her. She had once again been impulsively foolish.

Jacques returned with a tray of food and some wine. He placed the tray on the table beside the bed, then left. *Madame* poured a glass of wine and handed it to Jessica.

"Drink this, *ma petite*," she told her. "It will warm you. We have a long, cold journey ahead of us."

Jessica took the glass but did not drink. She remembered all too clearly what *Madame* had done to the tea. "Where are we going?" she asked, trying to delay drinking the wine.

"To France, of course. Drink your wine, *ma petite*."

France? she thought, panicked. If *Madame* took her across the Channel, she would never see England—or Damien—again. "Please, can't you leave me here? I won't tell Damien anything."

Madame laughed. "Foolish girl. Of course you would tell him." She shook her head. "*Non*. I cannot leave you here. You will come with us. Now, drink the wine." *Madame*'s voice became hard.

Despite her fear of the woman, Jessica refused to drink the wine. She needed to be alert, so she could try to escape.

Madame sighed in exasperation. "Jessica, please drink the wine. It will not make you sleep. It will only relax you. I wish for you to be awake when we leave. If you will not drink it, there are other, more unpleasant things that I will use to keep you calm. The choice is yours."

Jessica stared at *Madame* as she weighed what the woman said. She did not doubt that she would do as she said. Deciding she had no other choice, Jessica drank the wine.

When she had finished the glass, *Madame* handed her a plate of food and remained with her while she ate. By the time she finished eating, a warm, languid feeling began to spread through her. It was quite pleasant. She felt very relaxed. *Madame* handed her a second glass of wine, and Jessica drank it with no questions. With a tiny part of her brain, she realized she was in great danger, but for some reason, she did not care. Nothing at that moment seemed to bother her. She handed the glass back to *Madame*.

Madame stood and tilted Jessica's face up. "You will stay here for a little while. Do not try to get away. I will be back soon."

"Yes, *Madame*," Jessica answered obediently. She watched as the woman left, locking the door behind her.

As Jessica waited for her to return, she felt the effects of the second glass of wine begin to take hold. The small part of her brain which had told her she was in danger had been silenced. She felt nothing. She did not care what happened.

When *Madame* returned, she had two of her maids with her. She carried a bundle of clothes and a pair of scissors. Handing the clothes to one of the maids, she said, "Put these on her."

The maids replaced Jessica's clothes with trousers, shirt, and jacket. When she was dressed, *Madame* snipped off Jessica's long hair, creating a mass of short curls. With the help of a hat and cape, Jessica had been transformed into a boy.

Madame removed the locket which Jessica always wore, and retrieved a long lock of hair from the floor. With a satisfied smile at the transformation she had performed on Jessica, she told the maids to bring her downstairs.

Jessica had become a puppet, doing as she was told, moving as she was guided. She soon found herself sitting astride Aphrodite. Her wrists had once again been bound together before her, and her ankles were tied together by a rope which ran under her horse's belly.

Madame, also dressed as a man, mounted her horse. The group of riders, eight strong and all dressed as men except for two of them, began their flight to France.

CHAPTER 13

After donning the garb of *Le Chat*, Damien retreated to his study. He suspected the message from *Madame* would not come until very late, giving her time to get a head start. He tried to distract himself with some correspondence, but a pair of clear, blue eyes haunted his thoughts. The touch of silky skin heated his blood. The memory of inky, thick hair made his fingers itch.

That afternoon during her questioning, he had been merciless with her and unforgiving. Yet in spite of that, when she had thought him injured, she'd managed to escape his well-trained men and rushed to his aid, risking her own life. A flood of mixed emotions washed over him—admiration for her courage, wonder at her daring, and frustrated anger at her stubbornness. What if she truly did care about him? What if she had been telling the truth, that she knew nothing of Margaret's evil duplicity? If *Madame* du Barré took her to France, she would make Jessica disappear into the demimonde, the shadowy world of mistresses and brothels. A frantic fear squeezed his chest. He could lose—No! He couldn't finish that thought. Refused to finish it.

Something—an air current, a whisper of clothing—made him raise his head. He listened, every muscle tense, waiting. Then in an explosion of shattered glass, something heavy blew through a window and landed in the middle of the floor.

Damien bounded to his feet and scooped it up. A rock was tied to a small, unmarked package. He placed the package on a table then sank into a chair and stared at it, dreading what he might find.

Taking a breath, he untied the string and opened the small box. Inside, was a gold locket and a long, black, curled lock of hair. There was no note or message, only the two items. He picked up the hair and placed it in the palm of his hand. It felt soft and alive, and it brought to mind several nights when he had lost his fingers in the thick mane.

Anger thrummed through him. He knew what *Madame* was planning, and he had a good idea when she would implement that plan. He'd be damned before he'd allow her to spirit Jessica away. His fist clenched around the length of curl in his hand.

Leftenant Johnson barreled through the door. "I heard breaking glass."

Damien clenched his jaw and stood as he tried to school his face into a soldier's impassive mien. He held the silken coil tightly in his hand.

"We have received *Madame*'s message," he said. "Higgins should be returning soon to tell us they have left. We'll be moving out."

Johnson paused. "We'll get her back, Damien," he said quietly.

Damien nodded stiffly, annoyed with himself that he had allowed his thoughts to be visible, even to his friend.

Johnson left, quietly closing the door behind him.

Several minutes later, *Le Chat* and his men waited in the dark stable for Higgins to bring the news that *Madame* had, indeed, begun her escape. They did not have long to wait. The clatter of hooves on the road reached their ears, and soon after, Higgins rode into the mews. Damien went out to meet him.

"They have gone, sir," the young man panted. "There were eight of them. Two women."

"Good work, Higgins," Damien said. "And Wells?"

"He is following them."

With a brief nod, Damien mounted his horse and motioned for the others to do likewise. He led them out into the street. They rode without speaking, disciplined and focused on the task ahead.

When they reached the outskirts of the city where the road forked, they stopped and waited. Damien gave a low whistle. An answering whistle came, then a man on horseback emerged from behind a hedgerow and approached the group.

"Which way did they go, Wells?" Damien asked.

"They broke up into two groups, sir," Wells reported. "Five of them took the road to Dover. That was with the two women. The other three took the west road to the coast."

"Then it's to Dover," Johnson said.

"No, wait." Damien stopped him as he thoughtfully stared down the empty road. "Can you describe the three that took the west road?" he asked Wells.

"Two men and a boy, it looked like," Wells answered.

"That's it," Damien said grimly. "The group on the Dover road is a lure. Once we caught up with them, we'd discover we had followed the wrong group. We would never be able to catch up with *Madame*. We'd be forced to cross into France. Come on! A cask of Mr. Napoleon's finest brandy for every man if we can make it to the coast before that she-devil." He spurred his horse and raced off, his men following close behind. What he did not tell them was that they might be forced to cross into France anyway.

They followed the road for a time, then turned off, racing across the fields and through woods so they would not come upon *Madame* unexpectedly. They arrived at the coast well in advance of the woman. After a bit of searching, they found a cove with a small boat riding at anchor a few feet from shore. A man sat waiting at its tiller. This was *Madame*'s embarkation point.

Silently, Damien and his men dismounted, tethering their horses where they would not be seen. Then, melting into the shadows, they hid themselves behind boulders strewn about the beach.

They didn't have long to wait before they heard the sound of approaching hoof beats. Three riders came into view and rode onto the beach. Damien waited until they had dismounted, then he stepped out from behind the rock.

"*Bon soir, Madame*," he greeted her pleasantly. He brandished a pistol. "Are you taking a late-night sail?"

At his words, three people swung to face him — *Madame* and Jessica, dressed as men, and Jacques, *Madame*'s major-domo, who pulled out a very large pistol. *Madame* had her hand on Jessica's arm. She appeared to have to guide her. In the moonlight, Jessica's eyes stared at him blankly. What was wrong with her?

Madame recovered quickly. "So, we are finally met in the open, eh, my friend, *Le Chat*?"

Damien bowed gallantly. "At your service, *Madame*."

Madame glanced around. "Is it possible you are by yourself? You are the foolish one."

"Hardly, *Madame*." Damien's tone was dry.

As he spoke, his men stepped out of their hiding places and formed a semicircle, effectively blocking any escape by land. *Madame* would be foolish to try to outrun them to her boat in the opposite direction.

"Now, if you would be so kind as to allow the young lady to move to this side of the beach, we can conduct our business," Damien suggested.

Madame only paused a fraction before she shrugged and dropped her hand from Jessica's arm. Jessica did not move. She stood staring at Damien as if she did not see him.

"Jessica." Damien tried to gain her attention. Why wouldn't she come to him?

Madame smiled. "If you want the girl, *Monsieur Le Chat*, you will have to come get her."

Damien's eyes narrowed. There was something…Then he understood. Jessica had been drugged. She would not be able to react. One of his men began to edge toward her. *Madame* turned back her cape to reveal a tiny pistol pressed against Jessica's side.

"You will tell your man to move away, *Monsieur* Le Chat. The young lady is in danger of losing her life. I know you do not wish that to happen. So, you will let us wade out to our little boat and sail away."

As she spoke, she began to back away, taking Jessica with her. Jacques grinned evilly, then turned and splashed out to the boat. When *Madame* reached the water's edge, she ran through the waves and dragged Jessica behind, blocking any shot Damien or his men might have taken.

As Jessica was pulled through the water, she turned around to look at him, her placid expression transformed to terror as *Madame* roughly forced her into the boat. As soon as Jessica was aboard, she turned toward the beach. Damien saw her lips move once, then again as he witnessed the effects of the drug wear off.

"Damien!" Her scream was cut off abruptly as Jacques shoved her down into the boat.

Jessica's cry of fear wrenched at Damien He watched in dismay as they began to sail away. The only clue to his feelings was a tightness about his mouth and a muscle that twitched in his jaw. Inside, a part of him was screaming in rage and anguish. Higgins, who was standing next to Damien, raised his gun.

"Let me get off a shot at her, sir," he pleaded.

Damien put a hand on the man's arm to restrain him. "No. There's too much risk of hitting the Lady Jessica."

Without another word, Damien stuck his pistol into his belt and strode up the beach to where the horses had been tied. Leftenant Johnson reached him just before he swung himself into the saddle.

Remorse and determination warred within Damien as he turned to his friend. "*Madame* won this time, Edward," Damien said in a clipped voice. "I allowed her to escape and take Jessica with her. Arrange for transportation to France for me for tomorrow night. I have to go after Jessica."

Johnson looked worried. "You know this is a trap."

"What would you have me do, Edward?" Damien asked, his frustration escaping for just a moment. "I'm determined to free the Lady Jessica and capture *Madame*."

After a moment of hesitation, Johnson gave a nod. "I'll make the arrangements and tell the others,"

"No," Damien told him firmly. "I'm going alone. It's too risky for you and the others to come. We just barely made it out the last time with our lives. You will not tell the others of my plans."

Johnson remained silent as Damien mounted his horse. The other men arrived, bringing the abandoned horses with them. Damien gazed down at Edward.

"That's an order, Leftenant. Not a word to the others," he said sternly. Wheeling his horse, he rode off.

Two hours after midnight the following night, Damien rode onto the old, little-used dock just outside the port of Dover. A small ship was riding the gentle swells at the end of the wooden structure. The dock had originally been built for much larger ships, so it was above the level of the deck of the tiny ship which rose and fell at its end.

The whole area was deserted, and the sound of Apollo's hooves on the wooden planks of the wharf sounded unnaturally loud in the stillness. As Damien dismounted, a figure detached itself from the shadows on the boat.

"You're late," the man accused with humor in his voice.

Damien froze at the greeting he and his men used in France when they had become separated while carrying out their mission. In the next moment, he recognized his second in command.

"I was unavoidably detained." Damien gave the accustomed answer.

Before Johnson could answer, three riders approached. Damien scowled in frustration. There was nowhere to hide, and the last thing he wanted was to be seen by anyone. His trip across the Channel could be delayed because of these intruders. He needed to get rid of them quickly.

The riders rode onto the dock. Damien stood his ground, but loosened the pistol from the waist of his breeches. In the dark, he was unable to discern faces. They kept coming. He pulled out the pistol and held it down beside his leg. The group stopped several feet away and dismounted.

Damien scowled as he recognized them and turned to Johnson. "What the devil is this, Leftenant? A bloody going away party?" he growled. "I told you I was going alone."

Sergeant Higgins cleared his throat where he stood with Wells and Walker. "We didn't think you should, sir," he ventured.

Damien turned on him in a rage. "You didn't think...?" He took a deep breath to calm himself, then swung about to Johnson. "Leftenant, I gave you an order."

Johnson shrugged and grinned, unaffected by Damien's anger. "You have always told us to be resourceful. Have me court-martialed."

Damien shook his head. "I may just do that." He returned the pistol into his waistband with a sigh of exasperation. "As long as you're here, you might as well come along." He threw the reins of his horse to Johnson. "Since you brought so much help, you won't need mine to get the horses aboard."

He jumped down onto the deck of the ship and found a comfortable spot while his men boarded, and they made the crossing to France.

CHAPTER 14

"Fouché, never before have you questioned my intentions. Why do you start now?"

Madame du Barré paced before the fireplace in a small, ornate sitting room. In a chair, was a slight, handsome man watching her with the eyes of a fox. He was Joseph Fouché, the very powerful Duke d'Otrante, Minister of Police under Napoleon.

"Adèlée, I am not questioning your intentions," he answered smoothly. "I merely asked if it was wise to sell the girl at auction. She is, after all, the daughter of an earl. We are having enough problems with England as it is, without causing an international incident over some chit."

Madame waved her hand impatiently. "Her father is dead, and her stepmother does not care what happens to her. The auction is the best way to flush out The Cat. You do wish to capture him, do you not?"

Fouché inclined his head in agreement. "You are so sure he will come after her?"

Madame stopped her pacing and looked confident for the first time since Fouché had arrived. "He will come after her. Come, I will show you."

She led him to a door across the room and into another small room beyond. The two walked to the bed and gazed down at the unconscious girl laying upon it.

"Lovely," Fouché conceded.

"There is another reason for him to pursue her," *Madame* told him smugly. "She has been examined. She carries his child."

Fouché raised his eyebrows in curiosity. "How can you be so sure it is his?"

"It is his. In things such as this, I am never wrong."

Fouché turned back to the sitting room. "It will be to your advantage if you are correct, Adèlée. I was not overly pleased to discover that you had to flee England in order to save your precious skin."

Madame followed him. "It was because of that man that I was forced to flee. He will follow me here. He will come looking for the girl. I know he will. When he does, he is lost." *Madame* smiled wickedly and flexed her fingers as if they were claws. "You must allow me to make the arrangements for his capture. Revenge for his meddling will taste very sweet."

Fouché picked up his walking stick in silence and strode to the door which led out to the hall. With his hand on the latch, he said coldly, "You may make the arrangements. Keep in mind that the fool who allowed him to escape from France the last time has not been heard from since. I do not tolerate mistakes." Then he was gone.

Madame sank into a chair with a sigh of relief after the door closed behind the Duke d'Otrante. He was such a difficult man, and a ruthless one. But a smile of anticipation soon appeared on her face as she contemplated the capture and eventual demise of the man who was known as The Cat.

When Jessica awoke, the sun was high in the sky and streaming through the window beside the bed where she lay. The room was unfamiliar to her, and she wondered where she was. She felt dizzy and nauseous. Her arms and legs were stiff. She sat up slowly and swung her legs over the side of the bed. As she fought the waves of nausea, she realized she was wearing boy's clothing. Absently, she picked at the breeches while she wondered what had happened to her own clothes.

Her last clear memory was of having tea with *Madame* du Barré. Everything after that was a blur except for one moment that she remembered vividly. Damien, standing on a beach, watching her, surrounded by his men. Was that a dream or a true memory? If it had actually happened, why did he let her go? Why did he let *Madame* escape? Despair flooded her. Damien must have been relieved to have her taken away by *Madame*. She was no longer a problem for him.

Perhaps the whole incident had never happened. Her brain felt fuzzy, and she knew *Madame* had drugged her. She had to try to escape.

She stood up and wandered about the room to examine her prison. It was a pleasant space despite the sparse furnishings of a simple bed, dressing table and small chair. Her head felt strangely light, and she put her hand up to discover why. The scantiness of her once long tresses made her gasp. She rushed to the tiny mirror above the dressing table and peered at herself. Her mouth dropped open. Her hair had been cut off! She turned and twisted to see better and pulled at several curls, but her hair still remained short. She glanced down at the clothing she wore. Why had *Madame* gone to such lengths to disguise her as a boy? She combed her fingers through her short, cropped curls and heaved a deep sigh. Her hair and clothes were the least of her problems right now.

She tried the door but knew it would be locked. Two girls speaking French approached in the hallway, probably maids. She banged on the door and called to them, but they walked past. Frustrated, she slumped against the door. *Madame* had brought her to France, and she had no way to get home. She had a vague memory of a boat ride, and *Madame* making her drink more wine. After that, she remembered nothing. Except for that vivid image of Damien on the beach.

Jessica rubbed her eyes. Why was she here? What did *Madame* want with her? After all, the French woman was now safely back in her own country. *Le Chat* was no longer a threat to her. But she had no answers.

Striding to the window, Jessica peered out. The wrought iron bars and the steep drop to the ground dashed any hope of an escape in that direction. Groaning in dismay, she pounded her hand against the glass. She heard the sound of carriages and people nearby, but if she could not get out, no one could help her.

The door opened, and *Madame* du Barré strolled in with another woman. The woman was about the same age as *Madame*, but was gaudily dressed, with an overabundance of frills and bows on her purple gown, which barely contained her ample bosom. Her hair was a vivid, red-orange color. Jessica warily watched them approach.

"Well, little one," *Madame* said, speaking in French. "I see you are finally awake." She indicated the other woman. "This is *Madame* Rousse. She is kind enough to allow us to stay in her house for a while. She does not mind that you are here, but you must behave yourself. You will remain in your room at all times, no matter what you hear. If you do this, no harm will come to you. If you try to escape, or if you wander out of your room, you will be punished." Her eyes narrowed. "Do you understand?"

Jessica looked from one woman to the other. She understood very well. *Madame* was not the kind woman she had led Jessica to believe. Jessica should have heeded her father's warnings about not going near the woman or her establishment. There was danger there. Jerkily, she nodded her understanding.

Madame Rousse turned to *Madame* du Barré. "Are you sure you will not sell her to me, Adèlée? She is lovely. She would be very popular with my customers."

Madame du Barré shook her head and smiled slyly as she tilted up Jessica's face. "I am sorry, Colette, but I have other plans for this one. I will give you a share of what I get for her at auction because you have been so kind. She should bring a handsome price, don't you think?"

Jessica's blood froze in her veins as she guessed at what *Madame* was planning.

Madame Rousse appraised Jessica with a practiced eye. She nodded her approval. "She will bring a very handsome price, indeed. A pity you will not sell her to me. Ah, well. I must attend to my girls. I will see you later, Adèlée."

After she left, Jessica asked, "What is going on, *Madame*? What auction?" Fear tied her insides into knots.

Madame smiled. "You, little one, are bait to catch a very large fish. Or rather, I should say, you are the fish to trap a cat."

Confused, Jessica frowned, then her eyes widened. *Damien. Le Chat.* She stared at *Madame* in horror.

Madame laughed. "Yes, that is right. Your Duke. A pity. He is such a handsome devil."

Jessica shook her head. "He will not come, *Madame*. He hates me."

"Ah, you are so innocent, Jessica. Love and hate are so closely bound together that, at times, one cannot tell them apart." *Madame*'s voice turned cold. "He will come."

"And if he does not? What will happen to me?" Jessica asked, needing to know, at the same time dreading the answer.

Madame shrugged. "Whether he comes or not, you will be sold at auction to the highest bidder. You will become whatever your owner wishes, and I will make a considerable profit. Your Duke will have no need of you in Hell."

Jessica felt her chest constrict, making it difficult to breathe. The French spy meant to kill Damien! Despite his contempt of her, she had to stop this. She loved him. The realization surged through her like a bolt of lightning. She was determined to save him at any cost.

"You could send me back to England. I could pay you a fortune," she suggested, trying to sound nonchalant. "You know how well I gamble."

"Pay me?" *Madame* asked incredulously. "With what? Where would you play? And what of your stepmother and your poor little brother? Your winnings would go to them." She laughed shortly. "I am not so stupid, little one. No, I am afraid you will remain in France. Resign yourself that you will never see England again." She sauntered to the door. "Do not concern yourself with your future, *ma petite*. It is out of your hands. I will have some food brought up to you." She left, closing the door behind her with finality.

Alone and terrified, Jessica slumped on the bed. Tears welled up, but she dashed them away. Crying would do her no good. She got up and splashed water on her face. The cool water helped her refocus her thoughts.

She could not wait on the hope that Damien would rescue her. If he came, he would be walking into a trap, and she had no way to warn him. But she could try to escape. Since she was very good at gambling, somehow, she would use those skills to defeat *Madame*'s plans.

As she dried her face on the thin towel, the door opened, and a maid entered with a tray of food. Jessica tried to talk to her, but the girl said nothing, left the tray and hurried out, locking the door behind her. Jessica had no appetite. She threw herself onto the bed and stared up at the ceiling.

When the maid came back to remove the tray, Jessica tried talking to her again, but the girl rushed away without a word. No one else came to her room. Twilight softened the shadows, and the maid returned with another tray of food. Jessica tried once more to speak with her, but with no better results than the last time. She gave up trying to talk to the girl when she took away the tray.

With the night came noises of people laughing and talking. Several times, Jessica heard couples strolling past her door. Then she was grateful for being locked in. She had discovered the type of establishment *Madame* Rousse owned by listening to the conversations of those couples. The girls were *filles de joies*, paramours, lightskirts. Empathy for them welled in up in her. After the auction, she would belong to their society.

Her hand went to her belly, still flat, where she carried Damien's child. What would happen to her once the man who bought her discovered she carried another man's child? What would happen to the babe after it was born? She should have told Damien about the babe, as Donny had said. Now, he might never learn he had fathered a child. Regret sat heavy in her chest. She had been so naïve and foolish.

She rubbed her belly where her child grew. She was not alone. Together, they would somehow get through this nightmare.

The next two days were no different. She saw no one except the silent maid who brought her meals. She stripped and washed as best she could with the stale water in the small washbasin. After she dressed, she went back to counting the spaces between the floorboards.

She knew every inch of the room where she was being held. Occasionally, she would try the door to see if someone had accidentally forgotten to lock it, and several times, she banged on the door and yelled to see what would happen. Nothing. It was as if she did not exist.

During the afternoon of the second day of her captivity, the door opened, and *Madame* walked in. She was followed by the fattest man

Jessica had ever seen. He waddled sideways through the opening. Rolls of fat hung over the neck of the huge, velvet tunic he wore in place of shirt and coat. His arms were twice as thick as Jessica's waist. His eyes were tiny beads in his bulging cheeks. His face had the appearance of bread dough with a dot of strawberry jam in the middle where his mouth should be. He and *Madame* approached Jessica. All Jessica could do was gape at him.

"You see, *Le Cochon*," *Madame* said. "She is small, but very well proportioned. You must sell her as your last item. It will be worth a great deal to your purse."

The man reached out with his sausage-like fingers and grabbed Jessica's chin, turning her face this way and that. In disgust, she jerked out of his grasp. He threw up his hands in dismay.

"*Madame*, how can I make a judgment if the baggage cannot even hold still for me to look at her. And these rags! They must come off." His voice came out in a high sing-song.

Madame turned to Jessica. "Take off your clothes," she ordered.

Jessica blinked. "I beg your pardon?"

"I said to get undressed," *Madame* said testily.

Jessica shook her head and backed away a step. "No."

With an exasperated sigh, *Madame* explained, "Either take off the clothes yourself, or I will have someone take them off for you." She turned to the fat man. "She will be more amenable by the time of the auction, I assure you."

"There are those who prefer their purchases to have spirit, *Madame*," *Le Cochon* said. "Do not break her."

Jessica felt fear tighten inside her. She stared from *Madame* to the fat man and back again. If only there was some means of escape… Her gaze drifted to the doorway. *Madame* had left the door open.

The invitation to freedom was too great to let slip by. She did not know where she would go once she escaped, but she would worry about that later. With a leap, she side-stepped around *Madame* and bounded out the door. She bolted down a set of stairs, two at a time. At the bottom was a garishly decorated room—golds, reds, violets blurring as she ran through. In the far wall was a door leading to the outside and freedom. She kept her eyes on that door as she ran across the thick rug. She should have checked to see if anyone was around.

A very large body hit her from the side and threw her to the floor. She fell hard, and the wind was knocked out of her. As she gasped for air, she saw the grinning face of Jacques, *Madame*'s major-domo, hovering over her. Jessica screamed in frustration as he hauled her to her feet. He pulled both her arms behind her and held her wrists together in one large hand. Struggling was useless. Then he propelled her back up the stairs and into her prison.

"That was a foolish thing to do," *Madame* said. "You are fortunate that the auction is tomorrow night, and there will be little time for bruises to heal. Otherwise, the consequences of your attempt to escape would not have been pleasant. Perhaps, though, we can still find a suitable punishment." She turned to Jacques. "Strip her."

"No!" Jessica cried and struggled to free herself from Jacques's grip. "I will do it," she muttered.

Madame studied her a moment, then with a jerk of her head and a wave of dismissal, she ordered Jacques to leave. Frowning unhappily, he released Jessica and retreated out the door. *Madame* locked it behind him. Jessica slowly removed her clothes, folding each piece and placing it on the bed to delay. She was finally dressed only in a shirt.

"Remove that as well," *Madame* said.

Jessica was about to refuse when she saw the cold glint in *Madame*'s eyes. With a silent sigh, turning her back, she removed her shirt. Humiliated, she stood stiffly, her hands clenched at her sides.

Her head snapped up in shock when the fat man touched her. He squeezed her flesh, touched her here and there, turned her this way and that, smoothed his hand across her stomach and her bottom. Jessica endured it in silence, but when he pinched the sensitive tips of her breasts, she cried out and jumped away. *Le Cochon* turned to *Madame* with a satisfied nod. "She is valuable property," he said. "Beauty, good skin, responsive, spirited. It is a shame about her hair, but it will grow. I can start the bidding very high."

"How high?" *Madame* demanded.

He turned back to Jessica and regarded her thoughtfully. "Five-hundred gold guineas."

Madame's eyes gleamed with avarice. "You will be well rewarded, *Le Cochon*. Come down to the kitchen. I believe the cook baked fresh pastry today." As they walked to the door, *Madame* glanced at Jessica with a sly grin.

"Enjoy your last few hours of innocence, *ma petite*," she said. "After tonight, you will learn what the world is truly like."

Jessica pulled her shirt over her head and sank to the bed. Thoughts of Damien filtered through her head. Damien whispering to her, Damien kissing her, Damien loving her. The memories were all she had now. The memories and the child she carried.

Somehow, no matter how long it took, she would escape and let Damien know he had fathered a child.

Le Cochon, propped up on many pillows because of his enormous weight, slept the sleep of the innocent. Snoring thunderously, he did not hear the muffled scrape of a boot on the parquet floor of his bedroom. Nor did the soft hiss of a dagger drawn from its scabbard awaken him. Two dark shapes watched him sleep, one from beside the bed, the other from deeper shadows in the corner of the room. It was not until one of the shapes knelt on the bed beside him and pressed the cold steel of a knife against his throat that he became aware that he was not alone.

With a snort, *Le Cochon* reluctantly opened his eyes. He had been dreaming of roast pheasant with chestnut stuffing, of puff pastry filled with orange-flavored cream. It had been a wonderful dream. Now he was awake, and hungry. He felt the blade nestling between the folds of skin on his neck and realized it was not morning. He would have to wait before he could eat again.

"What do you want?" he demanded testily. He was not afraid. There were few who would dare harm him, no matter how much they desired his disappearance or demise. He was too valuable a source of information. And he had many safeguards in place as insurance.

"Please, *Le Cochon*," a silky voice entreated from a black corner of his room. "A little civility would be appreciated."

Le Cochon knew that voice. It was the only one which could inspire fear in him. A few months ago, that voice had kept him prisoner and hungry for two days. Two whole days! All because of some tiny bit of information *Le Cochon* had conveniently forgotten. Gingerly, because of the dagger at his throat, he turned his head toward the shadows and tried to make out the figure who lurked there.

"*Monsieur Le Chat*," he said meekly, "please forgive me. I did not expect to ever see you again."

Le Cochon felt, rather than saw, the cold smile which appeared on those handsome lips.

"Ah, you heard, then, of our misfortune, of our betrayal. Did you truly believe I had used up all of my nine lives, *Le Cochon*? Perhaps you know something more about the trap Fouché set for us?"

The knife against *Le Cochon*'s throat pressed harder.

"No, no, *monsieur*, nothing," he denied. "I know only what I hear in the streets, in the bistros." *Le Cochon* sent a pleading glance at the shadow hovering over him.

The pressure against his neck lessened.

A movement from the dark corner drew his attention again. *Le Chat* stepped forward onto the Aubusson carpet which covered the center of the floor of *Le Cochon*'s bedroom. He appeared to drift above the floor like some dark angel.

"Fortunately for you, *Le Cochon*, I have not come seeking revenge," *Le Chat* said. "I came for information. There is a woman. Small, beautiful, with raven hair and eyes like sapphires. I want her."

Le Cochon swallowed against the knife. He should have known the girl belonged to someone of significance, especially because of the lack of secrecy involved. Word about her had spread through the back rooms of bistros and the shady world of the demimondaine faster than the plague. That bitch, the du Barré, wanted her to be found. If he told this devil where the woman was, he would lose the tremendous profit he had been expecting to get for her. The knife wiggled against his throat, and he felt a sting of pain as the skin was broken. But he could still make this venture worthwhile.

"There will be an auction, *Monsieur Le Chat*. She is to be sold to the highest bidder." Becoming cagey, *Le Cochon* added, "The rest of the information, *monsieur*, you will have to pay for."

Le Cochon felt the anger emanate from the dark figure standing across the room as if it were something tangible. For a moment, he thought he had pushed too hard. Then, he sensed the tension release.

He had no doubts that *Le Chat* would appear at the auction. *Le Cochon* knew what the great spy was after. She was exquisite. He assumed that *Le Chat* had more than a nodding acquaintance with her. Why else would the devil risk returning to France? As for his payment, he knew he would receive that, also. *Le Chat* harbored an unusually honorable streak for such a ruthless rogue.

Damien had expected to pay this pig. He had used him as a source of information before, and the price had been steep. But *Le Cochon's* information was always accurate, so it was worth the exorbitant cost. Now, he prayed that it would be so again. If *Le Cochon* was wrong, then he and Jessica and all his men were lost.

"You will get your payment at the auction, *Le Cochon*," Damien said. "I will bid for the girl. And I will win her. You will get more than what you dreamed possible. Now, where is the auction to be held, and when?"

As soon as *Le Cochon* had given them the time and place of the auction, Damien and Edward slipped out of the bedroom. They had no fear of being discovered, for they had incapacitated all of *Le Cochon's* servants, having either knocked them unconscious or tied them up.

At the bottom of the stairs, they turned toward the back of the house. The rest of Damien's men lounged outside, waiting. As Damien emerged, Higgins pushed away from the garden wall.

"The cook's been tied up and hidden in a stable a few houses away, sir," Higgins reported.

"And the food?" Damien asked.

Higgins grinned. "Distributed to the poor of the city, sir."

Damien gave an answering grin. His revenge for the possibility that *Le Cochon* had been involved in his betrayal to Fouché was to deprive the man of any way to assuage his enormous appetite for a while. "Good. Let's leave here, gentlemen, and get some sleep. We have work to do tomorrow night."

CHAPTER 15

Late the next afternoon, the silent maid who delivered Jessica's meals arrived with several other servants who carried in a hip bath and buckets of steaming water. For a moment, she wondered at the sudden kindness of *Madame* du Barré, but then realized the reason for it. The auction would be held that night. She would be put on display like a horse to be sold to the highest bidder. It would be to *Madame*'s advantage to make her merchandise as attractive as possible. When the servants had filled the tub, they all left except for the silent maid.

"*Madame* du Barré said you were to bathe," the girl said timidly with her eyes downcast. "She told me to help. Please, don't get me into trouble." She glanced at the door as if she expected it to open at any moment.

Despite her own dire predicament, Jessica's heart twisted. The girl was obviously deathly afraid of doing something wrong and being punished. She was shorter and younger than Jessica, not fully grown. Fine, dark strands of hair escaped from her cap.

"I promise not to try to escape," Jessica said. "What is your name?"

The girl raised large brown eyes. "Marie." The word was barely above a breath.

"Why didn't you talk to me before, Marie?" Jessica asked.

Marie glanced at the door again before she answered. "*Madame* Rousse told me not to speak to you or she would beat me. Please, I should not be talking to you now." She silently indicated a tray of food that had been placed on a table beside the bed.

Jessica had little appetite, but she made herself eat for the babe. She looked forward to stepping into the heated tub. She hadn't had a proper bath since leaving Damien's home.

By the time Marie had finished Jessica's toilette, night had fallen. Jessica sat alone, naked, huddled in a blanket as she waited for whatever came next. She tried not to imagine the coming hours. The minutes seemed to crawl by. She prayed for the auction to be over quickly, so that she could at least be free from fear of the unknown. Finally, she heard the scrape of a key in the lock, and *Madame* du Barré entered. She carried a white garment over her arm.

Madame smiled. "It is almost time to go, little one. Stand up and let me look at you. And take off that hideous blanket."

Jessica's gaze went to Jacques, who hovered just behind the woman. His face was expressionless. He appeared to care little if Jessica was clothed or not. Raising her chin proudly, she stood and allowed the blanket to drop. There was no point in fighting. Her fate was already sealed.

Madame nodded in approval as she studied Jessica. "Very good. Marie has done well. I will have to tell *Madame* Rousse to commend the girl. Now, for the finishing touch."

She shook out the white material that had been draped over her arm. It was not a garment at all, but a large square of diaphanous, white silk. She wrapped it about Jessica, pulling it under one arm and tying two corners at the other shoulder. It concealed and revealed at the same time, for it remained open down one side of Jessica's body.

Madame stood back to survey her work critically. When she was satisfied, she held out her hand to Jacques who gave her a warm cloak. This she carefully placed about Jessica's shoulders and pulled the hood over her head. No one would guess that Jessica wore next to nothing.

"Now, you are ready, little one," *Madame* told her. "Just a short ride, and then you will enter a new life."

Jessica gazed impassively at her. She was determined not to reveal her overwhelming fear. *Don't let them know you are afraid.*

They descended the stairs and left the house by a side door. A coach was waiting for them. Jessica breathed in the chill, night air. She relished the tiny feeling of freedom it gave her. She had not been outside for many days, and the fresh air made her giddy. She climbed into the coach, followed by *Madame* and Jacques. With her head bowed, she sat in the corner of the seat and prayed that fate would not be too cruel to her this night.

"For whom are you praying, little one?" *Madame* sneered. "For yourself, or for your lover, *Le Chat*?"

Jessica's head snapped up at the mention of Damien. What diabolical scheme had *Madame* planned? Did she really believe that Damien would come after her?

Madame laughed. "Oh, yes, little one. He will be there tonight. Feast your eyes when you see him, for it will be the last time you will be able to gaze upon his handsome face." *Madame* shook her head. "A terrible shame to kill such a perfect male specimen. But perhaps he will only be captured, and I can turn him over to Fouché. Either way, I win, and he loses." *Madame*'s smile was cruel."

Instead of pleading or bargaining with *Madame* to let Damien go free, Jessica bit her lip to refrain from making a reply. Invoking *Madame*'s anger now might lessen any chance she would have to warn Damien of a trap. Once again, she lowered her head.

The auction was to be held in a country house several miles outside the city, less likely to be discovered by the authorities than if it were held in Paris. Jessica wondered what type of person actually attended these affairs. She knew, of course, of black slaves, and she had heard whispered rumors of the slave markets of North Africa where white women from captured European vessels were sold, never to be heard from again. Would she disappear into oblivion, also?

As the coach pulled around to the back of a large chateau, her heart quickened, and her hands began to shake. She was determined not to show her fear, and she clenched her fists to hide her tremors. Keeping her face expressionless, she descended from the carriage. With *Madame* on one side of her and Jacques on the other, she walked through the door to meet her fate.

They entered through the kitchen and passed down a long hall into a small sitting room. Jessica counted nine other girls waiting to be auctioned besides herself. They were all dressed in a similar fashion to what she wore. Some sat waiting quietly, some cried, the rest looked as if they were in shock.

Madame took the cloak from Jessica's shoulders, and then she and Jacques left. Jessica shivered in the chill air. There was no fire on the hearth. Glancing about, she realized that even though she had been left alone, escape was impossible. A very large, rough-looking man stood to one side of the door and watched everything closely. Jessica found an empty chair in a corner and sat down to wait.

It was not long before the door across the room opened and an older woman beckoned to a tall, buxom girl. Before the girl went out the door, she turned and waved to the others waiting. "Good luck, my friends," she called.

So, the auction began. One by one, each of the girls was taken out the door to meet her master. At last, only Jessica remained. The door across the room opened again, and the woman who had been escorting the girls entered. She held a length of long, white, satin ribbon in her hand. She stopped before Jessica.

"Hold out your hands, child," she said kindly.

Jessica gazed at her in confusion and did as she was told. The woman wrapped the ribbon about Jessica's wrists and tied them together, leaving a length of ribbon trailing on the floor. None of the other girls had been bound. Jessica raised questioning eyes to the woman.

"I was told to tie you," the woman said. "I do not know why. We only tie those who have been unruly." She gave Jessica a sympathetic smile and a gentle pat on the arm as she finished. "Come along. It is your turn, now."

Jessica knew that *Madame* du Barré had something to do with her being bound. Why else would she have been the only one?

The woman led Jessica through the door and into a room filled with people. The crowd was mostly made up of men, but a few women were scattered among them. A raised platform stood between Jessica and the crowd. The woman handed the end of the ribbon tying Jessica's wrists to the fat man, *Le Cochon*. He led her onto the platform.

Le Cochon began the bidding. "Our last sale of the evening, ladies and gentlemen. A lovely pearl from the shores of England. Gently born and raised. Intelligent, yet endowed with spirit, guaranteed to make bedding her an experience to remember."

At this last, he winked and grinned at the crowd, then placed his fat hand on one of Jessica's breasts and pinched her. Jessica gasped in pain. Knocking away his hand, she swung both fists and hit him in the arm, then moved as far away as the length of ribbon allowed. The crowd laughed and applauded. Jessica stared stonily at a spot in the wall straight ahead.

"The opening price is five hundred guineas!" *Le Cochon* announced. "Who will bid?"

"Five hundred!" came a bid from the right side of the room.

"Seven hundred!" a man sitting directly before the platform bid.

"One thousand!" a third man called out.

So, the bidding went on: eleven hundred, twelve, fifteen hundred, two thousand, up to three thousand guineas.

"I have a bid of three thousand guineas," *Le Cochon* told the crowd. He gazed out over the faces expectantly. "Come, come," he exhorted them. "Is that all you will bid for such a ravishing creature?"

He reached out and tugged at the knot at Jessica's shoulder holding her garment in place. It fell to the floor with a whisper. The people murmured with approval at Jessica's nakedness. Appalled, humiliated, she shivered, but raised her chin and stared straight ahead.

Le Cochon gave the crowd a sly look. "I have heard it rumored that she is the mistress of *Le Chat*. Gentlemen, does that not fire your loins? Imagine, having this beauty under you, moaning, knowing that you are taking the place of that devil *Le Chat*."

"Four thousand!" a dark haired man with beady, evil eyes offered.

"Forty-five hundred!" another bidder shouted.

"Five thousand!" the dark haired man returned.

Le Cochon waited a moment, but no other bid was offered. "I have five thousand," he said. "Is there another bid?"

He raised his walking stick to finalize the sale, and Jessica's heart sank. She knew the dark haired man would not treat her kindly.

Before *Le Cochon*'s stick hit the floor, a deep voice from the far corner of the room announced, "Ten thousand."

Jessica immediately sought out the source of the voice. Damien! He leaned against the wall with his arms folded across his chest, appearing bored with the proceedings. He was dressed as Jessica had seen him at *Monsieur* Montaigne's, as *Le Chat*.

The crowd babbled excitedly, and someone exclaimed, "*Le Chat*!" *Le Cochon* smiled happily at the large bid and rapped his walking stick several times to regain order. When the crowd quieted down once more, he looked questioningly at the dark haired man.

"Do you wish to bid against the rightful owner of this piece of fluff, *monsieur*?" he asked.

The man scowled and shook his head. *Le Cochon* brought his walking stick down sharply.

"Sold, to *Le Chat*, for ten thousand guineas," he announced.

Damien pushed away from the wall and made his way to the platform. He tossed two pouches, heavy with coins, at the feet of the auctioneer.

"You may count it if you wish," Damien drawled, daring the man to do so.

"That will not be necessary, *monsieur*," *Le Cochon* replied quickly. "You have always paid me fairly in the past."

A glance full of meaning passed between the two men. Damien finally smiled without humor.

"You would do well to remember that, *Le Cochon*," he said.

Le Cochon passed the end of the ribbon to Damien. "You have made a wise purchase, *monsieur*. There are those who would use the *mademoiselle* against you."

Damien's eyes narrowed at the oblique warning, then he turned to Jessica. Placing his hands around her waist, he swung her down from the platform. He removed his cloak, placed it over her shoulders, then guided her through the crowd and outside. He stopped just outside the door of the house and began to untie the knotted ribbon around her wrists.

Jessica remained silent as she watched his fingers work at the ribbon. Her feelings at seeing him, being near him, went so deep she did not trust herself to speak. She shifted her gaze to the dark beyond the lamplight to keep her equilibrium. A movement caught her attention out of the corner of her eye. It all happened in an instant and yet time seemed to slow to a crawl.

Madame du Barré stood in the middle of the lawn with Jacques beside her. A flash of light reflecting off metal revealed the pistol raised high in her hand, aimed directly at Damien's back.

A flash, and the report of a gunshot rang out.

Screaming his name, Jessica launched herself at him, knocking him off balance against the wall of the house. She felt a thud in her shoulder, then a white-hot pain. A second explosion rang in her ears, and she watched through a blur as Jacques crumpled to the ground. *Madame* disappeared into the woods behind her. The smell of gunpowder made Jessica cough.

"Are you hurt?" Damien asked, as he stuck his pistol into the waistband of his trousers.

"I'm all right." She could not worry about the searing pain in her shoulder. Impatiently, she tried to push him toward the drive. "Please, you have to get away from here. *Madame* was trying to kill you. Leave me here and go."

"Not bloody likely," he ground out between clenched teeth. "Do you think I came all this way to leave you?" He grabbed her arm and hurried along the front of the house, across the lawn and into a group of trees. In its shelter were two horses, one already with a rider. Jessica recognized Leftenant Johnson as he held the reins of Damien's huge stallion. Damien nearly threw Jessica onto the horse, then mounted behind her. With a nudge of his heels, he urged his horse into a gallop.

Waves of nausea and blackness washed over Jessica. Hot pain radiated from her shoulder at every jostle. Warm blood trickled down her side. She tried desperately to remain conscious. Damien did not need to be hampered with her inert form. But the world around her became blurred and fuzzy.

She was not really aware of where they went or how long they rode as she slipped in and out of consciousness. Only Damien's arm kept her on his horse. He had come for her. That was all that mattered.

They finally stopped before a tiny cottage. The horses were blowing heavily after their long, treacherous gallop through the dark. When Damien dismounted, Jessica flopped sideways from the horse. He caught her before she fell, and his hand slipped against her skin, wet and sticky.

"God's teeth," he muttered as he realized it was blood.

With his mouth in a grim line, he picked her up and carried her into the cottage. He placed her on the small cot in the single room. Pulling the cloak away from her shoulders, he saw the round, dark hole seeping blood where she'd been shot. He covered her with a blanket, then went to start a fire on the hearth. As he coaxed the kindling into flames, Leftenant Johnson entered after having secured their horses.

"We'll have to stay here longer than I had planned," Damien said. "Jessica has been shot. I want the others on lookout duty at the usual places."

"They're already posted," Johnson said. "Is she hurt very badly?"

"She was hit in the shoulder. I think the ball is still in the wound. I couldn't see very well." Damien straightened. "I'll need some water and something for bandages."

As Johnson left to gather the supplies, Jessica moaned. Damien grabbed the lamp and hurried to her side. Her face was pale, and she shivered. As he tucked the blanket around her, his chest tightened. She was so small and delicate, yet she had pushed him out of the way of a bullet that might very well have killed him. He knelt down and smoothed back her curls, short now that *Madame* had cut her hair. They looped around his fingers in silky coils. He mourned the loss of her long tresses.

At his touch, her eyes fluttered open. They widened in panic, and she grabbed his coat.

"*Madame* has set a trap," she said. "She means to capture you. Damien, you have to get away."

Damien smiled soothingly, disengaged her fingers from the front of his coat and held her hand. "It's all right, Jessica. We're safe for now. Rest for a while."

He placed a kiss on her fingers. With a nod and a sigh followed by a grimace of pain, she fell unconscious once more.

Johnson returned with a bucket of water and a handful of cloth strips. Damien helped him empty the bucket into a kettle hanging over the fire, then took him aside.

"We have to be away from here by dawn," Damien said. "We'll need a wagon to get Jessica to the coast. Have Higgins take one of the others and see what he can find. Tell them to be very careful. I'm sure Fouché will have patrols out all over the countryside. After you have spoken to Higgins, come back here. I'll need your help."

Johnson nodded briskly and left. Damien returned to the cot where Jessica lay. He unclasped the cloak from about her throat and pulled it off her shoulders. There was an ugly little hole where the ball had entered her soft flesh. It bled freely. He folded one of the cloth strips and pressed it against the wound, then tucked the blanket more securely around her. When he had finished, he put his hand to her cheek.

"Jessica," he said softly.

Slowly, she opened eyes clouded with pain. She smiled weakly.

His thumb caressed her cheek. "Jessica, I have to remove the ball from your shoulder. Do you understand?"

She nodded.

"It will hurt, love," he said. "I'll try to be careful."

"I know you will." Her words were infused with a confidence he did not feel.

He stood and scowled darkly at the wall before him. He was torn with guilt and apprehension, feelings which had never assailed him before. His guilt arose from his desperate desire to help the wounded girl who lay before him. She was a member of the family that had inflicted so much pain on his. Margaret's evil seduction of his brother. His brother's death in that God-forsaken duel. His mother's devastation. If he'd had any sense of justice, he should not have followed her into France to save her. He should have let her go to whatever fate *Madame* du Barré had planned. Instead, he found himself aching with a need to heal her, to escape with her back to England. When he had seen her exhibited at the auction, naked before all those leering eyes, he had wanted to strangle every man there with his bare hands. But even in front of that salacious crowd, Jessica had stood brave and defiant. She was magnificent.

An unfamiliar apprehension swamped him. His responsibility was to get everyone safely out of France, but he felt very unsure about the outcome of this mission. He had never worried about such things before, assuming a favorable outcome for every assignment. He knew his talents and those of his men and used them accordingly. He had trained his men to be resourceful in an emergency. With

Jessica injured, their progress to the coast would be slow, giving Fouché time to catch up to them. Resourcefulness could not make up for lost time. Since this slip of a girl had entered his life, he found he could not be sure of anything.

When Johnson returned to the cottage, Damien forced his dark thoughts aside and prepared to remove the ball from Jessica's shoulder. As the Leftenant held a light, Damien cleaned the wound with the heated water. He could see the ball just below the surface of her skin. Fortunately, it had almost spent itself by the time it entered her shoulder. He held his knife in the fire to clean it. Then with Johnson holding her down, Damien pried the ball from her flesh. She cried out, stiffened against the pain, then lapsed back into unconsciousness. Damien pressed a pad of cloth against the sudden flow of blood from the wound, then washed and bandaged her shoulder tightly. He sat back on his heels, and let out his breath in a rush. Sensing Johnson's concerned gaze, he frowned to cover his relief and stood.

"Have you checked our lookouts?" he asked, irritated that he had revealed his feelings about Jessica.

"If they see anything, they will report," Johnson said with a shrug. "Why don't you try to rest? You haven't slept in two days. I can watch over Lady Jessica."

Damien glared at him. Johnson grinned, reached into a pocket and pulled out a silver flask. As he tossed it to Damien, he said, "This might help your mood. Sir."

Damien hissed out his exasperation at his friend and caught the flask in one hand. He sniffed its contents. The pungent scent of his best brandy assailed his nose. He poured a liberal amount on the bandage covering Jessica's wound. As the alcohol painfully sterilized her wound, Jessica stiffened, mumbling gibberish in her unconscious state. Damien took a generous swallow, capped the flask, and tossed it back to Johnson.

"At least you're good for something," he grumbled. The brandy helped quell the anxiety that had assailed him since discovering Jessica's wound.

At that moment, Walker burst into the cottage. "Sir!" he exclaimed breathlessly. "A patrol passed me on the road, headed this way."

"We'll have to move. Where is Higgins with that wagon?" he chafed.

As he spoke, he heard the sound of horses drawing a heavy vehicle. It was the distinct noise of a well-oiled coach, not the wagon they expected. It stopped before the cottage. At a flick of Damien's hand, they quickly donned their masks, drew their pistols, and took up defensive positions. Johnson and Walker stood against the wall on either side of the door. Damien stood in the corner and guarded Jessica's cot. The door creaked open, and a man filled the opening.

CHAPTER 16

Just as Johnson was about to bang the man on the head with the butt of his pistol, the intruder spoke. "I've found us some fancy transportation back to the coast, sir."

"Higgins!" Damien exclaimed. "Next time, give us the warning call so we know it's you. Let's see this fancy transportation."

He followed Higgins out the door. Sitting incongruously before the cottage was a very expensive coach and four. The coach door opened, and a portly gentleman descended with his hands held above his head. He was followed by young Wells who aimed a pistol at the man's back.

"Good evening, sir." Wells grinned. "This is Citizen Boudreau. He has graciously allowed us the use of his carriage this evening."

Damien grinned and bowed before the man. "Citizen Boudreau, a pleasure to meet you, sir. Allow me to introduce myself."

"I know who you are!" the man blurted. "You are *Le Chat!*"

Damien raised an amused eyebrow. "You know of me, then, *monsieur*?"

Monsieur Boudreau's hands trembled. "I know nothing, *monsieur*," he protested. "I am just a poor merchant. I will give you all the money I have with me."

Damien looked askance at the elegant coach. "Just a poor merchant, *monsieur*? Then I must be a dear friend of *Monsieur* Fouché," he said drily. "We do not want your money, *monsieur*. What we want is your carriage and your silence and your cooperation. Now, kindly get back into this fine conveyance. One of my men will wait with you so that you will not feel lonely." As Boudreau turned away and climbed back inside, Damien winked and nodded his approval at Wells.

Higgins retrieved a bundle from under the driver's seat and handed it to Damien. "We borrowed his footmen's clothes, too, sir," he said.

Damien smiled. "Nicely done, Higgins. You can do the honors and drive."

As Higgins began changing his clothes, Damien gave orders to move out. He went back inside the cottage and strode to the cot. Jessica was still unconscious. When he put his hand on her forehead, he felt the hot, dry skin of a fever. He muttered a curse. He had to get her home quickly. After checking her shoulder to see that the bleeding had slowed, he wrapped her in another blanket, then doused the fire. His sharp gaze flicked around the space to be sure they'd left no evidence of their presence. Satisfied, he scooped Jessica up and carried her out to the carriage. He laid her on the empty seat with her head in his lap, then gave the word to leave. Johnson sat beside *Monsieur* Boudreau with his pistol pressed against the man's side. Their passenger looked like he was about to be ill.

"Is there something wrong, *monsieur*?" Damien asked mildly.

"What did you do to her, you fiend?" the man demanded.

"Do, *monsieur*? I did nothing to her."

The man gestured at Jessica's unconscious body and stammered, "But-but…"

"She was shot, *monsieur*, and, I assure you, not by me." Damien gave him a level stare.

"There was a rumor of a shooting at the auction, but I thought…" The man's voice trailed off once again.

"Ah, you were at the auction this evening," Damien said mildly.

Monsieur Boudreau looked frightened to death. Tiny beads of sweat popped out on his forehead. He mopped his brow with a lace-edged handkerchief, nervously wiped the palms of his hands, then wiped his forehead a second time. Damien decided to give the fellow a little more to tell his friends.

"What were you doing at the auction, *monsieur*?" Damien asked. "I did not see you bid on any of the merchandise."

Monsieur Boudreau's eyes bulged. "W-well, I—I…he stammered.

"Yes?"

The man swallowed. "I just went to watch, *monsieur*," he whined.

"To watch?" Damien repeated. The stiletto appeared in his hand. The blade caught a glint of moonlight as he leaned forward. "To watch whom?" he demanded.

"No one!" the man exclaimed, leaning as far back as the seat would allow. Then amending his lie, he said, "I mean, the girls. I went to watch the girls." He gestured in Jessica's direction.

Cold rage washed through Damien as he remembered that room full of men leering at Jessica. But he needed to be sure the man across from him was merely a bystander and not one of Fouché's men.

"I think not," he said. "I think you were there to catch a glimpse of *Le Chat*."

"No! No, no. He shook his head vigorously as he kept his gaze on the knife. "Only the girls." Then he pleaded, "Please, *monsieur*, I am a married man with children."

Damien believed him. The man's fear was too real. He needed to keep him afraid. He sat back and narrowed his eyes. "Then you should be home with them. I do not like others ogling my woman," he said as he tightened his hold on Jessica. "I do not think I like you, *Monsieur* Boudreau."

"But *Monsieur Le Chat*, I did not know she was yours," the man tried to placate. "I only heard…" His voice trailed off with a squeak.

"What did you hear, *monsieur*?" Damien asked.

When the man did not answer immediately, Johnson nudged him in the ribs with the pistol. *Monsieur* Boudreau jumped.

Quickly, he answered, "Only that there was to be a special item at the auction tonight. That you would be there." Fear made his jowls tremble.

Damien met Johnson's eyes. *Madame* du Barré had been busy spreading her venom. "You would do well to stay home with your wife and children next time," Damien said, his lips curled in disgust.

The portly man bobbed his head in vigorous agreement.

Damien turned away, ending the conversation. Eventually, their hostage fell asleep. In between his snores, Damien listened to Jessica's irregular breathing. He had never felt so helpless and prayed they would reach the coast without mishap. But after they had traveled for quite some time, the coach slowed and stopped. Damien and Johnson exchanged worried glances. Johnson nudged their captive awake.

"*Monsieur*," Damien said, "you will find out the cause of this delay and get rid of whoever has stopped this coach. Do not try anything foolish. Remember that my men are sitting above and will hear everything that is said. There will be a pistol trained on your back at all times. If there is any killing tonight, be assured that the first to die will be you." He motioned for the gentleman to get out.

Johnson carefully looked out and reported on what was taking place. "A patrol. I can see five, no, six men. Boudreau is talking to them. They seem to be accepting what he is saying. He's coming back. The patrol isn't leaving."

Monsieur Boudreau opened the door and stepped into the coach. He wiped his brow with his damp handkerchief.

"The sergeant insisted on accompanying me to my home," he told Damien. "He said the notorious bandit, *Le Chat*, was in this area, and it was not safe to be out alone."

Damien smiled widely, appreciating the irony of the situation. "I am glad he was so solicitous of your welfare, *monsieur*. A shame he will never know that he escorted *Le Chat* to safety. Is there a house close by?"

Boudreau looked out the window. "I think there is one about a mile up the road."

"Good. We will pretend it is yours."

Damien communicated the plan to Higgins through the little door in the ceiling. He prayed that one of the soldiers did not look inside the coach before he could be rid of them. Relief washed through him when Higgins turned into a drive.

"Thank the soldiers, *monsieur*," Damien instructed their prisoner. "Do it quickly and get rid of them."

Monsieur Boudreau stuck his head out of the coach and called his thanks to the patrol as Higgins drove slowly down the long lane, then stopped around a curve. They waited tensely for the soldiers to leave. Finally, he turned the coach about, and they continued on their journey.

They halted at dawn in a small field beside the road where a stream meandered through the grass. They were able to refresh themselves and water the horses. Jessica was still unconscious, and her fever had risen. Her skin was hot and dry to the touch. Damien bathed her face with cool water and forced a few drops through her cracked lips. Her eyes opened, and she stared up at him. They were glazed from the fever and an incredible, bright blue.

She reached up and touched his cheek. "Damien," she sighed. "Don't let our baby die. Please." She closed her eyes and a tear slipped out from beneath her lashes.

Damien gently pushed her hair away from her face. "The baby won't die, Jessica. I promise."

She sighed and fell asleep.

Damien sat back on his heels. A child? He should have known she would conceive. She'd been a maiden and had no knowledge of the ways to prevent conception as his mistresses had. He shook his head at his lack of foresight, at his stupidity. As he caressed her face, he knew her naïveté did not matter. He'd wanted her from the moment he saw her at the gaming hell.

The impact of this news hit him like a blow from a sledge hammer. He could not catch his breath. God's teeth, everything was different now.

She was with child… The daughter of the man who shot and killed his brother carried Damien's unborn child in her womb. He dragged air into his lungs and shook his head at the insanity of it. But he could not dwell on that now. He had to get them out of France.

He pushed all other thoughts out of his mind as he inspected her shoulder. The bleeding had almost stopped. After washing the wound, he changed the bandage, then gathered everyone together. They had to move on. Until they reached the coast, they would not be safe.

By late afternoon, they sighted the English Channel. It was a relief for everyone. They were all exhausted, and *Monsieur* Boudreau's whining and complaining grated on everyone's frazzled nerves.

They waited at the edge of the beach for Walker who had been riding several minutes behind the coach with the horses. Damien shifted Jessica off his lap and onto the seat, then he climbed down to reassure himself that all was well. He scanned the area. The beach was empty, and the woods and fields in the other direction seemed quiet. Their small bark was anchored several yards out from shore, just where they'd left it. As he walked to the water's edge, Higgins and Wells disappeared into the woods to attend to nature's call.

Damien watched the bark rise and fall gently on the swells. A sense of urgency flowed through him. They would not be safe until they were on board and sailing away from shore. Jessica's life and that of his unborn child depended on him. He swallowed, not wanting to think about what that meant.

A sound from behind made him swing about. He cursed. Their luck had run out. *Madame* du Barré sat atop the dunes on a horse surrounded by eight soldiers. They each held a rifle aimed at him. Two more soldiers were on each side of the coach, and they also had guns trained on the occupants inside. Damien glanced quickly towards the woods where Higgins and Wells had disappeared, but there was no sign of them. Walker had not yet arrived. *Madame* rode onto the beach followed by the soldiers.

Hiding his apprehension, Damien strolled toward the woman and bowed. "Good afternoon, *Madame*." He flashed a grin. "Did you come to see us off on our voyage?"

She laughed lightly. "You are a brazen rogue, *Monsieur Le Chat*. Always ready with the quick wit, eh? But I do not think you will be taking any voyages for a long time. As you can see, you are greatly outnumbered. I believe you have used up all of your nine lives."

Damien grinned. "Do not be so sure, *Madame*. Did you know that this spot is called Witch's Cove? Witches are known to have supernatural powers and are always associated with cats." As he spoke, he moved closer to her horse.

"Stay where you are, *monsieur*," she warned. "These men will get very nervous if you come any closer."

As she finished speaking, an eerie wail came out of the woods. It ended in unearthly laughter. The horses shied and pranced nervously. The soldiers fought to keep them still and exchanged frightened, worried glances.

"You will not fool me with your tricks, *Monsieur Le Chat*," she said sternly.

"Tricks, *Madame*?" he queried. "I have used no tricks. You have watched me. I have been standing here before you in full view."

As he spoke his last word, the sound of many horses came from the woods. They thundered across the ground, sounding as if they would burst out of the woods in a huge herd. The soldiers with *Madame* tensed, shifting their rifles toward the woods as they prepared for a large group of riders to emerge, but none appeared. Then, as suddenly as the sound had begun, it stopped. There was no fading of the sound into the distance, it merely ceased. There was deathly silence. Even the waves crashing on the beach seemed muted.

"Ghosts!" one of the younger soldiers exclaimed.

"Witches," another mumbled.

"Captain contain your men," *Madame* ordered to the officer beside her without taking her eyes from Damien.

Before the captain could open his mouth, the spectral laughter sounded again from the woods. Two of the soldiers crossed themselves, turned their horses, and bolted. Damien raised an amused eyebrow at *Madame*.

"Hold steady, men," the captain commanded.

"What are those noises, sir?" a very young soldier questioned.

"Quiet, soldier!" the captain barked.

Three huge, black crows flew up out of the trees, circled, and, cawing loudly, swooped past the group on the beach.

"Mother of God," one of the soldiers who was guarding the carriage mumbled. "Witch's messengers." He dropped his rifle and galloped away, followed by two more men.

As the remaining three soldiers and *Madame* were distracted by the commotion, Damien dug the toe of his boot into the sand and flung it up in front of *Madame*'s horse. The animal reared in fright. *Madame* fought for control, but without success and toppled off the horse. In a flash, Damien dropped to one knee beside her and held his stiletto to her throat. "If you do not wish to see this woman's throat slashed, gentlemen, I suggest you retreat back to Paris."

"Shoot him!" *Madame* screamed.

"I'm afraid I cannot do that, *Madame*," the captain told her with regret. "I have received other orders from *Monsieur* Fouché." He turned to Damien. "You win this time, *monsieur*. You are fortunate that *Madame* du Barré has outlived her usefulness." He saluted and rode off with the remainder of his men close behind.

"Cowards! Fools!" *Madame* screamed after them. "You will live to regret this!"

Damien smiled coldly down at his captive. "I think, rather, it is you who will live to regret your actions, *Madame*."

He stood and dragged the woman up with him. Whistling sharply, he waited as Higgins, Wells, and Walker emerged from the woods with the horses. *Madame* glared at Damien at the appearance of his men.

"You have not won yet, *Monsieur Le Chat*," she spat at him. "You will never see me go to trial."

Unmoved by her threat, Damien turned to his men with a smile. "Excellent evil spirits, gentlemen."

"I thought the crows were a nice touch." Higgins grinned.

Damien chuckled as he handed *Madame* over to the Sergeant. "Higgins, tie her up. Wells, tie up *Monsieur* Boudreau and start his coach back on the road to Paris. Someone is sure to find him sooner or later. The rest of you, get the horses aboard our ship. Make haste, gentlemen."

He strode to the coach and checked inside. Jessica was mumbling in her delirium. Johnson was holding her on the seat of the carriage with one hand, and with the other, he pointed his pistol at *Monsieur* Boudreau. Damien gathered Jessica into his arms and carried her out to the boat. His men would see to the rest. His first concern now was the courageous, wounded woman in his arms.

Half an hour later, relief washed over Damien as he watched the shoreline of France recede in the distance. This would be his final mission as *Le Chat*. It had nearly cost his men their lives, and it could still snuff out Jessica's. The thought of losing her made his chest constrict. Determined to do everything he could to keep her alive, he turned with resolute steps away from the ship's rail to tend the sick girl who lay in a bunk below.

CHAPTER 17

When Jessica opened her eyes, she found herself in a soft bed in her room in Damien's house. For a moment she thought she must be dreaming. Then she felt the tickle of a spring breeze on her cheek and she understood. Damien had succeeded. He'd rescued her and brought her safely home. Relief washed through her, followed immediately by apprehension. Was he angry with her for escaping him and forcing him to cross into France to come after her?

She was too tired to worry and felt strangely weak. She tried to move, but a sharp sting in her shoulder and tight bandages restricted her. Memories flashed through her head — the shooting, Damien and his men taking her to a small cottage, a wild ride to the ship. A rustle from the corner of the room drew her attention. She watched with trepidation as the Duchess of Wyndham approached.

"I am glad to see that you are awake, Jessica," she said gently. "You had us all quite worried. You were very ill when Damien brought you home."

"I'm sorry I caused you so much trouble, Your Grace," Jessica murmured.

She was ashamed that this woman, whom her family had caused so much suffering, had taken her into her home and cared for her. Struggling, she sat up.

"Please, don't move," the Duchess said. "You will open your wound and make it bleed."

"But—" Jessica began.

"Shh. Lie still," the Duchess ordered as she helped her lie back down. "It is no inconvenience to have you here. I would not have

195

forgiven my son if he had not brought you here to recover. Are you hungry?"

"Yes, a little," Jessica admitted.

"Good. That is a good sign. I will have Aggie make up a tray for you. Now, stay there and rest. Donny will be back soon to sit with you."

With a smile, she left the room. Jessica mused over the kindness of the Duchess. The woman seemed sincere in her concern, yet Jessica felt uneasy. She had been the victim of two other women who had appeared kind at first before revealing their true natures. She didn't think Damien's mother was like Margaret or *Madame* du Barré, but she was wary just the same.

Her musings took a different route as she wondered where Damien might be. He was probably quite happy to relinquish his care of her. She was surprised she wasn't in a prison cell, although she supposed not even Damien would have locked up a wounded person.

Through the open window, she heard a horse and rider arrive. Damien's voice drifted up to her as he spoke to one of the grooms. He sounded energetic and well rested. She hoped he would be lenient with her. She was still under arrest after all. Perhaps he would be kind enough to bring Jason to see her. She missed her brother terribly. She had no idea what would become of her now. With no means of gambling to earn the monthly payment for Margaret, she was doomed. Bleakly, she took a deep breath and winced at the ache in her shoulder. She would have to figure something out, otherwise Margaret would never allow her to see her brother again.

The door opened, and Donny entered with a tray. Her eyes crinkled at the corners as she tried to hide a smile. "I see ye finally decided to wake up," she grumbled. "'Tis bad enough ye try t'escape, but then t'get yerself shot on top of it…" Her voice trailed off in an unspoken accusation as she shook her head. She helped Jessica prop herself up, then placed the tray across her lap. "Had us all worried to death, ye did. An' His Grace havin' t'go t'France after ye."

"He doesn't seem any worse for the adventure," Jessica observed wryly as Donny lifted a spoon to her lips. She swallowed the delicious meat broth, already feeling stronger. "I just heard him arrive home, and he sounded very fit, as if he'd had a wonderful night's sleep.

"Aye, and that he has." Donny nodded, scooping up another spoonful of soup for Jessica. "The first in six nights. Yer fever broke last night, and he finally left yer side and went t'his bed t'sleep. Wouldn't leave ye no matter how much Her Grace asked."

Astonished, Jessica gaped at Donny. She didn't know which shocked her more, that she'd been unconscious for six days or that Damien had remained with her the whole time she'd been ill.

She was not about to reveal where her thoughts traveled. Instead, she asked, "Did you say he hadn't slept in six days?"

"Aye, brought ye here six days ago, he did, not lookin' much better than ye did."

Jessica closed her eyes, her hand moving to her abdomen.

"The babe is all right," Donny whispered, laying her hand on Jessica's cheek. "The doctor examined ye."

Jessica opened teary eyes and nodded her thanks.

"Eat yer broth." Donny said gruffly as she spooned up another mouthful for Jessica.

Jessica grinned at Donny's tone. The woman's rough bluster was merely a ruse, hiding a heart of gold. She finished most of the thick broth that Donny had brought, and then with Donny's assistance, she settled back into the pillows and fell into a deep, healing sleep.

For the next three days, Jessica slowly regained her strength. Donny remained with her most of the time, and the Duchess visited her often. But Damien was conspicuously absent. Several times Jessica heard him arriving or leaving. She heard his footsteps in the hall, but he made no effort to visit her.

He would probably be very relieved when she was strong enough to leave. Although she had no idea where she would be taken, she was quite certain that Damien wanted her gone. After all, he'd made his feelings for her quite apparent before she'd been captured by *Madame*.

On the fourth day of her convalescence, Donny and a new maid, Frannie, helped her out of bed to bathe and dress. Donny had quietly told her that Lucy had been let go for being a part of *Madame*'s conspiracy. Jessica felt badly for Lucy, for she had liked her.

She felt remarkably better after her bath and with Donny's help, ventured downstairs for a stroll. She couldn't help but notice that her guards had completely disappeared, and she assumed that Damien counted on her weakened condition to keep her close to the house.

During the next few days, she never encountered the master of the house. He was either out, or sequestered in his study. Two nights later, quite late, she thought she heard him stop outside her door, but she could not be sure.

Throughout her recovery, Jessica had done a lot of thinking and had come to a decision regarding her future. Of course, her future depended on what Damien and the courts decided to do with her, but if she were found innocent, she had a plan. She contemplated telling Damien about the baby, but then rejected that notion. She would not take his pity. She would approach another gaming hell and use her notoriety as her way in. The cost would be high. She was not the innocent fool she'd once been. Her reputation was ruined and without a protector like *Madame*, she would have to figure out a way to keep the men at bay while earning Margaret's payment. Perhaps she could hire a private guard. Maybe one of Damien's men would consider it. She would have to raise some funds first. But that required a trip to a gaming hell. The thoughts circled in a dizzying puzzle.

A week after she had risen from her sick bed, as she stepped from her bath, a knock came at her door. It swung open before Donny could answer it. Donny jumped to stand in front of Jessica to hide her nakedness, while Jessica clutched a towel to cover herself.

Damien, looking relaxed and rather pleased with himself, stood in the open doorway.

"Yer Grace!" Donny gasped in shock. "M'lady is bathing."

Totally unruffled, Damien's gaze swept past Donny to rest with obvious pleasure on Jessica. He smiled lazily. "I would not deem it improper to pay my respects to my fiancée."

Jessica's mouth dropped open. Moments passed before she was able to squeak, "Fiancée?"

"Yes, my love," Damien said, appearing to enjoy the effect of his words. "Fiancée: that term which is applied to one betrothed to be married."

"Married?" Jessica squeaked again.

"Married," Damien echoed with a nod. He crossed his arms over his chest and leaned against the door frame. "I believe it's customary for a couple to marry who are to be parents. Don't you agree?" When Jessica continued to gape at him, he went on, "Is it not your wish to have a legitimate father for the babe?"

"Babe?" Jessica gulped. How did he know?

"Yes, babe." Damien lifted an eyebrow. "You have thirty minutes to make yourself presentable, then I wish to see you in my study."

Jessica's temper flared. How dare he come into her room and announce that they would be getting married! He could not even summon the courtesy to propose properly. She grabbed a bar of soap and flung it at him. He ducked and the soap hit the door as it closed behind him. She could hear him chuckling as he strode off down the hall.

Jessica turned on Donny. "You told him. You broke your promise."

Donny shook her head. "Nay, child. I not be the one to tell His Grace. Ye be the guilty one."

"Me?" Jessica blinked.

"Aye. When ye be sick, ye said much ye had kept in yer heart."

Jessica groaned and sank to the stool near the tub. "But how did *he* find out? Didn't you tend to me?"

"He was with ye from the time he brought ye through the door until yer fever broke. Don't ye remember my tellin' ye that last week? He refused to leave your side until finally Her Grace ordered him to get some sleep while she sat with ye, but then he came back an hour later. Her Grace threw up her hands at his stubbornness."

Jessica's heart lifted at the thought that perhaps he did care for her if he had been so reluctant to leave her during her illness. Her mood immediately plunged back to the depths with her next thought. He probably only wanted to be sure his heir didn't die with its mother. She was good for nothing more than to give him a child. If that was what he wanted, so be it. But just because they were to be married, didn't mean she would allow him back into her bed, despite her desire for him. She would teach the arrogant duke a few things about manners and women.

Although Jessica had been ordered to appear before Damien in thirty minutes, she took her time getting dressed. Besides wanting to defy him, she decided that looking her best gave her an edge in this game. An hour-and-a-half later, she stood before the door to his study. As she smoothed the front of her skirt, she smiled as she imagined Damien's reaction to her high-necked, modest frock of black-striped, gray taffeta, so different from those she wore as the Lady Fortuna. Her dress was a suit of armor against his seductive charm. Steeling herself for whatever he had planned, she knocked on the door.

Damien's voice bade her enter. When she walked into the room, she discovered that he was not alone. A rotund little man with twinkling eyes stood as she entered. Damien's gaze slid over her, but his expression revealed nothing. Despite her modest dress, she felt herself grow warm.

"Ah, my fiancée," Damien drawled, subtly revealing his annoyance at her tardiness. He indicated his guest. "Jessica, this is John Soames, the family barrister."

The little man bowed gracefully over her hand. "A pleasure, my lady."

Turning to Damien after seating herself, she smiled innocently. "I'm sorry I took so long, Your Grace. I only wished to look my best."

Damien's brows drew together as if he could not decide between being irritated or disarmed. Jessica kept her sweet smile on her face, but satisfaction at seeing Damien unsure of her bubbled inside. His glance slid away, then came back to land on her.

He cleared his throat. "Jessica," he said, "Soames has drawn up a statement concerning your involvement with *Madame* du Barré. I took the liberty of giving him information from what you had told me before. Since you have been ill, we will do our best to have you excused from appearing at *Madame*'s trial. This statement will be submitted in your absence. However, it is necessary that Soames asks you a few questions. You will need to read over the final document to be sure it is accurate. Then you must sign it before witnesses."

"*Madame* is going to trial?" Jessica asked. "She is here in England?"

"Yes." Damien paused. "She found it expedient to return with us."

Jessica could not imagine how Damien had managed to get *Madame* to return. From what she remembered, they had been trying to flee from her, not the other way around.

Mr. Soames gave a discreet cough. "I must inform you, m'lady, that your refusing to give a signed statement to the court could be construed as collaboration with the enemy. There would be a lengthy trial which you would have to go through, and, I am afraid, your wedding plans would have to be postponed, perhaps indefinitely."

Jessica smiled at the man. "Since I was only informed an hour ago of His Grace's intentions, I'm afraid we have no wedding plans yet. But I have no wish to spend time in a prison cell. I will answer your questions and sign your statement, sir."

Mr. Soames beamed his approval. "Wonderful! I will return later this afternoon with my clerks to record your answers, if that is agreeable." He turned a questioning look upon the Duke. At Damien's nod, he said, "We will take your statement then." He stood and offered his hand to Damien. "My congratulations again on your forthcoming marriage, my boy. Your father would have been pleased with your choice. Your lady is most charming, most charming, indeed." He bent over Jessica's hand once more, then was gone from the room with surprising alacrity for one so portly.

Awkward silence fell into the room after the barrister's departure. Jessica kept her eyes lowered on her clasped hands in her lap. The return of the barrister in the afternoon gave her a perfect excuse for leaving.

"If you no longer need me, I'll return to my room," she said without raising her gaze. "I would like to put my thoughts in order."

What she needed was to be away from him. She was still angry about his arrogant proposal and his assumption that she would agree, but her feelings were mixed with gratitude for bringing her home and watching over her, along with sheltering her from the ordeal of a trial and the scandal of bearing an illegitimate child. And God help her, excitement rippled through her at the prospect of being married to him. Confusion was raging in her brain, and she needed to think.

"I would like you to stay for a moment, Jessica," Damien answered. He pulled a small object out of his pocket, leaned forward and placed it in her lap. It was a tiny velvet box. She looked up at him curiously.

"Open it," he instructed her gently.

She did and gasped. Nestled amidst the folds of black velvet was an exquisite sapphire and diamond ring.

"It's beautiful," she breathed. "I have never seen anything so lovely."

"It's yours," he said brusquely as he turned to gaze out the window.

"I cannot accept such a gift." She closed the box and held it out to him.

"It's the custom in our family for the Duke's fiancée to receive this ring upon their betrothal," Damien said. He turned back to face her. "I see no reason why you should not accept it."

Jessica stood and placed the box in his hand. His tone and attitude had brought her quickly to a decision. Raising her chin proudly, she said, "I will give you the best reason for not accepting it. I am not going to marry you, Your Grace."

Damien blinked, then he stood, towering over her. His eyes became hard, and a muscle twitched in his cheek. "You are a fool, m'lady. I offer security for you and the child for the rest of your life. How can you refuse?"

"Very simply, Your Grace. I merely say *no.*"

He was very quiet for a moment before he spoke. His tone was dangerously soft. "You cannot say *no.* I will not have it."

Incredulous, Jessica's brows went up. "*You* will not have it? It takes two *consenting* adults to have a wedding, Your Grace."

"I will not have my child born without a name!" he thundered.

"You forget the child is also mine!"

"You are a fool!"

"You are an arrogant bully!"

Blue eyes met green and clashed. Only several weeks before, they had meshed as one in a night of passion. Now, the distance between them was greater than that between earth and sun.

Damien's breath hissed between his teeth. "How do you propose to live?" he asked. "What will you use to live on?"

"I will live the same way I did before you disrupted my life," Jessica said haughtily.

His eyes narrowed. "*Madame's* is no longer in existence. Do you have entrance to any other gaming establishment?"

Jessica shrugged and turned away. "I met many gentlemen at *Madame's*. I'm sure one of them could gain me entrance to another establishment."

"For what price?" he demanded ruthlessly. "Didn't you declare that you would be no man's mistress?"

Jessica flinched as her words were thrown back at her. "I'm sure I can find an honorable gentleman who would not require that I go to bed with him merely for the small favor of an introduction," she said with more conviction than she felt.

Damien snorted his disbelief. "You are more a fool than I thought."

"Not so much a fool, Your Grace, as to marry an arrogant, tyrannical boor," she snapped back.

Damien took a step toward her and she braced herself as if for a blow. His words hammered themselves into her brain. "You may defy me, now, my lady, but marry me you will. Before the week is out, you will have this ring on your finger." He held up the velvet box, then set it on a corner of his desk as if throwing down the gauntlet of a challenge.

Jessica huffed her aggravation and impatience, then turned on her heel and stalked out. When she reached the security of her room, she gave full vent to her anger and frustration. She paced from wall to wall as her conflicting emotions warred within her.

She had gained her heart's desire only because of Damien's sense of duty. She would not be trapped into a marriage with a man who did not love her. He didn't even have the courtesy to ask her to marry him, but rather informed her she had no choice. He could not even bring himself to be polite to her. He must despise her that much.

Of course he would. Her family had hurt him terribly. He had lost his brother because of Margaret's immorality and her father's foolishness. Damien felt honor-bound to wed her because of the child they had conceived. This was not the marriage she had envisioned.

She had thought when she wed, her husband-to-be would love her, and she would love him. She halted in mid-step.

But she did love Damien.

She regretted her outburst. But he'd made her so angry. Her hand went to her still flat abdomen. Damien might not love her, but he wanted his child to have a name, and for that she was grateful. Sighing, she sat on a chair beside the window and gazed out at the sunlit day. She thought back to that night when she'd cheated at cards and ended up in his bed. So much had happened since then. She'd been wrong not to confide in him about her innocence. But her pride and naïveté had gotten in the way. Now they were locked in this battle, neither one willing to give ground. How could she make this right??

She stood once more and paced her room until exhaustion overtook her and she lay down on the bed. Wiping her tear-streaked face she closed her eyes. Somehow, she would make him see that she was not the cause of his pain. And somehow, she would make him love her.

Damien watched Jessica leave in silence. His hands clenched tightly at his sides. He wanted to throw something, anything. That woman would drive him mad. Perhaps she had already. What was he doing forcing her into marriage? Her family had brought terrible pain to the Wyndham family. She was obstinate, outspoken, proud. She was soft, vulnerable, desirable. He threw himself into a chair, leaned his head back and closed his eyes.

He had really messed up everything. What had happened to his manners and that charm that got him any woman he wanted? God's teeth, he had been a boor! If she weren't quite so lovely, or quite so naïve, maybe he wouldn't feel so honor bound to wed her. But he knew that was not true. His honor would dictate that he do the right thing no matter what Jessica was like. It was an added bonus that he found her so desirable, which was why he found himself in this position in the first place.

He had wanted to be gentle with her. Her illness and her pregnancy made him want to protect her. Yet, her relation to Braeleigh and Margaret weighed heavily on him. While he felt himself aroused by the sight of her and the memory of her passion, he couldn't get past the pain her family had caused. He was in a hell of a mess.

His glance fell on the little velvet box. He had to talk to someone. Edward was still in London. He was staying at his family's town house before returning to his duties. Rising swiftly, Damien scooped up the little box and deposited it in his pocket as he strode out the door to call on his friend.

CHAPTER 18

That afternoon, Jessica was summoned back to the salon because Mr. Soames had arrived with his clerks to take her statement. As she reached the door, Damien arrived at the same time. They stood, not moving or speaking. Then with a sardonic grin, he backed up a step and bowed.

"After you, my lady," he said.

Jessica could smell brandy on his breath. It was only early afternoon. "You've been drinking," she hissed.

Damien gave her a benign smile and swayed slightly. "I believe I have. Leftenant Johnson was most free with the cask of Mr. Bonaparte's brandy I had given him upon the completion of his guard duty here."

Jessica primly compressed her lips. With a snicker, Damien opened the door and waved her through.

Mr. Soames glanced between the two of them. He studiously turned to shuffle some papers, then suggested, "Shall we begin?"

Damien settled himself on the far side of the room in a high-backed chair. He rested his elbows comfortably on its arms and stretched his long legs out before him with his ankles crossed. Jessica frowned at him, but he only gave her a beatific smile. As her attention was captured by the barrister, she paid him no more heed.

After Jessica and Mr. Soames had been absorbed for about an hour, she heard a strange rumbling. Then she heard it again. It seemed to come from the far side of the room. She glanced in Damien's direction and discovered he had fallen asleep. He was snoring.

Mortified, Jessica's cheeks heated, but she pretended not to have noticed. Of course, the others were polite enough to ignore it. For the next half hour, the barrister's questions and her answers were interspersed with the low rumbles of Damien's slumber. When he finally roused himself, she sent him a dark frown. He only smiled at her innocently, as if there had been no breech of manners. Another two hours passed before Mr. Soames declared they were done. Jessica was relieved for more than one reason. She was exhausted, and her shoulder ached interminably, but she also could not wait to give Damien a piece of her mind.

When Soames and his clerks had gone, she turned on Damien like a hurricane. "How could you be so rude? You fell asleep!"

Damien shrugged. "I was tired." He yawned behind his hand.

"You snored the entire time!"

Damien grinned. "Did I really? How amusing."

"It was embarrassing."

"Ah, Witch, wasn't your magic working?" He reached out and tugged at a short curl.

Jessica batted his hand away. "You are insufferable. And to think I was going to tell you that I lo—" She caught herself just in time. She had almost revealed that she loved him.

"Tell me what, Witch?" Damien asked, his eyes shrewd.

"Nothing," she mumbled. "Excuse me, I am very tired." She swung about and hurried out of the room, away from him.

When she returned to her room, she was so exhausted she could not even think. She slipped off her shoes and climbed into bed without even undressing. *Madame* and her treachery and Damien's bad manners would have to wait.

She awoke with Donny standing over her, looking worried. Jessica stretched and yawned. The room was bright with sunshine.

"I must have overslept."

"Ye missed dinner last night," Donny informed her. "And breakfast, too. Are ye all right? Are ye sick again?" Donny felt her forehead.

"I'm fine, Donny." Jessica pushed herself up. "I was just very tired."

Donny nodded. "Good. Then get yerself up. Her Grace would like to see ye in the drawing room. She has a dressmaker here so ye can be measured for ye weddin' dress."

Jessica groaned and flopped back onto her pillow. Evidently, the Duke had received his domineering traits legitimately from his mother.

"Tell Her Grace there is to be no wedding," Jessica said. "I will have no need of a wedding dress."

Donny gasped. "Are ye daft? I cannot tell Her Grace that."

"Why not?" Jessica demanded. "You've never been shy before."

Instead of answering, Donny asked her own question. "Why ain't there goin' t'be a weddin'?"

Jessica sighed. "Because I can't marry a man who doesn't love me."

"Hmph. Then fool ye be," Donny declared. "I ain't goin' t'tell Her Grace no such thing."

Jessica glared at her maid, then relented. "Then tell her I am not feeling well and cannot come down. Tell her anything, but I will not be measured for a wedding gown I am not going to wear."

Donny harrumphed again and mumbled something about the blockheadedness of young people as she went out the door. Jessica sighed and got out of bed. Pulling on her dressing gown, she went to sit on the chaise near the window. She needed to make a plan.

Her immediate departure from this house was imperative. After the trial was over and her name had been cleared, she would leave. Until then she would do her best to avoid anything having to do with any wedding plans. And she would avoid Damien as much as possible. The less she saw him, the easier it would be to leave. She just had to figure out where she would go once she left. It would have to be some place where Damien could not find her, some place she could afford. That did not leave her many choices.

As distasteful as her plan of action was, it was the only way to avoid the agony of being married to Damien. That was something she could not bear. Her love was still a strong spark in her heart, but it was a spark she would have to keep hidden. She could not bear having it extinguished by Damien's distrust and bitterness. After all, she carried his child inside her.

As Jessica sat with her musings, a knock came at the door. She was not willing to entertain anyone, especially Damien. The knock came again, this time with more persistence, and the Duchess called out her name. Jessica sighed and went to open the door. Damien's mother had been kind to her, even knowing that her son had been killed by Jessica's father. Concern was etched on the Duchess's face.

"May I come in?" the lady asked.

Jessica stood aside and allowed her to enter, anxiety fluttering in her middle.

"Donny told me you were not feeling well," the Duchess said as she sat. She patted the chaise next to her. "Come, sit here and tell me about it."

Jessica approached but did not sit. She couldn't lie to this woman. "I am well enough, Your Grace. Perhaps your son would be better able to tell you why I am troubled."

The Duchess smiled gently. "I have asked him already. He told me that you would be able to enlighten me better than he."

Jessica blew out a breath and sank to the chaise. "I am not surprised that he places the blame for this confusion on me," she muttered, more to herself than to the woman sitting near her. She looked straight into the Duchess's eyes that were so much like her son's and said bluntly, "There is to be no wedding, Your Grace."

The Duchess nodded. "I had guessed as much. What has Damien done that has caused you to be so angry?"

Jessica dropped her gaze to her fingers entwined in her lap. "It is not what he has done, but how he feels," she answered quietly. "I cannot marry a man who hates me."

"Oh, my dear," Her Grace exclaimed as she placed her hand over Jessica's. "He does not hate you. Please, believe that. He cares a great deal for you."

Jessica shook her head in disagreement. "I have to believe what my own eyes and ears have told me, Your Grace." Hurt twisted through her. "It is not possible for him to feel any differently."

"That my son took advantage of you was despicable, but he is an honorable man and will set it right. His feelings for you at this moment are clouded by his grief for his brother and the horrible events which led to his brother's death. My two sons were very close, and Damien has not been able to put away his hatred for the creature who manipulated such a tragedy."

Jessica ducked her head. "I am sorry for the pain my family has caused you, Your Grace."

The Duchess smiled. "You have nothing to apologize for. You had nothing to do with the tragedy."

"But Damien still blames me," Jessica said.

The Duchess sighed. "My son's work in France has made him hard. It has made him forget his softer side. He needs a woman such as yourself to help his gentler nature to reemerge."

Jessica shook her head again. "I do not want to marry a man because he feels it is the right thing to do. I want him to love me for myself. Is that so wrong?"

The Duchess smiled. "That is not wrong at all. It is exactly what you should want. But I think you should also consider the child you carry. Do not act rashly, Jessica, so that you find yourself regretting your actions." The Duchess's smile turned into an impish grin. "I would not run away just yet, at least not for another day."

Jessica's eyes widened in surprise as she watched the woman leave. How had the Duchess known that she had planned to leave? She sat thinking on the lady's words. What the Duchess said could be the truth, that Damien cared for her. But the lady was his mother. Her idea of the truth might be clouded by prejudice.

Jessica was more confused now than ever. She liked the Duchess a great deal. Perhaps she would heed her advice and wait.

As the dinner hour approached, the maid, Frannie, appeared at her door. "Excuse me, my lady," she said, bobbing a nervous curtsey. "His Grace wishes you to join him at the dinner table this evening."

Jessica had no desire to dine with Damien. "Tell His Grace that I have no wish to upset his digestion. I will dine in my room."

Frannie cleared her throat. "Excuse me, my lady, but His Grace said to tell you that if you refused to come down to dinner, he would come to get you."

Jessica drew in a sharp breath. She knew it would do no good to defy him. He had come after her before. He would do it again. Frannie shifted from foot to foot. Jessica relented and smiled. She could not blame the girl if the Duke was acting like a boor.

"Tell His Grace I will be down as soon as I am dressed," Jessica told her.

Still, Frannie did not leave. "My lady?" she ventured.

Jessica sighed. Damien would leave nothing unsaid. He would make sure he had complete control.

"What else did he say, Frannie?" she asked.

"He told me to tell you — begging your pardon — that dinner is at eight o'clock, and if you are not downstairs at that time, he would bring you down even…" Frannie's voice faltered and trailed off.

Jessica knew what was coming next, but decided she had better hear it anyway. "Even what, Frannie?" she prompted.

Frannie swallowed and finished in a rush, "Even if you are not dressed."

Jessica's teeth clamped together. He was being as arrogant as ever.

"You may tell His Grace that he need not worry. I will be on time for dinner."

Frannie bobbed a curtsey, then hurried away. With a shake of her head, Jessica shut the door. Damien was acting like an ogre. She decided he needed to be tamed. The black dress she had worn the first night she had met Damien would be perfect.

As the clock struck eight, she arrived at the door of the salon. Damien leaned one elbow negligently on the mantle. He glanced up as she entered and saluted her with the glass he was holding. She felt his glance pass over her in appreciation like a warm breeze.

The Duchess rose and came to greet Jessica. "I am so glad you could join us for dinner this evening, Jessica," she said warmly. "Are you sure you are feeling well enough?"

Jessica smiled. "Yes, quite well, thank you."

She glanced at Damien, who had obviously not informed his mother of his threat to drag her to dinner. He smiled placidly and shrugged. The Duchess stood, and looping her arm through Jessica's, guided her to the dining room. Damien was left to follow by himself.

Dinner turned out to be a pleasant affair, and Jessica enjoyed it despite the presence of Damien at one end of the table. The Duchess was a practiced conversationalist and storyteller. With a sharp wit, she related gossip she had heard during the day, about the lady who had made a terrible gaff by wearing a morning dress for her afternoon visitations, and the young viscount who had been denied entrance to Almack's because he had arrived three minutes after the doors had closed, so he had tried to enter by climbing a ladder and crawling through a window. Jessica found herself laughing for the first time in months. Damien and his mother also kept up a lively banter which delighted Jessica. It had been so long since she had taken part in a family dinner where the people around the table enjoyed each other's company. She covertly watched Damien during the meal and noticed the softening of his features as he spoke to his mother, and the crinkles around his eyes when he laughed with her. How wonderful it would be to have him look at her with love, she thought.

When the meal ended, the Duchess excused herself to write some letters. Jessica and Damien were alone at the table. An awkward moment of silence ensued.

Jessica stood. "I will leave you to your brandy," she said.

Damien stood and took her hand. "Don't go just yet, Jessica. Come into the drawing room. I would like your company for a while longer."

Bemused, she did not object as he tucked her hand into the crook of his arm. A table with two chairs had been set up in the drawing room. A deck of cards sat precisely in the middle of the table.

"What is this?" she asked.

"I thought perhaps we could spend some time playing cards," he said. "That is, of course, if you are not too tired."

"No, I am not tired," she answered with a small smile.

"Splendid," Damien said. "We will play for…" He glanced about the room. "Rose petals." He pulled a deep, red rose out of a nearby arrangement. "Hold out your hands."

Chuckling, she did as he asked. He pulled the petals from the flower and dropped them into her cupped hands.

She smiled. "What will you use to gamble with, Your Grace?"

"Oh, I will find something," he said with a vague wave of his hand.

He seated her at the table, then took the chair across from her. Pulling several coins out of his pocket, he placed them on the table before him.

"It's not fair that you should use money while I have only flower petals to wager," she protested.

Damien captured her fingers. As he brought them to his lips, he murmured, "Flower petals from your hands are worth far more than the few miserable coins from my pocket, my sweet. I consider it an honor that you will accept my small stakes."

Jessica was charmed at his outrageous flattery. "You'll not consider it such an honor when you have won nothing but a withered petal."

"Who is to say that I will win anything? Perhaps you will bereft me of all my riches." He raised a teasing brow.

She shook her head. "I do not believe that."

"We shall see," he said with a glint in his eyes.

They played cards for well over an hour. At first, Damien won most of the hands. The flower petals piled up before him. Then his luck seemed to change. Finally, he had lost everything, but the round had not ended.

"I have a document here which I will wager, if that is acceptable to you," he said as he reached into his pocket and drew out an official looking parchment.

"I don't wish to take important papers from you, Damien," Jessica said. "This game was only in fun. I'm sure your document has great value."

"Its value is an arbitrary matter." He shrugged. "Will you accept it or not?"

"Well, if it means so little—" she began.

"Ah, but I did not say that," he interrupted. "I merely said that its value was arbitrary. Its worth is determined by the person who holds it." He held it up and raised a questioning brow.

She hesitated, then nodded. "All right. I will accept it."

They played out the hand and Jessica won. He laid the document before her and leaned back in his chair. "I think you had better see what you have just won, love."

Jessica opened the document and began to read. She was stunned into speechlessness. It was a document, signed by her stepmother, giving Margaret's permission for Jessica to marry the Duke of Wyndham in return for a small fortune. It nullified the need for Jessica to continue to give Margaret her monthly stipend.

"How…? When…?" she stammered. "Oh, no. No."

Damien covered her ice-cold hand with his warm one. "Do you hate me that much for what I have done to you?" he asked gently.

Jessica stared at him, her vision blurry from tears, not trusting herself to speak. If he only knew how much she did *not* hate him. She pulled her hand away, stood and walked to the window. She looked out into blackness, her mind in turmoil. What was she to do?

She sensed Damien move up behind her and prayed he would not touch her. She would dissolve if he placed just one finger on her. Her emotional defenses had been shattered with that document.

Damien waited quietly while Jessica sorted out her thoughts. He knew he had shocked her. That had been his purpose. She had defied him too long, this delectable witch. He had allowed his own rage to cloud his thinking. He was still angry, but he realized that Jessica was not responsible for what had occurred years ago. Hell, she was a young girl at the time, still in the school room. No, the blame lay with Margaret for luring his brother into her bed. And to be honest, his brother had been foolish to fall for that harpy. He wanted Jessica with every fiber of his being. He had to make her see that. The passion that flared between them was more than a momentary spark.

His gaze traveled over her back and came to rest on the tantalizing curve of her neck. The spot cried out to be kissed, but he knew that would have to wait. He sensed her reticence and respected it. It was time for discussion.

"Jessica, why do you defy me?" he demanded quietly.

She turned to face him. Her gaze was determined, as if she had come to a decision at his question. "I can defy you no longer, Your Grace," she stated coolly. "You have seen to that. You have bought me. You have won."

Damien was taken aback by her harsh words, but did not allow them to shake his determination. "You will not be sorry that you agreed to become my wife," he murmured as he raised her chin with one finger and leaned in to kiss her.

Jessica stopped him with a hand on his chest. "I will be your wife in name only, Your Grace. I will be mother to your child, hostess in your house, and convenient companion if you wish to go out in public, but you will not buy my body like a whore. I will have none of it."

Damien stiffened. His teeth clenched. This woman would drive him to madness. He had to take a moment to subdue his temper. Finally, he nodded.

"All right," he agreed. "I will grant you this one concession. For now. We shall see how long you will be able to hold to your own demand."

"Do not threaten me," Jessica warned.

"One thing I never do, my love, is threaten," he drawled lazily. "I state facts."

He took her hand and held it palm-up, then pulled out the small, velvet box that contained the betrothal ring which she had refused. He placed the box in her hand and closed her fingers around it.

"Wear it," he commanded. "Please. It belongs to you, and I would see it on your finger. Always."

Jessica's fingers clenched around the box. He had outwitted her again. The knave. Would he always command and expect her to obey?

With an abrupt nod, she said, "I bid you goodnight, Your Grace." Then swept from the room.

When she reached her own room, she threw the little box onto the chaise with such force that it popped open and the ring fell out. She stood glaring at it. The bright stones glinted in the candlelight. She had never owned anything so beautiful or so valuable. She reached out a finger to touch it, but the door opened behind her to let in Donny, and she snatched back her hand. She needed to consider all the ramifications of wearing it. She stepped away as, without a word, Donny put the ring back in its box and placed it on the dressing table. Then she helped Jessica undress for bed.

Sleep did not come quickly. Jessica's thoughts shunted between the two men who mattered most in her life: Damien and

Jason. Damien, with his outrageously large payment to Margaret, had indirectly seen to the monetary well-being of her brother. But Jason was still trapped with Margaret at Braeleigh. Damien would never consent to become guardian to the son of the man who had killed his brother. His contempt of her family was only momentarily subdued by his lust for her. She was not so stupid to believe he loved her. The wedding would be a farce, held only to give his offspring a legitimate name. How could she make him see that she was not the cold-hearted monster that Margaret was?

The next morning, Jessica was violently ill. She was dizzy, weak, and nauseous. Her shoulder ached abominably. When she tried to rise, she fell back against the pillows with a hand to her head and a groan. She wanted desperately to appear at breakfast, to be calm and remotely cool to Damien, to prove to him that she had meant her words of the night before, and to show him she would wear his damnable ring and keep her part of the bargain.

Donny was the first to enter. She made clucking noises as she went about straightening the room. "It's the babe." She nodded several times.

"Why haven't I been sick before this?" Jessica asked.

"Some mothers have the sickness early on, and some later. Some not at all." Donny straightened the covers over Jessica. "It will pass." Then she disappeared out the door.

Frannie was the next to appear with a tray of tea and toast. She made sympathetic noises as Jessica turned her head away from the food and told her to take it away.

"Her Grace will be in to see you soon," Frannie said as she set the tray on a table in the far corner of the room. Then she was gone, also.

Just as Jessica was recovering from another bout of retching into the chamber pot, the Duchess walked in. Sympathetic, she told Jessica to remain in bed and rest. The dressmaker would come the next day to take measurements for her wedding dress. The wedding plans would have to be finalized immediately.

As Jessica opened her mouth to protest that she did not require an elaborate wedding, the Duchess smiled her disagreement. One did not wed the Duke of Wyndham without pageantry.

Jessica had hoped for a quiet ceremony and then to go about her life without notice. She should have known better. Nothing Damien was involved in ever went the way she wished.

Her thoughts turned to Jason. The document that Damien had given her last night did not mention her brother. Because of her pride, she had sealed Jason's fate to remain with Margaret. Damien would not concede to any more requests or demands unless she gave him what he wanted — his conjugal rights. She sighed. Jason would have to wait. She would need some time before she could approach Damien and ask him to help.

By late morning, she was feeling physically stronger, but still gloomy. She climbed out of bed and wandered over to the dressing table where the little velvet box sat. She had told Damien she would wear the ring today. Even though she knew he would not come to her room, she took it from its box, slipped it on her finger, then stared down at her hand. The large stones winked coldly back at her, reminding her of the aloofness of the man she was to marry. If only he had expressed some little feeling for her…If only she didn't love him so much. She flopped down onto the chaise.

If only wishes came true.

CHAPTER 19

Jessica awoke with a start. The slant of the sun told her it was late afternoon. She'd fallen asleep on the chaise and slept for several hours. Someone had come in and placed a light throw over her. As she pushed herself up, a voice she knew very well spoke from her left.

"Good afternoon," Damien greeted her pleasantly. "I was beginning to wonder if my fiancée had turned into Sleeping Beauty and could only be awakened with a kiss."

"There is no kiss needed, thank you very much," Jessica answered tartly. She was immediately awake and alert, and would not let down her guard for an instant.

"Ah, my loss," Damien lamented.

"Why are you here?" She tried to make her question merely curious, but somehow it came out confrontational.

He rose and stood over her. Her gaze traveled over his broad chest covered in its sheath of white linen, up to his mouth—oh, Lord, that mouth—to his eyes. They told her nothing, so she forced herself to look away.

"I have something to tell you," he said.

His tone was serious, and brought her gaze back to his face. She waited for him to continue. He appeared uncomfortable, as if he were not quite sure how to say what he had to tell her.

His uncertainty, so unlike him, caused her imagination to run wild. Something had happened to Jason. He no longer wanted the babe she carried. She was going to be arrested as a spy. Her apprehension made the last, perhaps most important question tumble from her.

"Are you calling off the wedding, Your Grace?"

Damien grinned. "Hardly, my love. I am eagerly looking forward to the day when you will become my wife." He sat on the edge of the chaise. "No, what I have to tell you is dark news."

Jessica remained silent and anxious.

He took her hand and said seriously, "There will be no need for you to worry about your statement for *Madame's* trial."

Panic swept through her. She was going to be brought to trial. Damien no longer believed in her innocence.

"Jessica." Damien's voice captured her attention. "*Madame* du Barré is dead."

"Dead?" she repeated, not quite comprehending.

"Yes," he said gently. "It seems someone smuggled poison to her in prison. She was discovered this morning."

Jessica tried to assimilate the information. Then, it sunk in. She covered her face with her hands. "She killed herself. Oh, God."

Damien tugged her hands down and held them, his grip warm and comforting. "Jessica."

She shook her head, confused and appalled. "She was so kind to me when I first came to London. I know she only used me, but she was the closest thing to a friend I had. Why did she have to be a spy?"

"She did what she felt was right," Damien said gently. "I think her suicide was for the best. She had been disowned by her superior for failing to capture me, and she knew she would find no mercy here."

Jessica nodded sadly. "You are probably right. Thank you for telling me." She slipped her fingers from his grasp, not wanting to appear weak.

"I also wanted to return this to you." He held up a gold chain.

"My locket!" she exclaimed. "I thought I had lost it."

"*Madame* sent it as proof that she had you," he said. "It must mean a great deal to you."

"My parents gave it to me when I was a little girl." Tears sprang to her eyes at the memory.

"Is the woman's portrait of your mother?"

Jessica nodded.

"She was very beautiful. You look just like her." His tone was level, without emotion.

Jessica wondered what he was thinking. The other miniature portrait inside was of her father. Damien had shown great restraint by not destroying the piece.

"Thank you for returning it," she said.

He undid the clasp, leaned forward, and re-clasped the chain around her neck. As he sat back, his fingers brushed her neck. The touch was a reminder of what he could make her feel with those fingers. In that moment, she forgot about her anger, her hurt. She felt comforted by his presence. It would be so easy to say yes to him… She caught her wayward thoughts and inched back.

Damien quirked a smile as though he'd guessed her thoughts. "I have also come to change your bandages."

Jessica gazed at him suspiciously. "Donny can do that. There is no need to concern yourself about me."

"Why should I not be concerned about my future wife?" he asked. Without waiting for an answer, he said, "Donny has gone out shopping with my mother."

"Then Frannie, or one of the other maids can do it," she tried.

The last thing she wanted was to sit half undressed before him. She was much too aware of what his touch could do to her. She could not take back her demand of the night before.

"I have given many of the maids the afternoon off. They will be working long hours soon enough to prepare for our wedding. The other servants are busy." He dismissed any further argument by tugging at the ribbons on her dressing gown.

Panic gripped her. She was practically alone with him in the house. What did he mean to do?

Damien chuckled at her expression. "Believe it or not, love, I am not an ogre. I merely came to change your bandages and spend some time with you. Despite our intimacy, we have had little time to get to know each other. You are, after all, my betrothed, and I have seen you without your clothes. Please, unbutton your nightrail."

Jessica looked down and realized he already had her dressing gown untied. While she tried to decide whether or not to comply, he waited patiently. He had agreed to her demand of the night before, and her bandage did need to be changed. Yet, had he really given the servants time off to be generous?

She gazed into his face to try to guess his true intentions. His eyes locked with hers, and she could feel herself falling under their spell. With a great amount of effort, she managed to look away. The barrier which she thought she had erected about her emotions was not as strong as she had believed.

"Jessica," he said kindly, "I will not harm you, and I will keep to our agreement. For now."

Jessica slanted a glance at him. His return smile was all innocence. With a nod of assent, she unbuttoned her gown. He helped her pull it off her injured shoulder. Unfortunately, it was necessary to lower it to her waist in order for him to remove her bandage. Staring straight ahead, with blazing cheeks, she sat quietly as he removed the old dressing.

His hands were gentle and practiced. But the touch of him against her skin made her flinch more than once, not from fear, but from desire. She wanted to relax into him, to feel his fingers trace down across her breasts. Gritting her teeth, she suppressed a moan of desire that clogged her throat. How was she ever going to keep to the demand that she had forced on Damien last night?

Damien was having trouble keeping his desire tamped down. The swell of her creamy-skinned breasts laid bare before him nearly undid him. He had agreed to Jessica's preposterous demand of the night before because he could see that was the only way to get her to be his wife. Once that was accomplished, he would find a way to get her back into his bed. He had never wanted a woman so much in his life. And he wanted this woman. With more self-control than he thought he possessed, after one quick glance, he kept his eyes on the strips of cloth. He was damned if he would be the one to break their agreement.

With a flourish, he tied off the bandage and sat back, relieved he could give himself space. He helped her pull her clothes back on because she was still a bit stiff and confined by her bandage. And he needed to have her covered for his peace of mind.

She looked up at him with curiosity. "You seem very familiar with changing bandages," she observed. "Are you a student of the science of medicine, as well as a soldier and a spy?"

He smiled. "When one is an outlaw in the enemy's country, one tends to learn how to care for one's own hurts. I've had a great deal of practice in wrapping and unwrapping bandages, as well as a small amount of experience in surgery."

"Were you in France when you received the scar across your chest?" she asked.

The memory burst into his brain. He had nearly died from loss of blood when he had received that wound. Only Edward's nursing skills had kept him alive. He shrugged, ignoring the cold sweat that broke out on his back. "It was a minor disagreement with a gentleman who refused to allow us to kidnap his mistress. He was an excellent swordsman."

Her eyes widened. "How terrible! You could have been killed!"

Damien lifted an amused eyebrow. "I did not think you were so concerned about my health."

She blushed, but her voice was cool as she said, "I am concerned about the pain of all God's creatures."

"How humanitarian of you," he observed dryly as he rose and walked to the window. He stood gazing out. "Then you will be very distressed to learn that the gentleman who gave me the scar is missing the last finger of his right hand."

"Oh!" She covered her eyes as if to blot out the vivid picture. "How could you do such a thing?" she demanded. "How can you remain so unmoved?"

"Unmoved?" He swung around to face her. "I am far from unmoved at the things I have been forced to do to remain alive. I am not cold and heartless. I am, rather, well aware of man's cunning and deceit. Perhaps too much so. I have practiced it too long myself. I have not always enjoyed the role I played."

"Yet, you remained in it for several years," she accused.

He smiled ruefully. "Ah, yes, the contradiction. I think I can explain it best by asking you a question, Lady Fortuna. Did you always enjoy your role of adventuress at *Madame* du Barré's?"

"But that was different," she protested. "I did it because Margaret forced me into it. I did it because of my br—" Her words halted. "I never hurt or maimed anyone," she finished.

He wondered how she would have finished that interrupted statement, but he did not pursue. He would get her to tell him eventually.

He raised a cool brow. "Were all those gentlemen with whom you gambled so wealthy that they could afford to lose the exorbitant sums which you won from them?"

"I did not ask them about their financial stability when they sat down to play cards," she said in her defense. "If they had the money on the table, then I considered it fair to try to win it. If they did not lose to me, it would have been to someone else. I could not afford to be altruistic."

Damien smiled as he watched her realize that her own logic had lost the debate for her. "As I could not afford to be merciful," he said. "We are not so different, are we, my love? He strolled to the chaise and cupped her chin in his hand. "Perhaps our marriage will be a good one after all." He dropped a kiss on her cheek, then strode to the door. With his hand on the latch, he turned. "Rest for the remainder of the day. I believe an appointment has been made with my mother's modiste for tomorrow so that you may be measured for your wedding gown. I do not wish to dally any longer over the plans for this wedding than is necessary. I should think a fortnight would be long enough to ready yourself." He opened the door but did not leave immediately. Instead he paused, and, in a softer tone, said, "I enjoyed this discussion, Jessica. I hope to have many more with you after we are married." Then he left, whistling. But he knew the next two weeks of waiting would be torture.

CHAPTER 20

Two weeks later, the morning of the wedding dawned clear and bright, a distinct contrast to the weather which had preceded it. The birds chirped merrily, and the sky held no hint of rain. Jessica was awake early enough to watch the sky turn from soft gray to blush pink to bright blue. She listened as the house began to come awake and relished her last few minutes of solitude before Donny and the other maids descended on her to ready her for the grand event.

Thankfully, her stomach was behaving, and she was not queasy as she had been on many mornings of late. Her gaze landed on her wedding gown which had arrived from the modiste the day before. In a few short hours, she would be dressed in it and walking down the aisle to become Damien's bride. Despite their tumultuous beginning, she prayed that their marriage would be a happy one. *Whether it's happy or not depends just as much on you as on him,* an inner voice told her.

A knock came at the door, and it opened to admit Donny followed by two maids carrying steaming kettles of water for her bath.

"Aye and tis a fair day for yer weddin'," Donny beamed. "A fair day, indeed."

Jessica could not quite summon the same excitement. Butterflies danced madly in her stomach.

The morning sped past. She was pampered and perfumed, and felt somewhat like a pagan virgin being made ready for sacrifice before a heathen god. She realized the comparison was not far from wrong. Damien was very capable of cutting out her heart with just a glance from those damnable green eyes.

Finally, she was ready. She stood before Donny and the other maids as they inspected her for any flaw.

One of the maids sighed. "Lawr, just like a fairy princess."

Jessica felt like a fairy princess. Her gown was made of creamy satin and fell to the floor in simple lines. The toes of her matching shoes poked out at the hem. The neckline was cut low enough to tease, but high enough to retain her modesty. The long sleeves puffed at the shoulders and then tightly hugged her arms to the wrists. A train of the same material as her dress fell from her shoulders, held on by ties knotted in bows. Her hair was pulled up into little ringlets by a simple gold band studded with tiny diamonds. It had been a gift from Damien's mother on their last shopping expedition together. Covering her head and face and trailing down her back to the length of the train was a veil of Spanish lace.

The Duchess knocked and entered. She smiled warmly. "You look lovely, Jessica." She handed Jessica a white leather case. "Damien asked me to give this to you."

Jessica opened the case and gasped when she saw its contents. Inside, lay a magnificent necklace of sapphires and diamonds with earrings to match.

"It is the customary gift of the Duke of Wyndham to his bride on their wedding day," the Duchess explained.

"But I cannot accept these," Jessica protested. "These are your jewels."

The Duchess shook her head. "Not any more. In a short while, you will be the new Duchess of Wyndham. These are not mine any longer." She grinned. "Besides, they will look much better on you than they ever did on me. They always clashed with my eyes."

The lady took the necklace out of the case and clasped it about Jessica's throat. Then she clipped on the earrings. She stood back and inspected her handiwork.

"Perfect." The Duchess smiled. "We should go now. We have kept my son waiting long enough."

Jessica's heart fluttered, but she followed the Duchess out the bedroom door. She wondered how Damien was feeling at this moment. Was he as nervous as she was? No, that man was never ruffled. He would be cool and remote, as he always was.

She descended the stairs slowly, trying to keep her composure. Activity bustled all around her. A wedding banquet would be held in the ballroom after the ceremony. Jessica stepped out into the sunshine and climbed into the carriage. The Duchess and then Donny followed. Her nanny would take care of any last minute primping that had to be done. The carriage moved off, and she sat back to contemplate her fate.

The ride to the church seemed an eternity, yet not long enough to suit her. As they stood in the vestibule, the Duchess sent her a worried glance. "Are you all right?" she asked. At Jessica's faint nod, she whispered, "Be brave, Jessica," and gave her a quick hug. "It will be over sooner than you realize." Then she turned and walked down the aisle to take her place at the front of the cathedral.

Jessica stood alone in the vestibule. The lofty notes of the massive organ sent a shiver through her. She was grateful that her soon-to-be mother-in-law was kind and supportive. She didn't know what she would have done if the dowager Duchess had been anything like Margaret.

Donny fussed with Jessica's veil and her train. One of the footmen handed her a single, white rose and told her it was from His Grace. The organ music changed, and she sent a pleading glance at Donny. Her nanny just smiled broadly and motioned for her to start walking.

Jessica gazed down the length of the cathedral. She swallowed hard, and somehow, her feet began to move her forward. She had a fleeting impression of curious and smiling faces, but the main focus of her attention was the man dressed in elegant black velvet and white silk who watched her approach with glittering, green eyes. Beside him stood Edward Johnson, the witness to the wedding. His smile was friendly and warm, and gave Jessica a boost of confidence.

Damien held out a darkly tanned hand to her. As she placed her small one on his, she looked up into his face. He raised a brow and a corner of his mouth twitched up, then he turned to lead her to where the priest stood waiting. She had a sudden urge to flee back down the aisle, but she repressed the feeling. Both her unborn child and her brother depended on her.

She knelt beside Damien as the priest said a short prayer, then stood to exchange vows with the man beside her. She listened intently as he stated his vows.

"To love, honor, and protect…and I pledge thee my troth." His voice was firm and low, and he sounded as if he meant every word.

Before she had time to think, it was her turn to say her vows. Somehow, she managed not to stumble over the words. Then came the moment for Damien to place the ring on her finger. Her hand trembled but he held it steady as he slipped the wide, intricately carved, gold band on the third finger of her left hand. She stared down at the symbol that told the world she now belonged to Damien.

The priest gave them a final blessing. The ceremony was over. She was officially the wife of Damien Trevor, Duke of Wyndham. She belonged to him until death parted them. This had been her deepest desire, to be wife to Damien. But she had not wanted it forced on him. She had wanted him to want this marriage as much as she did.

Damien turned her to face him and folded back her veil. She looked up into his handsome face, and her mind froze. All her thoughts and doubts were stilled as her senses were overpowered by the man before her.

One corner of his mouth lifted. "I believe," he said quietly, "that it is customary for the groom to kiss the bride at this point."

His arm went about her, pulling her close. She braced herself for the ravaging of her mouth that she had come to expect, but instead, his lips came down on hers softly, gently caressing and surprising her into a response. The world seemed to spin around her, and her knees turned to jelly. She held onto his coat with both hands and swayed against him for support. Her lips parted, inviting him, beckoning. All thoughts of their bargain flew from her mind as his kiss deepened.

She had no idea how long they remained in their embrace. The priest clearing his throat finally brought her back to reality. As Damien raised his head, his green eyes glinted with heat and something else… She couldn't define it, but it made her breath catch in her throat. Then with a smile, the spell was broken. He tucked her hand into the crook of his arm. Together, they walked back down the aisle.

It had only been a short while ago that she had walked this path alone. Strange, how a few minutes of time could completely alter one's life. Before, she had been the poor daughter of a deceased earl, thrown out of her own home by her stepmother. Now, she was the Duchess of Wyndham, wife of a very powerful and very rich man.

They emerged into the late afternoon sun and hurried down the steps and into the waiting coach. A curious crowd had gathered outside the church, and there was much shoving and pushing to see the new wife of the Duke. Once inside the coach, Jessica sat as far into the corner as possible. She was suddenly very shy of her new husband.

Damien was unable to sit very close to her because of the long train of her dress. The creamy satin billowed around his feet and up over his knees. He pushed at it ineffectually and smiled ruefully.

"I think wedding dresses are designed to keep husbands away from their new wives as long as possible," His eyes danced with humor as he glanced at her. He took her hand and placed a kiss on her open palm. "You look beautiful today, my love," he murmured. "Delectable witch turned into a fairy princess." He flashed her a grin.

Jessica blushed and ducked her head. He could charm the feathers from a peacock with his flirting.

A few minutes later the coach pulled up before the door of Damien's house. He descended, then turned to help Jessica. As she gazed up at the front door, apprehension at meeting the guests inside, most of whom she did not know, made her stomach flutter.

Damien bent close and whispered in her ear, "Do you suppose we could sneak away for a private game of cards?"

She smiled up at him. "Only if you let me win," she whispered back, grateful for his attempt to help her feel at ease. Her heart swelled at the connection between them. Together, they walked up the stairs and into the house.

When they entered, they discovered all the servants lined up waiting for them in the front hall. Jacobs cleared his throat, then announced, "Their Graces, the Duke and Duchess of Wyndham." All the servants cheered and applauded.

Damien thanked them, then smiled down at Jessica. "It seems they have accepted you as their mistress," he observed.

With apprehension, she answered, "I hope I do not disappoint them."

The applause died, and Jacobs shooed the servants back to their duties, then he turned to Jessica and Damien. "May I extend my congratulations and best wishes to Your Graces," he said with a formal bow.

"Thank you, Jacobs," Damien answered. "That is most thought-ful of you."

Jacobs snapped his fingers and Frannie appeared with a tray that held a snifter of brandy and a steaming cup of tea. "I took the liberty of preparing a small libation for you both," he said.

"Oh, Jacobs, you are a dear," Jessica exclaimed as she took her cup.

The butler looked rather aghast, but pleased, at her informality "Thank you, Your Grace." He nearly smiled. "Now, if you will excuse me, I must attend to my duties." Bowing again, he left.

Jessica and Damien were alone, but only for a few moments. Damien's mother arrived along with Donny and Leftenant Johnson. The two women hustled Jessica upstairs, so she could refresh herself before meeting the guests. Halfway up, she glanced over her shoulder. Damien was watching her, his gaze warm, intense, possessive. A pleasurable shiver ran through her. Then Leftenant Johnson said something to him and the spell was broken. But as she continued up the stairs, she smiled to herself as she began to plan her campaign to make Damien fall in love with her.

CHAPTER 21

A fortnight after the wedding, Jessica sat on a quilt on the warm grass under a tree. Her needlepoint had fallen unheeded to her lap. She gazed back at the house—Damien's house—proud and regal, sprawling in the sun.

This was her home now. She was its mistress. A duchess. She could scarcely believe it.

The house was built in the shape of an H, with the main entrance in the center of the crossbar. In order to reach the front door, one had to climb a wide, sweeping flight of stairs. The large, open foyer, which was two stories high, was actually on the second floor of the house, along with the ballroom, the main dining room, the salon, and various other rooms for entertaining guests. The bottom floor contained an extensive library, Damien's study, a morning room, a parlor and a smaller, more intimate dining room where the family ate when not entertaining. On the opposite side of the crossbar on the ground floor were the kitchen and the other rooms necessary for the every-day running of the mansion. The two wings contained bedrooms and the staff living quarters.

Jessica took most of the first week to inspect the entire structure, and even then, there were parts she had not yet seen. She thought that she might have some reorganization ahead of her, but everything was running smoothly without her intervention. There was little for her to do. Out of deference to her position in the household, Hobbs, the majordomo, asked her opinion on the menus and the linens to be used for dining, but he was so competent that she felt superfluous.

And lonely.

Damien had not spent much time with her. He was immersed in reacquainting himself with his estate because he had been away for so long. He had occasionally taken her out for a ride in the curricle, but their conversations would center mainly on the sights or the history of the estate. Gone was the charming, teasing seductive rogue who had won her heart. Jessica feared that his polite but distant demeanor would define their marriage.

Now, she sighed heavily and poked at the needlepoint in her lap. The young maid who was sitting several feet away got up and approached her anxiously. Damien had instructed that she was never to go outdoors alone because of her condition. She supposed she should appreciate his concern, but she felt confined.

"Is there something wrong, Your Grace?" the maid asked. "Are you feeling ill?"

Jessica smiled to belay the girl's fears. "No, Mary, I am not ill," she told her. "I think I have done enough needlepoint for today. I am going back to the house."

The girl helped Jessica gather up her things, and walked with her back to the house. At the doorway, Jessica asked the girl to put her needlepoint away for her, then she made her escape to her bedroom.

The master bedroom suite consisted of two bedrooms which were connected by a large sitting room. Each bedroom also had its own dressing area. Jessica's rooms were decorated in shades of light blue and white. It was a pleasant room, situated at the back of the house and looked out on formal gardens directly below the windows.

Damien's room, which she'd only seen in passing while on her tour of the house, was on the side of the house, facing rolling lawn and forest beyond. His room was done in shades of darker blue and gold. The connecting sitting room was situated on a corner of the house, thus having two walls with windows. This room combined the colors of the two rooms on either side. Jessica liked this room, but found herself apprehensive about using it. She was always afraid she would meet Damien in it. For some reason, she felt it was his room, and she did not wish to tread on his territory. Bored, frustrated, she decided to raid Damien's library. At least a book would provide some companionship, even though it was imaginary.

At dinner that evening, Damien was quiet. He told her a poacher had been seen in the woods and to stay close to the house. After that, he lapsed into brooding silence. The only conversation was between Hobbs and whomever he happened to be serving at the time. As soon as she could, Jessica escaped upstairs to her room and left Damien to befriend his brandy. Her book would be much better company than her silent, overbearing husband.

Near dawn, a noise outside Jessica's bedroom door awakened her. She lay quietly and listened. It came again, a shuffling noise, then her door handle slowly began to turn.

"Who's there?" she called.

The door was flung wide, and Damien stood in the opening.

"You are a witch!" he announced. "You have worked your spells too well, Witch."

Jessica jumped out of bed and hurried over to him. Her heart pounded in her chest, but she could not tell whether it was from fear or anticipation. Her only thought was to get him out of her room before he woke the servants.

"You need to leave," she said as she tried to push him out.

"No," he disagreed, not budging. He draped his arm heavily across her shoulders and pulled her against him. "What I need is a kiss, Witch."

Before she could protest, his mouth descended and captured her lips. Caught off guard, still groggy from sleep, she kissed him back. Warm tingles ran through her and curled her toes. The taste of him, flavored with brandy, made her senses reel. Damien was magic.

Finally raising his head, he grinned down at her. "Good night, my Witch," he whispered. Then he turned away and sauntered down the hall, bellowing for Wilson as he went.

After returning to her bed, Jessica lay awake pondering her husband's strange behavior. He had been so distant and taciturn at dinner, she had been certain that he wanted little to do with her, that he had no soft feelings for her. The kiss he had just bestowed on her was warm with feeling. Her lips still pulsed from his stolen caress.

She turned impatiently in the bed as she tried to block out the delicious throb in her center and the confusion in her head. Sleep did not come easily for the rest of the night.

The next morning, Jessica found the dining room empty when she came down for breakfast. She had almost finished her meal when Damien entered and sat in his chair at the head of the table.

She was not about to sit through another silent meal. Placing her napkin beside her plate, she said. "If you will excuse me, Damien, I have things to attend to."

As she rose, he commanded quietly, "Sit down."

She remained standing.

"Please," he added.

She dropped back into her chair. Nervously, she chewed at her bottom lip as she waited to hear what he had to say, then forced herself to stop. She would not let him see how uncomfortable she was. She was a better card player than that.

Confusion clouded his eyes. "What are you trying to do to me, Jessica? I have honored your damn bargain. What more do you want?"

Jessica's mind raced. Except for the kiss of the night before, he had honored the bargain. She could tell him what she really wanted was his love, but that would be like rubbing salt across the open wound of her heart. That would never do.

There was something which she had wanted to speak to him about since their wedding day, but had not found the right time or the right words. It concerned Jason, who still remained Margaret's ward. Damien had power and influence. Perhaps he would be able to help her brother. But she was not about to relinquish her superior position in this battle of wits with her husband. Not yet.

Looking suitably puzzled, she asked sweetly, "Why Damien, whatever do you mean? Have I suggested that you have been anything less than agreeable to live with, gracious, or honorable?"

A pained expression flitted across Damien's face before he warned, "Do not play games with me, Jessica. I have very little patience this morning. You know I can make you tell me what I want to know."

Having her husband's attention in spite of his poor disposition, she decided to take advantage of the opening he provided. She sat back and ran her finger thoughtfully along the edge of the table as she searched for a way to begin. The best way, she decided, was to be direct.

"I have a brother," she said. "He is twelve years old, too young to shield himself completely from Margaret's influence. He inherited the title of Earl of Braeleigh upon my father's death, and several months ago, we learned he also inherited a substantial land holding in America. But he is Margaret's ward. She has control of everything — the money, the estate, and my brother."

"Fascinating," he murmured.

She glanced at him. Her husband's gaze was icy. Her family was far from his most favorite topic of conversation.

She took a breath and plunged forward. "Could you do something about the situation? Could you take over as my brother's guardian?"

Disbelief crossed his face. He responded with an incredulous question of his own. "You are asking me to become involved with *another* member of your family? Have you no sense of justice, Jessica? Or is this further punishment for what I have done?"

Jessica answered him with only one word. "Please?"

Damien's face closed over his emotions. Sardonically, he asked, "You would trust me more than your own, dear stepmother?"

Jessica answered coldly, "I would not trust Margaret to tell me the correct time of day."

Damien did not answer right away. He sat staring at her for so long that she began to fidget in her chair. What was going on behind those cold, green eyes?

Finally, his voice stony, he said, "I can do nothing for your brother."

He rose, apparently deciding the conversation was at an end.

Jessica had one more thing to say. "Then I will write to him."

Damien stopped and turned to her. "You may write to the Devil for all I care."

Jessica watched him stride angrily from the room. She had been stupid. She should have known he would want nothing to do with her family. She had asked too soon. She might have spoiled her chances of ever getting Jason away from Margaret.

At least she could write to her brother. Out of deference to Damien's feelings, she had only sent one, short note to Jason informing him of her marriage. Now, she would write to him regularly, whether Damien liked it or not. She only hoped that Margaret would not intercept the letters.

CHAPTER 22

Three days passed before Jessica was able to write to Jason. Many tasks occupied her as she learned how to run a house as large as Wyndham. The boredom she had experienced was gone, but Damien was still a missing piece in her life. They lived in the same house, but more like acquaintances than husband and wife. She had not yet figured out how to rectify that.

He had gone out early that morning with several of the servants to track the poachers who had been killing deer on their property and leaving most of the carcasses to rot. He would not return until late that evening, so she had a bit of time to herself. She was at a small desk in the morning room, a cozy room situated at the southeastern corner of the house, and had just begun her letter when Hobbs knocked discreetly.

"Begging Your Grace's pardon," he said. "The men have captured the poacher."

She was puzzled that the majordomo would relay this information to her. "That is good news, Hobbs," she said. "Has His Grace been told?"

"His Grace is still out searching the grounds." Hobbs discreetly cleared his throat. "Begging Your Grace's pardon, but I believe you would prefer to deal with this yourself."

Intrigued by his suggestion, Jessica put down her pen and followed him outside. A group of Damien's retainers stood about a small, bedraggled fellow. As Jessica approached, they parted to allow her through. A pair of dead rabbits lay at the poacher's feet.

"What is the problem, Hobbs?" Jessica demanded. "You caught the fellow red-handed."

At her words, the poacher raised his eyes and stared sullenly at Jessica. She was taken aback to see a smudged, pixie face glaring at her.

"Why, it's a girl!" Jessica exclaimed.

"Isn't she the smart one," the poacher said sarcastically.

The footman, who had been holding the girl by the arm, gave her a shake. "Watch yer mouth, wench. This here's the Duchess o' Wyndham."

"Well, la-di-dah," the girl sneered.

Before the footman could throttle the young girl for her insolence, Jessica held up her hand to stop him. "What is your name?" she asked her. "Where's your family?"

The girl just hunched her shoulders and stared at the ground. Jessica glanced around at the hostile faces of the men and had an inspiration. Putting her arm about the thin little shoulders, she said gently, "Come sit over here with me. We'll talk, just the two of us."

The girl resisted at first, but then she allowed Jessica to lead her to the step before the door. They sat down together as if they were equals.

"Are you hungry?" Jessica asked. Without waiting for the girl's reply, she said, "Hobbs, get something to eat for this child."

A few minutes later, Hobbs brought a plate of food, and Jessica watched the girl devour it. When she had finished, Jessica managed to drag out of her that her name was Mae, and she and her grandmother lived alone. Mae was the provider for both of them.

"Mae, how would you like to come work for me?" Jessica asked.

The girl looked at her suspiciously.

"You can work in the kitchen," Jessica added. "We will pay you fair wages, and enough food for you and your grandmother."

"Will I have to live here?" Mae asked.

Jessica surmised she did not wish to leave the old woman. "No, you can sleep at your grandmother's, but you must be back here every morning to do your chores." Jessica watched Mae think over her offer. Finally, the girl nodded. "Good. Hobbs, get Mae cleaned up and show her to the kitchen. She is going to work for us."

Jessica watched with amusement as Hobbs distastefully told the girl to follow him. She had to hurry to keep up, and Jessica heard

Mae complain, "'*Ey*, you ol' coot, wait up!" With a smile, Jessica returned to the house. Her letter to Jason was forgotten.

Damien did not arrive home until much later that night. Exhausted and hungry, he entered through the servants' entrance into the kitchen, for he had planned on raiding the larder and then falling into bed. Instead, he found Jessica sitting at the large, worn, kitchen table. Spread out before her was a small feast of a crusty loaf of bread, a hunk of cheese, cold ham, a large dish of strawberries and a bottle of wine.

She released a small gasp at his entrance and rose from the table. "Welcome home, Your Grace. Would you care for a bite to eat?" She indicated the food on the table.

His gaze traveled from his wife to the food and then back again. She looked delectable. Her color was high, most likely from being caught in the middle of her surreptitious banquet, and her luscious lips were stained with strawberry juice. Silky, dark tendrils of hair curled at her cheeks. He could not decide which enticed him more — the food or his wife.

"A feast!" he exclaimed as he slid into a chair at the table.

Jessica smiled as she sat beside him and poured him some wine. "Did you catch the poachers, Your Grace?" she asked.

He shook his head. "No. But I understand from Hobbs that *you* were quite successful." Damien placed his hand over hers and said, "You did well today, Jessica. I'm proud of you." He lifted her hand to his lips and kissed her fingertips.

She blushed at his praise. "Thank you," she murmured, "but I only did what I felt was right."

Her humble response awed him. He never would have thought of putting the girl they caught to work in the kitchen as Jessica had. The woman he had wed out of necessity was intelligent and brave and kind-hearted. She was beautiful and passionate. She made his heart sing.

He loved her.

Damien blinked. How could that be? He glanced at her, at her guileless eyes and soft lips. She entranced him.

"Jessica, I…," he began. His words trailed away, and his gaze dropped to the food before him. He shook his head. No, he could not say the words aloud. She was the daughter of his family's enemy.

He sensed Jessica waiting for him to finish, but he stared instead at his glass of wine and said nothing. Uncomfortable under her scrutiny, he felt heat rise across his cheekbones.

"Damien?" she prompted.

"Have a strawberry," he said as he hastily placed the bowl of fruit before her.

A tiny line of confusion appeared between her brows, but she did not press. Instead, she took one of the red fruits and bit into it. Juice dribbled down her chin as she began discussing her plans for a new garden. She giggled, grabbed a napkin and wiped the drip. Damien wanted to push the napkin away and lick up the juice, taste the strawberry on her lips. But he refrained. The discovery of his feelings for her were too new. He had to decide what to do with them. For now, he would merely enjoy her company, the rest of the meal, and pleasant conversation as they discussed the events of the day.

Jessica cherished each moment, for companionable times with her husband were very rare. When they retired that night, Damien escorted her to the door to her room and left her with a chaste kiss upon her cheek. Jessica felt that a permanent, warm glow would forever claim that spot. She thought he might attempt to seduce her into lying with him, but he was a perfect gentleman. Reluctantly, she entered her room alone.

She climbed into bed expecting to fall asleep immediately, but sleep would not come. She replayed their meal together in her head. Damien had seemed different somehow, more relaxed, more attentive. Perhaps she had begun to break through his reserve. She wondered what he had been about to say that would cause the flush across his cheeks. She might never know. But at least they had shared a pleasant meal.

As she stared up into the darkness, she remembered the unfinished letter to Jason which she had left in the morning room. She decided that since she could not sleep, she would finish it and send it with the morning post.

When she reached the desk in the morning room, she discovered with dismay that the letter was missing. She searched around the desk, in the drawer, on the floor, but it was not there. She thought perhaps one of the maids had taken it to her room, so she quickly returned there and began to search frantically. The last thing she needed was for Damien to find the letter and once more be reminded of her family.

As she searched, the door to the sitting room swung wide. Damien stood in the opening. He had never used that door. Something in his manner made her heart pound. He wore a long, dark green dressing gown belted at the waist. She had an uncomfortable feeling that he wore nothing beneath. He held up a piece of paper. Jessica recognized it as her letter to Jason.

"Is this what you were looking for?" he asked quietly.

Relief washed over her at his mild tone. "Oh, you have my letter." She started toward him to retrieve it.

"Aren't you being rather careless about where you leave letters to your lover?" he asked.

Jessica halted. "What do you mean?"

"Your lover," Damien repeated. He enunciated each syllable clearly. He glanced down at the paper in his hand and read:

Dearest Jason,

I miss you so very much. I wish you could be here with me, now, but I know that is not possible. Perhaps, soon, I will be able to come to you, and we can spend time together, laughing and riding together the way we did before my marriage…

He looked up at her. His lips twisted, and his face was stony. "How touching." Those two words dripped sarcasm.

Jessica was devastated at the sordid meaning he read into her innocent words to her brother. His manner was quite evident. He was furious. She backed away.

Shaking her head, she said, "You don't understand."

"I think I understand too well." He stalked toward her. "You have betrayed me, Jessica. You deny me the right to your bed as your husband, yet you pine to be with your lover."

241

"No, I—" She stepped away.

He prowled closer. "Do not deny it. You have written it with your own hand." He shook the letter at her.

Jessica had backed up to the bed. Damien was so close he only had to reach out to keep her where she was. The look on his face was terrible—a mixture of barely controlled rage and horrible hurt.

"Damien, don't do this," she said quietly.

"Do what? I'm not doing anything, while your lover…" He released a humorless laugh. "What does your lover do to you, Jessica? Does he shower your mouth with hot kisses? Does he caress your body to the point of forgetfulness? Does he excite you to ecstasy?" His voice became deceptively seductive.

Jessica shook her head. "No. None of those things." Then she realized by her denial she had admitted she had a lover. Her chin went up. "I have no lover."

"No?" Damien's mild tone contradicted the wrath in his eyes. "This letter says otherwise." He held it up, then let it flutter to the floor. "I would like to meet this paragon of manly virtue. How did he steal your heart, Jessica? Did he woo you with florid phrases of poetry? Did he pick innocent daisies for you? Or perhaps he placed chaste kisses on your fingertips."

Jessica sucked in a breath, hurt and frustration creating a heated tangle in her chest. This man—her husband—would always think the worst of her. He viewed her through the glass of her family and what they had done to him. He did not see her as herself, a separate person. And that made her very angry.

"You, my lord, are a half-wit," she snapped. "The letter is to my younger brother, Jason."

Damien blinked, stunned into confusion. Her words acted like icy water on the heat of his anger. He had been so sure of her infidelity. Was she telling the truth?

Her soft smiles and guileless eyes, her enticing curves and seductive walk tormented him. The restrictions she had placed on their

242

marriage drove him mad. He had agreed to them only to get her to the altar. And — God help him — he loved her.

The pain and betrayal he'd felt upon finding the letter had twisted inside him, blinding him to anything else. He thought by marrying her he would find some peace from the hurt of his brother's death that had haunted him all these years, but he had been wrong. All he saw was the deceitful betrayal by her family — Margaret's seduction, his brother's murder.

He searched her face for the truth. Her color was high. Her eyes were stormy. Her lips compressed in anger. That mouth, the bottom lip fuller, riper, begged to be kissed.

She stirred him as no other woman ever had. For a moment, he forgot the argument. She was his, dammit. All he wanted was to kiss her, touch her, possess her. He took a step closer, intending to do just that. And was stopped by a delicate but firm hand against his chest.

Jessica saw the change in his eyes from rage to desire. She watched as they changed color from cool green, cold and hard as two emeralds, to a darker shade like that of the sea. She wanted nothing more than to have him make love to her, but he would have to acknowledge the truth, acknowledge *her*, and believe her before she allowed him to touch her and break the bargain.

"Jason is my brother," she said quietly. "You agreed that I could write to him."

Damien blinked again and stared at her a moment. His gaze slid away, and he drew a breath. She watched as he seemed to rearrange his thoughts. When he looked back at her, his gaze was cool and remote.

"Of course," he said. "My mistake. I apologize." He took a step back.

Jessica realized that if he left, she might never have another chance to get him to love her. She might lose him forever. The time for truth had come. She had no other weapons to use in the battle for his love. It was a bet she did not want to lose. But she had to take the gamble. Time had run out. She curled her fingers into the lapel of his dressing gown and prevented him from leaving. He glanced down at her hand, then scowled at her.

"I am not Margaret," she said. "I do not manipulate people. I am not my father, who did the only honorable thing he thought he could do when he found his wife with another man. It destroyed him, turned him to drink, and eventually killed him when his curricle overturned." She shook her head. "I am sorry for your brother's death. But I had nothing to do with any of it."

He stared at her, his expression not revealing any of the thoughts behind those cool green eyes. He eased her fingers from his lapel, turned and walked to the door. Jessica's heart compressed into a hard lump in her chest.

She had lost.

He stopped before the closed door. And did not move. Jessica's breath stilled.

Seconds passed. He abruptly swung around to face her. "Is that why you made that absurd bargain with me? Because you believed I thought you had something to do with my brother's death?"

"Didn't you?" she asked quietly.

A crease appeared between his brows. A muscle jumped in his jaw. His head dipped.

"I believe I have made a mistake," he said, his tone low and quiet. He clasped his hands behind his back. "I owe you an apology. Another one. I would beg your forgiveness."

When he glanced up at her, his mouth curved in a crooked smile. He reminded her of a little boy whose hand had been caught in the jar of sweets.

Jessica's breath left her in a rush.

"I have been a fool," he said. "I had forgotten about your brother. When I saw the letter, I was furious. All I could think about was you with another man. That you had wed me because of some demented plan of your stepmother's and forced me to accept that bloody bargain. I was so jealous I couldn't see what you had told me only days before."

Jessica opened her mouth to speak, but he rushed on before she could say a word.

"I will keep to the bargain as long as you wish." He straightened as if standing before a judge. "I hope you can forgive me for being such a cad."

His humble apology overwhelmed her. It wiped the words from her brain. Her love for this honorable man swelled inside her.

At her silence, he gave a short nod, turned, and placed his hand on the doorknob.

She could not let him leave. She took a step forward.

"Damien."

He did not turn.

"Damien, make love to me."

He swung to face her. "I beg your pardon?" he asked, gaping at her.

Jessica smiled at his disbelief. "Make love to me," she repeated. "Please."

"But the bargain…"

She gave a little shrug. "I was the one who forced you to accept it. I can be the one to break it."

He took a step toward her. "Are you sure?"

"Yes." She tipped her head, feigning curiosity. "Don't you want to make love to me?"

He took another step forward. His mouth twitched up at one corner. "Of course, I do."

"Well, then." She pulled at the top ribbon of her dressing gown.

He stepped close, then pulled back as if she might break. "What about the babe?"

Jessica grinned. "I don't think he or she will mind."

A sly smile curved his lips. He pulled at the next ribbon on her dressing gown. "Well, then." He untied the rest of the ribbons on her dressing gown, then reverently pushed it from her shoulders. "We will do this slowly," he murmured. "You will tell me if you wish to stop."

Jessica swallowed. "Yes." She had no desire to go slowly or to stop, but she would not tell him that. She would let him care for her.

With a gentle shove, he pushed her back onto the bed. Leaning over her, he took both her wrists in one hand and pinned them above her head. She closed her eyes, finally able to break the bonds of his gaze. She felt his weight on the bed as he knelt over her.

Jessica sucked in a breath. Anticipation made her giddy.

She felt his lips on hers, demanding and possessive. His tongue slid across her lips, tasting, probing. With a sigh, she allowed him entrance.

His free hand slipped under her nightrail and explored until it found the mound of her breast. With his thumb, he teased the tip, causing it to harden and swell. Jessica shuddered in pleasure.

His touch, which she had denied herself for too long, was devastating. She had given him leave to claim his marital rights. He could have taken her quickly and been done. Instead, he seduced. He knew what aroused her, what made her mindless, and he used his knowledge ruthlessly. His hand moved over her body and awakened sensations that she thought she would never feel again.

His lips moved from her mouth to her neck to her throat to her shoulder, and left a trail of tiny butterfly kisses, making her breath catch in her throat. Somehow, her nightgown had come unfastened, exposing a breast. His mouth found the spot where his hand had been. A wonderful tingling ran through her body. A sound, somewhere between a moan and a sigh, escaped her lips.

She was helpless in his hands, as if he had cast some sort of spell over her. She could not break away. She did not want to. His mouth moved back up to her neck. He nibbled at the lobe of her ear. Her head fell to the side to allow him full access to the spot.

He sighed, as if a great weight had been lifted from him. "I love you, Jessica," he whispered.

She sucked in a breath, shocked and at the same time joyous at the words.

He braced himself above her. "Do you wish me to stop?" he murmured.

She opened her eyes and cupped his face in her hands. "No. Never."

She slid her hand to the back of his neck and pulled him down. Recklessly, her mouth met his, inviting him to taste. Her fingers curled in his hair, and her other hand slipped down his back as she felt the play of muscles under his skin.

His hands moved over her freely now, touching all over. She was exposed to his warm gaze and hot touch. He tasted first one breast, then the other. A heated glow spread through her body.

He stood and pulled her up with him. Taking the high neckline of her modest nightgown in both hands, he ripped it to its hem. It fell to the floor about her ankles.

"These are for virgins and old maids," he growled. "You are a woman, and I will not see you in them again."

A blush warmed her cheeks at being naked before him. She felt self-conscious with the slight roundness of her belly from her pregnancy. Half turning away from his gaze, she covered herself shyly.

"Don't turn away, Jessica. I want to look at you," he urged gently.

Very aware of his eyes on her, she slowly turned back to face him. He did not take his eyes from her face as he dropped his own robe to the floor, baring himself to her gaze. He wore nothing beneath it.

She could not tear her eyes away from his body, the broad expanse of his chest, the muscular sleekness of his hips and thighs, his proud manhood. He took her by the shoulders and drew her close. His body was warm, firm. All hard planes to her soft curves. He placed a warm, demanding kiss on her lips.

Jessica felt the coiled desire in him. The heat from his body matched her own. His hard thighs pressed against hers. His manhood throbbed along her hip.

"You are a witch, Jessica," he whispered against her mouth. "I want you so badly, I ache."

"Make me your wife," she whispered back, as her arms tightened around him. "Make love to me."

In one smooth movement, he scooped her up and placed her gently on the bed. He ran his hand the length of her body, from her shoulder, over her breast, to her slightly mounded belly, to the wellspring of her womanhood. His fingers caressed there.

Jessica shuddered and moaned. As he stretched out beside her, she ran her hands over his body. His breath rasped in his throat as he played in that tender spot between her thighs. She arched toward him as she writhed in her passion. Her body clenched and spasmed in delicious waves. When they receded, she saw him grinning at her with male pride.

"Your turn, Your Grace," she said as she reached for him. She wanted to pleasure him like he had pleasured her.

He groaned at her touch. "I need you now, Witch," he growled.

He pulled her on top of him and positioned her gently as he entered her. Her eyes opened in surprise and delight at the wonderful sensations he created. He began to move, and she caught his rhythm. They moved as one until a wild burst went surging through them both. She felt as if her world were coming to a spectacular end, that her life's energy was reaching an apex and then being sucked out of her. With a tiny sigh, she collapsed on top of him. Her world came slowly back into focus.

They lay quietly together, gathering their strength after the storm. She rested her head on his shoulder. He kept his arm about her and held her close.

Shyly, she circled a spot in the middle of his chest. "I love you," she whispered.

He became absolutely still, then with disbelief he asked, "What did you say?"

Jessica smiled up at him. "I said, *I love you.*"

Damien gathered her close and buried his face in her hair. "God's blood," he whispered. "I never thought I would hear you say that. I've treated you so badly. I think I have loved you from the first time I saw you at *Madame*'s, but I was too stupid to realize it or too arrogant to admit it." He paused, struggling with some deep emotion. "I worshiped my older brother. I wanted to be like him. He was charming, handsome, and everything he did seemed so effortless. He had a line-up of Papas with marriageable daughters asking about joining their family to ours. He could have been happily settled with several heirs by now. Instead, he became obsessed with Margaret, another man's wife. I could have shot him myself, I was so angry with him. And then he was challenged to a duel by your father. I begged him not to go. He laughed and said no one could best him at shooting." Damien shook his head. "I realized how shallow and foolish he was. When he died, I was furious at him, but even more furious with myself."

Jessica leaned back in his arms. She touched his cheek with her fingertips and gazed lovingly into those striking green eyes.

"Damien, I'm so sorry," she said in a husky voice as she hugged him.

"You have saved me, Jessica," he murmured as he brushed a curl from her forehead. "I was so blind."

Jessica took his hand and kissed his palm. Then she grinned impishly. "You were never blind. You were always ogling me."

Damien raised a brow. "How could I not help but stare when you always wore those clinging, low-cut gowns to *Madame*'s? My imagination would run wild as I thought of all the things I could do if you were wearing nothing at all."

Jessica smiled an invitation. "I'm not wearing anything at all now."

He ran his hand down her back as if feeling for something. "Hmm. You're right." He grinned. "I guess my imagination doesn't have to work so hard, now. Shall we see what my imagination can come up with?"

"Mm," she purred. Her eyes traveled down his body. "It looks like your imagination has come up with something very useful."

Damien chuckled as he lowered his mouth to hers. He was hers now. Completely. No one would ever take her away from him again.

CHAPTER 23

The days passed quickly for Jessica. The summer months were pleasant ones, for she was happier than she had ever been. She and Damien spent hours together riding in his curricle, walking hand in hand through his estate, talking about everything, frolicking like two children, or just sitting together in companionable silence. Damien had completely changed, as if a burden had lifted from his heart. He was caring and attentive, and Jessica found herself falling more deeply in love with him.

There was only one dark smudge on this bright picture. The letters from Jason were becoming fewer, and his tone was different. She could not point to something specific. But she knew something was wrong. She discussed her worries with Damien. He told her again, though in much gentler tones than the last time, that there was nothing he could do for the boy. Margaret was Jason's legal guardian.

Jessica stood facing her husband now, as frustration formed lines between her brows.

"Well, why don't we abduct him?" she demanded. "I know he would be much happier here with us."

Damien smiled. "I'm sure he would, but we can't just ride out to Braeleigh and take the boy. Don't you think Margaret would come after him? If she did, she would have the legal right to take him back. The law frowns on kidnapping."

Jessica walked aimlessly around the room in her frustration. Clasping her hands before her, she stared out upon the lawn.

"You are right, of course," she reluctantly agreed. "I may never see him again." She was on the verge of tears. "I'm afraid Margaret will change him into a cruel monster, who'll care only for himself and his money and nothing of others."

Damien came up behind her and turned her around to face him. He enfolded her in his arms and held her tightly.

"There is one way that we could force Margaret to give him up," he said thoughtfully. "I might be able to have her declared unfit to be your brother's guardian and have you named in her place."

Hope returned to her. "Do you really think you could?"

He brushed his lips across her brow. "I can't promise that it will happen. It will take a long time. All I can do right now is make some inquiries and get the legal work started."

"But at least that would be something," she said.

"I will have to travel to London," he said. "I will be gone almost a week."

"Oh." Disappointment made her shoulders droop. "You mean I can't go with you?"

Damien shook his head. "There is nothing I would like more than to have you with me, my love, but it would not be healthy for you to be in the city right now, not while you're carrying our child. You will be much more comfortable here, where it is cooler. You're too precious to me. I don't want anything happening to you."

Reluctantly, Jessica nodded her agreement.

Damien gave her a small squeeze and held her to him. "Don't be sad, love. I'll try not to be gone too long." He tilted her chin up with a gentle finger. "I will miss you very much."

The following morning, Jessica stood beside him in the early morning mist as he sat on his horse. She rested her hand upon his knee and gazed up at him.

"Hurry home, Damien," she said, her voice husky from unshed tears. "I shall miss you terribly."

Damien leaned down and kissed her tenderly. "I'll be back as soon as I can."

He straightened and touched her cheek, then wheeling his horse, cantered down the drive. Jessica watched as long as he was in sight, then, sighing, she went into the house. She missed him already.

Five days after Damien's departure, she was sitting in the morning room and embroidering a tiny jacket for the baby. She was restless, and she could not get the stitches even and straight. With a sigh of frustration, she threw the jacket down on the settee beside her and wandered about the room. Stopping before the window, she noted the clouds gathering. Thunder rumbled ominously in the distance.

It would be two days, at least, before Damien's return, and that did not lighten her spirits any. She had kept busy, and had done reasonably well in fighting off the loneliness while he had been gone. That morning, she had awakened with an uneasy feeling, but had decided it was only because she had not slept well. The babe's activity had kept her awake during the night.

A light tap came at the door, heralding the entrance of Hobbs. She turned, wondering what problem he had encountered that he could not handle.

"Excuse me, Your Grace," he began. "A letter was delivered for you." He held out a silver tray which held a rumpled, stained envelope.

Thinking it might be from Damien, she swept up the letter and opened it. She read:

Dear Jess,

This will be my last letter to you. I do not know if you received all the others, for Margaret always took them from me to post. Sometimes, she even told me what to write. I asked Dudley, the dairyman, to post this for me so that I would be sure that you received it. Margaret is sending me away to America with her uncle. She says I should see the land that I own there. I do not believe her. I think she does not want me around anymore. We are supposed to be leaving in a fortnight. I tried to run away, but she managed to catch me. She told me the next time I try, she will lock me in the attic. Please, do not let her send me to America, Jess. I am so afraid.

Your loving brother,
Jason

P.S. I will understand if you cannot help.

Jessica sank down onto a chair. Despair covered her like a shroud. How could Margaret send a young boy to America? What about his schooling? What about Braeleigh? Jessica knew the answer to that last question. Margaret wanted Braeleigh for herself. Jessica became thoughtful as an idea began to form.

She rang for Hobbs, and when he appeared, she said, "Hobbs, I am traveling to Braeleigh. Prepare the coach for me."

Hobbs looked surprised at her request, but he said evenly, "Very well, Your Grace. Will there be anything else?"

"No. Yes. I will want strong footmen, men who will not mind a fight."

Hobbs bowed and disappeared to do her bidding. Then Jessica went to find Donny and change her clothes for travel.

As Donny helped Jessica change, the little woman scolded, "Ye be crazy t'go there with that woman about. Ye ought t'wait for His Grace t'come back. He'll take care of it for ye."

"I can't wait, Donny," Jessica said. "Jason's letter said they were leaving in a fortnight, and Margaret might change her mind and send him away earlier. I have already waited too long." Affectionately, she put her hand on the woman's arm. "I have to go, Donny. Jason is my brother. Damien is not here, so I'm the only one who can save him from that woman."

Donny merely grunted her disapproval.

Later, when Jessica climbed into the carriage, she found Donny already seated inside. A mischievous smile curved her lips, but she said nothing to her nanny.

Donny grumbled, "Well, ye didn't think I would let ye go into that woman's lair alone, did ye?"

The driver cracked his whip, and they started off. The ride to Braeleigh would take them most of the day. They would not arrive until late afternoon. Jessica remained very quiet for most of the trip. She stared out the window and worried a handkerchief in her hand.

She wondered who Margaret's mysterious uncle might be. She had never heard her stepmother speak of any relatives. She decided it was probably just some story that the woman had devised to tell Jason.

As the coach finally came to a stop in front of Jessica's childhood home, she scrambled out of the coach and turned to Donny. "I think you should remain out here with the coach. If I can get Jason away, then I will send him out to you. If something happens to detain me, I will meet you at the inn."

She did not wait for any argument from Donny. She left the driver and one footman with her nanny, and took the other with her. Walking boldly up to the front door, she let the knocker fall. It echoed inside the hall. Soon, the door opened to reveal, not Foy, the majordomo who had been with the family since she could remember, but a man she did not recognize.

"Yes?" He looked down his nose at her.

"Where is Foy?" Jessica asked.

"Foy is no longer employed by Her Ladyship," he informed her haughtily.

Jessica raised her chin and disdainfully brushed past him. "You may inform Her Ladyship that the Duchess of Wyndham is here to see her."

The majordomo sniffed primly at such boldness and stepped in front of her footman, barring him from entering. Jessica ignored him and started toward the drawing room.

Just before she entered the room, she realized the man had not moved. "Well?" she prompted disdainfully. "Will you tell your mistress that I am here, or shall I have to find her myself? And please allow my footman entrance," she said in the most regal tone she could muster.

The man bowed, then hurried off to find Margaret. Jessica had her footman wait in the foyer and swept into the drawing room. She waited until the man's footsteps had died away before she went in search of Jason. Just as she was about to dash out the door, she heard Margaret's quick footsteps and the rustle of her skirt. She mouthed a silent oath as she hurriedly sat in one of the chairs and acted as if she had been waiting for hours.

Margaret was slightly breathless when she arrived at the doorway. Her calculating glance landed on Jessica, seated nonchalantly on the settee, and her mouth flattened when she realized who her visitor was. She sauntered into the room.

"Well, well, what is this? Some sort of charade? You are playing at being a duchess now?" she asked sarcastically.

"No charade, Margaret," Jessica answered her stonily. "You know whom I married. You were certainly paid enough by him."

"Ah, yes, I seem to recall now that someone did want to marry you. I could not imagine why the powerful Duke of Wyndham would want to marry such a little slut as yourself, but I suppose you enticed him into your bed. I see you are quite fertile, aren't you?" Her gaze landed pointedly on the small swell beneath Jessica's gown.

"I did not come to trade insults with you, Margaret. I came to see my brother." Jessica could not allow her temper to get out of control if she wished to accomplish what she had come to do.

"Really?" Margaret raised an elegant brow. "Jason is not here at the moment."

Jessica began to panic. What if she were already too late? She forced herself to remain calm. "Not here? Where is he?"

Margaret waved a hand. "Oh, he is out having a riding lesson, and then he was going on a picnic." She frowned, feigning confusion. "Or perhaps he was going to visit a friend. It is so difficult to keep track of children."

Jessica knew Margaret was lying. The woman had kept a very close watch on her brother when she was living in the house. She could not imagine Margaret suddenly changing her ways. However, she decided to play along.

"When do you expect him to return?" she asked.

"I really could not say," Margaret said. "It would not be worth your time waiting for him. He might decide to spend the night with his friend."

"Margaret, I did not travel all the way from Wyndham just to turn around and go back again without seeing my brother." Jessica stood. "I believe I will stay the night and wait for him. You may have my old room made ready. Donny is out in the coach. Would you tell your servants to inform her of my plans? I would like some tea and biscuits, and then I believe I will rest before dinner."

Jessica hoped her imperious manner would fool her stepmother. At the moment, she was feeling anything but imperious. The woman frightened her. She wandered to the window and looked out, waiting for Margaret's next move.

"My, my, haven't we become the high and mighty duchess?" she sneered. "Did your new husband teach you those manners? You certainly could not have picked them up in the gutters of London."

Jessica swung around to face her stepmother. "You would know about the gutters of London, Margaret, for I seem to recall that you were the one who told me of the establishment of *Madame* du Barré."

Margaret burst into shrill laughter. "A word or two about an exciting, seductive place dropped into an innocent ear was all it took to pull Miss High-and-Mighty down from her lily-white pedestal. You were so easy to manipulate, Jessica my dear, that it was almost no fun at all."

Jessica gasped at Margaret's revelation.

Margaret laughed again as she sauntered closer. "Oh, yes, my plan to get rid of you worked so well." She frowned. "But then you met this duke and landed on your feet again. I will have to think of something else."

"I will leave as soon as you let me see Jason," Jessica said, planning to take her brother with her.

"I have no intention of having you leave, dear Jessica." Margaret smiled. "Of course, you will see your darling Jason. I may even allow you to travel to America with him." Margaret gazed at Jessica thoughtfully. "Well, we shall decide that later." Margaret took her by the arm.

"Let go of me, Margaret." Jessica pulled out of her grasp.

The sound of a scuffle, and a yell of "Watch out, Your Grace!" came from her footman in the foyer. Then Jessica heard a grunt, and the thud of a body hitting the floor. Jessica's heart sank. Her footman had been overcome by Margaret's thugs.

Margaret smiled. "I can have my footmen escort you, if you wish. They will not be so gentle with you."

Jessica wanted to run, but she had to find Jason. She had already met one of Margaret's footmen, and had no doubt what would happen to her if Margaret allowed another near her. She had to protect her unborn child. And if she wanted to find Jason, she had to go along with her step-mother.

Margaret took her arm again. "You did say that you wished to rest? I have just the place."

She propelled Jessica into the foyer where Margaret's footmen were dragging Jessica's man into the back of the house. Jessica hoped no further harm would come to him. Her stepmother's fingers gripped her arm like a vise. Jessica was yanked up the stairs and down the hall to the door of a closet where linens were kept. Margaret unlocked the door and pushed Jessica inside.

"You can't keep me here, Margaret," Jessica said. "Donny and my other footmen are outside. They will come get me. And my husband knows where I am." She knew Damien was still in London, but she hoped the bluff would work.

"Donny and your footmen are well taken care of by now," Margaret said. "As for your husband, we will deal with him when he arrives. I should not think that will be too difficult."

She gave Jessica a shove. Jessica stumbled forward and landed on a stack of blankets. The door closed behind her, and she heard the key click in the lock.

"Have a good rest, my sweet!" Margaret called out.

CHAPTER 24

Jessica heard Margaret's evil laughter float away down the hall, then silence. The closet was as dark as a coffin. She could not see a thing except a tiny, dim line of light under the door. The scent of lavender, which had been placed between the linens, was quite strong and made her sneeze. She rubbed her nose, sat on the blankets and contemplated her predicament. Depression and fear settled on her like a weight.

She had accomplished nothing by coming to Braeleigh. Locked up in a closet, she still had not seen Jason and might never see him again. Her only hope was Damien. She had bluffed to Margaret, but she had also been voicing her own hope. Hobbs knew where she was. She prayed that Damien would return early. The chances of that happening were slim, but it was all she had.

For the moment, all she could do was try to get herself out of the closet. She pulled out a hairpin, slid to the door and tried to force the lock. Several times, she had to stop when she heard footsteps, but finally, by the time the light under the door had begun to dim, she heard the lock click open.

She crept out of the closet and carefully closed and locked the door behind her. A clock in the downstairs hall chimed the hour of eight. As the notes died into silence, she made her way stealthily down the hall to Jason's room. She had little hope of finding him there, but she thought she might find a clue where he might be.

By the time she reached his room, twilight had fallen. She dared not light a lamp for fear of being discovered. She knew the room as well as her own, and she headed straight for the wardrobe. His clothes seemed to be all there. Next, she checked the cupboard next to the bed. His copy of *Ivanhoe* by Sir Walter Scott, his favorite book, was still there. She knew that Jason would not go anywhere without taking that book with him. Her brother had to be in the house or about the estate, locked away somewhere. She could not consider any other possibility. It was too terrible.

Jessica scanned the room for anything unusual, but everything seemed to be in its place. She sat on the edge of the bed and tried to think of places where Margaret could be hiding him. As she sat there, she heard a small sound. It seemed to come from behind the wardrobe, but was not in the room. She walked over to the piece and listened. She heard singing. It was Jason.

She dared not call out to him. One of Margaret's spies might hear her. She realized where he was — the secret room between this room and the next one. She used to play in it when she was little. It was an excellent hiding place. There was only one way to reach it, and that was from a garret room on the top floor of the house.

Jessica hurried to the door and opened it cautiously. She checked to be sure the hall was empty, then she scurried to the narrow set of stairs which led up to the top floor where the servants' quarters were located. The stairs were dark, and she hoped the servants were still at their chores in the main part of the house. Taking a deep breath, she began to climb.

At the top of the stairs, Jessica pushed against the door, and it creaked open. She stepped out into a labyrinth of small hallways and tiny rooms. Most were empty now, for most of the servants had been let go. She remembered that the opening to the secret room was in the floor of a tiny room to her left.

In the dark, she slowly crept down the hall. She finally found the room where a faint rectangle of light shone through a trapdoor in the floor. A ladder, the only way into the secret room, lay beside it.

Jessica sank to her knees beside the opening and peered down. Jason sat on the floor with his back to the wall. There was no table, no chair, no bed. One short candle shed light.

"Jason," Jessica called softly.

Jason stopped singing but did not look up.

"Jason," she called again. "It's Jessica."

He scrambled to his feet and peered into the gloom above his head. "Jess? Is that really you?"

Jessica's throat constricted. He was trying to sound very brave. She smiled, hiding her own flood of emotions.

"Of course, it's me," she said with forced gaiety. "I'll lower the ladder down to you."

Quietly, she dragged the ladder to the edge of the opening and let it down to her brother. As soon as it touched the floor, he scrambled up. They hugged tightly for a moment, then Jessica held him away.

"Are you all right?" she asked. "Has Margaret hurt you?"

Jason shook his head. "No, I'm fine, really, Jess. I'm just hungry."

Jessica laughed softly. "Then I guess you're all right. I can't get you anything to eat right now, though. We have to get away from here. How long have you been down in that room?"

"Since Margaret caught me giving the dairyman the letter I wrote to you," he said. "I thought I was being really careful. I slipped out of the house when he delivered some eggs a few days ago, and I hid in the bushes until he came out. Margaret came into the kitchen to inspect the eggs and saw me give him the letter. I was surprised when she told the dairyman to post it. I guess she knew you'd come get me. I'm sorry, Jess."

"It's all right. I'm here to take you back to Wyndham," Jessica said. "All we have to do is find Donny and my footmen and leave."

She sounded much more confident than she actually felt. She was foolish to think she could have walked in and taken Jason away.

Quietly, they made their way down the narrow stairs to the floor below. Jessica was relieved to find that the hallway was still empty. They crept to the top of the grand staircase, stopped and listened. Voices came from the salon.

"We'll have to use the back stairway," she whispered.

Just as they turned to escape, Margaret emerged from the salon. They rushed to the other stairway.

"Get them!" Margaret yelled to her footmen. "They're escaping!"

Jessica and Jason started down the back stairs, only to be cut off by a large, forbidding man at the bottom of the stairs. They turned and fled back down the hall. Another large man came from around the corner and stopped their flight in that direction. They tried the nearest door, but it was locked.

"Run, Jason," she whispered. "You're faster than they are."

When he hesitated, she gave him a little push. He dashed for the grand staircase. But a third man had just reached the top of the stairs. He scooped up Jason and threw him over his shoulder. Jason kicked, yelled, and punched as he was carried down the stairs to Margaret.

The other two closed in on Jessica. She backed away, wishing she had a weapon. The closest thing was a fragile vase on a small table next to her. She whipped it at one of the men, then tried to run past as he dodged it. He swiped it into the wall with one hand while he grabbed her with the other. She tried to twist away, biting, kicking, but his fingers dug into her arm and held her fast. The other man reached them, and they each took one of Jessica's arms and led her roughly down the stairs. Margaret watched with a triumphant smile.

When they reached the bottom of the stairs, the woman said, "I have decided what I will do with you, Jessica. I promised you to Sir Percival Lowry in marriage. I think the time has come to keep that promise."

"Do you forget, Margaret, that I am already married?" Jessica reminded her coldly. "The Duke of Wyndham will not stand idly by and watch me wed to another. You cannot force me to commit bigamy."

Margaret dismissed the problem with a wave of her hand. "Your Duke will not be alive to see it happen. I have a score to settle with him. He will be rather unpleasantly surprised when he comes to rescue you. Come, my sweet. I have someone here who cannot wait to see you again." She turned to the two thugs holding Jessica. "Bring her into the salon."

Jessica was shoved into the salon behind Margaret. The footman holding Jason followed. When she entered, she was met by the salacious leer of Sir Percival Lowry.

He approached her and bowed. "My dear Jessica, how pleasant to see you again."

His eyes raked over her voraciously. Reaching out, he took her chin in his flabby hand and tilted her face up to his. Jessica tried to turn away, but his grip was too strong.

"Ah, do not turn away, lovely Jessica," he said. "You shall have to get used to my face, for we will be spending much time together."

"I would rather die first," Jessica spat out.

"No, no, not now, my lovely. Not yet." His smooth contradiction held menace. "Perhaps at a later time, when I grow tired of you, but not now. We shall have many hours of pleasure before that time comes."

Jessica jerked her head and broke from his grasp. She kept her face turned away from him. The man made her skin crawl.

Jason kicked and punched the footman who held him. "Leave my sister alone! Don't you hurt her!"

He squirmed and wriggled until the footman lost his grip and dropped him. Jason scrambled up and nearly escaped before the man grabbed him.

"Keep quiet, brat," the man warned, "or you're going to lose your teeth." He threatened with a raised fist.

"Leave him alone," Jessica said. "He's done nothing to you."

Margaret's smile was nasty. "I do so enjoy the family concern you have for each other. Isn't it heart-warming, Uncle Percy?"

Sir Percival grinned, equally vile. "Very much so, my dear niece."

Jessica stared in surprise at the ugly visage of Sir Percival. He was Margaret's uncle?

"You look surprised, Jessica," Margaret said. "Yes, Percy is my uncle, and he has helped me with several unpleasant tasks. You will be his reward." She settled herself on the settee. "I have sent word to Wyndham. I believe we should make ourselves comfortable while we wait for Jessica's gallant rescuer to appear. Tie those two into chairs," she ordered her footmen.

Jessica and Jason were dragged to chairs at opposite ends of the room and tied with drapery cords. She smiled bravely at her brother, but inside she quaked. Damien was not due back at Wyndham until the next day at the very earliest. He would need another day to get to Braeleigh. She hoped Margaret would not get impatient waiting for him.

Sir Percival hovered near Jessica and kept touching her as if he owned her. He disgusted her, but she gritted her teeth and pretended she didn't notice. Jason glared at the man, but Jessica warned him to silence with a shake of her head. She did not want her brother punished for protecting her.

The footmen left the room. Margaret sat in silence as she sipped a glass of wine. Sir Percival drank stronger spirits. He sprawled on a couch next to Jessica within arm's reach, and every few minutes he would pet her. Jessica wanted to sink her teeth into his hand.

The clock chimed nine o'clock, then ten, eleven. Jessica became stiff and sore from sitting in the same position for so long. Jason's head drooped, and he dozed. Sir Percival finally began to snore.

As the night wore on, Margaret began to fidget. She crossed and uncrossed her legs. She drummed her fingers on the arm of the settee. Several times, she got up and refilled her glass. She repeatedly licked her lips and clenched and unclenched her hand. Finally, she jumped up and stalked about the room. Stopping before Jessica, she stood with her hands on her hips.

"Where is this gallant husband of yours, slut?" she demanded.

Jessica gazed mildly back at her stepmother. "Are you getting nervous, Margaret?" she asked. "Are you afraid that you'll not be able to do away with my husband, as you had my father do away with Damien's brother?"

Margaret's eyes narrowed. "How did you learn that?"

Jessica shrugged. "It was no secret that my father was in a duel. When I discovered how the present Duke of Wyndham came into his title, it was easy to figure out the rest. But I am curious about one thing."

"What is that?" Margaret snapped.

"How could you be so sure that the Duke would die in the duel, and not my father?"

A conceited, smug smile crossed Margaret's face. "That was easy. Your father had scruples. I knew he would not want to kill the boy. I had Percy hide in the bushes with a pistol to ensure that the Duke would not live."

Jessica's eyes widened in shock. "That is cold-blooded murder!"

Margaret gave an amused chuckle. "So, it is. Percy was not very happy with the plan, but when I promised him a young, beautiful wench for his trouble, he agreed to it quickly enough."

Margaret sent a scathing look at the snoring figure of Sir Percival. He had passed out from his large consumption of rum. She gave his leg a kick. "Wake up, you old fool!"

"Wh-What? Is he here? Where is he?" he asked foggily.

"He could have come and gone, and you would have slept through it all," Margaret sneered. She moved the half-empty bottle beside him to a table farther away near the fireplace. "No more rum until we have finished this."

"Why do you wish to kill my husband, Margaret?" Jessica asked. "He has done nothing to you."

"Nothing?" Margaret turned on Jessica. "His father caused the ruination of my brother and my family. We were made paupers, and my brother was barred from all the decent clubs in London. We were ostracized by society. We were able to live only because of my friendship with several wealthy men."

Jessica stared at her. How had her father been duped by this woman? How could he have married her?

"Don't forget to tell her, Margaret, that your brother lost your family's wealth at the gaming tables. That he borrowed from my father, and proceeded to lose that as well," a voice said.

Margaret swung around with a gasp. Damien stood at the door of the room. Jessica thought he had never looked so dangerous, nor so wonderful. He held a sword, its point dipped to the floor at the moment. His gaze swept over Jessica, his eyes filled with love. She smiled, relief and joy a bubble in her chest. He glanced at Jason, who had awakened, and sent him a nod.

Margaret stiffened. "Those are all lies."

Damien shrugged. "If you wish. But I still hold the promissory note on several thousand pounds sterling with your brother's signature at the bottom."

"If you are dead, it will not matter any longer," the woman sneered.

Damien's lips twitched as if he were enjoying a private joke. "True."

Margaret called her footmen, but none came.

Damien said, "You won't receive any help from them, I'm afraid. They've suddenly become indisposed."

"You murdered them!" Margaret screeched.

"Hardly," Damien answered.

"They may not be able to help, but I can," Sir Percival spoke.

Since no one had been paying much attention to him, he had pulled a tiny pistol from his pocket. Aimed with precision, against a sword, it would win without question. He leveled the weapon at Damien.

Sir Percival heaved himself up from his chair and swayed unsteadily. As he passed in front of Jessica, she stuck out her foot. He tripped, stumbled against the table with the rum, and hit his head on the mantle. He was dazed when he fell to the floor. The bottle of rum crashed on the hearth and spilled its contents into the fire.

As the rum ignited, Margaret gave a wild, hysterical laugh. She grabbed a lit candle, ran to a window and set the draperies aflame.

"You won't take me from here!" she cried. "I am the Lady Margaret! I am the wife of the Earl of Braeleigh! All of this is mine!"

"Margaret, no!" Jessica yelled.

Damien tried to pull her away from the draperies, but she escaped and flung the lit candle onto a chair, where the cushion caught fire. Then she dashed out and up the stairs to the second floor. Damien let her go. He rushed to Jessica and started to untie her.

"Are you hurt?" he asked anxiously.

Jessica shook her head. "I'm fine. I'm so glad to see you."

Damien smiled at her and touched her cheek. "I'm glad to see you, too, love." As he went on loosening the bonds, he frowned. "I wish you had waited for me."

The concern beneath his annoyance warmed her and she smiled as she explained about Jason's letter. "How did you get by Margaret's thugs?" she asked.

"I had a little help. I found Donny and our footmen tied up in the stable. After I freed them, we found Margaret's men sitting in the kitchen. We merely showed them that the wisest thing to do was to leave Margaret's employ." He finished with a casual shrug.

As the last of her bonds fell away, Jason shouted, "Look out! Behind you!"

Sir Percival had roused, and he pointed his little pistol at Damien's back. Blood dripped from a gash on his head where it had hit the mantle. Damien swung about, and his hand went to his sword hilt.

"Not so fast," Sir Percival sneered. "The wench has been promised to me, and I mean to have her." He wiggled his little pistol. "I won't hesitate to use this. I killed your brother. It won't bother me to kill you."

Damien threw an astonished glance at Jessica.

"It's true," she said. "Margaret had Sir Percival hide in the bushes during the duel between my father and your brother. When they fired their pistols, he shot your brother to be sure he was killed. My father never meant to kill him."

Sir Percival snickered. "It was a simple matter," he gloated. "The young Duke was easy prey. He never suspected foul play. Why should he? He was dueling against the honorable Earl of Braeleigh." He motioned with his gun. "Stand away from the wench. She's coming with me."

Jessica stepped forward. "You'll have to shoot me right here, Sir Percival. I'll go nowhere with you."

As Sir Percival's attention was on Jessica, Damien gave his hand a little twist, and his stiletto slid into his palm. Like lightning, his hand came up and he flung the blade at the man. It hit its mark, piercing Sir Percival's upper arm. He cried out in pain, and the gun slipped from his grasp. Jason was quick to kick it out of reach.

Damien hurried to untie Jason. The fire had gained ground. It raged up one wall of the room and was threatening to engulf the door. Damien removed his coat and placed it over Jessica's head to protect her from the flames and heat. With his arm about her, and another about Jason, he hurried them out the door.

When they were safely outside, Damien had Jessica and Jason wait, then he returned to the house. Jessica waited several agonizing minutes until he reappeared with Sir Percival. Donny arrived with the footmen, and Damien handed the murderer over to his men. Sir Percival would be given over to the authorities and tried.

Damien wrapped his arm around Jessica. "I couldn't get up the stairs to Margaret," he said. "She had piled draperies and linen at the top of the stairs and set them alight."

Jessica, Damien, Jason, and the others stood and watched the house burn. They could do nothing to prevent the fire from spreading. It had taken on a life of its own, devouring whatever was in its path. The flames caused windows to shatter, and they licked up the side of the house. Smoke billowed, threw a shroud over the building and reflected the light of the flames back to the ground. The whole area was lit by the conflagration.

Margaret emerged on the roof and walked back and forth along a parapet. She carried a candle and seemed not to notice the destruction, nor the danger.

"Braeleigh is mine!" she screeched, throwing her arms wide. "No one will take it from me!"

There was a roar and a crash as a main beam gave way. The whole house shuddered as sparks blossomed above her head. With a piercing scream, Margaret fell to her death into the house she had fought so hard to keep as her own.

Jessica watched in horror. Margaret had been jealous, cruel, and, finally, insane, but Jessica had never wished such a horrible end for the woman. The house, which held so many happy memories for Jessica and so many painful ones, was now truly Margaret's. She had claimed it by setting it afire and dying in it.

Tears streaked Jessica's cheeks. Damien's arm tightened around her.

"You have a new home, Jessica," he reminded her gently. "One where you can create new memories, happy ones for our children. When Jason is older, he can return here and rebuild Braeleigh."

Jessica turned to her husband, away from the terrible destruction. Her tears soaked his shirt. In her heart, she knew what he said was true. The pain of losing her family home would fade, to be replaced by the joy of creating a home filled with love for the new family which would surround her.

She looked up into the face of the man who held her so safely. "I love you, Damien."

He placed a soft kiss on her temple. "You are my heart, dear one."

She had gambled her heart and lost it, only to win more than she had ever expected—the love of her life.

EPILOGUE

Damien rose from his chair near the hearth and paced the floor of the library for at least the tenth time that night. The fire which had blazed so cheerily earlier in the evening was beginning to die. With a sigh, Edward Johnson heaved himself out of his comfortable seat and threw another log onto the embers.

"Careful not to dislodge the holiday greenery," Damien warned his friend. "Jessica spent hours decorating the house for Christmas."

The holiday was only a few days away, and his wife had draped swags of holly and evergreens across all the mantles and down the main staircase.

Edward turned from poking the fire and grinned. "I would wager you don't mind all the mistletoe she's hung in the doorways."

Damien shrugged. "What's a man to do when his wife wants to decorate?" He walked to the door of the room, opened it, and listened. There was no sound from the floor above. "What the devil is taking so long?" he muttered.

Leaving the door ajar, he walked back to the fireplace, absent-mindedly picked up a glass from the mantle, and drained its contents. It was one of several he had left about the room during the long night. He glanced at his friend.

"You look terrible," Damien observed.

Edward smiled. "You would not pass inspection from the general either."

Damien had run his hand through his hair so many times that it stood up in spikes all over his head. Worry etched a deep line between his brows. Dark smudges of weariness shadowed his eyes. He fell into a chair across from Edward. Leaning forward with his elbows on his knees, he stared into the empty glass clasped in his hands.

"How can it take so long?" he lamented again. "It's been days since I left her."

At that, Edward laughed outright. "It has not been days, my friend, only hours. I am lacking in experience, but I know it takes time to have a babe. They come in their own time." He motioned to a dark corner of the room. "Perhaps you would be better off like that."

Damien turned to look where Edward indicated. Jason was asleep, curled into a ball on a settee. Damien had allowed him to stay up on this special night after the boy had declared he was a man, too, and would keep watch with Damien.

"I would not be able to sleep," Damien told his friend. "After you and Catherine are wed, and she is having your child, you will understand."

Incredulously, Edward asked, "What makes you think I am going to wed Catherine?"

Damien grinned. "You did not come here only to visit Jessica and me, Captain. We have seen very little of you since you arrived here five days ago. I am surprised that Catherine's father has not thrown you out of his house for harassing his daughter."

A flush darkened Edward's cheeks. "The squire has already expressed his fondness for me and has informed me I could visit whenever I wished." He shifted. "Of course, that was only after I made clear that my intentions were honorable. Catherine and I were only waiting for the babe to arrive before we made our final plans. We wanted to be sure that you and Jessica could attend our wedding."

Damien's face creased into a warm smile as he reached out and clasped his friend's hand. Just as he was about to congratulate Edward, there was a long, drawn-out scream of pain from the floor above. Both men froze, and their gaze traveled to the door. Damien's face paled. Within seconds, the thin wail of a tiny baby could be heard. Damien turned to glance at Edward. A look of relief and happiness and amazement passed between them. Damien lost no time in racing out of the library and bounding up the stairs, two at a time.

He stopped just outside the bedroom door. Doubts and fears suddenly assailed him. What if something had gone wrong? What if the scream meant that Jessica was dying? What if there was something wrong with the babe? Steeling himself for the worst, he opened the door.

The sight which met his eyes caused him more panic than he had ever known. His mother, Donny, and the midwife were all grouped around the bed. The slight mound under the covers, which was Jessica, was very still. When the three women heard him enter, they backed away from the bed. His mother came to greet him with tears in her eyes.

"Congratulations, Damien," she whispered. "You have a beautiful son."

Relief so strong his knees nearly buckled swept through him. Then, in a daze, he walked to the bed. Jessica lay with her eyes closed. Her face was pale, and damp tendrils of hair clung to her forehead and temples.

Her eyelids fluttered and opened. She gave him a tired, but happy smile. As he knelt by the bed, she reached out and touched his cheek.

"You look tired, Damien," she said softly.

He took her hand and kissed her palm, but before he could reply, she gently pulled back a corner of the blanket to reveal a small bundle in the crook of her arm. In the midst of the bundle was a tiny, red face topped by a fluff black hair. Damien gazed at it in amazement.

"This is your son, Damien," she told him. "I would like to name him, Brian, after your brother."

She unwrapped the blanket more to reveal four tiny, perfect limbs that began to wave wildly in the air. The small face screwed itself up, and a protesting wail issued from its toothless little mouth. Damien laughed delightedly and put his finger near one of the miniature hands. The little fingers clasped it eagerly.

"He is beautiful, Jessica," Damien said with a smile. "Thank you."

Jessica grinned as she covered the infant with the blanket once more. "You did have some part to play in this, Your Grace."

The look of love that passed between them would have melted the coldest heart. Damien caught her hand once more and brought it to his lips. Jessica sighed contentedly and closed her eyes to sleep.

The ghost of Damien's brother was finally put to rest. The hatred, which had germinated so many years before, dissipated like the morning mist before the golden rays of the rising sun.

"Happy Christmas, my love," he whispered, as he watched his wife sleep with a smile on her lips.

ABOUT THE AUTHOR

Patricia Barletta is a multi-published, award-winning author of historical and paranormal romance fiction. As a native of the Boston area, she has been inspired by its history, which influenced her stories, and probably had an impact on her decision to become a high school British Literature teacher so she could pay the bills. She received a Master of Fine Arts in Creative Writing degree at the fabulous Stonecoast program in Maine. She loves to travel, especially to do research for her stories. When she's not at a yoga class, gardening, or socializing with friends, she's writing about dark heroes, feisty heroines, magic, and other fantastical things in her historic old home in Boston.

Find out more about Patricia and her books at:
patriciabarletta.com

Follow Patricia Barletta on BookBub.

www.ingramcontent.com/pod-product-compliance
Lightning Source LLC
Chambersburg PA
CBHW030157200626
46812CB00017B/2263